The Well-Favored Man

Elizabeth Willey
The Well-Favored Man

The Tale of the Sorcerer's Nephew

TOR

A Tom Doherty Associates Book · New York

THE WELL-FAVORED MAN: The Tale of the Sorcerer's Nephew

Copyright © 1993 by Elizabeth Willey

This book is printed on acid-free paper.

A Tor Book
Published by Tom Doherty Associates, Inc.
175 Fifth Avenue
New York, N.Y. 10010

Tor® is a registered trademark of Tom Doherty Associates, Inc.

Edited by Teresa Nielsen Hayden

Library of Congress Cataloging-in-Publication Data

Willey, Elizabeth.
    The well-favored man / Elizabeth Willey
        p.   cm.
    ISBN 0-312-85590-7
    I. Title.
    PS3573.I44722W4   1993
    813'.54—dc20   93-25918
                                                        CIP

First edition: October 1993

Printed in the United States of America

0 9 8 7 6 5 4 3 2 1

To Anne-Marie Donovan,
my first-grade teacher at Roosevelt Elementary School,
who taught me to put my butt in a chair and write.

⌐ 1 ⌐

THE MANTICORE HAD RUN, PURSUED BY the silent and deadly dogs, up the ridge through the rhododendrons. Trampled bushes marked its passage. I spurred my horse, Cosmo, and ducked branches as he scrambled up after it. Even I could smell the pungent stink of my quarry, which drowned the homelier scents of pine and soil in an unpleasant overlay of dung and ammonia. Ahead, there was a snarling and a roaring.

A sandstone outcrop at the top of the slope had forced the manticore along rather than down. I turned and followed it; the outcrop became higher and developed into an overhang. The sounds of the dogs and the beast grew louder. There were boulders scattered around, a narrow foot-track threading between them, and the trees were fewer, straighter, and taller. The overhang was quite deep now, almost like a cave; fire circles on the sandy soil and soot stains on the roof showed where hunting parties had sheltered in the past. There were large splotches of blood in the sand also, punctuating the tail- and footmarks, and the sounds of the fight were immediately ahead.

Abruptly the ground dropped down steeply, and there before me in a broad open place beneath the overhang, I saw the manticore set on by my dogs. One, apparently dead, was fastened to its near hind leg, jaws locked; several others dead lay about on the ground, crushed or disembowelled by swipes from the beast's claws. The manticore was the biggest I had ever seen. I lifted my lance. Cosmo pranced and sprang forward at the touch of my spurs.

We call them manticores here in Argylle, but they are not the same as the manticore known more widely in Pheyarcet and Phesaotois. For one thing, they are more lizardlike; for another, they are less intelligent. The latter trait makes it possible for a single skilled hunter to kill one, rather than the usual coordinated group activity.

Cosmo stepped lightly and quickly around the beast, just out of its reach, as I whistled to my hunting allies. The dead dog on the hind leg had been trying to hamstring it. I decided that this was a good time to handicap my opponent further and whistled again piercingly. The manticore was annoyed by this and lunged toward me, hindered in its homicidal intentions by the overhang. Cosmo danced back out of range and I continued to urge him back and to one side, luring the beast out into the open. It swatted at dogs with its claws, but the remaining bunch were smart enough to avoid them and rush in for bites at the belly, harrying it after me, but hampering fast pursuit.

We emerged from the semi-cave area and the level ground dropped away steeply below me. I signalled the dogs to hold the manticore where it was now and whistled again. Before the manticore could snarl and bounce forward over the dogs, a black-and-gold war-hawk plummeted down onto its head and pecked at its left eye.

The moment for which I'd been waiting came. Screaming and flailing, the manticore reared back. Cosmo knew; he leapt when I kicked him and we raced forward. The hawk, as well-trained as the dogs for this work, disengaged and took to the air as we shot in on the manticore's left. It snatched at the hawk and then turned, too late, to us; one claw ripped through my cloak and scratched Cosmo's flank as my lance drove up beneath its chin into the brain.

I had developed manticore slaying to a fine art of late. They are somewhat more intelligent than a wyvern, but they have their patterns like everything else.

I let go of the lance and drew my sword as we circled away from the tail. No need, though; it was a good strike, and the animal was flailing about in death agonies. I called back the dogs and they collected in a pack nearby, out of range of the monster's thrashing. We watched while it continued dying. Meanwhile, I took out a Key, a bell, and a candle stub and performed a Lesser Summoning in the shadow of the overhang. My sister Belphoebe, who dwelt here in the forest Threshwood and is in a way its guiding genius, should be informed at once of my success in the hunt.

"Phoebe," I said, "I have made a kill."

"Where are you? Is that Beza Ridge?" I saw her in the globe of light from my candle-flame. She squatted by a stream on a broad, flat stone. Her short straight hair, russet-brown and pushed back behind her ears, was damp, as were her brief leather tunic and her lean, muscular legs. Evidently she'd been swimming. A string of fish in various stages of gutting and cleaning were in front of her, and she had taken her arm out of its sling for the moment.

"Yes," I replied.

"Hah, you will want me to come and help you clean up then."

"No, I'll fire the corpse myself. I wanted you to know, though, that I have never seen one so big."

"Measure it," she directed me.

"Very well."

"Gwydion," Phoebe said, stopping me before I disrupted the spell's line from me to her, "these things oppress me."

"They worry me also," I said. "We're seeing more of them these days, and they're stronger. I don't know why. I just don't know."

Phoebe nodded. "You said that you thought an Eddy might have ruptured."

I folded my arms, relaxed my stance. "I still think that's the most likely explanation, but it will take much work to test its soundness. We have not had such a rupture here."

"Perhaps we did not notice."

"I believe we would notice. Theoretically the natural state of the Spring—unlike the manipulated and unnatural Well of Fire in Landuc—should mean that we never see ruptures, because the Spring's forces move liberally."

"Yet it would account for the monsters intruding. And we have been, relatively recently, under great stress as regards the Spring."

Belphoebe knows a little—more than most laymen do—about sorcery, but she's no adept. I sighed. "I don't know whether the stress on the Spring was so great that it made an Eddy or that an Eddy so created would rupture rather than disperse gradually."

"The monsters are—" she began.

I interrupted her. "You know that I agree that the circumstantial evidence, the creatures intruding here, is strongly in favor of a nearby Eddy-world exploding very recently, but I don't have any idea why that would have happened all of a sudden."

I was frustrated by the problem. It certainly showed in my voice and expression. Everyone knows Eddies occur in Pheyarcet in the currents of Landuc's Well because those currents have been dammed and channelled to benefit Landuc; they hold worlds in their swift-swirling grips, worlds which come into being and go out of it unnaturally rapidly. When an Eddy flies apart under its self-induced stress, the vitality of the Well which has been pent in it is released and the world or worlds in the Eddy are destroyed. Some things from those worlds always survive and are cast willy-nilly into the surrounding area. However, we of Argylle do not bind or force our Spring's flow, and therefore the Spring does not spin such volatile Eddies, though they are common to the Well. Eddies from Argylle's Spring are uniformly slow and stable.

"Gwydion," said Phoebe, and her voice was like our mother's in its gentleness and tone, "I do not think you are negligent."

I blushed. "I don't either," I said.

"I have not felt any Eddy either. Yet I still deem it might happen without our noticing. I recall when an Eddy last ruptured near Landuc, the whole Empire was plagued by those horrid red long-clawed rats; none knew whence they came, for there was no other sign of the Eddy breaking."

"Phoebe, we agree on that. I am sorry to blow a stale wind at you. Certainly the characteristics of the creatures we've seen—the distortion, the strength—they are like those of the Eddy-worlds." We had reprised everything either of us had thought for the past half-year. Yet we might, sometime, see a new face in the old review.

"It is a canker-problem."

"When your arm heals—"

"Yes. I will go out, along the Roads from here, and follow the Spring's flow to see if there are any Eddy-like distortions. It seems that to go and see is all there is to be done."

"Thank you, Phoebe. I would go myself—"

"You have much on your mind. This is work for me."

"Enjoy your fish."

She grinned quickly. "Hah, caught in my disobedience by the physician himself." We nodded cordially to one another and I terminated the spell by snuffing the candle. I uncoiled a piece of rope from around my body and waited for the manticore to finish dying. It took a long time.

When the carcass had burnt out, foul oily black smoke rising high into the deep-blue evening sky, I started for home. The dog pack trotted around me, businesslike and satisfied and untroubled by the loss of four of their fellows. I chose to take the long way home, going through the forest and then along the Haimance highway; there was no convenient Ley or

Road anywhere close, and I wanted to unwind and think en route.

A good day's work. Phoebe, her arm broken, could not kill this one herself and had asked me to do so before it wandered from wild Threshwood to the nearby farmlands and really caused trouble. I had been more than happy to oblige. It is good to get out and kill something foul once in a while. It purges me.

The hawk circled over the trees; I could not see her now because of the darkness and foliage, but I knew she was there over the canopy. Little night noises began as the air cooled; the trees seemed bigger and darker, and their litter muffled our sounds until we reached the highway. It was a good five hours' slow ride home through the wood and fields. I had plenty of time to consider the manticore, all seven-and-a-half ells of it. Phoebe herself would have had trouble with that one on foot, I suspected. It had killed six of my dogs altogether, and they were all experienced with such creatures. It was bigger and faster than the usual monsters we saw here.

Usual monsters. That was the real problem: there had been too many of the cursed things wandering around, and Belphoebe had soberly told me when I had set her arm for her that she was now perfectly sure not all of them were left over from the problem we had lately had with Tython, whose ill-nature had drawn such creatures to him en masse. There were new permutations on the old standbys appearing, she said, and the old standbys had acquired a heightened viciousness and boldness. Her arm had been broken by a wyvern which had taken a fancy to sleeping in a farmer's stone barn in the south. Wyverns are usually shy and retiring creatures, occasionally nesting in abandoned buildings, but preferring caves, and shunning inhabited areas as much as possible—though occasionally a herd of goats or flock of geese will tempt them out of the wastes.

I resolved to spend the next day or so winnowing through the records and making a study of exactly what unusual things had been happening lately. I might find some pattern that eluded me now, discover some overlooked source besides that of a hypothetical Eddy's unlikely rupture. And once I knew what had caused this I would be able to rectify it. That was what Mother would have recommended. Collect information, think, and act.

After I had done my collecting and thinking, though, I must consult my elders before acting—my siblings, uncle if possible, and grandfather. This was more than a courtesy; any action would doubtless require cooperation from them, for one thing, and for another, they might see things I did not.

The City was peaceful, smelling of cooking and smoke. Golden light glowed from windows, bluish from the streetlamps' faceted balls, lighting my way from the Haimance gate to the Citadel's Island. I cleaned up and fed Cosmo myself and settled the dogs in for the night. The hawk soared up to the top of the East Tower. I felt I had accomplished something; in reality, of course, the greater problem was still there, lurking in the forest with the uncouth things like manticores.

Behind the tall rose-and-lily decorated doors, the Citadel was quiet. Guards saluted me and a few domestic staff nodded politely. I climbed up the winding central stair, intending to go to my study, but took the long way around the residential wing instead of making the sharp left that would put me by my rooms. I passed my older brother and sisters' rooms, Alexander and Marfisa and Phoebe's (never used), my mother's untenanted, locked bedchamber . . .

Gaston's apartment, connected to hers, was closed and silent. He was travelling, or so we hoped. It had been long years since anyone had heard from him. My grandfather Prospero, whose rooms were beside his, was down the Wye, in the seaport Ollol, having gone there this morning to meet Walter and the envoy from Landuc. I was the only family member currently in residence at the Citadel. There were many other people there, there always are, but it feels a bit lonely when I'm on duty, as I think of it, by myself. I unlocked and entered my own rooms.

Lonely, but not alone; when I was very tired, I often felt as though someone else were in the room with me. I felt it now: a silent companion's amiable, invisible presence somewhere just behind me or beside me in my blind spot, never directly intruding. Every family has its ghost, or ghosts. My siblings and Prospero had mentioned similar feelings. I had never dared ask Gaston when he was still here.

My foot hit something flat which had been slipped under my door: a concert advertisement from my brother Walter with a note on its reverse.

> *Gwydion, I'm home again. All went well. When I left Landuc about twelve days ago Avril asked me to give you this: personal, not official correspondence, he said. Come to the concert! You'll enjoy it. I have new music to show you. Small-ensemble works—just what you like best. Come see me tomorrow or I'll come see you and pry you out of here with true brotherly devotion. Walter.*

There was an envelope folded inside the announcement, sealed in three places with substantial blobs of red wax and impressed with a familiar ring. I opened the concert advertisement first, standing in the hallway and leaning on the vine-carven doorjamb to use the hall light for reading. Hm. Something called a brandenburg concerto by one Bohk. What might a brandenburg be? I sounded the word out. A horn, perhaps? Walter had wandered into the ever-changing outlands of Pheyarcet in his recent travels before this errand, and the music and instruments he had brought back were getting a varied reception. My own feelings were mixed. Some of it certainly was garbage, but some was very good, at least when adapted to the taste and instruments of Argylle.

The stuff from Faphata, played on twelve-tone glass-belled drums, was popular in Haimance now, I'd heard.

The heavily-sealed note was unaddressed. I broke the seals and opened it.

Unto Lord Gwydion of Argylle from the Emperor Avril his Uncle, Salutations. Walter's visit to us has brought to our full realization how long it has been since last we spoke with you. We hope that all goes well and request the favor of speech face to face, that we might but change a few words between us and assure ourselves (and Her Serenity, who agitates at times) of the health and well-being of our kin. By our hand with all affection, Avril.

I didn't believe a word of it, except perhaps the part about Her Serenity (the Empress Glencora) agitating to know how we all fared. Walter would surely have passed on to them any recent news when he was there. He had conveyed our cousin Ottaviano here from the Empire of Landuc at the burning heart of distant Pheyarcet. In addition to negotiating a trade agreement with Prospero and the merchants, Otto would certainly be absorbing as much information about Argylle as he could and transmitting it back to the Emperor. Avril wanted something else, and I thought I knew what it might be: something he could not ask of Walter.

I put the note on my desk and sat down on the bed. The City's mellow lights studded the darkness beyond the broad river Wye which flows around the island on which the Citadel is built. The hour was now very late; there were only a few isolated windows lit, and no coachlights moved along the roads. The moon was bright, a white oval above the countryside, but I lit a candle anyway for the friendly flame. Then I pulled off my boots and socks. Taking the candle, I went into my workroom to do a little sorcery.

Lenticular glass, firepan, sand, water, flower-shaped crystal bell, Keys, and the antithetical forces: put them together in the right way, with all due respect, and watch.

It was doubly difficult because Avril was in Pheyarcet, beyond Argylle's border. I had to call upon the Well of Landuc in my spell, but at this distance the power to be gotten was immeasurably small—the invocation served to expedite the process of getting across the Border and to ease my workings through Landuc's demesnes. One balances the three Forces when casting spells which reach past the Border or the Limen. People who have not assimilated another force cannot cast such spells into that force's domain.

My vision blurred slightly, as if a patch of mist had drifted into the room, and the mistiness clotted above the flame and thickened on the glass. Folding inward, but not moving at all, it began to make the image, full of color and brightness stolen from the fire. A soft bell sounded, sustaining itself, and took on other notes as the image formed, to become words, my words. . . .

". . . Summoning seeming and speech reciprocally."

Avril, the Emperor, looked back at me, settling down in a high-backed chair even as our eyes met.

"Ah, Gwydion." He nodded to me, smiling. He was at a table with his implements around him in artistically calculated disarray. Also a tall, deep-blue vase of dusty-gold roses. His robes were gold-bordered scarlet, a bit ostentatious—but that's Avril.

"Uncle Avril," I greeted him, also smiling.

"How are things in Argylle lately?"

"Nothing out of the ordinary has happened since last we spoke," I said. "And in Landuc?"

"Smooth sailing, as far as I can see. Yet you may guess that I didn't merely wish to trade pleasantries."

I nodded. "Not such smooth sailing, then."

"It is about your father. We have not heard from him in years. I am a little concerned." He sounded testy. "I suppose I do not need to know where he is; he's a private man, he keeps to himself, that is all very well. But I would just like to know he is alive. If you are in touch with him . . . ?"

I had guessed Avril's intention aright: he wanted Gaston. I said, "I understand. I have not spoken to him in a long time. He has been incommunicado."

"I know. How long a time has it been since *you* last saw or heard from him?"

"Years, I guess. At least . . ." I thought carefully. "Between twelve and thirteen years. I could make it more exact if it mattered . . . Yes, he came early in springtime thirteen years ago."

"You are not worried."

"Gaston has dropped out of sight for extended periods in the past, as I understand it. And he was . . . you know he was not happy. He said little before he left last time. He had not been here often anyway, just dropping in and out once or twice a year or sending a message."

Avril nodded, then sighed and ruffled his hair, not disarranging it in the slightest. "I see. I hope he is all right."

I debated within myself for a moment. Generosity won. "If you really need him, Avril, there are ways of finding him. But if it is not an emergency . . ."

"I know. Let us let the man grieve in peace. But his absence is felt here and, I am sure, there too."

"He has been gone longer," I repeated. "I am not concerned. The Wheel always turns, and it is best to let it turn in its own time."

"All right. People talk of searching for him."

That would probably be Uncle Herne and Prince Josquin, and perhaps Aunt Evote. "Tell them to hold off," I said. "He would not be particularly grateful to be found, I am certain of it."

"I suppose so. Very well, Gwydion. I shall bid you good night. And thanks."

"You're welcome," I replied, and snuffed the fire with

sand, which broke the spell's current and darkened the glass. I began putting things away.

Indeed it was as I had thought: Avril would not pry at Walter for news of Gaston, because Walter could not help him get it, but he would indirectly suggest to me that I set myself to discovering what he could not.

I wondered if Avril's nudging inquiries about Gaston and the trade agreements could be related. There was no obvious connection. Gaston had never been involved with our government. Probably Avril would like it very much if I did take the hint and look Gaston up, but if there were no pressing need to do so, I wanted to leave him alone. Also, though I was my Emperor-uncle's junior, I was not his lackey, and carrying out a request like this might make him think I was easily manipulated or dominated and inspire him to use me other ways. If I had believed him fonder of Gaston and sincerely concerned for his well-being, I might have heard his implicit request more sympathetically.

The Dominion of Argylle and the Empire of Landuc have stiffly polite relations. That two such different places, antithetical as the Fire and Spring that perpetuate them, have relations at all is a wonder, and it is unsurprising that we find it difficult to maintain them. There are historical reasons for the stiffness and also personal ones, and the politeness is mainly because we need each other and can't really afford to be at odds—again for historical and personal reasons. My late mother, however, always maintained that they needed us more than we needed them and had made her point in blood by winning the Independence War—one of the historical reasons for the cool relations between the realms now. Prospero considers the Empire an evil we could probably do without but are better off doing with. In Landuc they think that we need them more than they need us, but the trade between us is largely one-way. Partly that's intentional, because my mother didn't want the Dominion becoming dependent on foreign goods, and partly it is just that Landuc has little to offer that we cannot get locally more quickly and cheaply. Trade is controlled by strictly-enforced (on our end, anyway) treaties, and Walter had brought our cousin Ottaviano here as the Empire's representative to negotiate a new one, since the latest was due to expire.

My stomach growled, interrupting my meditation, and a sudden hollow feeling in my middle reminded me I hadn't eaten since my late afternoon snack while riding. I left the workroom and found my slippers by the window.

The night was lovely. I opened the casement and leaned out, elbows on the sill, looking around, down at the autumnal gardens. The near-full moon, the lively air, the liquid restless feeling of the Spring pouring over everything revitalized me. I began to think of staying up all night, though I was tired, and going for a walk in the City or outside. I hadn't done that in a long time: not going to bed because the world was too awake and exciting to leave . . . A shadow passed my head. I ducked, and something whumped onto my left shoulder.

"Ouch!"

"Prrrrt," said my familiar owl, Virgil.

"That hurt," I said coldly.

He bit my ear gently.

"Yes, it is a fine night. Why are you loitering here?"

Virgil fluffed and settled his feathers. He was feeling sociable, I supposed, and I pulled my head back in and straightened (the owl compensating for the change). My stomach growled again. It was time to raid the kitchen. Accompanied by Virgil, I went and did that, and then I went out and walked in the gardens for an hour or two, and then, as the night dew became cold and not just freshly chilling to my feet, I went in and climbed up to my bedchamber.

I turned in and dreamt of happier days, though I woke with tears in my eyes.

2

MY BROTHER WALTER HAS PICKED UP a bit of the routine drudgery of running Argylle. He really enjoys wandering around, talking to people, staying in touch with what they think. My forte is more in long-range planning, watching for changes, for potential trouble, for new opportunities. Accordingly, the next day I walked over to his tall stone-and-brick house, which is in the most densely populated part of town. There are always people around there, musicians, itinerant and settled peddlers, storytellers, carpenters (Walter is forever renovating or repairing), artists, all kinds of people, emphasis on creativity and good humor. It's a happy place, noisy and lively day and night.

Walter was pleased to see me, as usual, and we sat on a balcony in the warm autumn sun to watch the world flow by below, drinking a light Northern wine. Above us, an open window poured the sounds of a jazzy trio over the street. "I'm glad I returned yesterday. It's a song of a day," he declared, beaming.

"It is gorgeous. Not many more of these this year."

"Fine weather for hunting," he said. "But there's no one who knows that better than you."

"Yes. You heard about my manticore?" Phoebe must have told him, I thought.

Walter tipped his head to one side. "Rumor has it there is a great dragon come to the wood."

"It was just a manticore, but it was a big one. Seven and a half ells."

Walter whistled. "The damned beasts breed ever larger," he said.

"Yes. Walter, I came to ask you to start racking your

brains. I am looking back to see if I can pick up any pattern in these monsters occurring. So if you could be combing your memory for talk about them—when did people start really noticing them?—and keeping your ear tuned for current news, I would be grateful."

"Gladly, brother. And anything else curious, I'll pass on as well. There is a certain—I don't know, a tension—in the air. People laugh too quickly." Narrowing his eyes, he stared into the bright sky, following a cloud's shape changes.

"Hmph." I tipped back my chair and watched an old woman making lace on the balcony across the way. Tension. People around the Citadel had been edgy lately. Utrachet, the Seneschal, had actually snapped at my secretary Anselm this very morning. Most uncharacteristic. "Yes. That is true. —Avril's note was to ask that I Summon him for personal speech."

"Speaking of tension . . . ?"

"No, no. Nothing is wrong. He was wondering if we had heard from Gaston."

Walter sighed and shook his dark head. "He has probably found an impossible but just war somewhere in a hellish stagnant backwater of the Well's or the Spring's Roads and is fighting nineteen hours a day to keep himself from getting insomnia. Burning himself out." He became sad, wistful. "We were too happy too soon, Gwydion."

"Not Gaston."

"No. But the rest of us. Spoiled. Now the real work of life has begun and we must bend our backs and labor for our joys."

I thought about this. "You think happiness has to be earned?"

"Not like that, no. Not as the payment due for suffering. But it does seem that every life has sorrow and joy, some more of one or another, and we had much joy first. Mother's goal was joy for everyone all the time. I don't know how possible it is. Fortuna's Wheel does turn, as they say."

"It may not be possible, but it is a good goal. And I work for it joyously."

He smiled again. "As long as it is joyous work to you. . . . Are you going to look for Gaston?"

"No. I do not wish to intrude on him."

"Of course not." He looked down into the street, leaning on the balcony railing. "And our uncle?"

"What of him?"

Walter gestured loosely. "To find him . . ."

"Absolutely not," I said firmly.

Walter squinted back at me for a moment and then nodded. "Sorry, Gwydion. I do not mean to goad you."

"I know." To prove it, I sat with him a while longer and we talked about the City and countryside. Walter is a gossip sponge, a travelling newspaper, collecting and reporting rumors and news faithfully. Tactfully, he circled back indirectly to the subject of our missing relatives.

"I was talking to the Empress in Landuc," he said, watching me carefully, "and she said that she thought Gaston had perhaps gone off, as Prospero did, and found something . . . new."

"No," I said flatly.

"I do not know enough about it to say yea or nay," Walter said diffidently.

I regretted my somewhat abrupt answer. "It is possible, theoretically, but to liberate such a force as Prospero did here with the Spring, as Panurgus did with the Well of Fire, cannot be done without creating certain perturbations which are not undetectable. We know now what those are like, and I would recognize them, I am certain. Neither he nor our uncle has done anything like that. Besides," I went on softly, "Gaston . . . for one thing, he has never concerned himself with more than the quotidian applications of the most basic sorcery, what we use every day."

"That's so. He distrusts magic."

"And for another thing, Walter, I cannot see him . . . I

suppose I could have gravely misjudged his character, all these years . . . I cannot see him doing that alone. It might be possible that he would have done it with Mother, something for the two of them, but not alone, not as a solitary endeavor. It is not like him."

"I suppose you're right. People will do odd things when they are distressed, but they usually do them in keeping with their characters and past actions. Our uncle—"

"Again, I . . . I just don't think he would do it either, not in the state of mind he was in. More destructive than creative."

"You know him best. I yield to your superior knowledge. It was a pleasing notion."

I shook my head. "I am afraid it must remain only that. I do not think Gaston is enough of an adept for it, and I do not think our uncle is . . . in the mood. Besides the purely sorcerous evidence against it."

Walter changed the subject. "At Shaoll's house the other day—did you meet her? Oh, yes, that party—I had a good Romorantin wine, from the estate bordering this one actually, but I cannot recall the name . . ." and he indicated the bottle of Fidan we had been drinking.

I welcomed the change. Walter is a diplomatic man. "Those vines have flourished. Mother swore they would."

"And who would dare disagree? Yet they've been long in producing drinkable wine. I confess I had begun to think that perhaps for once she had erred, and it's reassuring that she was right." Walter emptied his glass and refilled it. He toasted me. "Your health, Gwydion!"

"Your happiness, Walter. I have seen no good Romorantin wine on my table, although I am pleased to hear you are seeing it on Shaoll's."

He chuckled. Shaoll was a weaver newly arrived in Argylle, and Walter was much seen with her. "I think they're keeping it in reserve, and a polite note reminding them of their obligations might bring some your way."

After perhaps half an hour of wine chat, I turned the talk back to business, to our ambassador cousin Ottaviano. "How is the Baron of Ascolet these days?" I said. "Did he sizzle and steam as you brought him through the Border Range into Argylle?"

Walter laughed, throwing back his head and roaring. "Ah me, I'd nearly forgotten that one." When I was a very small boy and had just heard that the Well embodied as fire, I had gone to Walter and demanded to know if this were true. He assured me it was, and he went on to explain gravely that when people from Landuc or the greater Pheyarcet around it tried to come to Argylle, they would vanish in a puff of steam, quenched by our watery Spring. Since I was old enough to know that people from Landuc never did come to Argylle, though not the genuine reason for it, this sounded wholly plausible to me. Only when I learned in a chance overhearing that Gaston was sometimes called the Fireduke was the truth of the thing explained to me; I ran in terror of his imminent demise to Mother and she had great difficulty sorting it out—and then blamed her father Prospero for filling my ears with fancies.

I laughed with Walter and then said, "But Walter, how is Otto?"

"Steamed. He sizzled indeed. He's affronted at being put under house arrest while he's here," Walter replied.

"He knew it would be so."

"Still, affronted. Not that he showed it, but I could see. He's going to be here for months, and he'll find it close confinement."

"He is only here until New Year. Mother would not have liked it," I said, "and Prospero certainly is annoyed."

"Avril wouldn't have dared send him to talk to her nor indeed to Prospero; he sent him because everyone there thought you would chaffer for Argylle," Walter pointed out, which was true. "Now that he's here, he's a diplomatic guest. It is nearly an insult—"

"I agree," I said, "but on the other hand Prospero will not want him roaming around, and at any rate he is bound by the same laws that govern others from Landuc when they are here, seldom though it is."

"No, I agree wholly with you . . . so we agree that he can't be kept prisoned in the guesthouse while he's here, and he can't be allowed free amble—"

I felt put on the spot. "I suppose we can allow him to leave the premises with a family member. You, me, Prospero, or Phoebe if she were inclined."

"That's still stringent—"

"It is more than Mother would have done," I said. "Tell him I said that, if he takes issue with the restraint. Don't tell him this: if he behaves himself we might loosen up. Let him go out with guards or a diplomatic escort. It would be better courtesy. And what reason has he to misbehave? —I don't know why Avril sent him and not Josquin. Josquin knows Argylle; people remember him kindly still from that visit years ago. I wish it had been Josquin." Josquin and I were good friends, and I had not seen him in too long. He was, in my opinion, the best of our Landuc family, the most like an Argylline. Temperamentally ideal for diplomatic work, he was witty, intelligent but not condescending, and his conduct and discretion were inerrant.

It *could* almost be construed as an insult, had I wished to be insulted—the Emperor sending to treat with his peer, not his Heir the Prince of Madana, but the Baron of Ascolet, his bastard son. Not that bastardy, as an idea, is current in Argylle—but Ottaviano had done things in the past which had given him a sulphurous aura, and though my uncle Dewar had a kind of rivalrous, hearty professional friendship with him, my mother and Prospero would not suffer his presence gladly.

I had picked up something of both attitudes. When I had met Otto in Ascolet with my uncle, he had seemed a good enough fellow, but all through my childhood before that I had heard his name spoken with coldness. I had decided to give him some benefit of the doubt: it seemed hard to forever damn a man for ill-doing he must himself regret, and by all reports Otto had repented heart and soul of the ungentlemanly conduct which had led the Emperor Avril to accuse Gaston of treason during the Independence War. Gaston did not commit treason; he lost the war because Freia was assisted by a mysterious woman named Thiorn who commanded the military actions. For Gaston, the truth of a matter sufficed. Prospero and Mother, however, both knew how to cherish a grudge, and had.

Walter, mollifying me, said, "I would rather have had Josquin as a guest again too."

"I would rather have done it in Landuc, but His Majesty made it impossible for me to refuse," I said, irritated with the memory of that discussion.

Walter spread his hands. "He's a vexatious man," he said soothingly, "and difficult to talk to. There's none who'd disagree with that. And he does have a point, albeit a small one."

"It is the point of a wedge. We must be careful."

"Yes. I will not allow Otto to stray into mischief, and Prospero will keep him leashed and muzzled straitly. But we cannot intern the man like a criminal when he is a guest. So this is just enough, all elements weighed and assayed."

"Just or not, it will have to do."

I went back to the Citadel and left him to rehearse an ensemble and choir.

Belphoebe was waiting for me on the steps. This was an enormous surprise; she rarely leaves her woods if she can help it.

"Brother Gwydion," she greeted me, not smiling.

"Belphoebe, what brings you here?" I had a sinking feeling. More bad news, surely.

"I come on the wings of ill tidings."

I led her to my private office and closed the door, leaning on it. "Tell me."

"There is a dragon on Mount Longview."

"A dragon?" I remembered Walter's rumor. "You're sure?"

Phoebe nodded, pacing around the room, up and down by the tall arch-topped windows. She's never at ease inside. "I have seen him myself. Gwydion, this is not one of the pesky little worms we have been plagued by of late. He is enormous. My hair stood on end when I glimpsed him."

"How did you see him?" I uncorked a bottle of wine from the sideboard and poured us each a cupful. It was not yet midday, and the morning had been long indeed.

Belphoebe sat on the corner of my desk as I sat behind it. "I had gone up to Beza Ridge to see where you slew your manticore and to bury the carcass, but you did a clean job and so I decided to hike out to the end of the ridge. There is a good view from there."

"Yes, you can even see Longview on a clear day." Longview is the highest mountain in the Southern Wall of the Jagged Mountains, which comprise the mostly uninhabited, rugged country between Argylle and Errethon.

"Just so. I had my spyglass with me and used it, scanning the forest. I have been thinking about establishing a base at Beza, although 'tis exposed in winter, and then as I stood there looking at the mountains of the Southern Wall it occurred to me that, although distant from the more habited areas, Longview would be a good place to set up a watchpost, to try to keep a lookout for these troublesome intruders in Threshwood."

"I suggested that to Mother more than once—I am sure Gaston did as well." In fact, the ruins of a gigantic tower lay tumbled on the stony, bare top of Longview. Someone had fortified the place once upon a time.

She shrugged. "There are reasons it is unfeasible . . . So I stood there looking along the range with the glass and I saw something moving behind Longview. I watched and watched and finally he drifted around, riding the thermals up from the valleys I suppose."

"The dragon."

"Yes. I could not guess at how big he must be, Gwydion, but I could see him quite clearly in the glass. He is very pretty: indigo tail, blue-violet-purple on his back, shading to darker, deeper violet and blue on his head, possibly white underneath."

I sat in my chair and leaned back, looking up at her sun-bronzed head. "Sun and stars, Phoebe—if you could see him coasting around Longview from the ridge, he must be simply gigantic."

Belphoebe nodded. "Exactly. As I stood looking at him, he turned his head and, I would swear, looked back at me, directly into my eye. Then he soared around the mountain again. I watched, but saw no more."

We were quiet for a moment. Then I slammed my hand on my desktop, frustrated. "Damn it, Phoebe! Where is this stuff coming from? The manticores, the erltigers, the wyverns, the karyndrasks, that damned pack of satyrs last spring . . . It is like when Tython was causing us all that trouble."

She just nodded again, her grey eyes serious, a furrow between her level brows.

"A dragon," I said under my breath. "Just what we need! They don't hibernate, do they?" It was autumn; if we could get it during the winter . . .

Phoebe, seeing my thought, shook her head ruefully. "The lesser ones do. The greater do not. That is a rule of thumb. There are exceptions. I know but little of the magical kind. I have never seen one."

"They tend to be fairly individualistic," I told her, "although there are common traits among them all."

"Such as?"

I rummaged in my memory for gleanings from tales and anecdotes. "They all tend to hoard something, although it varies from dragon to dragon. Gold and diamonds are most popular, but they will settle for other precious stuff. I once read of one who favored titanium. They like their prey kicking and screaming; perhaps it is the fear. And they get off on eating other sentient animals." I paused, thought. "I should add that everything I know about the intelligent ones is from books and hearsay. I have never encountered one myself. Just garden-variety dragons. The intelligent ones are very rare and are distinguished from the ordinary by size, habits, and naturally intelligence."

"And how intelligent are they?"

"I don't know. Probably no one has tested them."

She scowled at me. "Be serious! This is nowise laughable!"

"I know. At least he's fifty miles away at Longview. Let us pray he stays there until we can work out what to do."

"Kill him, naturally." Phoebe tossed back the wine.

I lifted my eyebrows slightly and looked at her. Oh, so? I thought, but did not say it.

" 'Twill be no joust, no child's play," she conceded, setting her cup down. "Marfisa and Alex will be delighted to have a share in the hunt, certes."

"There are so few opportunities for genuine heroism these days," I agreed drily. "Phoebe, it is very likely that one of our family is going to be dead before that dragon is."

She thinned her mouth. "How do you know?"

"The odds are for it. It is not like killing a wyvern in Jurlit's barn. Great dragons know who's who and what's what." I pulled a sheet of paper toward me. "I shall close the southern roads, I think." In an emergency like this, I couldn't wait to consult the Council, and legally I didn't have to.

"At once?"

"At once. It is autumn trading season and that road is heavily used. He may already have taken someone and questioned him. If not, we can make it harder for him to find anyone. Nobody is much around there, just a few mountain men . . . Perhaps," I went on, "I should route everything around him along Leys and the Road." That would require that I send Phoebe and Walter out to lead caravans of merchants . . .

"That seems a sound precaution."

"But he may well be able to follow anyway. If he is a real dragon, a magical one, he sees the Road and Leys as clearly as you see the lines on your palm; they are his natural paths. He knows without looking how they lie and where in the fabric of the world the pocket-worlds are stitched and how the Road leads in and out of them, among other things."

"Such as?" my sister prompted.

"Extensive knowledge of magic."

"Oh." She didn't say anything else for a while. I wrote a list of roads in that area and drafted a closing order and a mobilization and a few other notes to Gracci the Castellan and his subordinates. Anselm, my secretary, would draw the order up prettily, and Gracci would take some of the City Guard up toward Errethon border to enforce it.

"Should we talk to the others first?" Phoebe suggested diffidently as I pulled the bell.

"This is the best way to start. I will call a meeting for tonight."

"Then I'll tarry here. Till then I shall go watch the archers practicing." And sting them to better performance, I thought. She met Anselm coming in. I gave him my draft and told him to hurry. I wanted the closing official by sundown. The Councillors would squall; they were used to being consulted, but in times of emergency Mother had always gone straight over them, and I thought this was an authentic emergency.

I went to my workroom and assembled the materials needed to perform high-quality Lesser Summonings for my family, had a cup of bitter thick tea to fortify me for the physical drain involved, and began with Prospero.

The familiar preliminary words rolled off my tongue smoothly. The fire in the iron dish leapt up and showed me to myself in the mirror, the underlighting playing odd shading-tricks with the planes and angles of my cheeks and nose. I smiled at my reflection just to reassure myself. When I sprinkled three drops of water on the flames, my face was obscured in the disproportionate steam they made. I breathed on the glass, whispering. As the mist cleared, my image was replaced by Prospero's. We look much alike, so the change was not particularly dramatic; I seemed to acquire a beard, a few lines around my eyes, and a floppy blue velvet hat.

Prospero scowled when I told him about this latest headache. He was on a moored ship; the ocean and another ship moved asynchronously behind him, and a spit of land with a high white tower, the Ollol light, seemed unstable by its contrasting stability. The image yawed, too—he must have lit one of the gimballed lamps to bring my Summoning image as well as sound.

"What in the blistering hells—! A *dragon?* Whence comes this bestiary plague?"

I smiled in spite of myself. "I don't know. I killed a seven-and-a-half ell Argylle manticore on Beza Ridge yesterday."

He frowned more deeply. "Aye, and that wandering wyvern but a few days past. 'Tis one damned thing hot on t'other's heels, as they say. Tython's legacy haunts us still, may he twist in agony eternally and his deviant minions with him! I'll make my excuses here and be there forthwith; I must ride, as I rode hither and I'd liever not leave Blitzen."

"Good. I will call the others. By the way—"

"Yes?" he snapped, halting in mid-reach toward the focussing light.

"I know I ought to have asked you first, but I have already issued an order closing the southern roads. The Council will be complaining."

He nodded, and more mildly said, "Well thought on. You need not beg my permission, Gwydion, nor theirs; you are the Lord of Argylle."

I shrugged. Prospero's style was always high-handed. He smiled scantly and cut the connection. I cast my line upon the currents again. Punctiliously observing seniority protocol, I Summoned my eldest brother Alexander next.

"Alexander," I said as he appeared in the glass.

He was far away, in a green-draped alcove, looking at me via a mirror flanked by candles. It made a beautiful receiving focus. Behind him I could see a white marble corridor. His clothing looked formal. He glanced over each shoulder before speaking softly. "Gwydion. It has been a while."

"Not that long. Three months here? Yes . . ."

"Ah. What is afoot?"

"Not afoot, but aloft. We have a genuine dragon in Threshwood, on Mount Longview."

"A dragon?" He began to smile.

"Phoebe, using a spyglass, saw him quite clearly from Beza Ridge."

"Fifty miles away! Gods! It must be enormous!" He looked interested, excited.

"Precisely. I'm fairly sure, just based on the size, that he must be one of the real ones, not one of the mundane ones."

"Magical, you mean? Ley-finding faculty and so on?"

"Yes."

"Oho! But it can still be killed, no doubt." He smiled. "I misdoubt he'll move on simply at the asking. Who'll evict him?"

"If you can come to a meeting here, tonight, the topic will probably be touched on." Something about his eagerness to get the dragon to the taxidermist rubbed me the wrong way, but I had to be careful not to annoy Alexander. "I know it is very short notice, but we must move fast."

"Catch it off guard, perhaps. Yes. I'll be there." He glanced aside, shook his head, and turned away. I snuffed out the fire.

My next call was to Alexander's twin sister Marfisa, his junior by half an hour, like him in almost everything save sex.

This unnerved people, who often took her for his brother, especially when she was armored.

"Marfisa?"

"Ah—Gwydion." She was far, far away. Her voice was thin and remote from the lily-shaped crystal trumpet.

"You are wanted here, Marfisa. In Argylle. Can you come?"

"Now?"

"Yes. Or in the next few hours."

"Ah."

I thought we had lost touch for a moment, and then the glass fogged completely and cleared again and the image in it improved markedly. She was seated at a low table, cross-legged, in a loose smocklike shirt and trousers, in a tent it appeared. Her short-cropped curly hair was rumpled, her face expressionless in its classical regularity. A matchstub was between her fingers. There seemed but one light there, the one receiving my Summoning, and it stood some distance from Marfisa.

"Some emergency?" she inquired.

"Yes," I said, guessing that I had interrupted something.

A sigh. "Very well. What?" A line between her even brows, just like Alex's—"Father?"

"No. We have a very large dragon on Mount Longview. We are going to have to do something about it."

Her eyes narrowed and a spark of interest came to her face. "Such as kill it."

"Something like that, yes."

"When?"

"We will discuss and decide at our meeting here in Argylle this evening."

"How long from now by your clock?"

"About eight hours."

"I shall attend."

She pinched out the flame.

I sent a messenger to Walter with a note about the meeting

and then went back into my workroom and tried to raise Gaston and my uncle.

No answer, of course. Just wanted to feel sorry for myself, I guess.

We sat in the same order around the same oval table in the same long green-panelled room where Prospero had officially declared that I was the new Lord of Argylle. He had declared here to us once that he was worried about Mother, too, and announced a full-scale search. Mother had turned up on her own, apologizing for the fuss—she had miscalculated the speed of an Eddy's spin and overstayed. His son Dewar had been missing twenty-two years now, and Prospero hadn't bothered being officially worried. He had wandered the Road searching in every world he passed for a long time, and still went off periodically when he had a new idea about some place, but not even a rumor had he found. I had hunted around too, but if people want to hide, they can, and it is hard to find someone who does not want to be found, particularly an adept like my uncle. We knew he had bolt-holes, strongholds, retreats; we did not know where even one of them was.

This time I chaired the meeting.

"Belphoebe, please describe what you did today."

She obliged. I then tapped Walter and asked him to repeat the rumors he had heard about a dragon in Threshwood. He repeated them with cautions that they were rumors only; he hadn't traced any back to eyewitnesses.

"The timing is something we must ascertain," I said. "How long has he been there? What has he been up to?"

"Has he given our citizens cause for complaint?" asked Prospero.

"Farmers missing offspring or livestock and suchlike devilry? No. Not even a sighting as definite as Phoebe's," Walter said firmly.

"So he is but newly lighted here, taking his bearings," said

Alexander. One long finger tapped the base of his wineglass. He and Marfisa exchanged a glance, gold-sparked hazel eye to identical eye, a moment's nonverbal communication, no more.

"What do you know for certain about such creatures?" I asked my grandfather.

Prospero stroked his beard. "Hmmm. Since you told me of this, they've been much in my mind. Never have I faced one, nor would I gladly, though I believe your father Gaston did so ages past when he was a hot youth."

That was a long time ago.

"I did not know that," Alexander said. Marfisa lifted her eyebrows a hair's-breadth.

"'Tis but a tale I heard once, and the truth could be something wholly other. Histories alter day to day. Someone else in Landuc might remember better, or know more . . . There were dragons seen over the Palace of Landuc at Panurgus' death, a brace of them I'm told. The lesser ones, those that are like unto the Elemental creatures in form though not in nature, are commonplace in Phesaotois, to wit Noroison and its vicinity. Certain folk are wont keep the dragonets for guardian-pets till they grow large and ungovernable. Are you certain this is of the Elemental strain?"

I hesitated. I was not sure. "The size is extraordinary. Although I slew a manticore of unnatural size the other day, dragons are another thing. This one must be inconceivably big, and even if he be of the common run . . ."

"All creatures have appetites scaled to their size." Marfisa looked around at us all.

"Yes." I let that sink in for a moment. "We must act against him before he acts against us or ours."

"What kills those things?" Walter asked.

I spread my hands, shrugging.

"Father," Alexander said, a touch of black humor we didn't need.

"I can think of various things that would kill it, but many

of them would have undesirable side effects on the land-scape," I said. "It is likely that he shall be well able to defend himself against conventional and sorcerous attacks and to counter them in kind."

"Thus perhaps unconventional and nonmagical is the way to go," Alexander said.

"You have an idea?" I asked. It sounded promising.

"No. I merely offer a line of inquiry."

The discussion went on. Finally we winnowed out our choices:

One was do nothing and wait and see if the beast moved on. "Not likely," I said. "Mount Longview is an ideal dragon's roost. It's a major Node, with a strong upwelling of vitality from the Spring, and they prefer such places, I've heard. It has caves and ruins and the Errethon highway runs through Longview Pass to the east. Easy pickings."

Another was to attack him immediately with everything we had to hand, a preemptive strike before he had struck against us or established himself in his new abode. Alexander and Marfisa favored this, and Prospero did not conclusively speak against it. Phoebe chewed her lip and said nothing as they chaffered this back and forth, and finally looked at me and said, "You were serious before, weren't you."

"I usually am."

"About one of us being dead before the dragon is."

Everyone stared at me. I grew uncomfortable. "Fortune-telling is to neither my taste nor ability. But I think it quite likely."

Alexander looked suspicious. "I disagree."

"Your prerogative." I inclined my head to him politely.

He glared at me.

A third option was to do research, both abstract and ap-plied, and find out more about dragons in general before tackling this one in specific. I favored this choice. I pressed it by mentioning, during the debates over the others, how tactically sound it would be if we knew more about the thing we assaulted before we did so.

In last place was to attempt to coexist peaceably with the dragon. Belphoebe brought it up, she said, because Mother would have, although personally she didn't think it could work. We all agreed and shelved that one right away. Mother's ideas only worked, sometimes, for Mother.

More discussion and slightly-less-subtle leaning on my part resulted in consensus on the third choice. We would study, inquire of our Landucian connections, and find out what was definitely known about dragons. It was even possible that this individual would be known to someone. The draconid family in general live a long time. This decided, we adjourned to a sitting room and lounged around catching up on each other's lives.

My sisters and brothers and I get along well, better than many, which is good because we are a very small family by Argylle standards. There are tensions, conflicts, but we pull together more than apart. Gaston and Mother fostered this in us and with them gone Prospero continued to try to do so, with great difficulty at times. With only five of us siblings, and none but Walter who sought close long-term bindings with others, any genuine quarrel would split us fatally. We have not the cushioning structure of a real, wider family around us, and the loss of even one member of the broader group, let alone three, could have destroyed our fragile unity.

It has seemed strange to me that in Argylle, where everyone is bound to lovers, blood-kin, trading partners, and fellow-citizens generally by affection and goodwill, our family are all distinct, insular individuals. Perhaps it is because we were reared severally—a handful of only children—or because of something in our genetic makeup, or because of the Spring and the Well in us. We are each conscious of standing apart from the others, and we must each continually strive to stay connected.

This evening we were in effortless accord, though; there

was a problem to solve, something new and different and excitingly dangerous to confront, and we all love a good fight, except maybe Walter. So the conversation was animated, even cheerful.

It was quite late when we finished and turned in. Belphoebe knocked on my study door.

"I'm minded to head off toward Longview and camp nearby to keep an eye on our guest," she said.

"Do it," I said. "But for heaven's sake be careful."

"I understand. I'll send tidings twice daily."

"Or if anything noteworthy happens."

"As you wish. I'll leave at dawn." She left silently. I kicked myself mentally. I should have thought of that at once.

I had another thought, and I went to Prospero's door and tapped. He opened it immediately, a book in his hand.

"Prospero, do not speak of this to Ottaviano."

"Hm. Good thinking," he said. "I'll be mum."

"He may hear anyway—"

"From whom?"

I explained the decision Walter and I had reached that morning, to keep our emissary cousin mewed up in the guesthouse save when accompanied by one of us, with the possibility of more lenient treatment later—for the man had done us no wrong as an emissary. Prospero did not like it, but reluctantly assented. "If one of us escorts him, there's little mischief he can work."

"Just so. He speaks some Argos, I believe."

"Aye. Some. 'Tis folly to hope his 'some' is not greater than you think."

I shrugged. "At any rate, it's our problem, not his. I want no . . . interference. I'd rather he heard about it when it's over. I cannot think how, but he might find some way to use it against us when you bargain with him."

"True," Prospero nodded. "On the morrow I shall breakfast with Walter; I'll instruct him of this then."

"Thank you."

I lay awake in bed, unable to sleep, and finally lit a candle, took up pen and paper, and began making notes on things I would have to do, things I would have to have other people do, and things that might happen—three lists. I was growing concerned about the general population's reaction to this beast's sudden advent. How could I break the news to them? Rumors at first, then facts? Argyllines are a fairly level-headed, calm people, but a dragon is not an everyday occurrence. One of the fellows whose family's barn had been adopted by the wyvern was deeply terrified by the incident, and his wives and brother had wanted to move. Luckily they had a lot of relatives in the area who wanted them to stay. On top of everything else, I did not need a panicked exodus of villagers and farmers whose lands bordered on Threshwood.

This was going to be an acid test of their faith in me: would they trust my word, would they be calm and not panic if I assured them that things were fine, that we would cope with this one for them?

Early the next morning I called on Walter again and discussed breaking the news with him. On anything to do with public relations, his judgement was better than mine. He sucked a reed—I had interrupted him practicing—and thought about it.

"Less than full honesty will work against us," he said finally, around the reed. "Tell them everything."

"But all we know now is that it's there."

"Then tell them that, and tell them you're working on it. No secrets."

"If they panic . . ."

"Bah. When he eats somebody, then there'll be fireworks. Not before. Argylle always has odd things happening around the fringes. This is closer in, but it's still fifty miles away in Threshwood."

I walked back to the Citadel slowly, taking the river path, scuffling through leafdrifts under the big trees. What would

Mother have done? I wondered, and decided, yes, she would tell them. She had never hidden anything that affected the realm, and the people had understood this and backed her up whenever she needed it—with one noteworthy exception, which had taught them the value of compliance. Yes, I could gamble on their solidarity. The Archives were on my way, and I looked in on Hicha the Archivist and asked her to give me, top priority, today, everything there was in Argylle on dragons.

"Dragons?"

"Yes."

Hicha nodded thoughtfully, already mentally listing sources to check. "Whatever you want, Gwydion. Odd— Marfisa asked me that last night."

Marfisa had slept at Hicha's house, not in the Citadel. "Oh," I said. "Give it to me, and I will share it with her."

She smiled. "Very well. I'll send you what I find."

I found Utrachet the Seneschal looking for me at the Citadel. The highway closing had been received with bad grace and he suspected a lot of people were going to try to sneak around it, one way or another. The Councillors were offended because I hadn't consulted them, but were giving me the benefit of the doubt. Since Alexander and Marfisa had been seen in town, people realized something was going on.

"I'll make an announcement tonight in the Great Hall and explain why I've ordered it," I told him. He went off to arrange this, informing the Council first and then spreading the word through the streets.

The other thing I had to do was get our southern neighbors to close their end of the highway also. Our relations with them had been strained, but still cordial, since the Tython business. I spent the rest of the day drafting and redrafting, meticulously, a message to the Headman of Errethon and finally sent it via postal barge to Ollol and then to Errethon on a special clipper ship. He would have it the day after tomorrow, barring disasters.

* * *

The Great Hall was packed. My stomach fluttered as I glanced out over the sea of candlelit faces while I crossed the black stone dais from the side entrance that leads to the Citadel proper. Utrachet preceded me, announced to the crowd that the Lord of Argylle would speak, and sat in his chair a few steps below.

I took the Black Chair. Its stone was chill but comforting; I felt more in control of things there and less alone—the Chair still reminded me of Mother, and I still felt as if I were just keeping it warm until her return. Tonight more than ever I wished it were so.

After allowing the crowd to quiet down for a few seconds, I announced that a large dragon had been sighted near Longview Pass, through which the Errethon road ran. Until further notice, traffic headed south would have to go by ship. I explained that this was an intelligent, maleficent animal, unlike wyverns and manticores, and that it liked to eat people best of anything. If it captured and questioned someone, I went on, the risk to all would be augmented.

One way of getting through to Argyllines is to emphasize common interests. I saw heads nodding.

Someone stood and asked me why shipping was safe if the roads were not.

"I do not know that it is, but the Errethon road is a good sixty miles from the shore. My hope is that he is too lazy to travel the distance for a small return."

Another person asked if we were sure the dragon was hostile.

"Hostile is not what I said. But it eats people and it is intelligent and powerful. It is dangerous to everyone who would like to go on living. I think I speak for all of us there."

Tense amusement.

What would it eat if it could not get people?

"Other meat." I didn't go into details.

There were a few more questions about when I thought it

would be safe to travel and just what I was going to do. The answer to all of them was, "I do not yet know. We are working on it now." The assembly broke up quietly and people went home, nervous but trusting me.

This was scary. They were trusting me to protect them from something I myself did not understand.

Prospero joined me for a late supper. The twins, Alexander and Marfisa, had gone off to dine with old friends in the City, Alexander at Shervé Miruin's house and Marfisa with Hicha. We ate with little conversation until the fruit and cheese were served.

"Today I had a gossip with the fair Oriana," he said, picking currants off the stem and stacking them in pyramids. "She'd like a look at this guest of ours. She said the description rang familiar, but could not think just how."

"She said nothing definite, though."

He chuckled a little. "Oh, no."

"Perhaps," I said. The sorceress Oriana of the Glass Castle was always ready to meddle with magic, and Mother hadn't trusted her, although Prospero did and my tutor had. Sometimes. Oriana knows her sorcery, whatever else one might say about her. Mother wouldn't say anything, but her sniff spoke volumes.

Prospero steepled his fingers and looked across at me over them. "Thereafter I made a few other casual calls, polling about. Avril says the most draconic thing he's ever slain was a beast called a wantley, no dragon as we know them, when he was but a stripling: long ago. To my surprise, Prince Josquin says he's slaughtered many dragons, large and small, but nearly was dinner to the only great magical one he faced—'twas quite by accident. He escaped with a trick and his heels scorched, along the Road. It was a fleeting, or fleeing, encounter; he learned naught save that a dragon-slaying career is glorious but brief, and renounced his. He too believes your father Gaston conquered one, but knows no further."

I laughed as Prospero described Josquin's experience. My cousin was the last person I could imagine as a dragon-slayer; I would twit him on it when we met again. "You prompted him . . ."

"Nay, he volunteered the tale, rue-faced. Fulgens has never met a great dragon, although he's dressed a few of the other kind and their cousin sea-monsters. Herne has seen them on occasion, but says they've shunned his purlieus—wise creatures. He's athirst for a chance to prove himself 'gainst one; said naught of Gaston's prowess, but averred Ottaviano has spoken with a dragon." Prospero tried to keep the note of respect from his voice and did not succeed.

I was impressed. "Truly. And lived to tell the tale."

"Methinks if anyone in Landuc could, he were the man. Herne said 'twas his notion that Otto had done it of necessity, not curiosity. However, he did not kill it . . . else surely we'd heard more of it ere now." Prospero turned his attention to the currants, eating them stack by stack. "Herne's sifting the story behind Gaston's fighting one; thought it sounded likely when I spoke of it, but knew no particulars.

"Oriana has never slain nor seen one, but she said she'd made Gaston a gift of a book about them when she heard of his marriage to your mother." Prospero's mouth twitched slightly, an impenetrable expression, and he continued blandly, "I supposed his collection of such books has largely fallen to your lot, so I begged of her generosity naught but the title: *On the Ways of the Lords of the Air.*" He swept the remaining currants into his palm and ate them all at once. "The great difficulty that comes of your father eschewing our company," he said after we had sat for a while longer, "is that his memory goes back further than nearly any living man or woman I know, and largely in his head he carries matter that's nowhere found in books. I'm in no mood for necromancy to question, say, Panurgus. 'Twould be dear-bought information, too dear."

I picked apart a pomegranate. "I think our present resources are adequate," I said slowly. "Your experience and our—enthusiasm—"

He chuckled.

"Seriously, Prospero. Among us we share all the talents needed to kill this thing. I don't think we must beg help from Landuc. I don't think we ought to do a Summoning of the Dead. And I don't think we must hale Gaston out from his retreat."

Prospero drank wine, looking out the window at the city lights. "There I'm of one mind with you. We must honor his wish for privacy. He'd be a puissant ally against this creature—none better—but if his heart were here, here would he be, and have been." He tipped his chair back, lit a pipe, smoked thoughtfully. "You ought not to hesitate so, Gwydion."

"Hesitating?"

"You're groping, creeping cautious 'long the walls. Follow your humor. Don't falter so; don't wait for the world to choose for you your deeds, your plans, your thoughts. If you stumble, the fall will seldom be so great as to allow no recovery."

"I feel young for the job."

"You *are* young for the job. But you're carrying it right well."

We sat and drank the rest of the wine slowly. The sky was clouding over. The autumn storms would be settling in soon, and then the short dark days of winter would close around us. The wind rattled the glass as Prospero and I talked about the Landuc–Argylle trade pact. He had been in Ollol to pick up scuttlebutt on what the merchants thought of the present agreements and what they wanted to change.

"The conviction's widely held that Freia was overgenerous to Landuc. But I mind that at the time the Emperor cried we were most miserly—howbeit Gaston himself advised her to be more frugal with our wine." Prospero smiled. "He was not without selfish motives, stocking his cellar by betraying his own Emperor as 'twere ... Yet it's played against us, too; our cellars are full, with fine wines ripe and peaking, and every crevice with a bottle in it."

"The wine is what Landuc really wants. I understand it's become very popular."

His smile grew wider, gloating with satisfaction. "Exceedingly. They're hard-pressed and we can squeeze them dry. The bottleneck is that no one agrees on what we ought to get for it."

"Here, you mean?"

"Yes. Tobacco, coffee, silk: vice for vice. Perhaps 'twill become clear in time." He shrugged.

"Much does." And much does not. Where was Gaston now? "We have all winter to talk it over. And more pressing issues to consider."

"Such as the habits and physiology of dragons."

Having to spend the morning listening to the Council fuss meant I had no time to sit down and read in my study until the following afternoon. To my great relief, things held quiet; I heard no reports of murder or destruction from Longview Pass. Against reason, I hoped the dragon had moved on, but as I ate lunch Phoebe sent in a report that he was still there.

Hicha had turned up only eight books with substantial material on dragons. She also had a long list of references, but most of them were just a few words here or there. I curled up in the deep blue-cushioned window seat of my study and began to read.

Two of Hicha's books were ones I myself had added to the Archives; I already had gone over the copies in my own collection. I flipped through these just in case, but no, all was the same.

The others were more interesting. Prospero, Uncle Dewar, Freia, and Gaston were all book lovers of wide-ranging taste and had added freely to the Archives, collecting material from all over. One of the manuscripts I looked at now was very old and in Latin with a translation in my mother's minuscule handwriting on tissue paper between each page, the translation being sandwiched between two more sheets of tissue. She had also made editorial comments. I read a few lines and then closed it; her voice, evoked in my thoughts by the handwriting and the characteristic style, made me shake.

Two others were in archaic script, probably from Noroison via Dewar. I set them aside.

Oriana's gift to Gaston was a scroll in a pictogrammatic-looking brush-writing I didn't understand with an attached Lannach précis in Gaston's writing: "On the Ways of the Lords of the Air (dragons) with a description of their habits"—thanks, Gaston. Just what I needed, but no, he didn't translate the whole thing. Damn. Maybe somebody else could read it. The pictures were very pretty. They looked like someone working from a fifth-hand description had drawn them as accurately as possible.

One of the bound books was a standard hunting treatise and another was also a hunting treatise which contradicted most of the first's assertions about life cycle, feeding habits, and so on. They also disagreed on the best way to kill a dragon. It was clear that the unintelligent and nonmagical variety was intended, but I read them anyway.

That was all. I sighed and settled in with the books from Noroison. Had Dewar, I wondered, ever run across a dragon? He had not mentioned it to me.

These books were very informative. One of them, by a man I'd never heard of named Lord Uvarkis, even cited the other in a few places, agreeing and expanding in detail on cursory observations by the earlier writer, Duke Nellor Trephayenne. Duke Nellor was a legendary hunter, dead for many centuries before Uvarkis had written his sequel. When I read, I tend to hear the writer's voice, or to invent one for him; now I conjured up an image of the doughty, bass-voiced Duke Nellor and the dry, academic Uvarkis, who coughed occasionally and smiled a sidelong smile.

NELLOR: *"The lesser dragon be sluggish in chill weather and as the year wanes he groweth insensible in the greatest cold, which be to his disliking so he will fly if he be not injured or ill to milder climes to avoid this if he possess no lair or be from it sundered by accident. Yet he endureth the cold if necessary in a wakeful dullness of sense which passeth if he be roused by attack and if he be sundered from his lair. And if he be in his lair he doth nought but sleep all the season until the sun returneth. And in the days of winter-sleep the females lay their eggs."*

UVARKIS: *"Nellor states that the female of Draco sapiens will lay her eggs during hibernation. This is incorrect. She (and there are very few shes) lays them in the spring. Selecting a spot with good exposure to sun or other source of heat, such as a volcanic steam vent or hot spring, she will construct a sort of mound or heap and lay them in it, coiling herself about the pile during the incubation. The number of eggs can be many or few, but only one or two, possibly three, of the hatchlings will survive the cannibalistic feeding frenzy that follows hatching . . ."*

NELLOR: *"Purloining a souvenir object from a dragon's hoard be ill-rede, should you chance to find the hoard unattended. For he will mark the lack forthwithal and hunt you a-raged through Ocean and Vapor, Earth and Hell, until he recover the object and devour the thief."*

UVARKIS: *"Dragons brood over their hoards until they are intimately familiar with each item. In the case of the dragon of Li Changroven, the hoard numbered some eighty thousand jade objects great and small, each of which the dragon could apparently describe in detail, provenance and workmanship both, with a fair assessment of the item's current market value. It may be possible to appease a dragon by offering him a*

unique or novel item for his hoard, but I would person-
ally not rely on this."

NELLOR: *"The great dragon be solitary in his habit*
as a hermit, withal it liketh him to partake of fellow-
ship of men of passingly quick wit. So from time to
time will he suffer one with whom he hath held particu-
larly pleasant discourse to escape uneaten."

UVARKIS: *"According to Nellor, the great dragons*
are solitary creatures. This is true, and it is because
they are jealous of their hoards and their hunting terri-
tories . . ."

Uvarkis even gave an account of a conversation he had
had with one dragon, annotating it to explain the reasoning
behind his parts. They had talked for a day and a half. I read
it over several times. The key seemed to be to play Schehera-
zade, to keep the dragon guessing, wanting more, without
annoying him quite enough to end the chat.

I wondered how my scintillating conversational skills
would compare. Uvarkis had a masterful command of language; puns and anecdotes and double-entendres tripped
lightly along in a fluent, easy style, references to other dragons and ancient history indicating his wide experience and
familiarity with the species. Ottaviano had survived such an
encounter. I was not certain I could.

Dragon coloration seemed to be a random thing, rather
like spots on cats, not indicative of anything special.

Dragons favored high places near, but not too near,
human habitation. I knew that.

Dragons were attracted to magic and magical locales.
They could sense magic as easily as a dog could smell a
rabbit.

Dragons preferred warm climates, but the great dragons,
the biggest and oldest and most intelligent (they kept growing and becoming smarter with age) were impervious to the
cold. Nellor described standing next to one such as being

near a smelter's furnace, so great was the heat thrown off by the beast. This made sense, considering their Elemental pedigree.

Dragons' eyes were their principal weak spot, although Nellor had had good results when he had managed to pitch an explosive right down the throat of one yawning. It had annoyed the dragon so much it had gotten careless, and Nellor had been able to get in a clear swing at the head, decapitating it. I could not see any of us trying that. Maybe Herne would, but he was an impatient man and he was also lucky.

I closed the books and looked out the window. It was raining. I thought of the rain hissing and evaporating off the hot hide of our dragon. What had become of Uvarkis? Had he run across a dragon too smart for his wry wit? Had he gotten too close to the throne and been murdered, as happened to successful courtiers? Uncle Dewar might know. I sighed.

I picked up Gaston's scroll again and read his inscription once more. He was the expert on killing things. Phoebe and the twins knew a lot too, but the sheer weight of experience on Gaston's side was overwhelming, as Prospero had hinted the previous night. Prospero had never gone in for wholesale death the way Gaston had. Gaston had never gone in for sorcery the way Prospero had. They had widely different tastes in most things, despite being brothers.

I looked at Mother's translation of the Latin manuscript, which was a bestiary. The dragon part was nothing compared to the Nellor and Uvarkis books, being patently inaccurate or fictional. But it was pleasant to read her writing, to hear her quiet voice with its warm undertone echo dimly in my mind, and so I read on and on about the Camelopard and the Roc, the Oliphant and the Griffin (similar to but obviously not related to our gryphons). The light grew poor, and I learned of the Unicorn and the Wyvern (a local variant, perhaps) and the Beast Glatisant. The pictures were familiar, and I wondered if Mother had read to me from this, or just shown it to me and made up stories around the pictures, when I was a child. Soon the light was too dim for reading. I closed the book and leaned my head back against the wall, eyes closed.

"Gwydion."

I started and lit the lamp with a finger-snap invocation of an ignis. No one was there. Had I dozed through a failed Summoning?

I was tired from my sleepless night, my worried days. It had been Mother's voice I had heard: a hallucination induced by reading her manuscript. I slammed the books down on my desk and went off to find dinner.

⟶ 3 ⟶

BELPHOEBE HAD A BOW WITH SILVER- and gold-tipped arrows of black steel. Three black spears and a few throwing knives concealed about her person were her other weapons. She doesn't like armor, and we had pleaded with her to reconsider, but no, light mesh mail over her usual leather tunic was the most she'd have, not even more protection on her legs than her lightweight leather leggings.

Alexander was in silver-colored scale mail over leather; Marfisa's mail was coppery. They had lances, long swords, shields. Alexander was on his terrible horse Steel with its sharp teeth; Marfisa rode a beast I had not seen before with wild yellow eyes, clawed not-quite-hooves, and quilly fur that was almost scales. Still rather horselike. Her helmet was winged and her eyes, clear and neutral, scanned her brothers and sisters, cataloguing our weaponry.

Marfisa had had an intense, low-toned non-argument with her squire Tellin at the stables before we left the Citadel. Redheaded Tellin had firmly entrenched herself in the squire's duty to accompany her knight, and Marfisa had besieged her position with the knight's duty to train, not kill, her squire. Prospero, Alexander, and I had made ourselves scarce until Tellin, head high and face set and pale, left the stables. Alexander had brought no attendant with him; he never did when visiting Argylle, and Marfisa never had done so before. It was natural that the girl would want to accompany Marfisa, if only for the novelty of the adventure and the glory to be got, but Marfisa had the discretion of wisdom and experience and would not waste the girl's life, and rode out to join us alone.

I rode Cosmo and wore black leather and carried only one spear, a shield, and my favorite gold-damascened sword, Talon. Out of habit I had a small axe and a mace at my saddle, but I doubted I'd be using them. In the back of my mind, my memory ticked with spells, as I had spent the previous day and much of the night poring over my books and freshening my memory. Many of the spells I had reviewed I'd never actually used, though I'd learned them. The more powerful ones are more elaborate and take longer to say, because one must specify and control more things. Recalling a longer spell imperfectly meant that either it would be a dud, or that it would backfire on me, or that it would perform something—not necessarily what was intended—in an unpredictable manner.

Prospero was with us, the Black Sword at his side, an indicator if one were needed of how serious this was. He wore leather armor also, under a long mail shirt. He too surveyed us, seeming pleased with what he saw. His white horse, Blitzen, fidgeted, made nervous by Alexander's and Marfisa's peculiar mounts.

Walter had been counted out of this. I had wanted also to leave Prospero home to help Walter if every one of us were killed. The twins had shouted me down. "Every one of us has a right to go," said Alexander.

"Walter is going to need help if we get toasted."

"Prospero is a superb swordsman. He must come." Marfisa rarely expressed strong opinions like this. "It is essential that we hold nothing in reserve."

I threw up my hands. "What do I care, anyway? I'll be dead. So be it."

Government by committee has its drawbacks.

We had also bickered about armament. From Nellor's book, I had gathered that the right armor for going against dragons hadn't been invented. He had spent an entire chapter on the subject. Cogent arguments could be made for and against both leather and metal. Nellor had preferred a combination of leather and mail: leather because of the flames a dragon was likely to produce, and mail because of the teeth and claws. He also allowed that there was much to be said for plate—although it was bad in a fight with a lot of fire, it could be life-extending if you were going to be at close quarters.

I had passed this information on to the others and encouraged them not to wear plate. The twins had decided to wear part plate, part mail—mail on the arms and upper body, greaves and cuisses on the legs. I had decided to go for light weight and maneuverability. It was reassuring to see that Prospero had gone the same route.

Alexander grinned at Phoebe, who had just doused the Way-fire; I had opened a Way from the Citadel, a temporary Road in effect, to get quickly and (I hoped) unnoticeably close to the beast's roost. "Sister, lead us onto his slot," he said.

"Right gladly will I," she replied, and set off through the trees and undergrowth. Alexander trotted after her, then Marfisa and Prospero, and I brought up the rear, cold fear uncoiling in my stomach.

O Gaston, I thought, wherever you are, think of us today.

Maybe we should have invited Fulgens and Josquin and Herne along. The more the merrier. Safety in numbers. Et cetera. But of course we could not. To do so would imply that Argylle couldn't manage her own affairs. Mother had fought for years to prove that we could.

Cosmo followed Blitzen, snuffing. I could not smell anything unusual—maybe a slight extra freshness in the air. It was cold; the sky, overcast. We had had a few days of hard freezes. The predawn darkness made going difficult but not impossible; as we progressed, we left the taller trees below us and the ground became harder and drier.

The trail was one I had climbed before on hunting and picnicking trips. It winds around the mountain and then zigzags up one steep side. How far would the dragon let us get? Surely he had seen us. He'd cruised by after we arrived.

All the way to the top, it turned out. Of course, I thought; let us tire ourselves with the climb. Let our fear mature.

Cosmo grew balky, as did Prospero's horse, as we grew closer to the top. We passed areas of crushed trees, some still bleeding pitch and sap. Belphoebe fell back behind Marfisa—I had ordered her to, since she was the most lightly armed of us all—and preceded Prospero now. I could smell something like petrol or kerosene. Halting to listen, I could not hear the clatter and rattle of Alexander and Marfisa. A small, localized breeze shouldered through the rocks and brushed past us. I looked quickly behind me, nervous—there was no one there. Ahead of me, Prospero frowned and stopped too, loosened the Black Sword in its scabbard, and advanced through the rocky, narrow passage after staring around him with a preoccupied scowl of suspicion. I followed him.

The top of Longview is bare and barren, rock and stunted shrubs and the tumbled ruins of the tower. The dragon was draped comfortably around the tower, waiting for us. Alexander and Marfisa had their heads together to one side. Prospero allowed me to draw abreast of him and Belphoebe stayed out of sight, among the rocks.

"One is lacking," rumbled the dragon. Nothing I had read had prepared me for the voice, like a pipe organ. He spoke musically, with archaisms and a courtly manner. "Where is the squirrel who has been scampering about from tree to tree of late?"

I had advised my family not to get involved in a conversation they would surely regret. But Prospero smiled.

"Perhaps the squirrel has found a tasty nut to gnaw," he said.

"Perhaps. I am fond of squirrels. They amuse me. I am fond of people, too. They amuse me as well. I see that you have come prepared for . . . amusement."

Hypnotic, that was the word Uvarkis had used describing the effect of a dragon's personality. I shifted my attention to the haze of power that was tangible here—it was a vigorous upwelling, a substantial Node—and the dragon's head swung toward me. My head cleared as I began tapping the Spring via its emanations.

"Ho," he rumbled, a cathedral sighing. "The real opposition makes itself known." He examined me, the cilia-like whiskers around his huge mouth waving gently, testing the magical currents. "I do not know you, boy, though you smell of Landuc."

"Close enough," I said. I curtailed his inspection of me with a quickly-drawn shield.

"And your sorcery reeks of Morven. There was rumor of a bastardization of the two lines some time ago . . ." The great head lifted, tilted, looked from me to Prospero and back. "Ho. A true son of Panurgus, and a false one."

I urged Cosmo forward a couple of steps. Our agreed-upon strategy was that we would wait for the dragon to make the first move.

"The Stone of Phesaotois is in you," the dragon boomed, lifting his head higher and fixing his gaze on me. "It is defiled by your blood, bastard of bastards."

I twisted my mouth wryly. He reminded me of my conservative and parochial relatives, who had certainly had worse to say about all of us—though never to our faces. Indeed, the

Emperor of Landuc had at least legally cleansed all of us of the stain of bastardy by formally acknowledging our parents' marriage, though it was still a moot point there whether it was lawful for a man to marry his half-brother's daughter. Fortunately, in Argylle we reckon kinship differently, so nobody ever gave a tinker's damn about it.

"Your name and lineage!" he demanded. "I would know what I have before me here."

"What difference does it make?" I replied. Overhead, three of my dark hawks drifted in circles.

"It is a matter of consequence and reputation," he said. "I am something of a gourmet." He blinked lazily and turned his attention to Marfisa and Alexander. "A noble pair of Landucians, yes. It seems a shame to eat a matched set like that."

Prospero chuckled softly.

The dragon looked back at Prospero and me. "No, the real zest in this meal lies here. I cannot quite divine the connection. It is close, surely, but unclear. Not quite direct. Not quite father and son. No."

A feeling of closeness in the air around me oppressed me suddenly. I threw it off with a gesture. "Your manners are graceless," I said coldly.

"Bastard of bastards," he repeated, looking at me, and then at Prospero. "I had understood Argylle was ruled by a woman. That creature there is scarcely such." He flicked a look at Marfisa, who did not react. Alexander's jaw tightened.

"Argylle was ruled by a woman," Prospero agreed softly.

"Waaaas," purred the dragon. "Ho. Perhaps I should have paid my respects earlier, then. One dislikes to force oneself upon a lady, of course, but gentlemen may call freely on one another."

No answer from us. He continued to study us, concentrating his attention on Prospero and me again. "Prospero, son of Panurgus," he said. "That is it. I have heard of you." He seemed interested now. "It was you who claimed the Spring here."

Prospero smiled faintly.

"I am here principally because I was curious as to the result," the dragon went on. "There is more than I expected to find. Prospero, Maker of Argylle, and his heirs. You, bastard sorcerer, I think I know you now."

I froze the smirk that was ready to burst onto my lips and Prospero too controlled his face carefully. It seemed the dragon thought I was Dewar. Good.

"You appear to have the advantage of us, then. Perhaps you have a name also," I said.

"It would take several days to say it," he retorted. Dragons increment their names when they eat noteworthy people. "The first few syllables are harmonious, however. I am Gemnamnon."

"I have never heard of you." Prospero shrugged.

He blinked. "Nor will you again," he rumbled. "Your petty sorcerer and your pins and needles will not keep you from me, O Prince of Landuc and Maker of Argylle."

The fear, I remembered. Dragons enjoy fear. None of us were showing it. Alexander and Marfisa had their usual neutral, clear expressions. Prospero seemed amused. I was simply watchful.

"I did not come here to listen to a lizard boast," Alexander said coldly.

"But you have small choice, Sir Knight. I can keep you here as long as I wish now that you have come."

I felt a brief prickling in the flow of the Spring around me, as from a Summoning begun but suddenly cancelled. Belphoebe, perhaps? It was gone now. Gemnamnon didn't seem to have noticed and was speaking to Prospero again.

"Son of Panurgus, you may buy yourself a few additional heartbeats by telling me of the history of this place."

"Meseems you know it," Prospero said, unfazed.

"Apparently my source was outdated, if not unreliable."

"What source was that?" Prospero asked.

"Ho." He wasn't telling.

"We are not obliged to remedy your ignorance," I said. "Your impulse has led you astray if you expected to find easy pickings."

"Ho. No, it was largely curiosity that brought me, bastard sorcerer."

"Too bad."

He was examining me again. I shrugged off another magical probe.

"Those bother you, do they, boy?"

"Your source was very deficient indeed if you did not expect to find me," I said softly, gambling on Uncle Dewar's reputation and sending a short, sharp probe back.

Gemnamnon sneezed. A hot, acid wind puffed past us. The horses shied, rolling their eyes back. The dragon lifted his head and looked at me directly, but with no effect; my tapping of the Spring seemed to buffer me from the entrancing effects of his gaze. He projected an air of amusement. "But I did expect to find you. And, finding you, I am delighted to accept your challenge."

He exhaled, a sighing sulphurous breeze. A luminous ball of fire drifted toward Prospero and me, gathering speed. I shielded us and dispelled it.

The non-sorcerous part of our party, namely everyone but me, had been forced to concede that if magic started flying, they must retreat. Marfisa put her hand on Alexander's arm as if to remind him of this, but he shook it off and moved away from her. The dragon lifted his head a bit higher, higher, higher—his neck alone was perhaps fifteen or twenty feet long—and snapped his head around to puff a ball of fire at the twins.

I knew, I *knew* I should have come alone.

I managed to shield them from the worst of the blast and dispel it with a snap from one of the lines of Spring-force laced through the area, which I now commanded because I was drawing on the Spring.

Alexander said, "Hah!" and Steel reared up suddenly and danced to the right. Marfisa dropped back, lifting her lance. Alexander was holding his lance like a spear.

I summoned Gemnamnon's attention back to myself by casting a Steelburst spell, which sprayed fire and shrapnel into his face. At the same time, Alexander threw the lance at his throat. Gemnamnon caught it in his teeth like a pencil and crushed it, laughing a laugh that boomed back from the mountains. The spell had no apparent effect. He whipped a couple of coils of his body out from around the tower and a heavy, clawed leg appeared. It was as thick as two men, the digits a meter long, plus claws, and pale silver in color. His tail snapped out and Steel jumped over it as it whizzed by.

Prospero made a clicking noise with his tongue. "Lay on," he muttered, and drew the Black Sword. The blade flashed in the midafternoon light. Marfisa had meanwhile come over to the dragon's right side, opposite Alexander, dodging several passes of the tail. He was playing with them. I hit him with the simple Bolt of Death, which he parried with another fireball, but the aftershock seemed to rock him somewhat.

I wasn't shielding my brother and sister any longer; I couldn't. They had been warned.

Prospero suddenly swung his sword and splattered a series of small bolts of lightning Gemnamnon had thrown in our direction, at him, actually. I spurred Cosmo forward, lifting my black spear and my shield.

Gemnamnon laughed again and knocked Marfisa over with a puff of flame and gas, swishing her mount's legs away simultaneously so that it fell on her. She made not a sound as she went down like a stone. Cosmo bounded over the dragon's lashing tail and closer in to the tower, in the lee so to speak of a section of wall. The tail couldn't strike close in here, but the claws could. He lifted his foot to bat me and I shouted the words to a freezing spell. He hissed; the foot hissed and steamed too. I followed up with one of Dewar's special compositions, the Shower of Molten Iron, right in that huge face, and he hissed again and drew back, then bellowed, a deafening sound, as just in the periphery of my vision, to the left, I thought I saw a movement.

One of Belphoebe's spears was stuck in the side of his mouth—in his gum, like a weird whisker. He struck it away and sent a fireball poofing in the direction from which it must have come. I slammed him with the Locomotive Pile-Driver, knocking his head back as he brought it down toward me. A roar and a bounce, and Gemnamnon was up, suddenly rampant on the stones and ruins. I cried out Hand of Fire and the Bolt of Death and punched at his left eye. He jumped toward me, and Cosmo jumped back, away, and I barely had time to finish Thunder Fist, which made him pause, but not for more than a millisecond. Fire and acid smog shot from his nostrils. I heard a horse screaming somewhere. I drew a fast shield around myself and Cosmo and threw the spear I'd been holding toward the eye I had hit before, with a swift-spoken repetition of the Bolt of Death reinforced with the Pile-Driver.

With a deafening howl that made stones crack, Gemnamnon took to the air. The wind from his wings was corrosively smoky and stank of various gases. He dropped from the tower ruin and off the top of the mountain. I could not see his left side; I did not know what I had done, though plainly it had annoyed him. He dropped out of sight.

I was running out of really useful spells at the tip of my tongue; not one had wounded him mortally, nor had the most powerful done extensive damage, even in concert. To finish him off, I would have to come back. Nothing any of us had done thus far had had a significant effect on him except a few of my sorcerous sallies; I did not think I could keep pounding away at him, with the few which had thus far proven efficacious, and survive.

It was eerily quiet for a moment, and then the silence was broken by a soft groan and a thud.

I looked around. Prospero and Alexander were bending over Marfisa. They had just heaved her dead mount off her. Prospero glanced at me as I joined them warily.

"Best call the day's work done," he said.

"Yes," I agreed. Alexander was easing Marfisa onto his cloak. She was badly charred down the left side of her body; the leather had burned and the metal was simply melted. The smell of burnt flesh and leather around her nauseated me, but she was alive, breathing with difficulty, and in shock. A rattle from the rocks made us all spin around. Just Belphoebe, though. She sucked her breath in when she saw her sister.

I reached through the Spring for my birds, sent them soaring to find the dragon, then turned to her.

"Phoebe," I said, "I want you to get down the mountain and keep an eye on the place, as before. He is hiding in a cave on the north side, about a third of the way down, above that big scree slope. Be very, very careful."

She nodded once and sprang away through the boulders.

Prospero and Alexander lifted Marfisa. I prepared a Way and conducted us all back to the Citadel, after collecting a few small stones from the area and a handful of earth for use on a return trip.

My fear now was that Gemnamnon would strike at the City. All remained quiet. Belphoebe later reported that he had burned a postal relay station and eaten the three inhabitants before returning to roost at Longview. I set birds to watch him there at closer range than Belphoebe could approach.

We did what we could for Marfisa. I used sorcery to help her body begin to mend some of the worst internal damage. She would recover, I was sure of that, although it would be a long time before she had the full use of her left leg again; it was burned to the bone from foot to hip. A draught of the Spring might help her healing later; for now, she must rest.

Tellin sat with her, unnaturally quiet (she was a merry shield-maid to serve my dour sister), watching over her.

Alexander's condition was another care. He had inhaled a heavy dose of mixed caustic gases and was coughing blood, but refused my help—whisky, oxygen, and bed rest were his prescription for himself. Walter sat with him, playing on a harp, until he drifted off to sleep.

Prospero came to my study after we had cleaned up.

"I must attack him again," I told him. "No distractions. Sorcery is what will work."

"Take me with you," he said.

"No."

He stared me down for a moment and then shook his head. "As you will, then." But he pounded his fist on the table as he turned and left the room.

"Prospero!" I called after him.

He spun around, his face angry and hard.

"It will take me a day or so to prepare myself. I shall need to work without interruptions of any kind. Please, will you act for me?"

He nodded curtly and closed the door painfully quietly behind him.

Why was he so angry? I hoped he didn't blame me for the twins' injuries. They had had time to flee and had stayed, against my advice. I decided to take a nap before starting in swotting my spell-books afresh.

Curled up on my side in bed, I looked at a photograph of my mother and her brother. They are on a sailboat, Freia lying on her stomach and looking over the side and Dewar sitting beside her leaning on the cabin. His hand is on her back, ready to grab her if the boat should suddenly lurch. The photographer is on the cabin, perhaps next to the mast, and so the angle of the shot is downward and a bit slanted. They are not looking into the camera. Mother is gazing into the unevenly green water, her chin on her crossed forearms, and Dewar is looking down at his sister, smiling slightly.

Ottaviano had explained that he took this picture long ago when Dewar was making great efforts (in vain, as it befell) to reconcile his sister to their cousin and to reconcile his sister to boats, by coaxing her to join them in a swift Pheyarcet Eddy where Otto had a fine safe boat and calm waters. Otto gave it to me after her death and Dewar's disappearance, saying he had always liked it and he hoped I would too. I do.

I dozed, thinking of the slap of waves against the boat's hull, imagining the silence on the boat except for the sound of the wind in the sails and shrouds, and then the stealthy photographer's camera clicks and they both look around, startled for an instant, Dewar's hand tightening on Freia's shirt, his eyebrows shooting up, Freia lifting herself up on her elbows, chin on her shoulder . . .

I fell asleep with a pleasant feeling of being safe and secure, at home, and drifted into a dream of walking in my mother's garden outside the Citadel, looking for her, knowing she was always just ahead, around a corner, out of sight.

⟶ 4 ⟶

IT WAS DARK AND FROSTY OUTSIDE when I woke, dark and chill in my room. I ought to have lit the fire before sleeping. I remedied this at once, then pulled the bell to send the manservant who answered down to the kitchen for sandwiches and whatever was around. While he did that I bathed quickly and the place grew less cold. Finally I built up the fire in the study and sat beside it in my favorite leather chair, wrapped in a quilted black silk dressing gown, wolfing down my late supper or early breakfast.

In my dreams I had divined the reason for Prospero's anger: it was not directed at me, but at his son Dewar, absent Dewar, believed by most of the family to be wandering madly through the worlds crazed by the death of his sister.

If Dewar were here, I would not be in half the danger I was walking into. Probably we would have been able to destroy Gemnamnon between us, right away, rather than in this haphazard, fumbling fashion.

I wished he were around myself, but I was capable of finishing this. I was sure of it. I had Gemnamnon's present injury—I suspected I had damaged, possibly blinded, his left eye—working for me now. If I went in well-prepared and calm, I would live and he would die. My error lay in allowing the others to come with me at all.

The books Hicha had given me lay on the window seat. I leaned back and picked up the top one, Uvarkis'. There might be some clue in here as to what the animal's weak spots were and how they might best be exploited. I leafed through it, rereading stray paragraphs that caught my eye:

> *Dragons, being Fire Elementals, are impervious to most sorcerous attacks as most spells of destruction are based on Fire. Basing an attack on other Elements is not recommended, as they easily conquer all but the strongest manifestations thereof . . .*
>
> *The fortress of Vos was laid siege to and subsequently laid waste by the dragon Thembushskandriskar after the inhabitants rallied and attacked the dragon in his lair . . .*
>
> *Conversation with a dragon is always enlightening and usually lethal . . .*

Usually lethal? Yes, ours had been lethal.

Enlightening? He had insulted and goaded us, not enlightened us, and our conversation had been atypically brief.

Ottaviano had spoken with a dragon. If I had talked to him first, he might have been able to tell me about the beast's supernatural swiftness, its offhanded use of power and sorcery, its imperviousness—all of which had startled me in that first attack. I bit my lip and put the book aside. I had not wanted to bring him in on this, but if it were inevitable that he hear about it anyway, perhaps I should use him as I would any other knowledgeable source.

Prospero would not approve, and I misliked it myself. It was not good to appear vulnerable in any way to the Empire Otto represented, now or at any time. But he had encountered one of the things—possibly this individual, though I had no idea what the population of dragons in the Elemental Void might be, if that was indeed where they came from. The only source on that was dragons themselves, and Uvarkis said their stories varied and might be elaborate fictions spun to amuse themselves with our stupidity.

I did not want to get killed. Otto might know something I had not found in Nellor's and Uvarkis' helpful narratives. There was really no choice: I would consult him before I attacked again. In the morning, I decided, and opened Uvarkis again to reread him, searching for clues.

"Good morning, Otto. I hope it is not too early to ask you to strain your memory for me." I had invoked Ottaviano with a Lesser Summoning as soon as I was dressed.

"Hey, Gwydion. No, not really. I'm on my first coffee." Ottaviano hadn't combed his beard or brushed his hair yet, but he was clothed and alert-looking. The beard was a dapper touch; Otto is one of those blond fellows whose beards are rust-and-gold. It lent him dignity, a mature, wise look: fitting for an Imperial Envoy.

Now I faced another of those lightning decision moments. Generosity won again. Besides, it was better for me to keep myself available here in the City than for me to go to him in Ollol, two hours' ride along the Wye. "Come have your second here. I've not had breakfast, myself. I'll make a Way for you."

Otto hesitated a fraction of a second, nodded, and set his cup down. "I'm at your service, of course. I'd better leave a note," he said.

"Certainly." I cut off my Summoning and cast a new spell through my Mirror of Ways, seizing on a glass in the room where he now sat as my receiving focus. There was no difficulty in opening the Way between us; the opalescent, fluctuating compression zone was but a thin line, and so the impression was that my broad, tall Mirror in the Citadel was just a doorway leading to Otto's bedchamber—in Ollol.

He glanced up at me, smiled, signed his note, and left it on the desk where he'd written it, then came toward me and stepped through the Mirror.

"We're in the Citadel?"

"Yes," I said. "Come with me," and I took him down to the breakfast-room. Food was laid out on the table; someone had been there already, probably Prospero.

I served us coffee. Gaston and Mother were tea-drinkers. The kitchen staff had kept making tea and sending it up for a few years after her death, until I had to ask them to stop. The rest of us like coffee—which comes from Landuc, and is a luxury trade item because of the cost. Mother had never allowed anyone to import seedlings and start a plantation of our own, though the climate north of the Bevallin Coast was suitable.

"Good coffee," murmured my cousin.

"Your brother Josquin's own Madanese," I said. "Have some hash and eggs." We ate without talking much. I had not seen Otto for many many years, and never had I thought to see him in my own Citadel, and I was preoccupied, and all these things made me a silent host to my guest. Utrachet and Anselm came in and we rearranged some of the business of the day; it was all minor, relative to the dragon, and I postponed and referred everything planned before luncheon. I spoke Argos with Utrachet and Anselm, Lannach with Otto; they ignored Otto and Otto pretended to immerse himself in his food while the Seneschal was there.

"You're a busy guy," my cousin observed when Utrachet had gone.

"This is relatively quiet. It becomes hectic in midwinter, when people have time to think of reasons to petition me. I sit in the Chair every other day sometimes, especially after New Year's."

"I can see why you dumped the negotiations on your grandfather, though. I was surprised that you weren't doing it yourself, like Freia used to. As the place gets bigger, it gets busier."

We went to my office and settled into the comfortable tapestried armchairs. The tiled stove was warming the room so cozily that we could sit by the bookcases and not be cold. Though there was no wind, the remote sun's light had the edge of winter on it.

"Now to business," I said, meeting his acute eyes. "This has nothing to do with the Compact. I understand that you ran into a dragon once."

He lifted his eyebrows. "I heard a rumor that you have one in the neighborhood . . ."

Damn! So much for security. What else might he hear? I covered my dismay by saying, "Yes, there have been rumors to that effect."

"You want to hear all about my dragon, I take it." He grinned humorlessly.

"Yes."

Ottaviano nodded, dropping his grin. "I'm here to do some trading, so I'll make a trade with you now. I'll tell you my dragon story, and you'll tell me one."

"I know no dragon stories," I said stiffly. It would figure. Ottaviano wasn't one to give anything away.

He studied his fingers. "Not a dragon story. What I'd like, Gwydion, is the straight story about your mother's death. Almost nothing was reported in Landuc: simply that she was dead. We didn't get so much as an invitation for the Emperor to the funeral."

"We prefer to keep it to ourselves," I said, getting up and walking away from him. I stood at one of the windows, arms folded. A cold draft poured down its thick small-paned glass.

"I'd consider it a confidential matter, and I wouldn't repeat a word of it," Ottaviano said softly to my back. "I understand . . . how things are with Argylle, particularly as regards Landuc. But I knew your mother, and I've wanted to better understand how she died since the news hit. With Gaston, her brother, and her father in town, too: three mean guys, any of whom would cut his own throat to keep her alive. It just doesn't add up."

"It was an accident," I said to the window.

"What kind? Gwydion, I'll gladly tell you everything I know about dragons. I'm sure you think I'm true mercenary Landuc scum for charging. But I know there's no other way I'll ever hear the story, and I know that you'd tell me the unglossed truth. In a way you force me to act this way, you see? I sincerely want to know, not for anyone else or for any reason other than . . . it was a terrible shock, and I still can't quite believe it."

The fact that Ottaviano was here at all ought, I thought, to go a long way toward persuading him that it was true, that Mother was gone. I stared out without seeing a thing beyond the glass and thought about his offer. If he would swear to keep it to himself, then . . . there could be no harm in it. His curiosity was natural. Were Dewar around, he surely would have told Ottaviano himself, anyway, years ago.

On the other hand, I do not like to think about that day.

However, I did need to hear how he beat the dragon.

My realm was endangered by this dragon on Longview. Personal privacy was all very well, but quite a few people here knew what had happened to Mother and, really, it wasn't as if we had intentionally kept it wholly to ourselves, as part of some plot—we had simply not wanted to discuss it. If Otto could keep it to himself, so that we would not begin hearing hideously distorted versions of the truth with equally hideous interpretations, then there was no reason he should not know.

"All right," I said aloud. "You must swear to hold it in strictest confidence; if it were for general public distribution in Landuc, it would have been aired there. It's open to misinterpretation, and they always put the worst light on things."

"I guess that's true," Ottaviano admitted. "I will not repeat it ever, to anyone, by the blood in my body and the breath of my soul."

I nodded and turned away from the glass. After a moment, I sat down at my desk. "You first," I said.

He took out a pipe, shot me an inquiring look to see if I minded, and then packed it and lit it. The smoke had a fruity, ripe scent; I couldn't identify it. After a few minutes of quiet puffing and thinking, he started.

Way back when your Uncle Dewar and I were young and reckless—now we're older and reckless—we were talking one night about dragons. It was not long after I'd settled things between me and Landuc peaceably, and Dewar and I were spending a fair amount of time exercising our bodies by day and by night going on sort of celebratory pub crawls, chasing women, and generally living it up the way one is supposed to when one is young and reckless and well-heeled. By the time he knocked off and went to see his father and sister and I went back to Ascolet, we had a reputation as savorous as Josquin's was then.

We crawled back up to the Palace after a particularly good one and had a few nightcaps in the small library with that nice bar. There's a tapestry of a dragon in there, or there was, and Dewar started pointing out the anatomical inaccuracies.

I suggested that it was probably an imaginary dragon, and he got all snotty and said that in Landuc, it ought to be a picture of a *real* dragon.

"What do you mean, a real dragon," I asked.

"A real one," he said. "You know. You don't know. Intelligent and Elemental and more dangerous than anything spawned by the worlds you know. There are a few who domicile in Noroison and Morven. I suppose it's too tedious here for their tastes."

"Or maybe Uncle Gaston and Herne killed them all off," I suggested.

"No," Dewar said; "I think there probably haven't been any around here. If there had been, if Gaston and Herne had killed them, wouldn't we have a few heads and hides around the Palace?"

His reasoning made a sort of drunken sense. The trophy rooms were devoid of such. There were no, say, dragon-hide chairs or divans about. And he became even more, well, arrogant and said he'd show me a real dragon someday. Implied that he'd run into them before and they were no big deal for somebody as hot as he was.

Dewar and I, you have to understand, had been jockeying for the upper hand for a while. We had been competing lately in all the sports you can imagine, in spending money, in drinking, in, uh, um, the amorous arts, and a lot of other things I'm not going to describe. The funny thing about that was that no matter how much money changed hands on our bets, neither of us came out ahead for long.

So this put me into a competitive frame of mind. He was being damned cocky and I wanted to kick him down a peg or six. I started asking questions about dragons. When he told me that yes, they really do hoard stuff, I said "Enough, Dewar. Put it where your mouth is. We both go off and find a dragon and steal something from him."

"A capital idea!" he said. "Are we going to have a deadline?"

"Yes," I said, "let's make it interesting and give ourselves a one-month time limit. I'm sure I can find one of these big guys by then, and if you're so smart you know right where to look."

"Are we betting something?" he wondered.

I wasn't sure. We decided yes, we'd bet something, and we couldn't decide what to bet, so we figured the one who got back last with his trophy had to buy drinks for the other for a Landuc year including holidays—one year of rounds total, no matter how fragmented it was—and the winner got to keep both trophies.

Just to be safe, we wrote it all down, and although the next morning I'm sure he was thinking, as I was, that this was one of the dumber bets we'd ever made, neither of us dared suggest dropping it. We didn't tell anyone about it, because we were sure our elders would not like us roving off down the Road to pick a fight with something large, smart, and dangerous. For a cover we put out a story about a scenery trip to Musrie Gorge and took the Road that day from the Noonstone. When we were clear of Landuc, Dewar slowed his horse and looked at me.

"You're sure you want to go through with this," he said.

"Hell yes," I replied.

"Otto, I know I can do this, and I'd feel bad if you got killed."

"I can take care of myself," I said. "Any pointers?"

"They like to talk," he said. "They are suspicious, and paranoid, and very quick. They're attracted to sorcery and powerful locales. They can use the Road and Leys just as we can, or better. They like to eat you when you're most scared. Don't look one in the eyes or you'll be his next meal."

"Great," I said. "How'd you find all this out?"

"I learned it when I was a child." He shrugged. "It's part of the standard curriculum. Summon me if you get into too much trouble, Otto."

There was no way I'd Summon him to bail me out, but at least he was on record as making the offer. Slippery as a fish, Dewar . . . sometimes. I recall wondering if Avril or Gaston hadn't put him up to it somehow, as a good way of getting rid of me—though I'd been officially forgiven for my various trespasses, my relatives were not entirely happy about me. Prospero in particular appeared to have it in for me, and I knew Dewar was responsible for keeping him from simply cutting my throat and crying revenge for poor Miranda of Valgalant's death and other transgressions.

Dewar went on to tell me that I should get the name of the dragon I was stealing from. "They all have names, long ones, made up of various bits and pieces. Usually they have a few preferred syllables that they use."

"Why?" I asked.

In the tone of someone addressing a two-year-old, he started, "The names in their entirety can take a day to—"

I cut him off. "I mean why get the name?"

"Oh. So we know who he is. Then if I hear of him looking for you later I can warn you." He grinned.

We split up after more good-luck-mate chitchat. He stopped at a crossroad and went off somewhere after elaborate preliminaries—I suppose across the Limen to Noroison—and I headed there the hard way, not knowing the route in anything but theory and consulting my Ephemeris often. What I knew about dragons was entirely theoretical too; I was sure Dewar knew more, and I was sure he'd told me enough for me to be able to find one. So I wandered along the Road through every little pocket-universe world I passed, into the cul-de-sacs and out of them, favoring mountains and sparsely-populated areas, looking for caves and abandoned castles and places like that.

I asked people, too, if they'd heard of or seen a dragon in their area. I ran across a few small dragons that way, but nothing really big—none of the great dragons. I did kill one of the small ones, for practice, but its hoard was tacky trash and it had given its name as Neddy, so I figured it didn't count.

I kept track of the time in Landuc. Two weeks after leaving I knew that I was going to be in trouble if I didn't do better. I pushed myself into wilder places and hunted about there. After a few days, I ran across rumors of a dragon, and a day and a half later I found authentic dragon-created destruction in the form of a fire-levelled village by a lake. A few chewed-up corpses made me extra-cautious as I prowled around, hunting for someone who might be able to give me the latest news on the beast. Finding no one, I headed up into the hills for the night, where I encountered an old man who ran from me.

"Wait a minute!" I yelled. "I'm looking for the dragon!"

He just ran faster. I figured he knew something, so I followed him to his home—a cave, as it turned out. The steep, green hills were an extinct family of volcanoes, and they were riddled with unexpected openings here and there. He lived in the cave with a little old lady about as substantial as a dried-up leaf, and neither of them was pleased to see me. They barricaded themselves in their hole, peeking out through a triangular window in the door, which was made of bits and pieces of mismatched wood.

"Look, I don't want to harass you," I said, "but I'm looking for a dragon, a big one, and I'm wondering if he's somewhere in the area."

"Go away," the old lady yelled at me, and she threw a rock. "We paid our taxes. You go away. Brigand." And similar abuse.

I got off my horse and told them I wasn't leaving until they came out. And, figuring that bribery works where courtesy doesn't, I chucked a couple of gold coins into the cave at them.

"What do you want?" the old man asked after they'd had a moment to recover from this.

"I told you. I want that dragon." I'd considered asking to sleep in the cave, but the smell of the place put me off.

"He's gone," the man said.

"No he's not," she disagreed. "He's not gone. He's waiting. Mark my words, he's waiting."

"He's gone, you foolish old woman," the man insisted in a quavery voice.

"When was he here?" I asked.

"Weeks ago," the man said.

"One week ago," she corrected him. "Eight days exactly. He ate the King's tax collector. Good riddance to him."

"Too fat to run," the old man said. "It was weeks ago, weeks ago. Months."

She seemed more coherent than he, so I figured I'd trust her word. "What did he do?"

"He ate the King's tax collector," she said.

"Did he wreck that village?" I asked.

"No, the King's tax collector did that," she said. "You're a nice young man. Go away. Leave that dragon for the King."

"Shut up, you silly goose," the man muttered tremulously. "We warned him once, we did."

"King's job is killing dragons," she went on over his objections. "You let him get to it. Nobody ever thanked a volunteer."

"Where was the dragon living?" I asked.

"You never mind," she said. "You run along home now. He'll eat you up same as he ate the tax collector."

"I bet he's up in these hills," I said, looking around. "How long has he been around?"

"Long gone," muttered the old man, "long—oof!" He disappeared from the window and, though his mumbled complaints were a continuo to the rest of the conversation, didn't speak again.

"Oh, ages!" the old lady said. "Trust that fool of a tax collector to go stirring him up, trying to collect taxes from a dragon. Fat old idiot. He smelled like a rose, though."

"So the dragon was quiet until the tax collector tried to collect taxes from him," I said, "and has he attacked anyone since then?"

"He always claimed he was a vegetarian, too," the woman said. "The dreadful hypocrite. Heaven knows what he was doing with all that fish."

"Fish?"

"From the village."

I blinked. "The dragon was getting fish from the village?"

"Of course. Where else? Is he going to catch it himself?" She cackled.

"He's been quiet since he ate the tax collector, though?"

"I dare say. He's going to be wanting his fish, unless that tax collector choked him, and he's going to be fashed about the village being gone."

I recalled the state of the village. Maybe dogs or wolves had been at the corpses. "Does the dragon have a name?"

"Of course he's got a name. What are we going to do, yell 'Hey, you,' at him? What do you want with him anyway?" She squinted at me through the little window, suspicious.

"Just to talk to him."

She eyed my leather armor, lance, shield, and sword. "Hmph. You're pretty well set up for a talk."

"It pays to be prepared. What's he called?"

"Hunnondáligi," she said. "And you be respectful."

"I will, believe me."

"You go up to the Bowl Peak there," she said. "You'll find him."

The old man began arguing with her. I left them to wrangle it out and mounted my horse, Tango, and rode up toward a blunt-topped mountain that had to be the Bowl Peak.

It grew dark before I'd gotten more than a couple of miles from the village, so I camped for the night in the thick forest that covered the uncultivated part of the mountains. I decided against a fire, although it was chilly, and I slept with my sword under my hand. Tango was agitated when the wind blew from the mountain; I sniffed too but didn't pick up anything unusual. My night was quiet, if unrestful. A couple of times I started, hearing animals moving around in the undergrowth nearby, and once an owl went by.

I rose with the sun and Tango and I headed on up the mountain. I made my way to a sharp ridge and went along that to get to the bowl-shaped crater. Must have been a hell of an explosion that took that one off; it was like a miniature

mountain range in itself, maybe three or four hundred yea
old—still visibly a crater.

There was nothing to indicate where a dragon might have
his lair.

I spent the day going slowly around the edge of the crater,
studying the other sides through binoculars I'd brought with
me. I didn't spot any signs of dragon inhabitation and made
a fireless camp that night in a saddle between a couple of the
lesser peaks. That night, as I lay unsleeping, a dark shape
passed across the stars, blotting them out as it went over and
down toward the village. I scrambled up one of the peaks,
but I didn't see anything, though I watched for hours.

The next day I continued on my surveying circuit and
found a dirt road that went into the crater on one side and
down toward the village on the other by way of a modest
saddle. I hit myself on the head. Fish. The woman had said
he got fish from the village. Could they possibly be delivering
it? There were wagon ruts in the road. How had I missed it
on my way up?

I rode along it, extra alert, and Tango became more and
more fidgety as we went on. The road descended and then
bent to follow the curve of the mountains. It was more a
track than a road, not particularly well-constructed—used
infrequently. It ran along the base of a sheer wall of multilay-
ered rock—a slump, perhaps—and there Tango became
frantic. He rolled his eyes back, dug in his feet like a mule,
and refused to proceed. So I tied him to a tree there and
continued on foot. As I walked, I considered my own mortal-
ity and decided I would rather be a live rat than a dead lion.

I returned to Tango, fetched a few vital items from my
saddlebag (including my City Key for Landuc) and built a
fire, a big one using most of an old fallen tree, looking over
my shoulder often, as you can imagine. Then I opened a Way
to Landuc, but didn't use the Key. Instead I left the fire
burning there next to Tango and left the spell uncompleted—
that was a trick I learned from good old Dewar, accidentally.

.rudged back up to the dragon's lair with the Key on a ⌐ring around my neck, inside my breastplate.

The road disappeared here. The ground was hard and stony—no vegetation—and the sun beat down mercilessly. It occurred to me that this would be a good place to bask, if one were a large lizardy heat-loving creature. I poked along and found a sort of crack beneath an overhang. The crack grew wider and wider and became a dark opening, broad but not higher than about six feet. A chill draft from it bathed my face, the air having a peculiar chemical sort of smell. I wet my handkerchief and tied it over my nose and went in.

Of course it was dark.

I backed out, rummaged around in my pockets for a small electric torch, and found it. Those things are a hell of a lot more reliable than an ignis and easier to turn on. I don't know why more people don't use them. I checked for the extra batteries and tiptoed back in.

"It never rains but it pours," I heard, before I had gone three feet. My light didn't show me much. I went on. Something moved ahead of me.

Suddenly the whole passage was flooded with light, and with it came a blasting wave of chemical stink and a roaring sound. The dragon was testing his jets. I saw him clearly by the blue-white flames he breathed from his nostrils. The flames hit the wall and splashed about. He was very big. He filled the cavern beyond me, and he was perched on a mound of something white and glittering like ice . . .

His voice was huge, and his eyes were hypnotic. I forced myself to shut mine. His flame went off.

"I shall have to get a maid and have regular teas if these visitations continue," he rumbled, a gravelly sound as of an earthquake thinking out loud. "Stop right there."

I stopped.

"Your name and lineage?" he asked.

"Are you Hunnondáligi?" I asked.

"You are the intruder here, Knight," he said. "You must

identify yourself. I am testy today and I am little inclined to play guessing games. Kindly show your face."

Great. "Call me Otto," I said. I pulled the handkerchief down.

"Otto? Otto of where? Of what?"

"I think I'll keep that to myself until I know more about you, if you don't mind," I said, and that was the smartest thing I'd done so far.

"Hmmmmm."

I set my light on its most diffuse setting and saw him dimly—his head was up, and he was studying me. I realized that the pile of stuff was something like glass or quartz or crystal—though I suspected a dragon with a penchant for cut crystal would have different storage arrangements. His hide was of varying shades of green and gold, very pretty probably. I had difficulty not looking at the eyes. I looked at the claws instead. They were hypnotic in a different way.

"Hmmmmmmmmm," he mused, and hummed a scrap of Mozart. "Interesting, interesting. You're not a tax collector, I take it."

"No," I said.

"Not working for Mokis, either, I'd guess. That sort tends to swagger in and announce he's going to cut one's head off."

"What happened with the tax collector?" I asked.

"Apparently they've decided to tax savings accounts," he said, "and someone interpreted my bed here, which I have painstakingly assembled over centuries for my own comfort and pleasure, as a savings account. Six per cent.! I ask you, Sir Otto."

"Scandalous," I agreed. "Mokis must be hard up for cash."

"Oh, I wouldn't know. I stay out of local politics . . . So do you, hmmmm?"

Whoops. "I'm not from around here."

"I'd guess not." He moved. "If you're not working for Mokis, and you've actively sought me out, I can only assume you have some silly feat of derring-do in mind. I suggest you abandon it. As I said, I'm in no humor for it."

"Tax collector disagreed with you, huh?" I asked.

"Nasty little man. I never did trust people who wear too much scent. It's taken me days to get the stench out of here." His tail lashed and swished inches from my feet. I kept myself from jumping back with difficulty. "I came up here just to avoid unpleasant scenes like that. It will take me years to recover my composure. Years of meditation . . ."

Holy cow, a religious dragon, I thought.

". . . of exercises, of contemplation . . ." He picked up something round and sparkly—about as big as my head, but like a one-carat diamond in his claws—and examined it, then tossed it down. It rolled to a stop in front of me. I punted it back onto the pile. Too big anyway. He rumbled, laughing maybe. "If you are interested only in saying you have spoken with me, you should leave now."

"We've hardly chatted at all," I said. "I understand you're a vegetarian."

He sighed. "Lapsed, now, I fear," he admitted. "As I said, I shall have great difficulty disciplining myself anew."

"How'd you get into it?" I asked. "Aren't dragons carnivores by nature?"

"I encountered a philosopher, long ago, and after a most enjoyable discussion found myself agreeing with him on a number of fundamental points. Malcastraeus was a hermit, occupying a cave into which I had intended to move—and I did move in, but he stayed and I became his disciple. He was quite elderly and feared me not at all, which was why I had bothered conversing with him . . . At any rate, among the practices of his religion was the renunciation of all flesh. I did try, but potatoes and vegetable marrows simply didn't agree with me, and after some most unfortunate intestinal disturbances we compromised on fish."

"Did you try eggs? Milk? Nuts?" I wondered.

He puffed disdainfully, an ozonish whuff of breath. "It's

difficult to get them in decent quantities in the quieter locales I prefer. I always disliked eggs anyway—so slimy—and frankly, cheese becomes monotonous in all its guises."

"So he was vegetarian, huh?"

"Yes. Actually he was so desiccated and insubstantial that he hardly ate anything. Herbal teas and nuts and roots were his diet. Once he had some wild strawberries, and he liked them so much he abjured all fruit thenceforward."

"A real extremist," I observed. "What happened to him?"

"He died, of course. He did live a very long time, and we passed years in illuminating discourse. The local peasants revered him as a saint and started hanging about the cave praying and the like after word of his death somehow got out. I had to leave; it was simply too much public attention. I dislike being treated as a novelty to be gawked at."

"Were there miracles?"

"The usual nonsense. Spontaneous cures, resurrections, and divine interventions. I rather doubt that Malcastraeus was responsible. He had so little interest in the physical realities of life, it seems improbable that he would suddenly respond to importunities from women with clubfooted children and villagers fearful of plague. But there it was, and the ignorant hordes were unbearable in their adoration." Hunnondáligi snorted with disgust, then picked up another glittering pretty and scrutinized it, polished it against his breast, and set it down carefully. "Since then I've continued to meditate on my own, attempting to better understand the principles my teacher tried to convey to me."

"What are those?" I asked, still buying time, trying to think of a way to get something and get out of there in one piece. I hoped my fire wasn't burning out too quickly.

"Primarily they concern the denial of the self and attempts to distance oneself from the corporeal world, concentration on the unity of all Nature."

"I see," I said. "So your philosophy states that all things are one."

"All is one. In one is all contained." He took up another faceted stone and gazed into it for a moment.

"The universe implied in a single hydrogen atom . . ."

". . . or less," he agreed. "You are not the uneducated thug I took you to be, Sir Otto."

"I've been called a dumb jock. I did go to university."

"Oh? Where? There is a goodish college at Dom-Daniel."

"I know the place. I wanted a more grounded education than they give. More in the practical line."

"There is much to be said for that if one intends to lead a worldly life."

"Isn't Dom-Daniel primarily for sorcery? That can be a pretty worldly pursuit."

"It's best known for wizardry, yes, but the rest of the faculty is also quite sound, particularly the rhetoricians. . . . So it can, when misapplied. Pure sorcery has nothing to do with the physical, rather with the study and appreciation of the Elements and the ethereal energies that make up the world as it really is, in its most fundamental and natural form."

"Well," I said, "my appreciation of it is largely pragmatic, though I've known the other sort of sorcerers, the philosophical guys."

As we talked, I had continued to avoid his direct gaze and to glance around for something small enough to take away without slowing myself down and close to the exit. My eye had finally lit on what looked like a ribbon of small diamonds an inch or so wide, not too long. Part of a sash or something, perhaps. It had something blue and glittering near it, making it easy to spot, and I decided that was my prize.

"The problem is," I went on, "that it's very easy to talk about the purity of Nature as it exists fundamentally and very difficult to maintain anything in that state of purity for long—because Nature, as it exists fundamentally, isn't pure anywhere but in the formless Void outside the worlds or in the great Sources, whose natures are fundamentally opposed."

"I am finding it very difficult," Hunnondáligi said, "to return to my former state of repose, yes. You are suggesting it is futile to try?"

"It's going to take a lot of effort," I said. "Perhaps you should start by fasting."

He rumbled with dissatisfaction. "It appears that I shall be fasting involuntarily. The village with which I had my agreement for the provision of fish no longer exists."

I deemed that he might be feeling hungry. "There are still a few people living around the fringes down there," I reassured him. "Certainly new inhabitants will come, or old ones return, given time."

He stared into an irregular chunk of diamond—I'd decided that that was the preferred bedding of this particular dragon—and tipped his head this way and that to appreciate the way the bluish glow from his nostrils colored the stone.

"It will never be quite the same," he said at last, and exhaled a long, slender flame like a propane torch jet. "Indeed perhaps it was doomed to fail from the beginning, to deny my own nature in myself. The world entices, seduces . . ."

"Rise above it, Hunnondáligi," I urged him, having no desire to be his hors d'oeuvre. "Think of the bliss of enlightenment."

"Nirvana, or whatever one wants to call it. Yes. Have you known anyone who achieved that state?"

"Uh, no. Heard of a few, but none personally. I have known people who denied themselves things, who led lives of strict discipline, in order to serve an ideal, a goal, or to make of themselves a certain kind of person."

"You yourself, for example, you would never consider this rigorous life."

"I'm afraid I'm firmly stuck in the physical world. I can respect and admire the set of mind it takes to do that, but it's not the life for me, though I can work single-mindedly enough when I've something to work toward."

"You are the man of action by nature, I take it."

"Well . . . yes."

"Such usually come to an end in some action, Sir Otto. I recommend to you, for longevity, forgoing the riskier sorts of action . . ." His tail twitched erratically.

"We have a choice," I said, "of striving against our innate nature to conquer it and better ourselves, or of wallowing in it. One is certainly easier than the other, but holds less reward and attraction for the intelligent being."

"Innate nature," he puffed. "Elementary notion, Sir Otto."

"Elementary, yes, and like all elementary ideas profound in its simplicity," I agreed. "Mind if I sit, by the way?"

"I am a forgetful host. Please do."

I settled myself on a rock.

"Continue," he commanded, shifting about and reclining more indolently. The bulk of his body was great. It slithered and rattled over the diamonds, which tinkled as they rolled. "Are you implying that one must assume that one's own fundamental nature is base?"

The chain was near my right foot. I put my chin on my hand and looked down at it, thinking about how to answer his question. I realized it was a collar, about eighteen inches long or less, and the blue stone was a pendant. "Uh, no," I said, "but to overcome one's own most basic desires and instincts and do something superficially unnatural can bring deeper insights into what is truly natural. By controlling Nature, one understands it, and the best place to begin is within oneself."

"You exhort me to deny my own nature."

"You were doing well enough at it before you were interrupted," I pointed out. "One tax collector is no reason to throw it all over."

"There will be others to follow him. It is as certain as day following night."

"Relocate."

He twitched one of his wings around and looked at it for a few seconds. "Disagreeable, disagreeable to be forced to so much effort for so little return," he mused. "And I am still disinclined to accept your point, that denial of one's own nature yields better understanding than plumbing it."

"It is the privilege of a thinking creature to realize that he has a nature," I said. "Unthinking beasts follow theirs because nothing else is natural to them, and for them it would be unnatural to deny Nature—they do so only when rabid or ill. Thinking creatures such as we are able to view ourselves in perspective to the greater All, as you have spent so long doing, Hunnondáligi, and to alter our perspectives in order to gain new, deeper views of Nature."

"You are a nimble sophist, Sir Otto," he rumbled, exhaling twin streams of orangish smoke, appearing to grin behind them.

I didn't like his teeth. "You found your contemplations illuminating, didn't you? Didn't you find it rewarding to conquer your own nature and become something more than just yourself, something supernatural?"

He chuckled up and down a basso profundo scale. "Are you a natural creature yourself?"

"Yes," I said.

"Aaaaah," he said, and lifted his head and looked at me, and I continued to look more past him, not directly into his face. "So you are. So you are."

I had made a mistake, I feared. His air of recognition was too knowing, too shrewd—I recalled now Dewar's remark that dragons used the Roads and Leys as we did and that they sensed sorcery. Could he tell that I was a son of the Well?

"What is your nature?" he said, more than casually.

"What is *your* nature?" I retorted.

"I am Nature," Hunnondáligi said, stirring, half-rising. "I am made of Nature, of the most fundamental natural truth." His voice boomed and echoed, deafening me. "I am formed of the indestructible, the incorruptible, the Elemental. In my very existence I incarnate the ideal of Nature." He chuckled, a brazen, mellow sound but unbearably loud, like being in the tower when the bells are ringing.

I covered my head with my arms and bent forward, then fell to my knees. The object of my desires was between my knees and shins. "Calm down!" I yelled. "Nobody's questioning your existence!"

"None would dare," he chuckled again, but more quietly, and half-curled himself on his brilliant bed again. "Frail morsel of Nature, if you cannot bear my mirth, would you dare my wrath?"

I hit my ears, one and the other, trying to make them stop ringing. "Frankly, no," I admitted, straightening but not rising. "I'm not one of those heroic types." I brought my left foot forward and knelt on one knee, rubbing my forehead. As I did, I pushed the necklace under the top edge of my right boot, which fit loosely, and as I shifted my weight I felt it under my knee, just where I wanted it. If this didn't work, I would have to try something else, assuming that failure didn't kill me. I hoped it worked. I was running out of philosophy.

"Not the heroic type," he repeated. "Yet there cannot be much of cowardice in your nature, Sir Otto, else why would you be here? It is preternatural for a sane, intelligent creature such as yourself to deliberately invite a fiery death."

"Preternatural isn't quite the same as unnatural," I said, a little desperate. I had a sneaking, uncomfortable suspicion, with this reference to deliberately inviting a fiery death, that my origins were pegged, which was Not Good. That's just what you do at the Well of Fire. Of course, thinking back on it now, Hunnondáligi might have just made a lucky guess or a chance reference. Everything they say about talking to dragons is true: you're your own worst enemy. That's true of most Elemental creatures—dragons are just better at it, I guess. I went on, "There are plenty of things which exist in Nature which mimic other things in Nature, some indistinguishably. It's not wise to make conclusions about the nature of a thing until you've tested it rigorously—as you're certainly aware. Even diamonds can be made artificially, so well that the manufactured stones are all but indistinguishable from the natural."

"Hmmm—mmm—mm—mmmm," he hummed a few ominous chords. "Perhaps. However, the unnatural inevitably betrays itself by its excessively perfect mimicry of the natural, abandoning the variations and irregularities which are integral to Nature. Take this pair of stones—" He hunted around near his wingtip for a moment, and I shifted my weight again as he looked down, feeling the necklace going into the top of my boot. ". . . It was right here," he muttered, and ". . . your pardon, it will make this point quite clear—" He rose slightly and turned, a few diamonds big and small dropping off him as he did. I rocked back and scooped up more of my prize, and when he actually turned his back on me, I scooted forward an inch or two.

"If you're looking for a flawed stone," I said, picking up a diamond about as big as the end of my thumb and shining the light into it, admiring the rainbows I made everywhere, "I see your point. And I disagree. It can still be beautiful, yes, imperfect, but beautiful; but there's a clear standard in stones." I tossed that one back on the heap. The smaller ones were near the bottom, larger ones on top—self-sorted like a sand dune—which accounted for the large number of smaller diamonds around the edges.

"Here it is," announced Hunnondáligi, and delicately lifted a tennis-ball-sized diamond. "See? Here. One tiny, hairline flaw in the center." And he rose, undoing a couple of coils of himself, and approached me, holding two stones between three claws. "And see the other? A fake," and he steamed a bit, "which a very foolish sorcerer attempted to foist off on me as genuine. Identical in color, size, carat-weight . . . but different. Not as bright."

I had to stand, and so I did, and the necklace trickled down and settled coldly around my ankle. I hardly believed it had worked thus far. "Just toss them, all right?" I said, backing away.

To my surprise, he did. "See the flaw . . ."

I studied the stones and found the flaw after a few seconds. "Tiny. Yes. Imperfect. But still, the artificial, the unnatural one, is more beautiful, because it lacks the flaw: it surpasses Nature. Nice cut," I added, and made as if to throw them back.

"Just anywhere," he said, settling back. "Do you like my collection?"

"I didn't want to comment, not being sure of the etiquette," I said, "but it's quite pretty. Prettier with lights, though."

"I have light," he said, and flamed a short blue-white spurt.

"Where I studied," I said, "they were inventing things called lasers, concentrated beams of light which did astonishing things when refracted through stones like this. All sorts of scattering, and colors, and prismatic effects. Art enhancing Nature."

"Lasers," he repeated. "Hmmm. Perhaps I should have one. Would you like a souvenir?"

I shook my head and sidestepped the trap. "I'm a ruby lover, myself," I said. "And topazes. Anyway, diamonds aren't that hard to come by in some places."

"Rubies. Yes, they're not unattractive, but I always preferred the purity of diamonds."

"Even they come in colors. Blue, pink, yellow, and so on," I said. "In fact, stones can be colored by exposing them to certain artificially-made energies, turning yellow topaz blue and white diamond black, among other things. An example

of an unnatural impurity not detracting from—even enhancing—natural beauty."

Hunnondáligi chuckled suddenly. "So. So. You have me
there; I must agree with you. On that point but not in general."

"How long have you been working on this collection?" I
asked.

Humming, he thought for a moment. "Since . . . let us see.
In your terms, eleven or twelve thousand years, perhaps
more. Time has little meaning to dragons, Sir Otto."

"You are immortal, are you not?"

"I suppose so. One aspect of immortality is that one does
not think about one's own death, and the deaths of others are
of small import."

Speaking of death, my light was yellowing. It was just a
small pocket-torch, not meant for extended use like this.
"Hunnondáligi, my batteries are running down in my light.
If you'll pardon me I'm going to change them."

"That light," he said, cocking his head, "is that a laser?"

"No," I said. "Much weaker." I unscrewed the cap and
poured the dead batteries out on my palm, dropped the fresh
ones, and put in the dead ones again, then screwed on the cap
again and picked up the fresh batteries and pocketed them.
"You would like lasers, I think."

"Perhaps I'll get one. Or several. Where was it, you said?
The world has changed, it seems, since I last travelled. Lasers, hmmmm."

"Damn," I said. "These batteries aren't working either.
I've got a fresh set in the pack. Pardon me, I'll be right back
with the light—" and I stepped smartly back toward the dim
entrance, hitting my head on the low overhang, my back
tingling and sweating. I forced myself not to bolt, not to run
once outside. I was fairly sure Hunnondáligi would follow
me.

He did. I heard him slithering behind me, coming out. My

escape plan was very simple and it relied wholly on me being slightly ahead, out of sight.

"My pack's back with the horse," I called, and strolled along the way I had come.

The diamond necklace in my boot was still ice-cold, or maybe it was my blood. It was painful to walk with it there, rubbing holes in my ankle. There was my horse. There was my fire, burning still, smokily.

Hunnondáligi made a trumpeting noise. I drew my knife and felt the dragon thundering after me, shaking the earth and the trees, not making a sound after that first blast. Tango went wild as I slashed his reins and pulled out the Key, holding his bridle as he plunged about.

Hunnondáligi was moving toward me at about fifteen miles an hour, flaming a short, intense blue flame. I looked at the Key's wards and spoke the words to place it in its context and me with it. Precious fractions of a second . . .

That was the hardest piece of Way-opening I'd ever done, facing death by barbecue with a panicked horse dislocating my shoulder, but I said the spell clearly and stepped through the fire and into the Great Square of the City of Landuc as the heat from Hunnondáligi's flames began to singe my hair.

～ 5 ～

OTTAVIANO REPACKED AND RELIT HIS PIPE for the third time. He puffed a smoke ring thoughtfully, eyed it, puffed another smaller one.

"And?" I asked at last.

"And what?"

"Who won the bet?"

"Oh," he said glumly. "Dewar."

"You're kidding! How?"

He chuckled ruefully.

* * *

I just let Tango go, figuring he'd find his way back to the Palace stables eventually and that he probably needed to work things out on his own. He took off like a wild thing, flying out of sight. The Square was full of people, as usual; the loungers who were sitting on the iron railing enclosing the Keystone of the City got off the railing hastily and didn't look at me as I climbed over it and walked away.

The first thing I did was have a shot of whisky in the first bar I passed, and the second thing I did was have a double. Fortified and calmed, I went outside and around into a stinking alley usually used for other purposes—that necklace was still burning a hole in my ankle, so to speak—and took it out for a clandestine look. It was a stunner, fit for a queen. I thought I'd like to give it to Glencora, actually, since she'd been more than kind to me. I wrapped it in my handkerchief and put it in an inner pocket, took out my Key and kissed it thankfully (it was still hot), and then went out and marched up to the Palace.

First person I saw was Prospero, coming down the steps toward the stables, and I gave him the usual nod, no spoken greeting, and he gave me the same.

"Dewar's looking for you," he said as he passed me.

"No!" I said.

"Yes," he said, and shot a puzzled look back at me.

"Damn! No! Damn it." I kicked a watering trough.

Prospero snorted.

"I lost a bet," I explained. "Where is he, the—Where is he?"

"A wager?" A sardonic expression came to his face as he regarded me from two steps down. "Aaah."

I waited.

"He's at the Salty Cat," Prospero said, chuckling, and went on down, laughing outright by the time he reached the bottom.

Do you know the Salty Cat? The reputation is almost as

good as the real thing, believe me. After dumping my armor, I gritted my teeth and headed out to the city, found the unnamed alley in which its main door is (there are uncounted side doors) and allowed my eyes to adjust to the bad light just inside.

Dewar wasn't immediately visible. I edged past empty tables and around the corner of the bar, and there he was back by the wall at a round table with a wineglass and bottle in front of him.

An enormous, self-satisfied grin flashed across his face, and he smothered it almost at once. "Welcome back," he said, and signalled the barmaid.

I sat down. "Yeah," I said. "All right, you win—assuming you've got something."

"I do," said he, nodding.

A beer was thunked down in front of me and a piece of cardboard on the table picked up and punched all in one swift movement by the barmaid.

"How did you fare?" he asked, and I told him what I've told you, though I omitted any description of the prize. I wanted to see his face when he first saw it.

"Hm. I wonder if he might be Sorkal using a different part of his name," Dewar said. "He has a diamond collection, or a reputation of having one."

"How d'you know all this?" I demanded.

"I was brought up properly," retorted Dewar, with a dry smile.

"Here's your goodies, then," I said, with a sigh. "I was thinking it would be nice to give to Glencora," but he stopped me as I reached for my pocket.

"Let us wait until we are private."

I recalled where we were and nodded. "I'm starving, and I won't eat here," I said. "Got a cockroach in the only sandwich I ever tried."

"Allow me to buy you dinner at an excellent restaurant

I've discovered," he said. "My shout." But he handed me the tab for our drinks, smiling smugly.

We went to a pushcart called Armand's Pit on Fish Dock, almost as redolent of ambience as the Salty Cat, the cart specialty being delicious fresh fish steaks cooked right before our eyes at the grill by sweaty, singlet-clad Armand himself. We sat on the edge of the dock to dine and returned the shingles on which our repast was served to Armand, who chucked them into his fire. Dewar told me his story while we were eating, also not describing his loot, and we had another beer and went up to the Palace together.

In his rooms, we pulled out our separate hauls—his in a drawer, mine from my pocket.

"Holy shit," Dewar breathed, running the necklace through his hands and then holding it, shaking his head, and looking at the sapphire. "Ho-leee shit."

"Pretty nice, I thought."

"Rather."

He was obviously very, very impressed. I felt better about losing on execution, having scored points on taste and work-manship.

"Let's see yours," I said, and opened the round sandal-wood box he'd put it in. "Oh, my."

Emeralds and topazes, small ones, sparkling and twinkling together, a few diamonds scattered in . . . It was a tiara sort of thing, pure gold and glittering stones, not big, but intricate and lovely and graceful—curving wires giving a suggestion of gold-flowered green-leaved vines somehow, and perhaps the diamonds were dewdrops . . .

"Oh, that's gorgeous," I said, and it was, delicate and charming.

"Dwarf work. —So you wanted to present the necklace to the Empress?" he asked me.

I thought about it, looked out the window, looked at the wall, looked at the necklace. I thought of something else I might like to do with it. "On second thought, that wasn't such a good idea. Hard to explain where it came from."

"That presents no problem." He shrugged. "Or does it. Yes, I suppose it might."

"She'd tell Avril, but no one else, I think," I said.

"Avril," agreed Dewar. Avril had jerked his leash a few times lately, testing his loyalty or just testing his limits.

"However," I said, "if the other lady to whom I'd also like to give it would accept it . . ."

Dewar set the necklace down. "I don't know," he said after a moment.

An awkward silence lumped along for a minute or so.

"I think not, but if you wish to try you may." Dewar spoke in a not-optimistic tone.

I reminded him, "It's yours to dispose of as you see fit."

"You ran the risk." He shrugged again. "Anyway, I won the wager. Take it and give it to anyone you choose, or have it made into a watch chain."

"Tacky," I said. "Nouveau-riche and vulgar."

"But impressive."

He put the tiara away with a smile. I had a feeling I knew where it was going, and I was dead wrong as it turned out. Me, I presented the necklace to the Empress Glencora as a token of appreciation, gratitude, and so on.

"Who did you think was getting the tiara?" I asked. I could guess: Luneté of Lys.

Otto chuckled and shook his head. "A gentleman never tells," he reminded me.

I'd seen Mother wearing it dozens of times. It sat in her hair and caught the light, not flashy but a touch of color here, there, and the gold wires shining.

Otto said thoughtfully, "I saw Freia a few years later at a formal banquet at Landuc, wearing that and emerald-green velvet. I had to admit he'd done the right thing. It suited her better than it would anyone in the family or out of it." He smiled reminiscently out the window. "God, those were the days."

"How so?" I asked softly.

He shook his head. "Everything was . . . simpler. Being younger helped, I suppose. The longer I live, the more complicated even the simplest things look."

I smiled slightly and stared at my blotter. A final point about his story occurred to me as I compared his experience to Uvarkis' and Nellor's notes.

"I have been under the impression that dragons do not brush off such intrusions as yours lightly," I said, "and that they will spend a lifetime in pursuit of a thief. Did Hunnondáligi not follow you?"

"He sure did," Otto said, "and I knew he would, so I was out of Landuc, in an Eddy I know along the Road, when he found me."

"Oh?" I raised my eyebrows.

"I managed to appease him," Otto said.

"How?"

"With a contribution to enhance his collection." Otto smiled.

I waited, but he said no more. Typical of him, and, irked by his silence, I wasn't going to give him the satisfaction of asking. "I wonder whether Dewar's dragon pursued him," I said. "Do you know?"

"I never thought to ask him about it; he trekked off to visit over here for a while after that. Have you heard from him?" Otto asked.

"No," I said. "I don't know where he is. No one does."

"If you do, tell him I'd like to see him, to talk to him."

I nodded. We sat for a minute or more in silence, and then I got up and found a half-bottle of wine in my sideboard and poured us each a glass. We sipped it, and without thinking I launched into the story that was Otto's fee.

* * *

It began innocently enough. We had six days of bad weather and another ten of abysmal weather, heavy snow mixed with rain and then just snow. The New Year was still a month away. True, most of the forecasters had predicted a snowy, wet winter (based on the wet spring, summer, and autumn we'd had, the average length of growth of the horns of wood-elk, and the placement and depth of hibernation burrows by their resident rolies), but expecting it and liking it are two different things altogether. This is particularly true in Argylle, where snow by New Year is something unusual and a cause for celebrations by the sledding set.

At any rate the weather was foul and I couldn't go hunting, which is the natural late-autumn occupation. Confined to the Citadel because the roads were impassable, I played hide-and-seek with my birds, got under everyone's feet, read and reread books I didn't particularly like, and foiled my own best efforts to amuse myself.

Mother was away, Gaston was away, Prospero was away, Dewar was away—everybody in my family was away, even Belphoebe, who had decided to go down to Errethon and see just what the would-be sorceress Dazhur was doing there. Did you ever hear of Dazhur? I suppose there's no reason you would have. In Pheyarcet, she would have become like Oriana or, more likely, like Neyphile, chaffering her charms for power. In Argylle, since we do not barter with our Spring, Dazhur was a frustrated minor witch who had forever been snatching at shreds of sorcerous knowledge and who had forever been rebuffed by Prospero, Dewar, Freia, Gaston, Marfisa, Alexander, Belphoebe, Walter, and myself.

Dazhur had travelled to Errethon after our diplomatic exchange visitor Prince Josquin had returned to Landuc, and something she was doing had put the wind up my sister. I, therefore, was alone in our family's chimney of chilly stone.

Freia had appointed me to sit in the Black Chair for her. It was my first time in charge alone, and I was anxious to discharge my duties creditably. Dewar had stayed for a few months (the good weather) the first year I was on and had roused me before dawn one crisp autumn morning to announce he was for the Road. That was a few years previous to the winter of which I speak, and my family had, it appeared to me, been avoiding Argylle since. I suspected I was being either hazed or tested.

Mother had spent a lot of time on me, with me, and so had my tutor and my grandfather, far more than for any of the others, and the perspiration-inspiring realization that I was destined for Great Things had often crept into my thoughts. Nobody had said anything explicit, but I was very conscious of Freia's spot quizzes that began, "What would you do if . . ." or "Suppose such-and-such happened. What response could we make?" or, apropos anything, "But what do you think?" And then, for my trial by fire, Freia popped me onto the Black Chair and went away to submerge herself in a complex biological research project, something vague which would involve visiting her friend and research colleague Thiorn in whatever cul-de-sac or Eddy it is where Thiorn and her people live: nobody knows, they are secretive. Mother therefore had been obscure about her destination.

"I'll see you in a few years," she said, and kissed me.

"Please stay in touch," I said.

She patted my cheek. "I'll be unavailable, but when I can, I will." In practice, she had sent one letter by way of a sour-tempered black bird which had flapped away slowly after discharging his errand, and I had heard no more.

My faithful Virgil was getting a bit restive himself. He didn't consider that entertaining me was part of his job description, and my Hooded Owl Brahms, though he was happy to play games like catch-the-mouse or ring-toss, was a more nocturnal creature and thus more inclined to glide away when he'd had his fill of athleticism, perching at the top of the Core for a comfortable doze when I'd exhausted his energy and patience.

Brahms had, in fact, just done that, and Anselm had just wordlessly offered me letters to sign, which I'd signed, and lunch had just been eaten—in fact it was early afternoon on the third day of our being snowbound by this freak storm, and I realized I was at the end of my string.

Not that I wasn't occupied by business and catching up on postponed chores of government—I had cabin fever, as my uncle would call it.

I sat at the table reassembling the wing bones of my lunch and began to feel the smallest bit put-upon. It was so difficult to get around, I couldn't even invite people over for dinner. Utrachet had been caught up North by the lousy weather and was probably stuck there in a village tavern. I was bored, and I sat and tried to think of things to do.

Fly a kite. Indoors. No, that would just annoy people—I could stir up a wind with sorcery easily, but the place was drafty enough already.

Chess with myself? I had little taste for it. I always knew what my next move would be.

I could practice fencing. I'd done that four hours a day, every morning, religiously, since being Gaston's squire. I had a superb fencing-master, Dresmayer Tilas, whom I had recruited from an obscure, filthy city off the Road, but he had his other students in the afternoon and I didn't want to try his good humor.

Music. No. Poetry, writing of. No. Lover: stuck in Ollol by the snow—which was too bad, because being snowbound with Rhuil would have been anything but dull. Snowman-building, no; experimental cookery, no; reading, no; bird-harassing, done for the day; sorcery, to what end? No . . .

I yawned. I could always go to sleep. I'm usually good at that.

Virgil pushed open the door and plopped onto the table.

"I am bored and see no remedy," I told him.

He groomed himself.

"I bathed already today, thank you. Have you any other suggestions?"

He looked right at me, into my eyes, and then fluffed and smoothed his feathers and flipped his wings, making for the door.

It seemed he did have an idea. Interested, I followed him.

Virgil, in beautiful, deliberate curves, spiralled down the Core around and around the stairs and walkways. I went down the regular way, watching him; he always stayed on the same level as I was on myself, keeping up with me as I descended quickly. At the bottom, I glanced around for him and didn't see him at first.

The guards at the door to the Black Stair, though, were both looking up and back, over their shoulders. Virgil sat on the pediment over the door, waiting for me on top of the carven gryphon's head.

Down? I wondered, and nodded to the guards, who stood aside while I unlocked the door. Virgil, feather-light, dropped to my left shoulder and nibbled my ear affectionately. With a minor Summoning I got an ignis fatuus to light us down the stair and then closed the door.

It boomed in the blackness. I had only been down here a few times: to drink of the Spring and later to do advanced sorcery work with Dewar. Now, as I began going down the stairs in the pillar, my ignis starting glints of reflections from the rough black stone, I realized that I'd never descended alone. I recalled the huge, cavernous space, vaulted, arched, pillared, and frowned to myself. There were sections called the Maze and the Catacombs. The Maze, allegedly, shifted position—or rather, once you were in it, it shifted around you, changing. The Catacombs are what everything that isn't the Maze are called. I'd never been in the Maze, and I wasn't sure where it was supposed to be; the Catacombs aren't proper Catacombs providing a repository for the dead, just ... space and pillars and high-vaulting arches and occasional walls.

Contrary to popular belief, we store no wine beneath the Citadel proper—the old tower. The wine cellars are under the kitchens, and one doesn't go down nearly so many stairs to reach them.

A prickle of interest went through me. I smiled.

"Excellent idea, Virgil."

He clucked, pleased.

We spent the next days exploring. I couldn't understand why I'd never thought of it before. I'd spent my childhood and youth climbing on, crawling in, and investigating every nook and cranny of the Citadel and the Island, rooftops down, and it seemed amazing that I'd never thought of exploring the Catacombs, even when Dewar and I were working the Spring. I supposed the air of sanctity and respect around the Spring had put me off. And possibly the guards wouldn't have let me down there anyway. Mother had at various times put several areas off-limits, including the top of the Citadel proper, and certainly she'd not want me getting lost down in the darkness. Dewar had explained why the Spring was where it was and what the function of the Citadel tower was in relation to it, but that was academic, almost a civil engineering comment on Argylle's structure. We'd never come down here to see the Source of Argylle during that part of his ad hoc curriculum.

The Spring lies deep underground among the massive black pillars that bear the Citadel, and, I fancy sometimes, all of its Island in the broad Wye or even all of Argylle. The Spring is a darker spot in the black floor, an upwelling of . . . it looks like water, and the wholly insensitive might call it water, but it is more and less than water, even as Landuc's Well is more and less than fire. The Spring itself, to look upon, is perhaps a dozen feet across, perfectly black except when it is not, and without clear-cut boundaries. Gradually it solidifies into the floor, which is made of gigantic paving-stones, and it is the Source of All that is not Pheyarcet, Phesaotois, or the Void.

I liked the primal darkness. It whispered around me, and I could feel the energy from the Spring, sheets and currents of it, pouring out into the world, unrestrained in a way so different from Landuc's Well which is channelled and tapped and forced to a form—I cannot describe it. The feeling of vitality, of power, is several orders of magnitude stronger than it is even a relatively short distance away in the Citadel itself.

The second day I went down, I took lunch with me and prowled here and there, wondering at the gigantic blocks of stone—who had put them there? Why? When? Had Prospero built the place? I had never thought to ask, and no one had ever said. The stones fit together perfectly; they were all of precisely the same dimensions, as far as I could determine, and they were all of that same black stone that I'd seen nowhere else in Argylle save here and in the Great Hall where the Black Chair sat.

Each day I would go to the Spring and then walk away from it in a different direction. Virgil would accompany me, noiselessly flying through the darkness like a bat, coming and going on air currents and others. The massive columns, made of curved blocks of the black stone, reached up like the trunks of the mightiest trees of Threshwood, spreading vault-ribs instead of branches. There were no sounds save those I made; Virgil moved noiselessly on his muffled wings. My light cast hard black shadows on blackness. The air was cool; the Spring rushed past me and I became so habituated to its strength that to ascend the Black Stair again at the day's end was like decompressing after diving deep in the ocean. I forgot about the snow and my boredom; instead, I wandered in a dazed, appreciative dream though my own cellars where I had never been, until I found the door.

I found it in a corridor that led I knew not where, a corridor set in an arcing section of wall that also enclosed or excluded I knew not what because I had walked along and along it for hours and found nothing but wall to my one side and the pillared, vaulted dark to my other. The corridor had been welcome relief; I'd started down it and scarcely a hundred steps on found the door, the only door I'd ever met down there, more than twice as tall as I was and about eight feet wide.

It was strong-looking and I stood in front of it for a long time, studying it. It showed no lock or bar. It perplexed me, and I spent the rest of that day seeking to open it without success. Over the following days I tried all of the many ways I knew to open doors and none affected its closedness. Virgil watched or dozed on my haversack on the floor or assisted me as I tried spells of many different kinds, and they did nothing either. I couldn't mark it with an axe or a blade. Fire didn't scorch it. It didn't make anything but a hard, solid thud when I kicked or hit it.

Finally I gave it up, made note of the damned thing and its location, and plodded back upstairs. The snow stopped, and the sun came out and shone on the people shovelling, scraping, and sweeping, and I found other things to do. There were many: we had problems with piracy and banditry at the Errethon border, spring drought, disagreements among every group everywhere, incursions into the settled areas by the wild things from the woods and wastes, and poor crops to cap all. I coped with them all frantically, wishing my mother would take pity on me and return. It did seem as if all the difficulties had waited until she took her holiday.

Uncle Dewar was as intrigued by the door as I was, but he took it far more to heart. He muttered and paced, tried many of the things I had on it including an axe, and finally said we ought to ask his sister, if that were acceptable to me.

"Fine," I said. "Why would I object?"

He shrugged. "You might feel this is a private mystery."

"Wouldn't Prospero know? It's his Citadel."

"He might at that, but he hasn't been around much to ask."

The tensions and bindings between Prospero and his children are difficult to trace or understand. From his tone and inflection, I got the impression that Dewar thought his father's absence was somehow calculated to offend. It seemed safer to avoid the subject. "Then I'll ask, or you can ask, Mother when she comes home. Have you had word from her lately?"

"No," he said, "she said she would be unreachable, if you recall." He picked up most of the gear we'd been using, and, with a last glare at the door, started away. I collected the rest and followed him and the light.

As it turned out, Mother stayed unreachable for the next six years. At the six-year anniversary of her departure, Prospero declared he was concerned because such a silence was unlike her. We all began searching for her. After two years of fruitless searching my siblings had mostly given up, and shortly after that—a couple of months after Dewar finally returned without luck, on the edge of depression—Mother came home without announcement or fanfare.

At that time, or rather, a month or so later, Dewar took her down into the Catacombs and showed her the door. She didn't like it; it was not hers, she did not remember it being there, and she had Hicha the Archivist search for the maps Freia had made long, long ago of that place under the world. Then Mother went away again, after telling me I was doing very well but adding a long list of areas and specifics in which I could do better. She went with Gaston this time and let it be known that she did not want to be interrupted, although she did send notes via Gaston, who returned from time to time alone.

The problems I had been having before, both political and natural, worsened steeply in that year. When Gaston came round late that autumn to collect the news and leave me a note from Mother with a couple of books on economic forecasting she thought I might benefit from reading, I told him I was feeling overwhelmed. Prospero was in Errethon, skirmishing in the Jagged Mountains with brigands and the hideous beasts which had infested the forest, and Dewar was off in some pocket-world or other of his in an uncharacteristic foul temper.

Gaston must have told Freia that I was running under heavier weather than expected, because twenty days after he left they both returned together. I ceded the Chair gratefully to her; she listened to my report of woes and disasters calmly and told me she could not stay for long at a time, but that she would stay for a few days now and speak to me with Summonings often until we had gotten Argylle back on course. And, with her unerring gut instinct, one of the first things she wanted to address was the problem of that door.

Hicha found the maps, though not all of them. Mother had been thorough in her cartography, but the documents dealing with that section of the Citadel were missing. When she realized this, she Summoned us to a meeting: Prospero, Dewar, and me.

We sat around a table with crinkly old maps and smooth young wine, and I described how I had found the door.

"I'm sure I never put anything like that down there," Dewar said. "As sure as I can be," he added, muttering.

Freia cleared her throat, directing our attention from Dewar. "I know it is not mine." My mother, her brother, and I all looked now at Prospero.

"No, none of my making," he said. "Nor do I see your hand there, Dewar; though knowledge of the deed might have left you, it was a hallmark of your state that you shunned the Spring and would not approach it so nearly as this would require."

"True," he said curtly.

There was a brief, uncomfortable silence, because it is not really polite, in Argylle or anywhere else, to remind a man that he went over the edge of sanity into madness and lived there for a while, no matter how long ago it was. And Dewar had been . . . odd lately, anyway, following highly personal and highly charged interactions with the Countess Luneté of Lys and Freia which I could not follow, and which had worried me and frightened Freia. I hoped there would not be a quarrel. He had agreed only grudgingly to come to Argylle for this conference.

Freia ended the awkwardness.

"We ought to have a look at it."

Prospero lifted an eyebrow at her. "We?"

"Dewar has seen it, Gwydion has seen it, and I have seen it. You have not. I think we should all go down there and focus our collective intelligence on figuring this out. I don't like the idea of something . . . something not of our making in the Catacombs . . . I just don't like it. Particularly considering the other things that have been happening. The monsters, the general unrest—you must agree, Prospero, something's wrong. Somewhere. I never had such problems. It's not Gwydion—it's something else, and it's just started while he was here . . . or perhaps it waited . . ." she added to herself, half-audibly.

Prospero nodded reflectively, looking over the maps. " 'Tis an ill chance that the maps beyond that place have strayed from Hicha's keeping," he said finally, "far more than I'm inclined to grant to time's slow disordering of all things and blind, impartial Fortune."

"Obviously," Dewar said. "Which is why I'm for going down there now and canvassing the area as thoroughly as we can."

"Good sense." Prospero nodded. "And further, we should not take you with us, then," he said to his daughter.

"Oh?" she replied.

"If this be dangerous—"

"It is a matter pertaining to the realm," Freia said, and her chin went up, "and I am not letting anyone delve into something that potentially important unless I am there." She stared at her father, defiant, until my uncle broke the mood.

"We don't know whether it's dangerous," Dewar said indifferently. "It might just be one of those things."

"What *things?*" Prospero snapped.

"Things. Part of the Maze, maybe. It may be that it's drifting into that area of the Catacombs. Maybe it will engulf the Spring."

"That would present a challenge," I observed. "Perhaps the Spring wants more protection for itself."

"The Spring is not personifiable," Dewar said. "It doesn't want things or do things; it exists."

My mother caught my eye and forestalled the embryonic argument with a hair's-breadth shake of her head. I nodded and looked at the piece of paper closest to me carefully. Dewar moved in his seat, fidgeting.

"It's grown too late to go questing below today," Prospero said, "though one can say that it's dark in the Catacombs day and night, still we'd be better fitted for the unknown when rested tomorrow morning. Let us meet then and all go together."

Freia nodded.

"It's the Day of Reflection," I protested. I had plans for the holiday, the first day of the three which mark the end and beginning of the year.

"No better day for such an investigation as this," Prospero said.

"Indeed, it's singularly appropriate," Freia agreed.

"Eat a hunter's breakfast, or we'd best bring lunch," I suggested diffidently.

"Well thought of; it may be quickly undone, or may be not," Prospero agreed.

Another brief silence, and Prospero rose just as Freia said, "I don't think it is from the Spring."

"Everything here is from the Spring," Dewar said in a fight-picking tone.

"I mean, something the Spring has generated for itself. Or

for us. It did not feel like that. It is a . . . a real barrier. Not a . . ." she hunted for words.

"A straw man?" I supplied.

"Straw wall. Whatever." She smiled quickly, nervously.

Prospero sat down again. "What feeling did it stir in you?" he asked me.

I thought. "Resistance," I said finally. "It felt . . . stubborn. It wasn't about to give way."

"You?" He looked at Dewar.

He dropped his obnoxious manner for a moment. "I found, and find, the idea of a locked door in our own cellar which resists us threatening."

Prospero looked at the maps again and the forefinger of his right hand tapped.

"We'll go armed," he decided.

"I wonder—" I started, and stopped.

"What?" Freia urged me.

"A foolish thought," I shrugged.

Now they all looked at me, and Dewar shrugged, then looked down for an instant, biting his lip. "Go on anyway," he said.

"I wonder which side of the door we're on."

Whichever side we were on, it didn't have much to distinguish it.

Lanterns at our feet (Dewar and I had chosen to use them rather than sorcerous lights for conservation purposes), we stood in a crowded semicircle in the black-walled hall and looked the door over again. Mother shivered and pulled her mantle around herself more tightly. Prospero suddenly squeezed her shoulder.

"I feel as you: 'tis none of ours," he said in an undertone.

"And old," she whispered.

"Yes. Something ancient is worked into it . . . What lies on the other side of this wall in an analogous position?" Prospero asked, turning to me and pointing at the side of the corridor.

I had never thought—or been able—to check that. So, using a length of string (Mother had insisted we each carry a rather odd assortment of items, and a ball of thread was one of them), Dewar and I measured the distance to the mouth of this corridor and then, he standing at the mouth, I walked along the wall the same distance away.

"Nothing," I called, and regretted it, for the sound echoed horribly.

Dewar didn't answer, and I had a prickling and unpleasant sensation on the back of my neck as I walked back to him where he waited, thread in hand, as I rolled it up into the ball again.

"Nothing," I repeated.

"And more nothing," he said. "What's twice nothing?"

"Nothing again."

"Can you be sure it's the original nothing again, and not another nothing?" He grinned, quick and tense.

"Indeed," I agreed, my mood not supporting repartee.

We rejoined Prospero and his daughter, who were touching the door gingerly.

"I don't like it," she was whispering, and her whisper slid along the stones to us.

"No more do I, Puss," he said, and jumped and whirled on us, half-drawing before recognizing our lights. "Ha! —I advise that you not do that again," he said, relaxing.

Dewar said, "Gwydion found nothing."

"Nothing?"

I shrugged. "The wall is the wall."

"It goes on straight, in short?"

"And long. Yes."

"Hm. No discontinuity . . ."

"No."

"Then this must go, one way or another," Prospero declared, turning back to the door and glaring at it in such a way that most sensible doors would open at once without any backtalk. This one remained stubbornly immobile.

"Decree what you will against Nature; she'll break your law if it pleases her," Dewar said, folding his arms. "Just how do you propose we remove it?"

Prospero thumped the door angrily. "This thing is against Nature; Nature decrees its removal. Fire touched it not, you said."

Dewar held up his hand, which was suddenly outlined in white fire, and laid it against the door mutely. Nothing, though the heat thrown off by the flame was oppressive in the small space.

"I see. Not fire. Nor axes."

Dewar blew on his hand and the flame disappeared, though it wasn't his puff of breath that had extinguished it. Half of the best sorcery is showmanship, he'd said once to me. "No sorcery Gwydion or I knew."

"Crowbars?"

"I tried that," I said. "I couldn't get a purchase. It just slipped all over."

Freia was running her hands lightly around the perimeter of the door, as high up as she could reach, as we spoke.

"You didn't hurt yourself, did you?" she asked me, looking over her shoulder with widening eyes, her brows coming together.

"No," I said. "I was careful, Mother."

"You're thinking of something," Dewar said.

"Not thinking . . ." She ran her hand down one side of the door, touching the corner where stones and wood met. They joined seamlessly; there was no crack to work at. The fold of her mantle she'd put over her head had slipped back off her hair. Prospero, holding the lantern for her above her head, watched her and waited.

"You're sure it's none of yours." Freia rose and turned to her father, standing from where she'd been studying the stone floor.

"Certain."

She looked up at him and nodded and then turned back to the door. We contemplated it with her, three large men, one holding a lantern, one with his hands jammed in his pockets, one expecting his owl to land on his shoulder at any moment and scare the living daylights out of him.

"Could I . . . could I borrow that silver dagger of yours, Dewar?" Freia asked presently.

"It's yours." He bowed slightly as he presented it to her, hilt-first. She accepted it without turning around.

Prospero lowered his head and a frown crept over his face.

A ripple of power came into the hallway where we stood looking at this dead end, and a stronger current followed it. It came from the Spring; it came at Freia's bidding, and she was building it up in herself and preparing to give the door a blow with the dagger.

I had tried that already with the axe and a number of other implements, but it is best not to interrupt someone who is concentrating that way. Dewar caught my eye and shook his head, tolerantly superior—he had tried it too. Prospero closed his eyes for a moment and I felt him boost the current, adding his own demand to Freia's and increasing thereby the power tenfold because of his affinity. Freia's body swayed as he did, and then she adjusted herself to the greater power and I felt her assent to it.

She lifted the dagger, gripping it, and poised herself. I braced myself for the discharge and sketched a quick screen around me. Dewar did likewise. It was coming to a peak, coming closer, I could feel the surge building up—

Moving so fast I only saw the gesture when she'd completed it—or perhaps I never saw it and my mind reconstructed it from the start and finish which I did see—Freia moved her right dagger-holding hand down and her smooth left hand up and slashed the palm of the latter with the blade in the former and slammed her left hand hard and flat against the door as she slammed it simultaneously with the Spring's built-up power.

The noise was a thunderous one. It must have echoed through the realm and out to Argylle's Border Ranges, booming and reverberating so loudly that the Catacombs could not contain it. I felt the Spring's rush pass me by and pass through her bloody hand and smite the door, and I felt something give.

Dewar shouted something, but it was lost in the noise of the blow.

Mother did not do sorcery. She always relied on Dewar for anything of that sort. But she had an instinct for it, which is only natural, and this utterly unorthodox and unregulated stunt must have been something her instinct prompted her to try.

Freia was leaning against the door, her body a tight arc, pushing her hand against it, eyes closed and face contorted. The blood was running down from her gashed hand where it was pressed to the dark wood, and the stained dagger was still in her right hand.

We stood very still, breathing stopped, all trying to figure out whether anything had happened.

I felt something giving in the door's monolithic resistance.

Freia sighed and pulled her hand away, and Dewar, quick as a hummingbird, was there beside her to wrap his handkerchief around her hand and press the deep cut until no more blood welled out. Prospero stared at the door, which had a widening hole in the thick cross-grained wood where Freia's bloody hand had struck.

"What did you do?" I asked. We had tried things just like that, but without the blood, again and again.

"Told it *I* am in charge," Freia said, catching her breath.

Prospero and I bent and tried to look through the hole, but there seemed to be just darkness on the other side. I lifted a lantern and held it up and back, trying to shine light in there, and we muttered back and forth about whether we saw rock or dark nothing. The door was evaporating, disappearing as if it had never been there. The bloodstain crept outward and fringed the opening as it widened.

"Gryphon's blood?" I whispered. It is corrosive under some circumstances.

" 'Tis potent stuff," muttered Prospero, raking his lower lip with his teeth.

"What's over there, then?" Dewar asked. His arrogant disdain had evaporated as he bandaged his sister's hand.

We didn't answer. We didn't know. I turned to see how her hand was. There were a few bloodspots on the floor, but they were just spots of blood, not acting as the blood on the door was.

"Stings, eh?" Dewar said to Freia, finishing his improvised bandaging job.

"Not yet," she said.

"I could take stitches in that," I said. "It will mend better so. We can go up and return—"

"Thank you, but no, I think we should keep going right now," Freia said. "This will serve well enough. Thanks, Gwydion."

"We didn't bring a medical kit," I said.

"It's all right. It's a clean cut." Freia smiled at me quickly, then went to peer through the hole with Prospero.

"The other side," he said, "looks much as this one."

"As one might expect."

The hole was big enough to crawl through, but I was reluctant to risk touching the expanding edges. I was immune to the corrosion, but my clothes were not.

We waited, the four of us, watching the door vanish decorously. I half-expected a sound when the line of the bloodstain reached the floor and walls and ceiling, but it just stopped there, leaving a very fine red line of fresh blood. Freia's blood.

"Let us go on, then," Freia said, and led us across the sanguine threshold.

The corridor we were in continued there. Freia pulled her mantle up and folded her arms as she walked beside her father. Prospero carried a lantern in each hand. I had all my sorcerous senses at full alert, but there wasn't anything to sense: this was strange itself, because Freia had just released a great wash of the Spring's force through here, and there ought to have been perceptible remnants of that; yet I felt nothing of that, and nothing of the Spring. I was unsure whether this was my error or truly so, and so I said nothing of it. My tutor lagged behind us all, lifting and lowering his lantern, studying the blocks of stone that made up the wall. They were the same as the rest of the stones in the rest of the Catacombs.

The corridor came to an end—rather it opened up into a wide junction where several others opened. Prospero and Freia, ahead of me, paused and then looked to the right, and he said something indistinct and she nodded and went to the right with him. A moment later I was there, and I did not see them.

"Prospero? Mother?" I called, and looked down the first right-hand corridor, holding my lantern up high, and then a nasty realization clutched my head and shook me hard with both hands.

We were in the Maze.

"Dewar! Dewar!"

No answer.

"Shit!"

No answer.

I stepped back into the intersection, which was still there though I could not see the corridor where the door had been. I tried to calm down and to remember what I had been told about the Maze.

It changed shape around one.

Freia had been lost in it once, and she had never been sure how long. To the Citadel staff, it had been a day's absence, but to her the time had seemed three or four days.

No one else that I knew of had ever found the Maze, though everyone knew about it. I had asked Dewar if Mother hadn't just been lost and he had said no, the Maze existed, but only Freia had penetrated it. She'd been mapping down here, making those maps we'd consulted before this trip, when it happened, but those maps had placed the Maze in another place entirely.

Perhaps the Spring *had* put the door there, for our own good, and now here we were . . .

"Damn," I murmured.

I couldn't recall if she'd applied a rule to get out or just blundered along. The right-hand rule was the one that was supposed to work most of the time, wasn't it? I'd use it, then.

Thus, with a sinking feeling in my heart and a lantern in my hand, I started slowly away from the last place I'd seen them.

I walked for hours. I turned right so often it became difficult to think of the word left. I stopped a few times and had a snack from my haversack and a few drinks of water, but I was very afraid of using my supplies before I really needed to, and so I conserved them. I tried to sense and tap the Spring, but there were no currents in the area to orient or guide me—the place was a blank, like the Border, which was frightening in its own way. So I walked.

When I thought I must have walked nearly thirty miles and seen nothing but black stone, I had to stop. Jittery and worried about my family, I sat down and then lay down, turning my lantern down to save fuel but reluctant to turn it off and be alone in the crushing darkness. I dozed.

Prospero woke me, shouting at me.

"Gwydion!"

"Wha'?" I jumped and started awake and shouted back, "Prospero!"

We could see one another; he was running down the hall toward me.

"Stay where you are!"

I stayed, standing and yawning.

He arrived, and we hugged one another breathless in a paroxysm of relief.

"Where is Mother?" I asked him.

"Curse me for a wooden-headed fool," he said, grabbing my shoulders and staring at me. "She lagged but a half-step behind me as we went 'round a corner, and in my next breath I walked alone—"

"Hell!"

"She hasn't a light." He still had two, hers and his.

"Oh, no!" I almost said "We've got to find her!" and realized before I did how simple this would sound. "When?"

" 'Twas hours ago meseems. Since then I've wandered, and called at every corner, but I've seen no living soul save you. And a welcome sight you are." He pressed my shoulders again and released me, but kept one hand on my arm. "Your uncle?"

"I was alone. I don't know where Dewar is."

Without optimism, he said, "It may be he escaped or never was taken in. This is how it caught her in its coils, she said. She did not apprehend that she was lost until too late, too deep. Put out your lamp. We've no need to squander fuel, and I've enough here . . ." He twisted his mouth and looked up and down the hall, clearly blaming himself again.

"Are you tired? Would you like to sleep?" I suggested.

"Yes. I saw you sleeping; are you rested?"

"Yes." Even if I had not been, the excitement of being lost in company would have revived me.

"Good. Then I'll sleep, and you shall watch in case one of them comes nigh. So long as we stick to one another like burrs in uncombed wool, perhaps we shall not be separated." Prospero sat down heavily, ate an apple and drank some water, and then stretched out and was asleep in seconds. I sat down at his head, pulled his cloak around him more closely, and pushed my bag under his head to make a pillow. He snored lightly. I dozed, sitting up, keeping my hand on his shoulder, afraid he'd sublimate away beside me and turn into a wall.

While he slept I gazed at the black stone wall across from me, barely distinguishable in its darkness under the single yellow flame's light from the unlit stone beside it. My eyes strained at the emptiness to either side, looking for any sign of movement or any faint glow from another light, and seeing nothing they strained all the harder.

Gradually it seemed to me that the darkness or something in it moved and shifted, never when I gazed on it directly, but at the edge of my vision. I shook my head and looked determinedly at the stone wall, daring it to disappear or mutate while I watched.

It did. Very slowly the stone's substance began to move, rearranging itself in a pattern. At first I ignored this and then paid it closer attention; it accelerated and the winking flakes of brighter stone caught in the black shifted and darkened. It seemed that I stared at a face, which acquired definition and clarity as I studied it, emerging in deep bas-relief from the stone around it and regarding me.

The lips moved, slowly shaping meanings, but I heard nothing. The face's expression was cold and intent upon me. The lips moved again, and this time I heard it, as faint as a draft of air:

"Kill him," said the face of stone.

I was sure I had not heard aright.

"Kill him," it said again, a soughing icy command.

"No," I whispered.

"It is your desire," the stone face whispered. "His death will bring power. Kill him."

I seemed to feel the stone behind my back crawling and changing, and I sat forward and glanced back at it. There was nothing there, but the stone did seem to writhe under my eyes, and the stone voice said, "Kill him, and you shall live forever."

I might live forever anyway, I thought, but I did not say

that. "No," I whispered again. Something stirred beside me—not Prospero—I looked down and saw that somehow I had half-drawn my sword Talon. Prospero slept on by my thigh.

Suppose I did kill Prospero, I thought; he would never emerge from the Maze, and none would ever know what had become of him. Dead, he would not be there always in the shadows and backgrounds of Argylle, brooding on what was and was not his; dead, he could not approve or disapprove anything. My mother, lost without a light, might be dead already, and Dewar—

What was I thinking?

I turned hot and cold in the same instant and slammed Talon back into the scabbard.

"No!" I shouted, or thought I shouted.

The face twisted into a hideous grimace, mouthing something I was unable to understand. I closed my eyes, whispering "No, no, no, no . . ." like a child willing something to unhappen, and when I looked again the wall was just a wall: black, flecked with bright specks, with a dimly less-black area under the lamplight.

The face had faded, but I stared on. Then, with a fearful jerk, I grabbed Prospero's shoulder. He was still there. Deeply asleep, he rolled onto his face and sighed. I relaxed my hand.

I had broken into a cold sweat. I pulled my cloak around me and leaned against the wall. Was it a hallucination? I was not that tired. A vision? How sent, and by what agency? Tempting me to the most unnatural crime, to kill my mother's father Prospero—to what end? I had power already; I could not think of any enhancement I might gain from his death. The idea made me ill. For either it had happened, and the Maze was far worse a place than Freia had ever said, or I had imagined it, and my own mind was alien to me.

For the rest of my watch beside Prospero I stared up and

down the corridor anxiously, wondering what other visions might come. Nothing happened, which was excruciating in its own way.

When Prospero yawned and rolled over and woke up, he grunted a greeting to me and took out his water flask. A drink and a bite to eat later, he rubbed his eyes and neck and said, "A quiet night, as it were?"

I nodded.

" 'Tis well." He looked up and down. "Alas, you've done your duty with too much diligence, Gwydion, for had you broken faith and nodded, perhaps we'd have awakened outside these damnable walls. Naught's altered."

We got up, stretched and rubbed our stiff muscles, and walked slowly on, along the corridor the way Prospero had come to me. We walked hand-in-hand to keep from being separated. When I came to an opening and turned right, he chuckled.

"In this unruly place, you impose rules?"

"It was the only thing I could think of," I said defensively.

"I do not think our powers of reason will release us, no more than powers of sorcery can. We are lost to reason and the Spring until this thing sees fit to spit us forth at one end or t'other."

"I hope that's soon. I'm already tired of it."

We walked awhile, and I found the silence unbearable.

"I saw something while you were asleep, Prospero."

He didn't seem surprised. "A mirage or a . . . seeming?"

"Yes."

"I too have seen such. Spare your thought for better things. They are vile nothings; they are less than wraiths; they are no more than . . . influences." He spoke with vehement certainty and contempt.

Influences. Influencing me to kill Prospero? Mocking me for not doing so? For wanting to? It was good advice, not to worry about it. The very thought made my stomach wrench. How had my sword come to my hand? I must have drawn it, fearing the face . . . I pushed the thoughts away, as he advised.

A few minutes later we came across something that made us stop and consider.

The corridor was flooded. Prospero lifted up his lantern and then brightened it to see the extent of the flooding, and it seemed to me that I could see across it.

"I think there's something white over there."

"A small thing, pale, perhaps a rock," he said. "It lies at, oh, eleven o'clock . . ."

"Yes."

Prospero looked at the dark water which lay without moving against the dark stones. "How deep, I wonder, can this water be? Dark in darkness: I cannot plumb it with my eye."

Still holding his hand, I stepped in. Shallow at the edges. I took another step. It covered my boot tops.

"Belike it falls off of a sudden, as the shore, or belike it masks a stair or cavity," Prospero pointed out, and I came back.

I emptied the water from my boots. "I can swim."

His mouth twitched, not succeeding to smile. "So can I. By the way, I trust the stuff is no more unwholesome than the water 'twould appear to be."

I looked hastily at my feet. I bent down and sniffed the stuff. It smelled like stale, dirty water.

"I think it's just water."

"Let us hope this does not mean we have a leaky foundation beneath our Citadel," Prospero muttered. " 'Twould weaken the building beyond buttressing."

We looked at the white thing, the only thing that wasn't black in the whole world.

"Well then, needs must undertake the swim if we're to go onward, and truthfully 'tis a change from this walking. Keep your lantern and pack dry," Prospero said after a minute of reckoning the distance. "It seems not far."

We put my haversack and lantern on my head, and Prospero held the lit and the unlit lanterns he had in his left hand, and we set forth. It was water. It came up to our knees, and up to our thighs, and then the bottom did drop out. I pulled Prospero's free arm around my neck, and he held the light high while I swam.

"It's farther," I said, "than it looked."

He said nothing.

I swam.

The white thing was my target. I swam straight toward it. My arms began to ache. It was hard work, swimming for two, and my boots were full of water.

I decided I'd better keep them on and kept swimming.

Prospero held the lantern up high, though his arm must be stiff and uncomfortable.

Finally my hand hit something; I barked my knuckles on stone and scrabbled to grab onto it. And we were in a very curious place. We were at the bottom of a wall, from what my hands told me, though my eyes told me I was looking straight ahead, level across the stone, at the white thing . . .

I conveyed this to Prospero.

"Close your eyes."

I did.

"Now, without looking—nor shall I look—move you along, yet keep a hand upon the wall . . ."

I did this, and bobbed along through the water, Prospero around my neck still, kicking to help me. I don't know when it happened, but the wall became easier to grab suddenly, and without even thinking about it, I pulled us up and out, opening my eyes.

We sat on the floor next to a puddle of water perhaps six feet broad. I wondered what would happen if I tried to jump across it.

"I don't like this place," I said, a small shake in my voice because I was tired with all that swimming.

Prospero, his hand still on my shoulder, bent and picked something up.

"An apple core," I observed. It was brownish, but not bad.

"One of the others has passed this way—unless you dropped it, for I've not done so."

"No," I said, and then, feeling inspired, said, "Mother was here."

"This is an eloquent apple, to tell you so much," he said, lifting his eyebrows.

"Dewar eats apples core and all, and so do I for that matter. Mother does not."

Prospero smiled and patted my head. "Brilliant, Holmes," he said.

"What?"

"Pay me no mind; I maunder. You're observant and nimble-witted." He ate the apple core himself.

I thought of Mother sitting by the puddle and eating an apple in the dark. She hadn't a light, after all. "She was alone," I said, "when she dropped it, because Dewar would have eaten it if he were with her."

Prospero swallowed and nodded, looking bleak. When I'd caught my breath, we went on.

Our clothes were dry by the time we met the next illusion. It ran toward us.

"Dazhur!" I called.

"How now, witch, how camest thou—" Prospero began, and he grabbed my arm and yanked me back. I had let go of him.

"My Lord!" she gasped, dishevelled, tear-streaked and smudged, blonde hair coming undone.

"How did you get down here?" I asked.

"I don't know," she whispered, "I was Summoned hither by you, my Lord Gwydion . . ."

I shook my head. Something bothered me about her.

"Dazhur," I said, as it came clear to me, "what did you do to your hair—"

She vanished with a terrified scream, blowing away as a cloud before wind.

"Women! So squalled your mother when once I asked her that," Prospero said wryly after the scream had faded from our ears. "Speak or be silent, a man's damned either way. What of the wench's hair?"

"Hicha said she'd cut it."

Prospero laughed, really laughed. "In the new fashion! I did not know that. Recently?"

"Just a few weeks ago."

He laughed harder and then made a rude noise. "Hah! 'Tis points for our side."

The stone around us remained unmoved by his mirth.

"Let's go on," I said, wearily. On we went.

The next encounter came after another rest stop. Prospero watched while I slept, and I watched while he slept. I was undisturbed by further illusions, but I wondered about their source. Prospero didn't say whether he saw any or not. Given the nature of mine, I supposed he might not be inclined to discuss them. We ate bread and cheese and apples, drank water, and shook the kinks out of our bodies without talking.

The corridors went on and on and on. A glimmer of color· ahead was a welcome change in the monotony, illusion though it be. Prospero saw it too. "Hmph," he grunted, ready to be unimpressed.

It neither moved nor made a sound as we approached nearer and nearer. I could not remember if the first illusion I had seen had really made sounds or not, as Dazhur had. It had been less substantial than she had seemed, certainly, and more demanding.

Prospero stopped just as I resolved the colors and shapes and tried to speed up; he jerked on my arm and halted me. We faced a T-intersection. Dewar sat against the wall, his low-flamed lantern beside him, and he held Freia, and they were both asleep. From his uncomfortable attitude—head tipped back and lolling to lean on hers, which was on his shoulder—he must have dozed off on watch. He had a bruised scrape on his forehead and a ravelled tear in his dark-grey doublet. Freia had lost her mantle and had Dewar's blue-green cloak around her, over her dress, and her left hand, with the scabbed line from the knife gash black on her palm, lay loosely open on his knee, a gold spark where her wedding-ring nestled in the crease of her finger's base. His left arm encircled her, lest they be parted as they rested no doubt.

"Prospero," I whispered.

"Shh."

I looked at him. I was sure they were real. Prospero put his finger on his lips and shook his head at me.

He didn't want to wake them up. I smiled and thought that was nice, and he nodded and we walked up to them as quietly as possible, then sat down when neither of them twitched a muscle.

A quarter of an hour later, Dewar's lantern guttered and went out, and the only light came from Prospero's lantern—we had used up all the fuel in one and had abandoned it, and now we kept mine in reserve. Freia stirred, snuggled closer to Dewar, sighed, squirmed the way one does when trying to find the least discomfort, and then sighed again and relaxed. Dewar mumbled, "Hmmm . . ." and slumped down, then started awake.

"Holy Sun in the Spring!"

"Hush," said Prospero.

Dewar regarded us both suspiciously. Freia, with a "Humm? Wha' now . . ." sound, woke up and blinked fuzzily. Though she had slept, she looked tired and her face was pale in the lamplight. Dewar's eyes were shadowed and taut lines of tension fringed them and his mouth.

"Are you real?" Freia asked plaintively, still hugging Dewar.

"Yes," Prospero said.

"Of course you'd say that," Dewar retorted.

"Hell's bells," Prospero said, "why, then believe we are not, if it likes you better so, and ignore us. But a moment past your oil burned out, and we've light to spare."

Dewar grabbed his lantern and shook it; empty, no question about it.

"Did you see anything?" Freia asked me.

"Yes," I said, looking away.

"What?"

"I don't want to talk about it," I said.

"You are real," she decided, which was annoying. "A false Gwydion would tell me something." And she smiled as I looked back to protest.

"How do you know?" Dewar demanded.

"I expected him to answer when I asked, and when he did not I was surprised but recognized that it was in character nonetheless."

Dewar nodded, satisfied by this motherly logic. Freia yawned and shook her mussed head, smiled at Prospero too, and said, "I shall forgive you for leaving me in the dark."

"Though 'twas none of my will's doing, I thank you for your forgiveness," he said, and let her hug him. She still kept a hand on Dewar, though. "You two may sleep again, if you would," Prospero said over her shoulder. "We'll stand guard 'gainst ghosts and dreams."

She shook her head and said something too soft for me to hear. Her father hugged her harder, closing his eyes for a moment.

"This is an inconstant and perilous place. I've feared what harm might come to you, and it eases my heart to see the two of you hale and well," Prospero said to them when he let her go. My mother reached over and tidied my hair.

"Well we are, if you call being lost in the Maze with nothing to eat well," Dewar said. "I hate to be a bludger, but have you any food?"

"Yes," I said, and during the ensuing conversation I learned that Freia estimated her total subjective time lost as being around six days, and that for three of them she'd been alone in the dark without food or water. I told her about the apple core.

"Ah, that was the time I lost Dewar," she said. "It was in my pocket."

He still had one hand on her shoulder. This became understandable when they explained that they'd met once shortly after her separation from Prospero, walked for a ways, and been separated at that puddle. Dewar had taken a running jump across it and, naturally, found himself alone on the other side. Freia could not see how wide it was when he was gone, and she had sat down on the edge to eat the apple and then wandered away, giving up on a speedy reunion with her brother. They had met again three days afterward, not parting for an instant since, and had eaten the last of their food the previous "day."

"The stuff nightmares are made of," I muttered.

Freia nodded.

Dewar found our encounter with an illusion of Dazhur intriguing.

"She's involved with this somehow. I met her myself directly after getting lost."

"What did your illusion look like?"

"I think it was indeed Dazhur," he said. "Her hair was short, bluntly cut the way the Northern girls are wearing it, her dress was one I've not seen before, and she bragged that I was going to be begging for her favor real soon. I didn't know she'd cut her hair."

"Oh?" said Prospero. "Dazhur." He frowned; my uncle shrugged.

"Phoebe said something about . . . rituals," I said. "About Dazhur's rituals in Threshwood." There was something else about Dazhur, too . . . I strove to recall it.

"She said she was raising a power Phoebe couldn't understand," Mother said. "That was why Phoebe chased her down to Errethon where I presume she carried on—and carried on—as usual."

"What power could she raise?" Dewar said. "There is only the Well in Landuc and the Spring here, and she has partaken of neither. I know she hasn't been to Morven."

"I don't know," Freia said. "I trust Phoebe's instincts, though."

"So do I," I said. "Dazhur was getting into very arcane stuff, from what I could tell."

"She seduced Josquin when he was here while you were Gaston's squire, Gwydion," Freia said.

"No!" said Dewar, his eyebrows shooting up. "Jos? Surely you're mistaken. It'd be utterly unnatural for him . . ."

Prospero snorted.

She shook her head. "So it seemed to me. Artificial. Contrived. I wondered at it, but I couldn't stop it; it was none of my affair. I supposed Josquin must know his own mind, and he never mentioned her to me. Everyone in town knew about it, though, and of course Hicha did too, and I think that he was the reason Dazhur left Hicha. I wonder what seducing him might have done for Dazhur. Ever since never, she was always hotfoot after . . . you know, all of us."

"Arcane stuff indeed! I wonder what it might have done for him," my uncle muttered. "Clearly I left town too soon that winter."

"That was it!" I said. "She was still living with Hicha then. She was with Hicha, do you recall it, Dewar? You told me so when you visited Gaston and me."

"I did, she did—The maps!"

We looked at one another: Dazhur had certainly had ample opportunity to rifle the Archives when she was Hicha's lover, in Hicha's confidence.

"Raising a power," Prospero muttered. He looked at us all, frowning. "Well-a-day, this gossip is not getting us out of the Maze. Let us move along and see what the place has to offer us."

"And let's stay together this time," I said, standing.

Freia stayed close to Dewar. He kept an arm around her waist or over her shoulders, or she would hold his hand or arm closely to her side. Her free hand held mine; I held Prospero's, and he held the lantern. Now we walked along the corridor away from the T-intersection where we had found my mother and uncle.

"This feels different," Dewar said after a moment.

"Hm," his father replied.

"Do you . . ." Dewar didn't finish the question.

"Yes, I feel it," Prospero said slowly, after half a minute's slow walk in silence. "I do feel it. 'Tis not quite like the Spring, though."

"It's altered, but I cannot put a word to it," Dewar said.

"It's wrong," Freia said.

I hadn't picked up on whatever it was they were discussing so cryptically.

"Gwydion," Dewar said, glancing at me over Freia's head, "do not clutch at it, for it is not quite there—you must look for . . . currents."

I tried that. The lack of Spring-force had previously made this a frustratingly blank exercise, but now I saw what they meant: there *was* something there, similar to the Spring but not quite like. It was going . . . "Inward," I said aloud, as this became apparent to me.

"Drawing toward . . ." Prospero said, "toward . . . No good can come of this. Freia, you ought not to have come," he said to her, almost angrily.

"Papa," she replied in a warning voice.

He growled and let go my hand for an instant to loosen the Black Sword in its scabbard, a slithery metal noise. I dropped Mother's hand automatically, cued by the sound, and checked Talon; as I let go of her, she touched my shoulder and left her hand there, pulling me to a stop and with me Prospero and Dewar.

"What is it?" Dewar asked, low, looking around.

"Something's ahead," Prospero said. "It waits."

"What sort of thing?" Dewar said to Freia.

"Dark," she said. "Do you see?"

I stared into the lightless walls and hall and saw nothing but dark, though I could now sense, if I tried, the sinuous trailing line drawing us on with our own curiosity.

"Onward." Prospero tugged at me and the others gently to move us forward again, and his lantern went out. He lobbed it with a curse into the cavern which had opened out from the corridor—the Maze was gone.

We stood for a few breaths in darkness so complete that the darkness behind my closed eyelids seemed brighter.

"The Spring!" I cried. It was there, coursing around us, and Virgil hooted thrice as he landed on my left shoulder.

"No . . ." Prospero said uncertainly. It wasn't the Spring really. There was that same alien tincture in it.

"Aha," Dewar said. Suddenly he swung his staff speaking quickly, and a haze of light followed its end, streaming like a banner, and then clotted, hissing, at the top, a huge ball of fire illuminating the perfect chill blackness around us far better than any common lamp: no ignis fatuus, but a Salamander, bound there to light us and to be used as a weapon if Dewar chose to release it.

The darkness curled and coiled and rose like smoke, high up, and rumbled, "Usurper."

"You are the usurper here," Prospero said.

It glistened; it made a sandpaper sound, flowing and settling into a shape as tall as the pillars. The Salamander-light showed it: black, scaled it seemed, with two oblong patches of even blacker blackness on either side of a head that was not human-shaped, nor like anything else I recognized.

"This . . . is . . . mine," said the dark thing, a voice that filled the darkness with worse.

"It is mine; my blood has made it, my blood has shaped it," Prospero cried, "and you are an interloper and shall be cast out." The Black Sword was in his hand. "By the Spring

I command you speak your name," Prospero shouted, and gestured. I felt the Spring, our Spring, wash over and around us, and Dewar said, "Aaaah," and stepped to his right a few light steps as I circled to the left, behind Prospero.

Freia stood stock-still.

The Spring flowed out to us, gathered, and receded toward the intruder; I drew on it also, and I saw it forming into a deceptively lacy network, growing around him and constricting, compelling—

"I am Tython, who was here before all," roared the intruder, throwing off Prospero's command, and a blackness cut toward Prospero from Tython's right hand as he swung it. He had a black weapon, difficult to see in the darkness and against the darkness that was him. Freia ducked under the blow, which swept through where she had been, and rolled and came up by a pillar.

Prospero raised the Black Sword and met the blow. White-gold light flashed out from the meeting, like lightning struck between clouds; Prospero staggered, but so did Tython.

Dewar, at the same time, hit him with the Salamander, a comet of hissing fire.

"You are a leech, a loathsome lifesucking maker of nothing," Prospero shouted, "and there shall be no mercy for you, vile parasite."

I drew on the Spring and drew Tython's attention by doing so. It seemed that sorcery, under the circumstances, might not be the right weapon for this battle. "Sprat," he hissed, and I used the Spring to shield myself from his other hand, buffeting me. It didn't work—he was slowed by it, but not stopped, and he laughed until I slammed Talon through the palm of that hand and pulled it out, blackish blood flowing smokily with it, as I twisted and dodged away around a pillar.

Tython screamed; by the light of the Salamander which was winding itself around his right sword-holding hand like a bracelet, I saw that his tongue was forked.

"Gwydion, back! Ward thy mother, boy," yelled Prospero at me, furious, and I fell back toward her. He was right—she had neither Art nor arms.

From behind us, I heard laughter, incongruous bright soprano merriment.

"Dazhur," Freia said, whirling, her face settling into an expression I had never seen before—hard and cold, angrier than I would have thought possible. "You have done this."

"I, I," Dazhur laughed, "and you shall not be the Lady of Argylle long." She approached my mother, who folded her arms. By the Salamander-light I saw that Dazhur's blonde hair was short, as Dewar had described it, and that she wore floating white robes. My mother was grubby from her journey through the Maze; her hair was straggling out of its knot, and she presented not nearly so majestic an appearance as Dazhur, who shone in the vaulted dark.

"Fool," said Freia, her voice sharp. I hovered a few paces behind her.

"Gwydion, drop!" shouted someone, and I threw myself down against the base of one of the great pillars; a hot blast passed over my head. Dazhur laughed again and made a gesture with her hands, and the heat caught and collected there, darkness in her pale fingers. She held it over her head. It glowed, inside her hands, inside itself, dull and unlively.

"Get *back,* Gwydion!" Dewar cried.

I got away from the flashes and crashes of the fight against Tython, closer to my mother.

"Catch," Dazhur cried, and hurled that ball of Otherness at Freia.

Freia lifted the hand that had destroyed the door, her left hand, with the mark of the knife still on it, and the ball exploded into light, dissolving.

"There is more to the blood of Argylle than a draught of the Spring," Freia said, white with anger. "Dismiss this thing you have conjured and you may keep your life!"

Perhaps, I thought, Mother didn't need help—yet she was vulnerable to conventional attack.

I glanced around to see how Prospero was doing; he and Dewar were harrying Tython, trying, it seemed, to cut at his knees. The monster had left the Spring, and was smaller and solider than he'd been; he had tusks, as well as a forked tongue, and the sinewy way he moved made me think he had no real bones, only joints in his limbs. Dewar's Salamander was flying at Tython's face; Tython knocked it down at Dewar, who had to throw himself aside to avoid being incinerated by the Elemental he'd Summoned. This is the problem with them in a fight: they don't take sides. The match seemed even enough, and I returned my attention to the others.

"Oh, how generous of your Ladyship!" Dazhur retorted, sneering. "You, who have jealously kept everything of the Spring to yourselves for eternity, you would so kindly grant me my life. I tremble before your mighty justice—"

Prospero was fencing with Tython's claws, his back to the pillar behind which I stood. Dewar was not with him. Yet I was engrossed by the clash between my mother and Dazhur, and I tarried before helping him—he was holding his own, and he had ordered me to guard Freia—and he might resent aid when he didn't really need it.

"You have never understood the true nature of Argylle," Freia was saying. "The Spring is not kept; it is keeper, sustainer, donor. This thing of your greed will kill all if you don't banish it. Indeed—I believe you are not strong enough to dismiss it, and in that case you will keep neither your own life nor anyone else's." She seemed to glow. I could feel the Spring's power flowing around and into her like a whirlpool. Mother didn't use sorcery or the Spring, not as Dewar and I could. I think though that sorcery and the Spring could use her.

"The Black Chair shall be mine and you—" began Dazhur, and Freia made a sharp, chopping gesture with one hand: enough.

They stared at one another, the one malicious and hate-filled, the other coldly determined to do what was necessary, as she always had.

I wondered what the best way to jump in with Prospero was; clearly Freia didn't need help just now, and I could hear Prospero's quick steps and panting gasps as he fought. Virgil decided that for me; soaring in from the darkness, he hovered before Tython's face as the Salamander had, distracting him for Prospero. I held back again and watched the two women.

"You see nothing," Freia said, "but what you desire, Power. You are blind to the rest of the world. This thing you have raised is greater than you, but not greater than the Spring, which is not to be possessed."

Someone shouted, a quick short startled cry. Dazhur laughed again, and I knew that even if Mother did need my help, my uncle or Prospero needed me more.

I shifted Talon to my left hand and went around the stone column. Prospero, to my right, was doing well; some distance away, Dewar lay on the floor—he must have taken a blow. The Salamander was gone. Virgil was flying close around Tython's head, making him hiss and snap and snatch, but always escaping. I drew on the purling Spring, strengthening arm and blade, and struck at the back of Tython's scaly-clawed hand while bracing myself on the column. It was the diversion Prospero needed.

"Hai!" said he, and in the same moment brought down the Black Sword two-handed and hacked the wrist half-through. Tython screamed and the blood sprayed in a fine mist from his maimed arm; Prospero and I both darted out of its way. The hand flopped on a piece of skin and sinew. Tython tore at it with long teeth.

Freia had run to Dewar to help him up; I could not spare them more than a peripheral glance, being busy dodging a long line of hot-feeling force from Tython's other hand, which he wielded like a whip. It swished through the air. Tython howled again; Dewar had thrown his sword into the monster's side, where it stuck, and enraged Tython turned and swatted at him.

The blow missed him; he dodged it.

Freia leapt back and away, but not quickly enough.

Tython struck her.

I heard her gasp where I stood, my heart stopping in my chest.

Tython's handless arm knocked her into the air. Dewar screamed and jumped toward her; he could see what I could not at once, that her trajectory was taking her too close to the Spring.

Prospero snarled like an animal and hurled the Black Sword at Tython's head, where it smote his eye and stayed there.

I heard an inhuman shriek coming from my own throat as I recklessly ran forward, swinging Talon wildly, and felt the blade bite into Tython's groin.

Freia seemed to hang in the air a moment, just beyond Dewar's leaping reach. She fell into the dark, liquid Spring of Argylle. I saw her body jerk and twist as it surrounded her, and the Spring was dark and liquid no longer; in an instant there was an ardent eruption from it, a jolt of pure, unchannelled, undirected power and light and sound which caused Tython to howl as he vanished, erased from the world, and which blasted past me, overloading my senses and confounding interpretation.

Dazhur screamed madly, shrill and high.

The momentum of my swing threw me off balance and I fell to my knees.

The Black Sword rang and rang again as it struck the floor. Something else made a clattering sound nearby.

Dewar and Prospero sprawled on the floor at the edge of the Spring. Prospero half-lay over him; he had tackled

Dewar to keep him from falling in also as he failed to catch his sister. One of them was shouting incoherently.

The Spring had a halo of polychromatic light over it like a bubble, which faded as it returned to serenity.

Dazhur was laughing hysterically, her arms upraised in triumph.

Freia was gone.

Ottaviano let me sit and recover from the telling for a long time. The clock ticked more loudly than I breathed. He moved after many minutes, slightly, enough to end the moment.

"What happened to Dazhur?" he asked softly. "She Summoned that thing . . ."

"I beheaded her while Prospero sat on Dewar," I said. "We were mad. Stark mad."

I opened my desk, rummaged around for a can, and prised off the lid. I stuffed the herbs in it into my pipe and lit them with hands that were icy-cold and slippery with perspiration. Recollecting my manners, I pushed the can over to Otto, and he sniffed, smiled quickly, and knocked the dottle from his pipe to fill and light it too.

"Gwydion," he said, "I'm . . . Hell. It shouldn't have happened."

It should not have. Dazhur had been laying her web of evil in Argylle, seducing Josquin and Hicha, stealing information from the Archives, retreating (only in seeming) to Errethon and insinuating herself into the confidence of the old Headman there, promising him Argylle and herself. I clenched my teeth. "We were *asses.* Complacent. Unaccustomed to the idea of an enemy. There was Dazhur, all that time, collecting scraps and bits, enough to raise an evil thing with a grudge greater than her own. Phoebe recognized what she was doing as unnatural, but couldn't counter it herself—and none of us who could have acted, did."

"She's perceptive," he said, and drew on his pipe.

The mild sedative effect of the stuff, a local herb usually infused for headaches and as a muscle relaxant, began to hit me. I felt my pulse going down to a normal rate. Mother always frowned on this kind of drug usage, maintaining that a person should be able to govern himself, but even she sometimes failed to follow her own preaching. Crutch or not, I couldn't have gotten myself under control without it, couldn't have survived those first couple of months or those first couple of hours.

"Hit your dad hard, didn't it," Otto half-asked.

"Still does," I said.

"He's been away a long time."

"Wish I could be," I said, and it was true when I said it, although in all my travels I've never found a place I like better than home.

Ottaviano stayed another half-hour, and we just smoked together without talking until I got up and opened the Way to Ollol for him, back to the guesthouse and his mercantile diplomacy. I wondered why he had asked about Freia. In Landuc, they claimed he was in love with my mother, but in Landuc, they'll say just about anything about just about anyone. Except, really, Mother. People don't like to talk about her, not even gossipy Aunt Viola or foaming Fulgens. They press their lips together and look away, or say, "Such a shame," in a hurried mumble, or they shrug.

I had Anselm reschedule my afternoon appointments and went to my mother's study, where I spent the afternoon browsing through her books. I had another evil to face, alone this time.

⌐ 6 ⌐

I BEGAN BRIEFING MYSELF PAINSTAKINGLY THAT evening, first reviewing the spells that had had the most effect on the dragon the first time and then adding others of similar power and impact. If only there were some way to take a book of spells into battles of this sort, or notes at least—but there isn't, so a sorcerer facing a contest first conquers his own shortcomings, and if he fails to do so he will fail in his fight. Most sorcerers who lose such duels do so because their memory flags and leaves them speechless. Though it is best to be primed with freshly-swotted Destructions and Summonings, it is also well to be ready to cast some spell—any spell—no matter how incongruous. Dewar claimed a duel had been won by someone who, in the desperation of the moment, changed the challenger's horse into a pig. In the time so gained, he did the same to the sorcerer.

My review took the rest of the night and most of the following day. I paused for another nap and a big meal—no point in letting myself slip below peak in any way—and checked outside my door for any notes Prospero might have left for me. One, dated that morning:

> *Marfisa's mending; Alexander still coughs, but no blood. He'll live. The Councillors send respects and grovelling beg for news; I've answered them. Tell me ere you set forth. Belphoebe reports that Gemnamnon keeps to his billet, nursing his own grudges. Prospero.*

It was late afternoon. I was as ready as I could ever be. After building the fire up, I stretched and took out some pieces of sorcerous apparatus. With a bit of the soil I had picked up and certain other things, I composed a spell of passage to the mountaintop. Then I closed my eyes and reached along the gossamer lines of pulse and counterpulse connecting me to my three hawks.

My birds were still in place, meaning that the dragon had not relocated. Yet he might have gone out and returned.

Since I had my Mirror of Vision in front of me, I performed a Lesser Summoning of Phoebe and got a confirmation of Prospero's report: Gemnamnon was still there, in a foul mood; he had gone hunting again and returned to the tower ruins, presumably having killed and eaten. She hadn't heard yet whom or where.

"Thanks," I said. "I am attacking him again tonight. Stay off the peak. Go down to the south or southwest side, without being seen."

"Alone," she said, "you go alone?"

"Yes."

We regarded one another.

"You should not," she said finally.

"It's my risk to take," I said firmly. It was. Moreover, it was my duty to face things that threatened Argylle in person, just as my mother had always done.

Belphoebe sighed, still looking at me.

"This is sorcerous work," I said.

"You could—" she cut herself off.

"Could what?" I was sure I knew what she'd say, anyway.

She shook her head, once. "You know what you do. I cannot . . . I'm sure you've thought it through with all care."

"I have."

"Good luck, Gwydion."

"Thank you."

"Send a bird to me if you . . . if you need help."

What could she do? Get toasted herself. "Thank you, Phoebe." I broke the spell. No point telling the twins or Walter. They were out of this, and I didn't want more dissuasion or nervous advice. I wasn't letting myself think too hard about the whole proceedings at this point.

I dressed and armed myself. From Marfisa's and Alexander's injuries, I concluded that I wanted padding and a gas mask. The gas mask would have hampered me too much, and anyway the dragon's exhalations could be dispersed with simple transmutation spells, so I skipped that and layered on body protection. The dragon had shown a tendency to use his claws and tail, so I wanted more than just leather this time.

Sword, buckler, a knife in each tall black boot, heavy quilted gold-embroidered gambeson and over it my gold-tinted scale mail on leather (a present from Dewar, the work of dwarves he did business with at times, ensorcelled to repel most conventional damage, including fire), a helm, a couple of stilettos concealed here and there, and a long slender dagger with a leaf-shaped blade on my belt, with my sword. Certainly I'd use only the sword, but I felt better with lots of hardware. Confidence is what you make it of, Gaston used to say. The padding interfered with my freedom of movement, so I walked around and stretched and swung my arms until I was comfortable.

Last of all, I finished entering my passage spell in my logbook. Before using it, I went to Prospero's apartment. He was there by the fire in his study playing a lute to himself, fooling around fugally, his head bent over the instrument, his eyes half-closed, his expression abstracted, distanced.

"I'm leaving now," I said, moistening my lips.

Prospero looked up at me, frowning slightly. " 'Tis night."

"I don't need light," I said. "Anyway there is a full moon."

He sighed, resigned. "Gwydion, have care . . ."

"I will." I nodded to him and left before he said anything more or forbade me to go. In my own rooms I put on my helmet and cloak, performed the spell, and stepped into the Mirror of Ways.

There was a Summoning-pull for a moment, which faded. Strange. It had happened before too.

I was about a hundred meters from the open area at the summit, standing among scrub and stones. I stood allowing my eyes to adjust to the moonlight, and a soft scant weight dropped onto my shoulder. Virgil. This was no place for him, rather for the great war-hawks. I petted him and sent him to wait with Belphoebe.

The war-hawks had roosted for the night around the base of the mountain in trees which had good views of the summit. I closed my eyes and stirred them. The birds took to the air and begin drifting over the mountain to give me aerial reconnaissance. They showed me that Gemnamnon was curled around the tower ruins again, his left eye socket burnt and blackened. He was alert now, sensing my magical activity nearby. His tail twitched slightly and then stilled.

The moon was full. I could feel the energy running like water here, rushing through me and seemingly fountaining from the mountaintop. Closing my eyes, I moved with it, letting its pulse become mine. It took just a few seconds because the current was so strong. The poor light hardly mattered now; when I looked around I saw more clearly and with better understanding, with the near-prescience that the Spring-currents of the Node brought. I could readily understand why a magical creature like a dragon would choose this roost.

Now to the attack.

Gemnamnon lifted his head and exhaled, "Hooooo," as I leapt lightly onto a boulder across from him. The hot breath and deep, musical note blew by me.

I didn't bother making conversation, but stood with my hands on my hips. He seemed to gather himself together, and as he rose slowly, gracefully, I hit him with a simple lightning bolt. He jumped and dodged it, though the end of his long tail got singed, and reared back with his wings opening. They seemed as wide as the mountain. He fanned them and I threw another lightning bolt through the membrane of one. A series of snorted fireballs was his reply. As I parried them he half-soared toward me, pouncing.

He pursued me around the top of the mountain as a cat might a mouse, but in this case the mouse was sending fireworks back into the cat's face. I was trying to blind him, although it might not inconvenience him severely since dragons have other senses on which they rely more than vision. I did succeed in singeing off the cilia on the right side of his face and behind his head with a Fireflower.

A blue-white, brilliant Flashbulb incantation dazzled him for a moment when he had cornered me briefly against a fragment of crumbled wall. I vaulted to the top of the wall and followed up with the Locomotive Pile-Driver and Thunder Lance, a classic one-two punch that rocked him back and actually stunned him briefly—perhaps three seconds. He shook his head, recovered, and parried the Bolt of Death combined with Flashbulb again as he swung a clawed foot at me, hissing hot, sulphurous gas. I shielded myself and drew my sword, using it to make a complicated pattern in the air as I said a word. The sword flashed gold-white and the gas became so much settling dust. I pointed the sword directly at his right eye, using it for a focus, and cried the concluding words to Block of Ice, freezing the eye in his head as I jumped from boulder to boulder, getting away.

He screamed and reared back, wings fully spread, and a volley of fireballs and gouts of blue-white flame followed me, scorching the stones and making them crack and explode. Shielding was all I had time for until I got a small distance away.

I hurled back a few fireballs myself and also heaved some of the boulders, tossing them with stirrings of the energy of the Node—burping them, one might say, or bouncing them the way one might bounce wads of paper on a piece of cloth held taut and rippled. He batted them aside like cricket balls, advancing on me, driving me back and back with fire. I cast a simple electric-shock spell and Thunder Lance, which didn't slow him at all, and pitched a golden, tentacled fireball at him. It tangled itself around his leg and he destroyed it with a blast of his own flame.

I suddenly realized that I was approaching the cliff on the north side of the mountain. He had been herding me—

Gemnamnon laughed deafeningly and coughed short, intense bursts of fire. Rocks exploded around me. I dodged and shielded and cried the Falling Wall's keywords. He shrugged it off and pounced. I twisted, trying to roll aside, and his foot fell heavily upon me.

My head hung back over the edge of the cliff. I was pinned by two of his digits, my legs immobilized. Wind sighed past my ears, and then all was still.

He stopped flaming to bend his head over me and breathed softly, "Bastard of bastards, I am Elemental. You cannot conquer me, mongrel." He pinched me slightly, flexing his claws. I felt one of them slide into my left shoulder as if the mail were not there. Bones crunched.

"You *are* conservative," I gasped. I had few spells left. Most of them would certainly kill me and probably not kill him, given what I had seen tonight.

"Bastardy is one thing," he said, "but the mixing of two such noble lines is a degradation to both, particularly through such perversion as—"

A huge, crackling, ozone-stinking bolt of electricity slammed into his head from the left, dazing eye and ear with light and thunderclap. Not releasing me, the dragon reared back and threw flames in that direction. They spattered, hitting a shield, and another lightning bolt followed. Who was this? Prospero? Phoebe? A friendly million-watt generator? No one in Argylle commanded such raw power these days.

I had my sword in my hand. It had fallen behind me, under me. I drew it forth slowly, with great pain. If he leaned over me again, if I could lift it, I might be able to drive it into an eye, into his brain. Gemnamnon, however, pushed himself up and away, crushing the breath out of me as he reared back to meet this new opponent. I wheezed and gasped, trying not to black out, trying to see what was happening.

Three more smaller lightning bolts sizzled in, low and fast, splattering on Gemnamnon's gut. He laughed and crouched again, but he seemed to be slowing down a bit. Possibly that initial whack on the head had had an effect. Flames shot out and played against the newcomer's shield, a coruscating line of forces undulating and adapting efficiently to the changes in flow from the currents of the Spring. A blue-white sizzling ball drifted toward the dragon, growing as it came, attenuating, becoming a gauzy, curling, jellyfishlike thing: the biggest Salamander I'd ever seen Summoned from its Element. Its heat baked me where I lay. Gemnamnon reared up and blew a shrieking, fine line of ruddy-gold fire at it as its undulating tentacles touched him, tangled around him undamaged by his fire, and he thrashed and wrestled, crushing boulders as he tumbled to one side—

There followed a brief, violent blast of wind which moved boulders to grind on one another and toppled part of the ruined wall, an earthshaking thunderclap, and then silence. The dragon was gone.

I managed to suck air into my lungs, although it hurt to breathe. My head reeled. I was not certain that I was really conscious, or that I was not dying. The black edges that had been closing in around my field of vision drew back, though the moonlight was so blue and thin compared to the brilliance of the sorcerous fires that I saw little.

I couldn't move, but I could sponge up the loose power on the mountaintop Node, though it was turbulent from the dragon's recent passage. I did that, floating like a drowning sailor on the ocean's breast. A soft wind washed over me, cooling me and whispering sadly among the stones. I felt a strange sense of presence without object.

Footsteps came near, slowly, rustling grasses, disturbing

gravel and rocks. A ruddy ignis came to hover obligingly, illuminating me. My rescuer moved into its light, pushing back his cloak hood, rumpling his dark hair as he did, setting his staff down, flicking an eyebrow as he knelt by my side.

"Dewar," I whispered voicelessly, thinking I hallucinated.

Dewar's eyes met mine, and he smiled gently. He had a short, neat beard, and his sea-colored eyes held affection, amusement, reassurance. "Shh. Let's see . . ." He spread his hands and the Spring shimmered and danced at his finger-tips. His breath puffed white in the ignis-light.

I closed my eyes, nursing my blown-out vitality on the Spring's energy. Dewar pulled me back from the cliff's edge and went to work; things began to realign themselves, some-what painfully, inside me. I hissed once or twice and grunted when he set the bones in my shoulder. The crushed ribs took a long time.

"Half done," he said finally. "Let's get you back to Argylle and finish the job while you're in shock. Ariel—"

A gust of wind ruffled my hair and then localized to become a whirlwind, a dimly shining, flowery, graceful shape, not unlike the thing that had removed Gemnamnon from the mountaintop but smaller: a spinning short-throated lily. A sweet, soft, pealing bell-like voice spoke from it. "Yes, Master? What may I do for you?"

Dewar nodded. "Firewood, Ariel. For a bonfire of depar-ture."

I was beginning to guess where Dewar had been, what he'd been doing.

"Easily done, Master." Ariel gusted apart and blew off around the mountaintop, picking up branches, twigs, and brush in his whirlwind. Dewar watched, smiling slightly still, holding my hands in his. The woodpile, now big enough for a bale-fire, deposited itself on a flat outcrop ten paces away. Ariel asked, "Is it well done, Master?"

"Very good." Dewar hissed a command and pointed; the ignis shot into the pile and it exploded into flame, then settled down to burn more naturally. "No, Gwydion—don't stand. I'll carry you."

He did, too, and although it hurt like hell when he lifted me after opening the Way, I didn't black out. Ariel did not seem to accompany us. Dewar had made the Way into my own workroom; he set me down on the table. I'd left a green-shaded lamp burning by the Mirror of Ways. Hazily, by its tinted light, I saw him go and listen at the door for a moment. Then he nodded, satisfied, and returned to pick me up again and carry me to the bedroom.

"Do you still keep a surgeon's kit in here?"

"Yes. Cabinet behind the workroom door."

"Hang on then." Dewar squeezed my hand and whisked out, returned with the medical kit, and pulled a chair over to the bedside. I turned my head—my neck was beginning to stiffen—and looked at him. He smiled faintly and held a goblet of wine to my lips. I sipped and swallowed. It had a sweet taste under the fullness of the flavor: dosed.

"The dragon isn't dead, only displaced. Seriously displaced. But he may not care for a rematch," my tutor said. "You did very well."

"Not enough," I whispered.

"You could have wiped him out with a vortex," he agreed. "But I don't know how good an idea that would be, so close to Argylle City and the Spring." He stroked my forehead gently. "Rest, Gwydion."

Sleep dropped over me like a bag.

There was light, wan grey snow-filtered light, when I woke. I was alone. My body was cased in bandages and laced with aches and pains and smarts. I fell asleep again after a few minutes.

My second waking was dark and light. A fire burned brightly in the fireplace and candles were lit around the room, the deep-blue curtains drawn. Prospero was sitting beside me, holding the picture of his son and daughter, looking down at it. He smiled sadly as my eyes opened and set it back on the table.

"Good to see you," he greeted me.

"Happy to be here," I rasped.

"Hungry?" he asked.

"I'd better restrict myself to liquids."

He nodded and produced beef-vegetable broth, spooning it into me carefully, not talking until I had had enough. I sipped a glass of wine between mouthfuls. My arms were splinted and immobilized.

"You ought to have come to me," he said then, scrutinizing my face as he spoke. " 'Twas late, indeed, but I kept vigil on the Citadel and heard naught from you, though your lights and your explosions lit the heavens and shook the stones. I'd have gladly mended you. I'm no novice at treating such wounds as yours seem to be."

Had Dewar disappeared without making himself known?

"I . . . I wasn't thinking clearly," I said. "How long has it been?"

"Today's the second day since your assault, and noon's long past. Errethon has sent a snowstorm north to us, winter ice 'gainst dragon-fire perhaps," he added. "No connection to your battle, I assume."

"None I know of. How are Alex and Marfisa?"

"Alex mends apace, so well that his accustomed cussed self chafes at the mending and would undo it. Marfisa lies abed yet, in less pain today, also fairly cussed at confinement. Walter is their gentle jailer, warding them from their own inclinations, and Tellin ministers to Marfisa under Walter's eye."

"Good." I closed my eyes as though tired. I *was* tired.

"What befell you?" he asked.

"Got stepped on," I said truthfully, if indistinctly.

"I did so surmise. Your surgeon bound you well. How came you home again, Gwydion? Gwydion?"

I didn't answer, taking refuge in invalidism. Silence was better than lying outright, though I'd prefer to tell the truth all the time, and I expect to hear it, too.

He didn't say anything more.

Naturally he realized that I had had help in bandaging myself up. I didn't think I could tell him who had done it. Had he wanted anyone to know, my tutor would have stayed.

Dewar was alive and sane and somehow keeping tabs on events back home. And Ariel—that was a strange thing, that Ariel, given liberty by Prospero at the beginning of the world, should call Dewar "Master" now. Strange and wonderful. Dewar . . .

I fell asleep again, smiling.

A NOTE WAS PROPPED IN FRONT of the photograph beside my bed:

> *You need but one pair of eyes to sleep. I'm robbing*
> *Hounds at cards. Call if you've need of me.*

The Hounds is a nickname for Marfisa and Alexander, Gaston's Warhounds they are called in Landuc sometimes.

My little bag of magical essentials lay next to the note.

I tested myself. I didn't feel wonderful, but I certainly was closer to being in one piece than I had been during the past week-and-a-half of sleeping and waking only to eat, usually attended by Walter or Prospero. I got up very carefully and slid into my dressing gown. My arms still ached, but I took the splints off: by drawing on the Spring as Dewar had taught me to do, I had hurried the process of healing and sustained myself through the period when solid foods were impractical.

The curtains were closed, but brilliant sun leaked around them; by that light I tottered into my workroom and sat down on a stool. The mirror before me showed that I was on my way to having a beard. I scratched at it and thought I'd let it keep growing. Beards seemed to be the fashion in the family these days.

For the hell of it, I tried a Lesser Summoning of Dewar, but of course there was nothing, and I wasn't about to essay anything more elaborate in this condition. I invoked Belphoebe instead.

"Gwydion! How now? All's well?" She grinned, delighted, standing on snowshoes in a pine grove, the trees heavy-laden with snow. A candle burned in her hand, to focus my Summoning.

"Not so ill as I could have been," I allowed.

"And hast thou slain the Jabberwock? I saw great doings from Little Baldy's shoulder." Watching from there, she would not have seen specifics of Dewar's work.

I had to smile, and I blushed and found half a truth. "No. But I don't think he'll return soon."

"Fled and not dead. A rout is still a victory! Good work, Gwydion."

I felt uncomfortable about taking the credit for this. "That's what I'm here for, Phoebe. Anything new or unusual happening?"

"No. Just snow."

"Good. Talk to you later."

I wanted a pipe, but suspected that smoking was not healthful for my abused lungs. Instead I pulled the bell and asked for soup and applesauce and easy-to-eat food like that, and lots of it please. I was famished. They must have been keeping it warm for me, down in the kitchen; beaming Serge brought an overloaded tray up in less than ten minutes. I sat in my armchair by the fire and ate slowly.

My first impulse was to drop everything and shoot off to find Dewar, my tutor and mentor. He meant the world to me.

My parents had called him in after I had blown up a barn whilst visiting in the Westlands. It was a derelict barn anyway, a local eyesore. But Gaston was furious and Freia was annoyed, and, I realized now, amused. I stared in the fire and, smiling to myself, recalled Dewar's casual entry into my life.

"Damn it, Gwydion! Thou hast better sense than that. 'Twas not thy property, for one thing, and the Ellilizeës are wroth, justly so. Thou wast to build ties there, not tear them down." Gaston has never struck any of us except in training us in the arts martial. However, he has damaged furniture. This time he pounded a fist on the great oak table, which bounced under the blow, adding emphasis to his words as he paced up and down.

I flinched. "I'm sorry," I said lamely. He had not raised his voice the whole time and I felt deafened.

"Sorry! Shalt be sorry. I ought to make thee build them a new one, by hand. They've offered to take recompense in labor: we could apprentice thee seven years to a stonemason there."

Seven years? In the desolate Westlands? I caught my breath. Gaston was quite capable of disciplining us as he disciplined his enlisted men, I had heard tales from Alexander and Marfisa—

His eyes flashed as he rounded on me. "And the stupidity of using such sorcery, untrained! Why didst never ask if thou'rt curious?"

"I didn't think—"

"Obviously not," he said bitingly.

I had meant to say, I didn't think anyone would approve. There was a distaste for magic in Gaston, I had detected it clearly. "I would have—"

"But thou didst not! Lagwit! If thou knew'st enow to do that, thou knew'st eke 'twas dangerous. Flaunting folly! In the future—" He was interrupted by a knock.

Freia came in, flicked an expressionless look over me, and nodded to her husband. Gaston followed her out with one word to me: "Wait," flat and hard. He was really, really angry. I swallowed, shaking. He might be angry enough to make me swear not to use sorcery again, not to experiment with it or study it . . .

Mother had just shaken her head at me and said, "That was an ill-considered thing to do, Gwydion," when the El-lilizeës had haled her out there. She had come back with me on the Road and said nothing more. Gaston had berated me for about an hour. Now they must be deciding what to do.

I leaned against the tall window behind me and covered my face. The clock ticked. Outside, below in the burgeoning garden, someone pushed a lawnmower back and forth, the blades whirring and clucking rhythmically, whick-whick-whick. Insects buzzed. It was summer.

They had been planning to raze the barn anyway. Did it really matter how it got knocked down? I gritted my teeth to keep from crying. Gaston was so angry, and Mother so icily cold . . . He was right, I was supposed to be impressing them with how nice we were . . . I had blown it, for Argylle, not just for myself. There was no way to repair the damage.

The door opened and closed and I jumped, dropping my hands.

A man I'd met only twice before in my memory stood looking at me quizzically, then approached slowly to stand by me and look out the window. Taller than I, he had a short beard and looked less like Mother than I would have expected: her brother Dewar. I didn't know much about him except that he was liked hesitantly by most people in Argylle; that he was Prospero's son through a woman from Noroison and there was something about that nobody wanted to talk about; and that he was a sorcerer of already-legendary ability, bidding fair to outshine his famous father. His cloak, heavier than the day warranted, was dark blue-green, and his quilted tunic was a nondescript sandy color. His hair was longer than Argylle men usually wore it, curlier than Mother's and tied at the nape of his neck with a blue-green ribbon. He wore mottled grey trousers and high brown boots, also unseasonably heavy and spattered with light-red mud, and on his hands were brown gauntlets that he slowly drew off as he peered down into the garden.

He turned to me suddenly and laid a hand on my shoulder. "Come," was all he said, pulling me forward toward the window, and he gestured and spoke a word. We passed through the window, but not through it. The world flipped around us. We stood in a manycolored desert surrounded by towering piles of weathered rocks, under a triangle formed by two massive monoliths tilted together. The light was ruddy, from a low, swollen red sun. I realized he had taken us through a Way without my even being aware of it. The window had been the focus—

"Show me what you did," Uncle Dewar directed me, interrupting my thoughts.

I stared at him.

"Go ahead," he said. "Do it."

Trembling, I did. A pile of rocks shuddered and fell. It was a spell for loosening the bonds between objects, useful for disrupting, say, stone walls . . . or barns.

"You worked that one out for yourself?" he asked calmly, when the dust had begun to settle.

"N-n-no."

My uncle nodded as if I had confirmed his worst suspicions. "What have you been reading?"

I told him: *"Doctor Mervyn's Compendium of the Arts Magical."*

"Garbage, pure garbage. Forget it. Sloppy stuff. You're putting six times as much effort into that spell as you need to. Where'd you find that, anyway?"

He laid his hand on my shoulder again, murmuring something too quick and low for my ear to catch, and in a step we were in a musty room. How had he made the Way? I wondered. Uncle Dewar frowned and opened a couple of windows. The workaday sounds of the lawnmower, of insects, floated in. We were in Argylle again.

I looked around, trying to be inconspicuous. So this was what Uncle Dewar's rooms were like. I had never been in them. The windows were high, diamond-paned and arched, and at the tops, in the arches, were curled stained-glass vines on which a sun and a moon and various planets and stars grew among heart-shaped green leaves. Comfortable, if dusty, leaf-patterned cushions were in the window seats. Immediately behind me was a high black-bordered mirror, and I supposed that we had come through it, if it were a Mirror of Ways. All along one wall bookshelves rose from floor to ceiling; in the middle of the floor stood a long black-topped worktable and tall stools; and on the wall opposite the bookshelves were glass-fronted cabinets filled with things I could not clearly see through the dust-veiled glass: sorcerous instruments of metal and glass and wood, small caskets and rows of glass jars. There were small, elaborately-patterned multicolored rugs here and there on the stone floor. Two tall closed doors were to either side of the instrument cabinets, one beside the windows and one near the door that led into the hallway, and there was a sink in one end of the workbench. There was a drafting table in one corner and a rolltop desk, closed and locked, in another, with a green-globed lamp hanging from a chain above it and more bookshelves built into the walls around it, and all the bookshelves were filled with books, overfilled with books, books bound in black and red and brown and blue and green leathers, brown folios, books made of carven slabs of wood and sheets of bark, books whose bindings were ornately tooled and gilded and books whose bindings were rotting, books held together with string and several stacks of parchment pages weighted with strangely shaped bits of metal or mineral specimens or round color-dappled polished glass balls, books stacked on top of each other and books double-layered on the shelves, books laid on top of the shelved books and books with bits of ribbon lolling out like weary tongues to mark pages, thick books and thin books and long narrow books and several round black jars of scrolls in wooden cases.

I answered his question. "I, I found it in the Archives, and, uh, Dazhur gave me some ideas . . ."

He shook his head and tsked. "Let's start with the idea of balance," he began, pointing to a three-legged stool and taking off his cloak to hang it on a plain peg behind the hall door.

Thus began my first lesson in sorcery from my uncle, who was now my tutor, and who thenceforward went almost everywhere with me—Argylle and its demesnes, and later Morven and Phesaotois and the Great Court at Noroison. Golden-blonde, voluptuous Dazhur, who lived in a cottage on the dark fringe of Threshwood, did not even look at me again, which was too bad, because she was something to look at herself. I overheard part of the explanation for that by accident, the day after he arrived. My window was open and Freia and Dewar were in his rooms below, the window also open. I happened to be reading in my window seat, feet up, head down, poring over one of the books Uncle Dewar had given me to study.

"He's picked up a few very bad habits from Dazhur," Dewar said, "but he's young and he'll lose them fast once he's learned the right way to do things."

"From Dazhur! Dazhur?" My mother's voice was horrified.

"Yes, I'm surprised she's still—"

"Dewar! He's sixteen years old!"

A few seconds of silence. "Oh. I'll speak to her."

"*I'll* speak to her," my mother said, meaningly. "Libidinous bitch! She thinks I'm a pushover."

"You are. Let Gaston—"

"He'd just kill her."

"Do you think—"

"No. *I* will talk to her, and *you* won't mention it. Agreed?"

"As you wish, madame." He chuckled. "Argylle wouldn't be the same without her."

"You have no taste."

Another chuckle.

I wondered what was so bad about Dazhur. She had been very friendly to me. My old school dictionary didn't have "libidinous" in it, and when my uncle told me it meant "salacious" I supposed it had something to do with chemistry.

Dewar had been as much a parent to me as Gaston or Freia, and I loved him as dearly as either of them. I had learned most of what I knew of sorcery from him, here and at Noroison, and had studied further on my own with his guidance. Our master-apprentice relationship was unusual in that Dewar had taught me complete spells. The common practice—since the apprentice you train today will be your rival tomorrow—is to give the most miserly training possible and bind your apprentice to you with the Oath of Blood and dependencies of many kinds while using him for all he's worth for whatever dirty work comes to mind. That was how Dewar had been taught by his mother the Black Countess Odile and that mightiest sorcerer of Morven, Paracelsus.

Uncle Dewar had thumbed his nose gleefully at that tradition. He used his own and his father's grimoires and notebooks to teach me things that most sorcerers take years to figure out for themselves. He gave me complete spells, special ones he had developed himself, and encouraged me to tinker and modify and make mistakes. Most importantly, he had taught me his way of spinning spells with all three forces available—the Well, the Stone, and the Spring—something no one else in the world could do. This generous attitude raised eyebrows in Phesaotois, at the heart of which Morven lies like a stone in a net, and many were the voices that promised doom to come because of it.

It also, I flattered myself, resulted in me being a precociously well-equipped young sorcerer with more power available to me than any other had ever had at my age and a better understanding of what I could do with it.

"I wasted so much time with this . . ." Dewar would say, or "It was so damned frustrating to do this before I figured out . . ." and he would explain an elegant simplification, or "If only someone had shown me this when I was learning that . . ."

He had taught me languages, history, mathematics, logic, geomancy, everything. Dewar had guided me on the Road and answered, honestly and evenhandedly, questions about everything from politics and poisons to sex and family history. He had filled the cup for me at Argylle's Spring when I drank of it and secretly brought me to the Stone on Morven in Phesaotois. I could ask him anything and I would do, unhesitatingly, anything he asked me to. I relied on him for good advice, good arguments, and good companionship— we shared tastes in a number of things.

How had he known I was in imminent danger of being eaten by Gemnamnon? I wasn't perfectly sure, but I suspected that Ariel was capable of keeping watch on people and events anywhere and reporting to Dewar on them. It was part of the nature of a Sylph that all places be the same to it. But how could Dewar have bound Ariel again at all? Ages ago, Prospero had kept his word and freed Ariel forever, under duress. He did not like to talk about it.

Like all sorcerers, my uncle was continually working to expand his repertoire, although unlike the vast majority of the others Dewar was moved by curiosity rather than a craving to enhance his prestige or the need to maintain his territory. His position of perfect security in Argylle, without rivals against whom he must continually guard and defend as in Phesaotois and Pheyarcet, provided him with an ideal base for his investigations into . . . into anything that caught his attention. Yet he was not always in Argylle.

He had residences scattered along the Roads, throughout the worlds dependent on the Well and the Stone, but Argylle was home to him. In this he was as his peers, for I had always known he carried out other experiments in those places, work too intense, too difficult, too dangerous to pursue at home. Dewar, greatly as he had trusted me, had kept certain things dead secret—among them, the locations of his personal, private hiding-places and what he did there. I had asked him once, and he had said that a secret known to more than one person is no longer secret and refused to discuss the subject further.

It seemed that one thing he had done in seclusion was to teach himself of the binding of Elementals. His father Prospero had been the preeminent Master of the Elements before his involuntary retirement. Conquering their will with one's own is the supreme triumph for a sorcerer. Dewar certainly had the strength of mind for the feat, and by all evidence had accomplished it. What would Prospero think?

For now, I would keep my mouth closed, I decided. Nor would I pursue Dewar in any way. I was fairly sure that I could find him swiftly if I wanted to, if there were a desperate need for him, but I also knew that doing so would be dangerous for both of us and would certainly bring in an angry sorcerer in a far-from-amiable frame of mind.

I turned my thoughts to the dragon Gemnamnon. What had Dewar done with, or to, him? He had said something equivalent to "not dead but displaced." Using Ariel's capacity to shepherd winds, perhaps with a Way (I would do it thus), he had removed the beast—I hoped not to a populous, hospitable, or easily-departed region. Dewar had not thought the dragon would be back, but I suspected he would, eager for vengeance, and he would start right here. Otto's Hunnondáligi had trailed him through a Way, along the Road. Gemnamnon had far more reason for revenge.

* * *

Marfisa and I tottered about the Citadel, I under my own steam and Marfisa with her squire Tellin tucked under her shoulder. Worn by incessant pain, my sister leaned on Tellin's judgement as well as her arm, and Tellin minded her mistress's health better than Marfisa would have done. Alexander recuperated quickly and was soon down in the practice yards pulling a bow, fencing with Prospero and anyone who'd go up against him, and engaging in his usual fanatical physical training. Belphoebe reported that the incursions of monsters had abated entirely. We speculated that they had been related to the dragon. Prospero returned to Ollol and the wine negotiations and I returned to the Chair, finding that a new respect had infused the behavior of petitioners and Councillors.

Marfisa continued with crutches and then a cane, though Tellin was always beside or behind her. Her left leg was withered and twisted. When she could mount a horse (a chariot was out of the question and she wouldn't use a coach), she had Tellin pack their saddlebags and the two of them went to Landuc with Alexander, who seemed to blame me for the whole fiasco. Whether Marfisa did or not I could not discover, but I thought not; Tellin was as open and friendly to me as before the fight. Had Marfisa blamed me, surely Tellin would have turned a cold shoulder to me out of her love for Marfisa.

I was truly sorry to see them go. Their company had been diverting in the darkening days of midwinter, but they left before New Year's, which is celebrated at the Winter Solstice in Argylle. Morosely, I wondered if they even remembered the significance of the day to our family and then shrugged. The loss was theirs, if they didn't care enough to stay.

As was my custom, however, I took a lantern and went down the long black stone stair in the Core of the Citadel to visit my late mother.

I sat on the ornate iron park bench from the Argylle City Botanical Gardens which someone had thoughtfully placed

there—I suspected Freia or Dewar; it was their sort of joke—
and looked at the dark pool, washed in its currents of life.
Light from the lantern illuminated nothing in or around the
Spring. Taking my Keys out, I chose Freia's and held it,
running my thumb over it. Then I closed my eyes and concentrated on the faint taste of personality in the sensations
the Spring evoked.

In the past I had managed, I believed, to make a connection with her. But not this time. I felt an awareness but it was
not open to me. I waited there for a long time, hoping she
would change her mind, but there was nothing.

Finally I opened my eyes and rubbed at my temples. "Very
well," I said aloud, "be that way."

No reaction.

At the sound of a footfall behind me, I turned and glared,
annoyed at being followed. Prospero stood there, no light in
his hand, at the edge of the circle of mine.

"Call as you will; there's none to answer here," he said,
and joined me on the bench.

I was faintly embarrassed. "I am superstitious, I guess," I
replied.

"Nowise . . . She haunts us yet, too attached to part so
untimely soon. Poor girl. Drowning, more than drowning . . ." He looked around at the massive stone pillars and
the full darkness beyond them and then back at the insubstantial Spring. " 'Tis a pity it could not be one of the Node-
founts, if water must be her doom. Outdoors, in open air,
among the folk she loved. Best were the one in the Square.
The market bustle, the people's neverending comedy . . ."

I thought he was mocking me. "Next time I'll bring flowers," I snapped.

He glanced at me and I saw that he was serious.

"It is a wretched sort of tomb," I conceded.

He nodded. "Mine's far pleasanter." A ghost of a smile
came and went. Prospero's tomb is already built, owing to a
family tradition, back in Landuc's royal repository, which is

in a breathtakingly lovely park in the Palace grounds. When someone is born in Landuc, the family selects an auspicious location and builds his tomb or puts up a marker with the name and the birthdate on his gravesite. Just to keep them on their toes, maybe. Prospero has more than once expressed his preference for a common grave over "that pompous compost heap," meaning the Imperial Tombs.

"But this is close to home. She can keep an eye on us here."

"And does," he concurred. "You asked me once about that feeling . . . 'twas years ago now. Perhaps you've forgotten."

"No. I still get it sometimes. It hurts. It didn't used to."

"Hurts?" He looked at me with sympathetic interest.

"I am forgetting, Prospero. I do not want to forget her. She will slip out of our memories and soon we will not quite remember her voice, or the way she gestured when she talked, or how it felt to dance with her." I tapped my foot and looked away. Tears sprang to my eyes. I ordered them back.

Prospero inhaled slowly. "Ah, damn," he sighed. "Yes, that is how it goes, at first. And later as hard time grinds on, you gaze on her likeness frozen in paint or stone, and you say, 'I love you still,' yet 'tis no longer clear why you love her, or why you ever loved her, and would you really love her still were she here today? As well love a snowflake or a blade of grass. The likenesses we treasure in early mourning are but soulless paint and stone. Oblivion claims us all, and forgetfulness seals our fate. There is no difference.

"Methinks Gaston left because he couldn't bear it. We stay because we must: heavy burden it is. I was more than half inclined to smash this all and blow the place back to the primordial Elements. I should have. It would be a cleaner end than this, this slow tormentous dissolution of the heart."

I thought of her husband. Gaston, Gaston, what must your grief be like if ours still twisted in our guts? Our love was bound by blood, yours by choice. On the first day of New Year's, the Day of Reflection, she kissed you and said, Prospero and Dewar and Gwydion and I are going to investigate a peculiarity in the Catacombs. And perhaps you kissed her again and said, Be careful, love, to which she would tenderly reply Always, for you. She was careful, too. It was the rest of us who were careless.

I shivered and stood, went to the Spring and looked in, and took my leave to hurry back to my rooms to loathe myself in decent privacy. For I knew better than Prospero: she *was* haunting us. She was there, trapped within the Spring, and she could only be freed if one of us offered himself in her stead.

⌐ 8 ⌐

WHEN I WAS MYSELF AGAIN, I had a whisky and then another and splashed water on my face. My eyes were red-rimmed, making the irises brilliant in comparison. Outside it was dark already and fireworks were booming over the Wye, flowers of colored light for Freia.

A Summoning commenced to embrace me and then faded. "Cut it out, Mother," I said aloud. "If you want to talk, do it."

I straightened and stared back at myself in the looking glass.

When that had most recently happened, I had been on top of Mount Longview with Gemnamnon. Both times. Before that, in my study, reading, and before that—many times over the years.

But that it came now, when I was thinking unhappily about my part in Mother's death and continuance in that state, seemed to connect it to the occasional feeling I had that she was about the place still. Freia's haunting was nothing ridiculous, you must understand, no lights and footsteps, nor moving furniture and sourceless music. Simply a feeling that if I turned around, she'd be in the room. Or I might think I heard her voice. That had happened rather more often. Mostly, I might feel an imminent Summoning that never came: a feeling of sourceless attention, of unexpressed intention.

But when it had happened on Longview, it had apparently been the Sylph Ariel I'd sensed; I hadn't been thinking of Mother at all . . .

I stood for a moment, my thoughts skipping like a stone over half-a-dozen diverse topics, and then I ran to Dewar's rooms, below my own. The door was locked, but it popped open for me easily with an elementary spell. He had never worried much about security here in his trusted family's stronghold.

Lighting a thick white almond-scented candle, I went to his workbench, which was a bit tougher, and finally managed to open it up and searched for his neat index of spells. It was an outside chance only that he would have left it, a remote possibility . . . Eureka! I found the boxes, names of spells and descriptions tidily filed alphabetically, and looked through them. Yes, here it was. Dewar was a careful fellow.

Elementals: A Summoning of Elementals in the manner of my Lord Father Prince Prospero with particular note of Sylphs, read the card, and it indicated a certain notebook, title and page: a copy of one of Prospero's grimoires. Prospero had destroyed his books, but by then Dewar had already gone through his collection and copied down a small part of the spells. This was one of them.

I turned to the dusty bookshelves and by the light of my candle scanned them, up and down the ladder, looking for the book in which this spell was written.

Hunting and hunting, I peered and brushed at cobwebs and several times got shocks and nips from warding spells still set. I found nothing of the book I wanted.

Conceivably, Dewar could have left it in his rooms in Landuc, but I happened to know, because he had once told me, that he had never left anything of the sort in Landuc because he didn't trust anyone there.

Regrettably, I had never had much interest in the Elementals. Prospero had seemed to disapprove of the idea of binding one as a familiar, and Dewar hadn't had one, and somehow it had just seemed like something Not Done and I had concentrated on other areas of sorcery . . . Regrets, regrets. For if I had, odds were I'd have copied that and similar spells myself.

I put the card files away (keeping the Sylph one for myself for some unarticulated reason) put his desk back in order, locked up again and left. I hadn't been in there in a long time. It too was haunted, but differently.

I sat down in my rooms and doodled on my workbench blotter. Virgil watched me from one of the shelves overhead. My other owl, Brahms, dozed on his perch. He was getting old. He'd always been just a pet, not a familiar as Virgil was.

Now I thought I knew two things: that Dewar had somehow bound Ariel to him anew and that Dewar was using Ariel now to keep an eye on me and mine. Which was kind of him, but I would prefer that, if he were really interested in what was going on, he simply move back home or call.

Sylphs, Sylphs, Elementals. I cudgelled my brain and wrote the few keywords that fell out on the blotter. Something about binding, unbinding. It was as difficult to loose them as to bind them. Was it not? And they were the ideal servants, especially when willing. Ariel had served Prospero willingly. They had had a good working relationship, one might say.

An Elemental had the ability to be anywhere in its Element, if not instantly then very rapidly. Salamanders were swiftest, but being destructive made bad familiars; Sylphs were nearly as fast, Sprites third and the slow Sammeads last.

The Spring, the Well, and the Stone were also Elemental in nature—Water, Fire, Stone of course.

For the first time in my life, I wondered what connection

the Elementals could have with the source manifestations. I recalled that Dewar had often denied vigorously that any of the great Sources had native intelligence, yet when the conversation was not about that subject directly he had always appeared to consider them as living beings with opinions, thoughts, and tempers. Furthermore, it is customary in Phesaotois to address the Stone directly and indirectly as "Ancient One" or "Most Ancient One" with plenty of deferential respect. The Stone was spoken of as a living being might be.

My thoughts slowed down and began stumbling.

Mother had been destroyed by the Elemental Spring, the Source of Argylle. More or less. How much of her might remain? I had thought of her as "haunting" the place. I knew that something had survived her immolation in the unrestrained power of the Spring. How long could she persist? Might she be gone now? I had not felt her this year. Exactly what happened to a person who died as she had, anyway? Did she somehow become an Elemental? Was it possible?

I puzzled over this until I had a headache, and then I sighed and stopped. Virgil made soft friendly sounds at me while I paced aimlessly around my apartment, ending up at my desk in the study. I poured myself another whisky. This clandestine Elemental binding worried me. What was Dewar about? Why had he not told me? I would not have betrayed his trust, he knew that. I had kept other confidences.

Considering the circumstances under which he had left Argylle, I suspected his secrecy had something to do with Freia and that horrible New Year's Day. Dewar was an intense man; he kept a façade of glacial cool over emotions as strong and inexorable as tides. In the state of mind he had been in, he might have vowed anything—undertaken anything.

Dewar, plainly having just completed the major preparations for a complex and far-sending spell of Passage, stood over the Spring below the Citadel in the midst of his spell's golden web. His eyes were closed. His face wore an expression of deep concentration over the haggard lines of new grief. There was a bruise on his jaw where Prospero had hit him to knock him unconscious earlier.

The Spring had slain Freia hours before. Dewar had always had a morbid streak.

"Dewar?" I asked.

He glared at me. "Be very quiet. Be sensitive. Open your ears. Close your eyes."

I folded my arms and bowed my head, following his instructions. Ten minutes later I looked up slowly and met my tutor's gaze through the rippling light. "Something is here." It was clearer, stronger than the subtle draught of wrongness Tython had made in the Spring.

"Something. Yes."

"Why did you come down here?" I asked suddenly. He could have opened the Way from his workroom.

"It suited my purpose. You are too easily distracted, Gwydion," he said coldly.

I closed my eyes again and listened. The feeling was as if someone were about to speak, but it went on and on, an unexpressed thought hanging in the air.

Dewar broke the silence again. "It's much stronger as one works the Spring."

Another ten minutes passed. Dewar was wholly involved with the Spring, Summoning I realized, an intricate and powerful command whose object I could not guess. I watched, said nothing more.

"Freia, I still love you," my uncle whispered suddenly. "I would follow you . . . Where shall I find you now? Where?"

A wave of light rose at the perimeter of the Spring, a roseate glow in the darkness, and rushed inward toward the center, discharging around Dewar like a fountain, its splash of energy dissipating along the lines of the web that supported and insulated him. My hair stirred with the power and the feeling of present personality was stronger: it felt as though she were standing in front of me, ready to speak.

"Damn it," cried Dewar. "If you can take her away, you can bring her back! Do it! I ask you by the Gryphon, by the Source of the World, by Stone and Sea and Sun and Sky!"

Another shower shot up, a silent brilliant tower twelve feet tall, and fell back, rose again roaring loud as an ocean's worth of breakers with a strange high keening note in its spectrum.

"You don't need her as much as I do!" Dewar shouted over the storm, nearly invisible inside the fountain of sparks and polychromatic light.

I shuddered, covering my ears against the roar, and hid my face, expecting him to perish just as she had.

"What good is she to you?" he screamed.

There was a silence so abrupt my ears rang and I thought I hallucinated: "Dewar, stop shouting. I'm here."

He gasped. Opening my eyes, I felt faint. My mother, in the dusty red dress and Dewar's blue-green cloak which she had been wearing when she disappeared in our Spring, stood next to Dewar in the web of the spell he had constructed over the Spring, which had become dark and perfectly tranquil as usual.

For an insane, joyous moment, I thought: it was a mistake. All a mistake. All's right again.

"It is not simple," she said very gently.

He reached for her. "It has to be. It's all the same, isn't it? Matter converts to energy, energy to matter . . ."

She shook her head and seemed to recede before he could touch her. "People have said I was the very soul of the realm, dear heart. I was not. Tython's insinuation into the Spring meant that he was. I have displaced him. If I leave, he may find a way to return."

"We got along well enough before Dazhur stirred Tython up and polluted the Spring with her piddling amateurism," Dewar said.

She looked at him: one of her intense soul-peeling looks.

"I'm sorry about the business with Luneté," he added suddenly, a note of bitterness in his voice, looking down. "I was . . . a shit."

Freia shook her head slightly, smiling but sad. "I understand."

"You always do. Everything. It's not fair. Were you really surprised by this?"

"This what?"

"The Spring . . . consuming you."

"I think the same thing happened to Panurgus and possibly to Primas. I'm not certain of that, but . . . I think it did. I'm new to the trade."

"What trade might that be, Freia?"

She looked puzzled. "I am learning that still. It is here, being here . . . The view's grand. I can see everything, all Argylle, if I wish." She paused and her face changed, her graceful brows drawing together. "Gaston—"

"He needs you. You're his life. You can't run out on us, Freia!"

"On you."

"So I'm selfish."

She tipped her head on one side and looked at him, smiling. "Not so very," she said.

"Do we need a soul for Argylle? Right away? In the Spring? We didn't have one before! What's wrong with having it walk around with you?" he cried, anguished.

"Dewar." Her voice was a caress, a lover's murmur.

"Don't say my name!" He turned away from her abruptly and pounded his fist in his hand.

She was silent a moment. "But I know I am the right one for this."

My stars, I thought. I knew that tone. She was wavering. I sat transfixed on the iron bench and watched her, luminous creature of blood-red and sea-green. Dewar spun back to her.

"What if I followed you, jumped into the Spring? Right now? What would happen?" he shouted.

Frightened, she cried, "Don't! No! I don't know!"

"At the least, I would die, true?"

"That's what we're always told—"

Dewar snarled, "Panurgus was a notorious liar. You're not dead. You're transformed."

Freia spread her ghostly hands. "Death is a transformation. Let us not start on that. We have agreed to disagree, long ago."

"Why does the Spring need a soul, Freia?"

"Something must . . . inform it. To . . . make it . . . persist."

"The Spring should already have a soul: Father's. He opened it—we say he made it, gave himself to it; he founded the City. Why should it need another? Why you and not him?"

"Just making it is not sufficient. Tython was able to invade our Spring because there was nothing to ward it." She seemed to think or listen for a moment, head tipped again. "It is said in Landuc that the Emperor . . . is the World."

"The idea of identifying the ruler with the realm is standard. Avril's still running around making a nuisance of himself."

"Panurgus . . . is not . . . but he is, still." Freia spoke so softly I had to strain to catch the words.

"Do you mean to say that he has become part of Landuc's Well? That he really *is* Landuc, is Pheyarcet, as the Well is?"

"Yes . . ." She nodded slowly. "I can . . . hear him."

"What is he saying?" Dewar's hysteria had calmed, subjugated by his curiosity.

"I . . . think I shan't say. It is rather coarse."

"Flaming old bastard. All literally true."

She laughed, a sweet sound that echoed through the colonnaded darkness, her hands going up to cover her mouth.

"So why can you not continue to be part of the Spring and

still have a body, the way the Emperor does? And why you and not Prospero? He started this!"

Freia was clearly struggling, trying to understand it herself as much as to explain it to her brother. "Prospero . . . He has already . . . done all that he could do. He . . . his nature is not . . . it does not allow him to . . . he is too volatile."

"And your nature is stable. Yes. Were we right about transfiguration, that time with Esclados? Is that what what has happened, but on the Elemental level—to the Spring in your case, the Well in Panurgus'?"

"A different kind of being. Yes."

"You've made the transition successfully?" He spoke with professional briskness.

"I am still . . . making it. Every minute . . . it changes, I change. Together." She gestured, lines that hung in the air.

"So you could still be unchanged. Restored!" His hopeful note tore at my heart.

"I don't know."

They stared at one another, her chin tipped up to regard him from her lesser height, he with hands on hips.

"Ask Panurgus. We need you more than he does. Horny old lecher. I bet—"

"Dewar!" She started laughing again, interrupting his rage.

"Think about it, sister! Think. And do you tell Panurgus, if he will not teach you to reverse this, that he shall not tenant the Well of Fire much longer." Dewar snarled the last sentence.

My blood froze. A deep stillness fell in the Catacombs.

"You wouldn't . . ." she said in a hushed voice. "Dewar?"

"I would. And he can think about this, too. I will go in unprotected as you did. No ritual, no preliminaries, no buffering. Displace him, if my guess is correct. Or possibly, given my nature, I'll destroy the Well. He can wonder which will happen. It is of no consequence to me."

The silence grew heavier.

"You wouldn't . . ." she whispered again, becoming less substantial.

"What have I to lose?" he half-shrieked.

Freia looked at him. She darkened and was less transparent again. She searched his face.

"You see I'm sincere." Dewar folded his arms and regarded her defiantly, wild-eyed, quivering with tension.

She whispered, "I can see it." She listened again. "Panurgus says, there is a price."

"Nothing worth having is free. I know that."

"Someone has to . . ." her voice trailed away.

"Whoa. Ransom your soul with his? Take your place? Provide a body?"

"All."

"Can that be reversed, undone? If, later, you decide to . . . disincarnate, this person is freed as you were?"

"No. It is . . . permanent. The Spring will not permit it, he says. Now it is . . . I am part of it. Imprinted. The one who followed me must be utterly banished: dead, true death, not . . . immured here as I am."

"Let Panurgus worry about it. My threat holds. You shall be restored, or I shall destroy as much of Landuc as I am able."

"Dewar, he says that if you would extinguish yourself for me, 'tis well, you are a fool and a fool's soul is worth naught. If you can persuade someone else to do so, that is also acceptable. But it must be done soon. Before I . . . forget," she whispered.

"I say to him again, I shall go directly from here to Landuc and immolate myself, because life without you is no life at all." He was shaking, breathing hard, hands clenched.

Freia looked down, moved her feet and shifted about in a most unghostlike way. After a moment, she said with a slight quaver, "You didn't feel so a little while ago."

Dewar didn't answer at once. "Yes," he said finally, in a small voice. "I was wrong." He looked up at her. "So come through, Panurgus! Give me my sister or Landuc's thirst to engulf Argylle shall be slaked better than ever they dreamed."

"Panurgus says, 'Go thou, essay it,' " Freia said, the quaver stronger. "I say, do not! Dewar, I shall be with you always—whenever you are in Argylle or her demesnes. It would be wrong for someone else to die so I could live. Nobody else can do this as well as I can. You don't need me there physically! Please, Dewar—" She stepped toward him and moved her insubstantial hands as if to touch him, then stopped herself.

Dewar tightened his arms against himself, and the web grew brighter, more intense as he drew on the Spring. "I do. Gaston does. Father does. Gwydion does. All your children do. We need to watch you prune your apple trees and pick roses for you. We need to dance with you and walk with you, drink wine with you and laugh and listen to the ocean. I still can't steer a toboggan, you know."

Freia covered her face and vanished with a truncated, miserable wail, half a sob, in which Dewar's name was barely discernible.

"No!" Dewar screamed, grabbing at the apparition.

He disappeared.

My ears rang and the sound of *No* echoed back and forth through the Catacombs, up the Citadel, through Argylle.

I sat in stunned silence for a moment. The Spring sparked and flared opalescently, boiling and churning, luminous colors and darknesses appearing and disappearing in its surface and depths.

I watched the light fluctuate. "Mother?" I whispered.

But she wasn't talking now.

It was a fitting end to that nightmarish Day of Illusions.

⟵ 9 ⟶

I SAT AROUND CHAIN-SMOKING AND DRINKING, telling Virgil .
my troubles, feeling morbid and unhappy and powerless for
a while, and then decided I was hungry. It had gotten very
late; the Citadel was the closest it ever gets to being quiet.
People were resting up. The New Year's partying would start
at dawn and go for two days more.

It had begun to snow, too; the darkness beyond my window moved when I peered out past the draperies. The flakes
pirouetted and leapt in the chaotic air currents by the wall,
making the most of the long way down. New Year's snow.
This fresh coating would add a heightened festivity to the
celebrations.

Feeling nothing like partying myself, I headed for the
kitchen. I went through the Core in order to find out whether
Prospero had left the Catacombs yet. The Core is the central
part of the Citadel, the oldest part of it except possibly the
Great Hall and the Black Chair, which are attached to it. It's
a tower, surrounded on all interior sides with walkways and
with a spiral stair down the middle—the same stair, really,
that continues down to the Spring. Doors from various
chambers and wings open onto these walkways, which are
also interconnected with secondary stairs. It's a tangled,
improvised-looking snarl, but we like it. Visitors give themselves headaches trying to figure out how there can be windows to let in the sun when they *know* there's a room on the
other side of the wall. I have heard that Belphoebe as a child
used to terrify Mother by walking all the way up and down
the Spiral on the banister, barefoot. It's a grand place to play
Tag and Hide-and-Seek when you're small.

Argylle is a peaceful place, but out of habit we do have a

few guardsmen around the Citadel. Two are always by the door to the Great Stair. There is also a sentry post by the Iron Bridge that arches over the Wye to the City and two inside and two outside the main door. Mainly they answer questions and pass messages along, although they will also keep people out if necessary when it is not office hours, with exceptions of course for those known as household intimates.

I came slowly down the spiral stair, which was illuminated by oil lamps every few steps, and overheard quiet chuckling from the guards at the door. One looked up and saw me and nodded, squaring his shoulders: Akrak. I lifted a hand in greeting.

I was on the opposite side of the spiral when I heard Akrak shout, "Hey!" It echoed up and down. Virgil stiffened on my shoulder. Surprised, I stopped, foot in midair, and then sprinted around the column to the other side so I could see.

Akrak and his partner Valgez were moving forward toward someone in a dark, hooded cloak, who was smaller than they and backing away, looking about. I heard exclamations indicating that the Black Stair guards were also alerted to this intruder.

"Hold," I said. Akrak and Valgez stopped. The cloak whirled, obviously startled and confused.

"F-Father?" I heard a girl's voice call shakily—light, uncertain.

Still a full turn of the Spiral above the floor, I stumbled and caught myself on the banister. The voice, the word—Out of the deeper and irrational part of my mind stormed the conviction that Freia had somehow returned. She had ascended the Stair from the Spring. It had all been a misunderstanding. It was over. She was here, alive as she ought to be, asking for Prospero.

"Mother?" I tried to say, but there was no breath to utter the word.

Akrak glanced up, and she must have seen him do so, because she whirled about again and stared at me. I saw a pale face in a dark hood, and my head spun. The light was poor. I flipped my hand and said a word, and a sparking, annoyed gold-white ignis dropped through the dimness and hung above the tableau, illuminating all of us.

She had straight black hair held back from her face by a simple black ribbon under the hood, which fell off as she tipped her head up. Her face was oval, rounded, with a touch of childishness in it. Her eyes were light-colored, her skin fair. The hood was lined with green-and-grey striped silk, the cloak a dark grey-green. Her dress was plain and dark, of heavy stuff.

She was definitely not Mother. I collected my scattered senses. I had made my own New Year's illusion, born of too much reflection.

"Whom do you seek?" I asked her, still holding the banister tightly.

She inhaled, looking at me. I could see she was frightened. Virgil launched himself off my shoulder and swooped down for a better look at her, perching on a railing. She jumped. "I—I didn't mean . . . I . . ." she stammered, and then collected herself with a visible effort. "I was supposed to go home."

Home? I studied her face, its shapes and colors. "Come with me," I said. "Akrak, Valgez, I'll deal with this."

"She just appeared, sir," Valgez said. "Came out of the Keystone." They fell back to the door, still staring at her.

I went down the stairs, bowed, and offered her my arm with a smile. "Upstairs," I said, "we can have a glass of good wine and a quiet conversation."

Virgil glided to my shoulder again.

She took my arm: thin fine-boned hands. She was not short, but was not particularly tall either. I flicked my fingers and dismissed the ignis as we ascended. The Core seemed very dark when it was gone.

I led her to a comfortable room my mother had often used, lit the lamps there, and poured two glasses of good red

Argylle wine at the sideboard. The room was cold and the air musty; I put logs in the green-tiled stove and kindled a fire. We sat in chairs to either side. She seemed to have gotten over her initial fear, but she watched me do these homely things with wide anxious eyes.

"The first thing I want to know," I said, "is your name and lineage."

She swallowed. "M-my name is Ulrike. My father's name is Gaston the Fireduke of Landuc and my mother was Freia the Lady of Argylle. This—this is Argylle, isn't it?"

"It is."

"Are you Gwydion?" She said it timidly.

"I am." I looked at her closely. "It is perhaps rude to question you so nearly on your first entry into the Citadel, but . . ."

"I was to go home. Father said so."

"Ulrike, you must start from the beginning. But wait— you left him but recently?" Valgez had said she came through the Keystone, to which a Way opened with a Citadel Key must lead.

She bit her lower lip and nodded. "Yes. I looked for him when I had passed the fire and he was gone."

"Just now? Damn! At least he's all right. We've not heard from Gaston for much too long." I felt hurt and concealed it. A sister! Why hadn't Gaston trusted me enough to tell me? Here she was, anyway. "Now for the story. Please. To beguile a winter's night."

She smiled suddenly, shyly, and as suddenly it faded. "I don't have a story," she said. "I don't remember my mother. Nanna said I was only an infant when she died. I grew up in Fenshuyan, in the mountains. It is a great fortress; it sits across a pass high in the clouds and fogs . . . Father is the warlord, he keeps peace throughout Huhanwa. Everyone knows him." She sounded proud of this.

I nodded encouragingly.

She continued, "After Nanna died three summers ago,"

and her voice trembled, "he told me about Landuc and Argylle, about my family and their history and, and how the Well makes the Road and sustains everything and said that sometime he would take me to the Well and induct me as one of its own. A, a few days ago he came to me and said we were going to Landuc, and he brought me there along the Road. . . . that was a strange journey, such places we passed, the things he did at, at the Gates . . ." Ulrike shuddered. "He smuggled us into the Palace grounds, and took me to the Well there in the garden of tombs. It was all flames. I was afraid, terribly afraid it would kill me, but I . . . I went into the fire." She stopped again, swallowed. "When—when I was done, he said we would use a spell of passage to leave and made a fire for it."

Ah-hah. I could foresee what had come next.

Ulrike went on, "Father did the magic; I was still giddy from the Well and I don't know very much about that anyway. Father said I would learn more later. He opened the Way and told me to go through. I had to step into the fire again . . . I thought it would burn me . . . Then . . . I . . . I was here . . . and he didn't follow me." Her expression became one of bewilderment and fear. "He didn't follow," she repeated.

"He feared what we'd say to him for keeping you to himself so long." I smiled.

Ulrike did not smile. She looked down at her hands, which were clutching her winecup. I looked at them too; they were like my mother's hands, save that the nails were bitten.

I went on, "If you would like to return to Fenshuyan, you can. But if you would prefer to stay here awhile and get acquainted with your family . . ."

"All of them at once?" she asked, nervously.

I shrugged. "However you like. We could have a coming-out ball if you like, or you can just take a set of Keys, invoke them all with Lesser Summonings, and frighten them half out of their wits."

She giggled nervously. "Sometimes . . . after he told me . . . I did wish to do that," she said. "There are not many people to talk to, really talk to about things, there. There weren't any children in the fortress. After Nanna died, I would have been so lonely without my books and the stories Father told me."

I wondered if Gaston knew where she was. "Gaston told you he would meet you at home, did he?"

"N-no. I guess not," she said. "He said he was sending me home. I heard him put that in the spell, too. Sending me *home*. He wouldn't just leave me like that! All alone!" Her face crumpled with a child's distress.

"You are hardly alone," I pointed out. "If he sent you here deliberately, he knew someone of your family would be here." Especially, I realized, since it was New Year's—before Mother's death, before Gaston had pulled his smothering grief around him and left Argylle, the Argylline New Year had been a time of family reunion for us. He certainly knew it was New Year's here; he had the tables and formulas for calculating the passing of times in his Ephemeris.

Ulrike, however, was visibly dismayed by the idea that her father had sent her away by herself. I spoke again to forestall tears from her.

"Perhaps he saw someone coming and was detained," I said, "or perhaps the fire ran out of fuel. It is even possible that he made a mistake in construing the spell and sent himself elsewhere." Neither of those possibilities seemed terribly likely to me, though they reassured Ulrike. Gaston could make anything burn for as long as he desired it to; and to suppose a man who had opened a Way as often as Gaston would err, when he was under no discernible pressure, was to insult him.

Ulrike nodded slowly. "It seemed awfully complicated," she said.

"Did he give you a Key so that you could Summon him? Did he teach you the Lesser Summoning?"

"A Key?"

She did not know what I meant. "Hm. I guess he didn't."
I sat back and sipped my wine, which was warmed up to the
right temperature now. Ulrike tasted hers cautiously, like a
cat lapping unfamiliar water.

I did not believe the alternate explanations I had invented.
It was certainly unpleasant to think she'd been . . . packed
off. But Gaston would have given her his Key, had he intended to keep in touch, I thought, and he would have taught
her to invoke him with a Lesser Summoning. Ulrike had been
pushed out of the nest, from the Well to the Spring, and
whatever Gaston's reason for doing so, the deed had been
done intentionally.

Strangely, my sympathy lay more with Gaston. She was
like his lost love. It must have been painful to see the resemblance.

On the other hand, sending a timid creature like this alone
into the world could be signing her death warrant. Gaston
was protective of Freia's children and ruthless where threats
to them were concerned, and I suspected he had planned
Ulrike's initiation very carefully. Perhaps something had
thrown his plans out.

She had said he said he was sending her home. It was
actually possible that he had meant Fenshuyan. Gaston was
not a sorcerer. He used minor magic. The more I thought
about it, the more I thought about Gaston, the less likely it
seemed that he would deliberately dump a child so ill-pre-
pared even on her own family where she would be welcomed.
Perhaps he *had* just been vague, sloppy in his construction of
the spell of passage for them. "Home" is not precise. If he
had made an error of focus, meaning to send her to Fenshuyan but thinking that Argylle was truly her home, the
deeper intention might prevail. Many sorcerers routinely
construct spells with such layered meanings, to hide their
destinations or other things.

Ulrike had been thinking too, and she had hidden two

yawns while I thought. "I think . . ." she said, hesitating when I looked at her, "if it's not too much trouble . . . I would like to . . . could I stay? Just a little while?"

I smiled. "This is your place too," I said. "When you have drunk of the Spring you may use it to return to Fenshuyan if you choose."

"Oh! I don't think I'd like to do that. N—not right away." She shivered.

"As you wish," I replied. "It's late now. Let us find you rooms to call your own. In the morning we can discuss all this further."

Next to my own apartment were a series of guest rooms. I opened one, found it guest-ready, and gave her the key after lighting the fires for her. "I'm right here." I pointed out my doors. "Prospero is down the hall a ways. I'll send a maid around in the morning—oh." I struck my forehead.

"What's wrong?" she asked anxiously.

"It is New Year's holiday. Three days of nonstop revelry. The staff has largely deserted us. We will just make do."

The concept of three days of partying seemed wholly foreign to Ulrike. "Three days? Of celebrating a New Year?"

"Argyllines mark the last day of the Old Year, the in-between day which is no year's, and the first day of the New Year," I said. "Tomorrow is the first of those. At any rate, I shall look you up at a respectable hour. Good night, Ulrike. Welcome to Argylle."

"Good night, Gwydion. Thank you." The tiny smile again. She closed the door.

Virgil was waiting over my door. I beckoned to him and he went into my rooms with me. I went straight to the bathroom and opened the window. Brrrr. Snow still fell steadily, dia-monding my cuffs for an instant before transforming to dew.

"Wake Prospero," I told my owl.

The candlelight flashed on Virgil's wings as he glided out into the darkness, banked, and swooped up to perch on Prospero's snow-upholstered windowsill. He rapped smartly on the glass with his beak. It took a long time for Prospero to notice.

"What in Hella's name is it?" he mumbled as he opened the casement. He batted at Virgil, who floated back to me. "Gwydion?"

"We have a visitor," I said.

"How now?" Prospero's bleary gaze sharpened and he leaned out to look around.

"A nonmilitant, frightened one. Open the door, would you?"

"Ha. Know you what hour o' the clock it is? What visitor's discourtesy to his hosts surpasses yours to your kin? This gem had better outvalue the setting, Gwydion." Scowling, he slammed the window closed so that the panes rattled.

He was waiting for me in his dressing-gown and slippers and had put a pair of logs on the fire to brighten the sitting room up. " 'Twas warm in here ere you sent your subaltern to the glass. Is your humor so imbued with air that you cannot walk and knock as other men?" Prospero grumbled.

"Your bedroom has no hall door and I had no wish to wake the house pounding and yelling," I said, sitting down. Had I done so, Ulrike would have heard me. "Guess where Gaston's been."

He stared at me, his glowering look lightening. "Gaston's back?"

"No."

"Gwydion, I'm in no temper to play your foggy guessing-games. If there's urgent news, speak it; else leave me to my rest and my curse on you for breaking it." He sat down heavily.

I noticed a lot of broken glass in the fireplace: dark-brown wine bottles. Oh. He had observed the end of the Old Year too, probably feeling much as I had about it. "Your pardon, sir; I meant no offense," I said, looking away. "I have another sister, and she arrived but an hour ago by a Way through the Keystone."

Prospero's jaw dropped, but he recovered quickly. "Your mother's daughter?"

I nodded.

"Gaston! Ah, that skulking sire of yours," he said, and hit the arm of his chair with his fist. "Years ago, ere your mother fell, while we were battling with Tython's accursed minions in the Jags, I half-suspected she'd something 'neath her apron, but the minx kept close-mouthed. Meseemed wiser not to ask her, confidence of mine eye failing me. You remember—she was ever gadding off, never saying whence or whither. She had glib excuses for her absences, yet 'twas all out of nature that she'd leave Argylle in such a pickle for any common reason . . . All out of nature, and wholly natural . . ." He shook his head. "She showed herself alone, this girl, without her father to construe his own unnatural silence? How is she called?"

"Her name is Ulrike. She said Gaston took her to Landuc and initiated her clandestinely at the Well. He opened a Way that sent her here afterward. She said he had said he was sending her home. I suspect he may have been vague; home is a big word . . ." All at once I wasn't sure. Deliberate or not? I ought to tinker with passage spells and see if it could happen accidentally.

"The world's a wide place; anything's possible," Prospero muttered. "Well, well, well." He scratched and smoothed his beard, staring at me.

"For the nonce, she is around the corner from me on the east side," I said. "Seems a bit . . . I don't know, shy or frightened. I wonder what Gaston has told her."

"We may hope, the fundamentals."

"I hope so."

He leaned back. "If he has sent her here mistakenly, then he's sure to find his slip as soon as he fails to find his child. Indeed, must have done already: he'll be in a panic, if she's here by way of error, for he'll have no way to know where she'd be."

I related, word-for-word, her description of Gaston's actions.

"He gave her no Key? And he sent her from the Well's fire to the Way's?"

"No and yes."

Prospero frowned. "Then 'tis clear to me she's here by his intent. It could be that she heard amiss, were she still bedazzled by the Well." His fingers tapped on the arm of the chair.

I could not decide, and I was becoming a bit dazed with the late hour myself. And I had never gotten any supper. "It does look that way. If that's so, he probably did not return to this place Fenshuyan, knowing she would seek him there at once."

He shook his head. "There's naught of Gaston in this; 'tis timed too pat, too near the heart aimed, to be true. Could it be she lies?"

"About what? I believe she's telling the whole truth. She was scared." I had lost him.

"The whole tale! What fear, what guilt, could so vitiate Gaston's nature as to turn him from his children and then his child, could sway him to slink like a thief into Landuc? Why *there,* indeed? He could have brought her *here.* He could have *brought* her here, nursling though she be, twenty-three years past, when her mother half-orphaned her and your siblings. Why, by all the winds of the south, her *mother* could have . . ." His hand tightened into a fist and pounded the chair arm once. Then he opened the fist slowly and began tapping his fingers again, as some new thought apparently balmed the offense. "Although . . . Your parents have ever affirmed the safety of their brood before all else."

I watched him, unsure whether to respond.

Prospero gazed into the fire, narrow-eyed, thinking aloud. "Certes, there's method here, though it seems lunacy. Whenas we'd floundered through that fight with Tython, that ended in her murder, 'twould be out of keeping with his character for Gaston to fetch the child hither. He'd not expose her to that danger—for we knew not that Tython was no more, and indeed we cannot be secure of him even now.

"No. He'd lair somewhere and keep his nose in the wind, biding till he adjudged she'd take no harm here. Nay, and Freia'd not have wanted the child at our Citadel, with all out of sorts and overturned, war lurking and monstrous moil in the wood. She'd do as with the others—excepting present company—slink away to bear the brat, out on the Road in some unheard-of pastoral Eddy, naught saying in words or looks to betray herself. Sly. She was *always* sly . . . I cannot believe none marked her . . ." he growled, and punctuated this with more thumps of his fist. His jaw moved, grinding his teeth.

I opened my mouth, but had nothing to say. It did not seem the moment to point out that Mother's reasons for sneaking away for her first four children were directly connected with her and Gaston's concealment of their illicit marriage, which had finally become known when Walter was a boy. The Bad Old Days, Dewar called the following years of feuding. Not until after I was born were ruffled feathers shamefacedly smoothed and stiffly courteous diplomatic and familial relations gradually resumed. To bring this old sourness up now would only curdle the conversation.

"Even so . . ." Prospero stood and paced. "I cannot envisage Gaston turning the girl out thus. It lacks the ring of truth. Or perhaps 'tis my knowledge of Gaston lacking." Prospero folded his arms, twisted his mouth, and glared into the coals. They burned a bit brighter.

"I thought perhaps he found her too like Freia. Perhaps the likeness pained him."

He shook his head again. "Bah. You look like your mother, but your face does not put me out of countenance." After drumming his fingers for a moment, Prospero got up and left the room. "Come," I heard him say. I followed him into his study where he was preparing for a Lesser Summoning.

The mirror clouded and began to clear . . .

A sense of imminent completion, the beginnings of an image . . .

Fiery brightness shot through the mirror and the spell shut off. We gazed on ourselves. Gaston had invoked the power of the Well, drawing it around himself, concealing himself in its flow.

That convinced me. "I wouldn't wish to speak to anyone, either, had I just sent a young daughter into a passage spell all alone," I said.

"In all likelihood you've the right of it there." Prospero grabbed his Ephemeris from a shelf and began flipping through the index, stopped, and indicated a place on the page. No Fenshuyan in the index: *Fens* (many subheadings) and *Fenslach (var. Phinslech).* " 'Tis his wont: Gaston ever goes to earth in stagnant dead-end places. Can you locate this Fenshuyan? Belike they've word of him there; he may return, if he's made himself a leader in the place."

"I can certainly try. All right."

He snapped the Ephemeris shut. "As for the girl—let her be subtly put to probation, but tell her not so; take her not so deep into confidence nor so near to your bosom that, if she be hostile, we're made vulnerable. Let her be welcome, be at home among us. Yet I want Gaston to avouch her blood-kinship ere she go near the Spring."

I considered a moment. He was not being unreasonable. A wary attitude to her seemed wise, for the Spring is only for our kin, and it was not inconceivable that someone, seeking to play on our heartstrings, had invented Ulrike and her tale. I had no hard evidence of anything, really. "You are right. If we can get outside confirmation, fine; otherwise, we ought not to trust her."

"Just so. Let your welcome be nice, not overcool nor warm. When you've found Fenshuyan—"

"It were simpler by far to find Gaston."

He blinked at me.

"I can send him a note requesting the favor of a reply. I think I shall. I resent this, and I would like him to explain it." I stood. "Good night, then."

Prospero nodded. "Good night, Gwydion."

Back in my workroom, I Summoned three of my strongest-flying birds and sent them away after Binding each of them to Gaston via his Key. I had insufficient information about Fenshuyan to locate it thus, but Gaston's Key was part of him.

My hawks, like Virgil and Cosmo, are not entirely ordinary creatures, but they are more natural than my familiar or horse. *Natural* is an odd word to use—it seems to me that the closer something is to the Spring, the more natural it must be, but the common parlance has it just the opposite. At any rate, they are magical creatures too, and I can use them in ways that the austringers who handle lesser birds will never know.

Like Virgil, they can seek and find things, though they are slower than he.

The three would return when they had found their search-object. The hunt could be swift or slow: they would sweep through Argylle's Dominion and the Border quickly enough, but once across the Border in Pheyarcet they would be hampered by the twisted Roads there. Each hawk bore a simple message: "I request confirmation that Ulrike is indeed my sister. Gwydion." He could write, call or ignore it.

"What do you think, Virgil?" I asked him as he settled onto the head of my bed.

He ruffled his feathers and smoothed them again.

"Is she genuinely ours?"

He nodded once.

"You think so, huh?"

A nod.

"You've been right before. But I still want a word with Gaston."

If she were my sister, why hadn't he told us? Did he not trust us? What had we done?

Prospero's reasoning that Gaston and Mother had thought Argylle too dangerous for a baby stung sharply, implying as it did that we were incompetent, that we were untrustworthy, that we would not have delighted in another sibling.

I liked it little, but I liked less the opposite: that Ulrike was lying, that she was not one of ours, and that she was here to attempt a theft of what could not be freely given.

⌒ 10 ⌒

ULRIKE OPENED THE DOOR TO MY knock.

"Care for breakfast?" I smiled.

She didn't smile, but she nodded and said, "Oh, yes. Thank you."

"I hope you rested well."

Still no smile. She was uncommonly serious for a girl her age, and her manners were stiff—very unlike Mother. "Yes. Although the fireworks startled me."

"The festivities started at sunrise," I said, leading her to a small dining room.

Prospero was there already. Standing, he smiled, minutely scrutinizing her. "Gwydion has told me of your coming," he said warmly. "It is a great happiness to meet you, Ulrike." Prospero can be a surpassingly genial man when it pleases him.

An uncertain smile from Ulrike. "Thank you. I am happy to meet you at last, too." She took his outstretched hand and he bowed over hers, then straightened, looked down at her, and embraced her gently, still smiling.

"Welcome."

"Grandfather," she said softly.

"Just Prospero," he said curtly, and released her. Discomfited, Ulrike blushed and nodded in confusion.

I should have warned her. Prospero hates, *hates* being called Grandfather. And this atom of incident clicked in my mind with another thing: Gaston very likely would not have thought to mention that. He probably didn't even know it.

Prospero was utterly charming during breakfast and managed to put her more at her ease. She seemed very young. I wondered if time in this Eddy Gaston had chosen was slower than our time, a backwater of the Well; the whorls of vitality can be swift or slow, or both at once. Why had he suddenly decided that that part of her life was at an end, though? Had he been unable to bear the sight of her? She did look like Freia.

I had intended to go over to Walter's house during the New Year's festivities. We did little along those lines at home in the Citadel since Mother's death. I suggested that they join me. Prospero nodded, eyes half-lidded, watching her.

"Walter lives in the City most of the time," I told her. "Phoebe is generally in the forest, and the others are in Landuc or perhaps Montgard."

"That is what Father told me," she said. "I would like to go, yes, thank you." She looked down at her frock, the same travel-stained one she'd worn last night. I understood.

"I'll have clothes sent to you," I said.

"Thank you," she said again.

Prospero decided to join us and said he would show Ulrike around the Citadel. We would all meet again at noon.

When I had left them to their tour, I realized that finding suitable clothing for Ulrike was likely to be less simple than I had thought. I supposed I could go quickly to Walter's now and ask his lover Shaoll, a weaver and noted fashion-setter, for help, but it was quite possible she would be out, having much to do around town for the day's festivities. The shops were mostly shut or on short hours. There was no stock of spare women's clothing around the Citadel for me to raid—

Of course there was.

I went to my mother's rooms. None of us had faced up to the wrenching job of cleaning out her closets and chests. The staff, out of habit or homage, saw that her three-room, three-storey apartment was cleaned as ever, dusted and kept fresh, and the issue of destroying or giving away her effects had never come up since.

I could have moved into her apartment. No one would have opposed me. It was the pick of the Citadel, with wide views over the City and landscape beyond, but I had not wanted to do that. Nothing had been discarded; her jewels lay in intricately-decorated cases in her bedroom, her books stood in ordered array on the shelves in her study below; and in her office, below the study, her appointment book and pens were still on her desk with an absentminded sketch on the blotter of a sailing ship or the moon surrounded by birds or stars.

Candle in hand, I quietly opened her office door and went to the central spiral stair that connected the three high-ceilinged chambers and ascended its polished treads with one hand on the grapevine-carved banister. The draperies were drawn and no fires were lit here today, although to keep the rooms dry they were usually heated in the winter. The topmost round room was her bedchamber. I glanced instinctively to the left where a door led to a sitting-room between her and Gaston's chambers, then lit a triple candelabra off my single light and carried it over to the wardrobe. A draught of herbs and staleness whiffed past me as I opened the double doors. Twenty-three years, and the fabrics had aged hardly at all—unfaded, clean, neatly folded or hanging waiting. Twenty-three years, and I could still remember occasions on which she had worn each garment. I hesitated.

Don't be a fool, I told myself; Mother would hardly have disapproved lending the girl a couple of her frocks. I touched a sleeve, green velvet with roses, then looked further away from the center, where less-frequently-worn things were likely to be. As I took out a blue-green gown with silver fish frolicking around its hem, I noticed a seamstress's box with string still tied around it lying on the floor. Curious, I laid the gown aside and picked up the box, biting the string. Inside lay, folded as the maker's hands had left it, a new ensemble never-worn: a rose-colored chemise and a moss-green woolen gown. Odds were, I thought, Mother had gotten it for New Year's. A frisson went up my neck. I set the gown with the other and chose two more, quickly, hardly thinking about them, and closed the wardrobe.

I carried the clothes to Ulrike's rooms and laid them out near the fire to air for her. She had clearly not yet returned from her tour with Prospero. Then I dressed in more festive clothing myself and hunted down Argylle's Seneschal, Utrachet, in the stables, to tell him what was going on.

"Remarkable," he said. "I heard part of it from Akrak this morning as he came off duty."

Utrachet said he would take care of establishing her in the family wing of the buildings and suggested renovating some north-facing rooms near my late mother's.

I hesitated. "I don't want her to be isolated," I said, and we decided to leave her as she was for now. Utrachet would find a maid to help her settle in after the New Year's bash had done. I asked him to pass the news to Anselm and the general staff. "They'll have no trouble recognizing her," I said.

At noon I found her and Prospero in the Core near the front doors.

"Thank you for the frocks," she said.

She was wearing her own cloak and the gown with busy fish embroidered at the bottom. It fit passably. "I thought you'd prefer the green-and-rose one," I said.

Ulrike bit her lip anxiously. "I do like it, but it is creased— should I change? Would it be better?"

"No, no, no," Prospero said, " 'tis well enough, so let us be off."

We walked to Walter's house through the City. The snow decorated everything. Firecrackers popped everywhere. Vendors were selling food and toys, gauds and trinkets, and anything you can think of in the streets, which were thronged with people. It was a perfect introduction to Argylle; they were all too busy or too drunk to really notice Ulrike, who shrank against Prospero nervously.

We passed a brass band playing polkas for a dancing crowd at the entrance to Walter's street, which has a strip of park in the middle where people were building snowpeople, snowbirds, snowdogs, a snowgryphon, and a snowdragon, painting them and having snowball fights. Walter was assisting in the construction of the snowdragon with its glittering icicle teeth. The double front doors to his house were wide open.

He waved at me and a snowball whizzed by my left shoulder. I nailed him squarely in the chest with a return shot. We covered each other and a few innocent bystanders with snow. It ended when he got close enough to holler, "Who's your date there? It's about time you held something besides a pen! Or is she Prospero's?" They had retreated from the field of combat and Prospero was apparently regaling her with a story because she was actually giggling, hands over her mouth.

I grinned. "Come over and meet her, Walter."

He had ice and snow in his beard and hair and, with a broad smile, stuck out a sopping mitten. "Hullo!"

"Ulrike, this snow-covered abomination is your brother Walter, which you might not be able to descry," Prospero said drily. "Walter, Ulrike, your younger sister."

Walter stared at Prospero, at me, at Ulrike, dumbstruck. *That* was something, indeed. Ulrike stared up at him. "Is Gaston back?" he asked Prospero finally, and suddenly took off his mitten and extended his ruddy hand to her, smiling warmly. She took it shyly and he kissed her on both cheeks. Ulrike blushed again and ducked her head.

"No," I answered.

"How . . ." Walter gestured and looked from me to Prospero and back.

"A long story," Prospero said, "and 'tis a short wintry day."

"I am a poor host indeed," exclaimed my brother, and shepherded us into his house, which was full of children in theatrical costumes, including a three-part purple dragon, and musicians tuning up and madrigal singers rehearsing and wonderful cooking smells and people moving furniture around and wistful accordion music. Walter explained over his shoulder something about the grammar school theatre, old friends from out of town, and a dance, most of which was drowned in the general racket. The second floor had a ceilidh warming up. We climbed to the third floor, which was relatively peaceful (a harpsichord player was feeling his way through formal dances), and Walter closeted us in a sunny room with flowering plants in the windows, a fire in the stove, and overstuffed furniture arrayed in conversational groups.

Ulrike was overwhelmed.

Walter grinned at her happily. The more the merrier, is his philosophy. "Let me take your cloak," he offered, and lifted it neatly off her shoulders. He laid it on top of his own, a beautiful new one in shades of brown and touches of green— unquestionably Shaoll's New Year's gift to him, given a day or so early. He went on, "Pray be seated. A bite? A drink? Lunch!"

"We breakfasted not long ago," I said. "Let us toast the Old Year."

He rang for a servant and sent for wine. "Now," he said, "I would hear this tale." He sat down across from Ulrike, brushing the melting snow from his hair and beard carelessly.

She didn't quite know how to start. "You mean, who I am?" she said.

"Heavens! Yes! And where is Gaston if you are here, and where has he been, and where have you been all this time, and why didn't anyone know!" he exclaimed.

She looked around at me. "I did tell Gwydion last night . . ."

"Walter is a bard, as Gaston may have mentioned," I said. "Let him hear it from your own lips. He'll pass the news to the rest of the family."

"Walter's news service and hotel," he agreed with a chuckle. "Famous from Here to There and Back."

The servingwoman returned with two bottles of dark ruddy-brown wine—Corydol—and glasses.

"Aaaaah," said Prospero, smiling in his beard, and he nudged the cork from one and poured.

"Gaston's favorite," I said, sniffing. Walter must have opened a few bottles, decanted and breathed them, for the day's libations.

We inhaled appreciatively for a few moments.

"That was a good year," Walter said, eyes closed, his smile fading. "I remember that summer. Gaston kept saying it couldn't last. Perfect weather. It lasted and lasted and lasted. He was beside himself when picking began. Just enough sun, rain, and fog. We knew it would be good. And it has only gotten better."

"Someday it will lose the edge," I said.

"And we'll lose that summer. So let us enjoy it now, while we may." My brother rose. "The Old Year."

"The Old Year," and we drank. My nose and taste buds performed a happy sensory duet.

Walter swallowed. "And may the New be dragon-free. Now, madame. I plague you once more, having allowed you to organize your thoughts and whet your palate with the very finest wine in Landuc or Argylle or between."

She smiled tentatively. "I wish Father were here. He could probably explain things better than I. I don't know why he didn't tell you. I am sorry—"

"Young lady," Walter said gravely, "never apologize for your existence. Continue."

"But it seems to be such a shock. I wish I knew more. But Father never told me." She looked around at Prospero, standing by the white-tiled stove. I had sat on the arm of the sofa Walter was on. "He said that I would learn what I needed to know in time. He told me of the history of Argylle, how it was made," and she looked quickly at Prospero, "the two terrible wars and why they happened, and how Mother shaped it. And he told me of Landuc . . ." She paused.

"Where did you live?" Walter asked gently.

"In a fortress, Fenshuyan, in the Wenshay mountains. There is always war there, one petty noble against another, but Father keeps peace in the lands he holds. It is always wet and misty there; everything is very green in summer, very snowy in winter. Fenshuyan is a pass, and travellers come through, many because they hear that Father does not rob people and that the roads that he commands are safe." This sounded very like Gaston. "But I never saw much of them; I stayed away. Nanna and Father did not like me to talk to people, or even to see people much. I have never seen anything like this place," Ulrike said, looking around.

"It is New Year's," Walter said. "What did you do in this fortress?"

Ulrike thought and said, slowly, "When Father was there he would teach me, and when he was not Nanna taught me or I played. He brought me books. We would fence—"

Walter grinned.

"—or ride together in the summer. And I played with my dolls that Nanna made, and my kitten. Nanna taught me to weave and sew. In the winter there was not much to do but fence and read and sew. That was what I did."

"No music?"

Ulrike nodded, wide-eyed, eager to please. "Oh yes! He taught me the notes and the fingering on a harp, a lap-harp he gave me. Nanna taught me songs. Sometimes I would play and sing, but I preferred reading. I don't care for fencing, but he said I must. And we'd play chess and turnstones too. I never liked those very much—"

Walter chuckled.

"What is funny?" she asked, confused.

"Gaston's daughter disliking fencing and chess," he said. Prospero laughed as well, and I smiled.

"Why is that funny?"

We looked at one another. "Why is that funny?" Walter repeated. "Good heavens, girl! Many would give their eyeteeth, and an eye too, to spend a few years playing chess with Gaston, just as they'd pledge their souls to study sorcery with Uncle Dewar."

"Oh."

"Gaston is modest," murmured Walter. "So you lived in this place Fenshuyan with Gaston managing your education. And Nanna. Is Nanna your nurse?"

"Yes. She . . . three years ago she died, in the winter when it was so cold . . . I miss her." Her childish face took on a look of sadness. "Father and I did more things together after that. He made me learn to use the bow."

Gradually, Walter pulled out of her the tale of how she had been brought to Landuc and sent to Argylle, and he lifted his eyebrows when she said Gaston was left behind.

"Left behind?" repeated Walter.

She nodded. "He wasn't there."

"But home, to you, meant Fenshuyan." Walter picked this up too.

"Yes, it was very odd. I do not know how it happened. I went from the Well to the front door here, in the Citadel, or just inside, but I didn't know where I was. There were guards who were as startled as I. Then Gwydion came and talked to me and I understood where I had come."

Walter looked around at me. "I suppose you have tried the obvious."

"The obvious, and now I am onto the not-so-obvious," I said.

He nodded and turned back to Ulrike. "So Gaston seems to be missing . . ."

"I don't know . . ."

He tipped his head to one side, lifting his eyebrows. "Isn't he going to be worried when he gets home and you're not there?"

She nodded. "I'm afraid he will be, yes, but—but couldn't you use a spell to find him? Doesn't magic just find people for you?" she said.

"It could, but Gaston has been hiding for years and still is," I said. "We have tried Summoning him already."

"You didn't plan anything for when you had been to the Well," persisted Walter.

Ulrike seemed puzzled. "I—No. I thought we would just go home. Has something happened to him?" She looked at me.

"No idea," I said. "As I said, your story is the first certain indicator we have had that he was even alive."

"Landuc," Walter said.

"Possibly," I replied. "I'll sound Avril later, perhaps."

"The Emperor?" she asked. "Surely he knows where Father is." She looked from one to the other.

Prospero's mouth twitched. Walter snorted. "Not necessarily," I said. "Gaston is a private man, and he has never taken kindly to Imperial interest in his life beyond the duties he owes the Empire and Emperor." Less than kindly.

"Hmph," said Walter, drinking his wine. "So. Young lady, unless you care to set out to find Fenshuyan along the Road—wherever it is—you are here for now, and who knows where under the Sun Gaston is. He will turn up when he is ready."

"People usually do," I said, thinking of Mother and Dewar and Prospero, who all had that habit.

We spent the rest of the day at Walter's house. I liked the

noise and bustle; it kept me from sliding into the endless circle of my own thoughts about Freia and her death and what I could or should do about it. There was an elaborate buffet replenished continuously downstairs; we lunched off that, and Prospero, Walter, and I took turns introducing Ulrike.

"Gwydion," Walter said to me as Prospero acquainted her with Hicha and a pair of Archive assistants, "Ulrike is a very ghost."

"What?" I exclaimed, a little too loudly, and people glanced at us and away.

"She's so like Mother . . . I admit the dress is much of it—Why is she wearing Mother's gown?—but there's something about her that's purely Mother."

"She looks like her," I agreed, "and, well, she didn't bring any luggage and needed something to wear."

"Oh. I thought perhaps you were making a point of some kind . . ." He lifted his eyebrows.

I shook my head.

"Phew. Hah, there's Shaoll's brother—I have to talk to him," Walter said, and began wading through the crowd toward one of the doors.

I watched Prospero and Ulrike. Yes, she did look like Mother, especially from here; and clearly she was giving people a turn, because they would start when they first saw her, stare a moment, and then smile. She was the hit of the day, despite her shyness and tongue-tied embarrassment at all the attention.

I was very, very startled when, as I was telling her in an undertone the names of three notable people—two painters and a bookbinder—who had just come in, a finger tapped on my shoulder and a familiar voice said softly, "The seated Lord of Argylle is famous for his fine taste in all things."

Ulrike did not hear it, but she looked at me, surprised, as I spun around.

"Otto!" I exclaimed.

"Heya!" Ottaviano grinned as we clasped hands. He was cleanshaven now; it made him look very young. His eyes, blue and shrewd, flicked over me and Ulrike quickly.

"What brings you here?" I temporized, interposing myself between sister and cousin.

His grin was unabated. "I was invited. How could I be here otherwise?"

Ah. I guessed that Ottaviano had cannily touched Walter when the latter, normally distrustful of him, was in his most hospitable and benevolent frame of mind owing to the New Year, and Walter had impulsively invited him here. Doubtless he'd forgotten to mention this in his excitement over acquiring a younger sister. Under other circumstances, it might be diplomatic. Now it was awkward. "Good to see you again," I said. We hadn't met since that breakfast before I'd attacked Gemnamnon.

"It's good to see you, too. Until I talked to Walter, I thought you might be a dragon's kebab, spitted on your own lance and roasted in the flames from his muzzle. But Walter told me otherwise, in glorious and probably fictitious detail. You look sound enough."

I smiled. "I should have told you the end of the tale, I guess. Walter did mention that I did not exactly come off unscathed."

"Yes, he told me, and I understand Marfisa convalesces in eastern Madana . . . Anyway, cousin . . ." and Ottaviano glanced past me at Ulrike, smiling.

"Yes?" I said.

"They say you can't hide the sun under a bushel basket."

"They're right. It would burn up." Besides Otto's sterling efforts to stay on Mother's bad side over the years, he was presently an emissary of the Emperor. I had not thought beyond introducing Ulrike to our sisters and brothers and friends here in Argylle; was she ready for the Empire too?

"You could save me a lot of sleep," he said, watching me.

I smiled. "What is it worth to you?"

Otto laughed. "Let's see. What have I got? Nothing new on dragons, unfortunately. Hm. Might be able to give you a pointer toward a missing person."

"Oh?"

He raised his eyebrows. "Interested? Of course, this is really a freebie on my part, isn't it?"

I laughed.

"Murder will out," he intoned, grinning.

I supposed he was right. I had not considered splashing Ulrike into the family so suddenly and abruptly, but I could not walk off and refuse to introduce her. For one thing, he would easily find out who she was from someone else—in fact, he probably knew already and was just angling for the introduction.

I cleared my throat as all this passed rapidly through my thoughts.

"Ulrike, this is Ottaviano, Baron of Ascolet. Ottaviano, allow me to introduce Ulrike . . ."

Ottaviano bowed gracefully.

"You are first and second cousins," I said.

Otto nodded slowly, getting the point.

Ulrike blushed, finding his close examination disconcerting.

"Pleased to meet you, my lady," he said less forcefully than he'd spoken to me.

"Thank you," said she, barely over a whisper, and belatedly offered him her hand, "cousin."

He smiled brilliantly, taking her hand and bowing again, catching and holding her gaze as he straightened, his smile fading slightly. "Cousin," he said, "I am at your service."

Ulrike looked down, up, and down again, clearly unsure what to say now. I thought "Hullo" would have been appropriate, at least, but she said nothing.

I cleared my throat once more and raised an eyebrow.

Otto released Ulrike's hand; she had stopped blushing, which was an improvement.

"Ah," he said, still looking at her. "I should caution you that this is not real recent news."

"All right." Worth what I paid for it, no doubt.

"When Dewar first disappeared," he said, finally facing my gaze, "I was worried, as everyone was, that he was going to do something . . . outrageous. He . . . you know how he . . . But nothing happened. I wanted to get in touch with him, but he's been making that difficult. So I settled on the simple expedient of leaving a note in his apartment in Landuc."

"A note?"

"Right. I figured that eventually he'd drop in for one reason or another. I left it on his desk in plain sight, just a single sheet of paper with my message, and locked the door behind me. Fine. I checked it periodically and not long after I'd first put it there—less than half a year—it had been moved."

I was skeptical. "How could you tell?"

He grinned foxily. "I had written it with lead pencil and broken the pencil as I wrote. Left the snapped-off tip on top of it."

"Ah." Simple, but effective. "How do you know it wasn't the charwoman?"

"They won't touch his rooms."

"Why?" I was taken aback.

"Afraid of the mad magician's ghost or something. He's got a wild reputation over there, you know. The place is a mess. He's going to be furious. Probably is."

I laughed and shook my head. Yes, it was old information, very old: I had had hard evidence of Dewar's good health and good frame of mind personally on Longview. "I think that one was worth what I paid for it. But thanks. It means he was alive. Maybe he still is. The Wheel turns."

Nodding, Otto smiled, oddly wistful. "We can hope. I miss the bastard. It's too quiet without him."

"Yes," I agreed. They had been close friends. Why, I had never quite grasped; in many ways they were antithetical. But

Dewar liked flirting with danger, playing with fire, and Otto was certainly that, treacherously unreliable. His position as second, natural son of the Emperor was insecure, and improving it must always be his first care. It was Otto who had unkindly pried into my parents' lives and blazoned their marriage to the Emperor, which discovery had caused great difficulty for everyone. Otto had subsequently apologized to Mother and Gaston for the deed, blaming and excusing himself, but although Gaston had coolly accepted his repentance, Mother never did.

Ulrike had listened silently, clearly not understanding most of the conversation. Ottaviano turned to her with a smile. "But your word means little, Gwydion. Argylle's dark lord keeps his secrets to himself." He looked from her to me.

"So he does," I concurred. "And so shall they be kept."

We stared each other down.

"Does being a monarch always turn people into such hard-asses?" he asked.

"It requires one to think much," I said.

"You always thought too much," he said. "It's well-known that's dangerous." He glanced at Ulrike again. "My lady, it is good to meet you, good to know I have another cousin."

She smiled shyly and blushed rosy again, looking down, peeking up at him and then looking down again. She slipped her hand through my elbow.

"Now," Otto went on with a grin, "I'm going to run off and grab myself a good seat in the back garden, because it's getting on toward the time when those rug rats will do their thing."

"Adieu, then," I said. "We shall be out anon."

He bowed to Ulrike, lifted a hand in farewell, and moved away through the crowd.

"A very good lesson in Landuc manners," I remarked to Ulrike, guiding her along the buffet toward the hot food. A cup of mulled wine and a snack would be good before going out to watch the play.

"Why?"

I halted by a dish of bite-sized meat dumplings, picked up a plate, and put a few on it. "Obviously you were connected to me, but how? It could be important someday, but also it is inevitable that your identity will be known in Landuc eventually. He offered to trade me a piece of information about a missing person for information about you: who you are."

"Why did he not just ask? You, or someone else?"

"For one thing, he wanted to be introduced. For another, to protect you, I might not tell him." I lifted an eyebrow and ate a dumpling. Spicy. I helped myself to a couple more. We edged along and I signalled the servingwoman on the other side of the table for two cups of wine.

"Is he really dangerous?"

I just looked at her. "In Landuc, everyone is dangerous. Except, hm, probably Josquin. —I introduced you, indicated that you are my sister. He paid with the outdated but provocative news that Dewar had been in his rooms in Landuc a while back. Note that he did not tell me whether Dewar ever contacted him. He also let me know that he thinks I know more than I am letting on about Dewar's whereabouts, and I let him know that he was to keep your existence to himself. He acknowledged that I had a right, in a way, to demand this, but that it seemed silly, since sooner or later you will go to Landuc and meet your assorted kindred."

"But you said nothing like that!" Ulrike tried a bite-sized fruit-and-cheese turnover. I picked up several.

I laughed. "All was there."

Our wine was handed to me; I gave one to Ulrike and sipped mine. Ulrike tasted the wine. She swallowed. "If Josquin is the only safe relative I have—"

I pointed at her with my fork, trying to impress the necessity for prudence on her. "Oh, no, no. But you should not speak freely to anyone from Landuc. Always remember that although we are related, we have different goals and histories. Very different. If you would like to meet Josquin, that would be nice. I haven't seen him in a long time. Josquin doesn't usually have conversations like that. By the way, you did very well, saying nothing."

"I didn't know what to say."

"Even better to say nothing, then."

Someone rang a bell at the balcony that ran around the room at the second storey and cried that the Children's Theatre would present a play in the back garden in a quarter of an hour. This was followed by a surge of bodies toward the door, which frightened Ulrike. I pulled her against me and into an alcove while they went past.

"Someone will save us seats," I said. "Walter or Prospero will, to be sure. Drink up your wine; it's cold outside."

She nodded, wide-eyed, watching the people pass. Some stopped and bowed to me, greeting me, and I greeted them and exchanged a few words before they went off. Mother never liked being fussed over in public; this had become an ingrained expectation among her people and they had transferred it to me. All to the good; I dislike being fussed over too. There is always a certain deference and respect, and people tend to leave physical space around the members of our family, but we do without pomp and circumstance.

The hall had largely emptied, save for a few clusters of people talking so intently that they plainly meant to skip the play. I drew my sister along, outside.

We were among the last to arrive. I espied Walter, his lover Shaoll, and our cousin seated on the front row of benches. We joined them and I put my cloak around Ulrike so that she didn't freeze during the proceedings; hers had been left upstairs. She was already pink-cheeked. Ulrike sat down beside Ottaviano and I beside her. I would rather have sat between them, but asking her to move might start something I had no desire to pursue. Walter rose as we arrived and bounded up onto the stage.

General applause. He bowed hammily. More applause, far more vigorous than necessary, and a few cheers.

"Thank you, thank you," Walter cried. "I am delighted to see you all here trampling my garden."

Otto chuckled. Ulrike looked down at her feet guiltily.

"I am even more delighted to see you emptying my cellar and pantry in good health and good spirits," Walter went on, smiling, "and I bid all my guests welcome and wish you all a New Year as fine as this day."

"Thank you!" was shouted back at him from various hecklers amid general cheering, and "Same to you, Walt!" and the like.

"There is no activity more fitting to the final day of the Old Year, the Day of Reflection," my brother went on, "than to review the events of the past year, be they good or ill, to examine them and extract what lesson, if any, they hold for our edification and improvement. However, this requires concentration and a sober cast of mind, both of which are notoriously in scant supply during these three days of festival. Thus I am very happy to announce that the Children's Theatre have most congenially done our thinking for us, bless their pointy little heads. Now I shall step aside and allow them to present their view of the past year to you, in short as it were, and I encourage you to grant them your most courteous attention and support. Good guests, friends and neighbors, *The History of the Dragon of Longview.*"

"Oh *no,*" I said, feeling my face redden as the crowd laughed and applauded.

Walter vaulted to the ground and claimed his seat, grinning wickedly at me.

It is the custom in Argylle to present an Old Year's play highlighting a notable event of the past year. I had been the target on several occasions in the past. Sometimes the plays are serious and sometimes side-splittingly comic. A number of them have entered the standard repertoire and are played from time to time still. Every community does at least one, but the best appear in Haimance and Argylle City, with placers from time to time turning up in Ollol; our most notable playwrights are not above penning the books for them and have done themselves great credit in the past. Baudrin Leshy's tragedy dealing with the death of my mother always completely shatters its audience's composure and is something I treasure for the comfort it proffers, and Gant Harro's history plays about the Independence War became classics centuries ago.

However, works like that are not produced by grammar-school theatres. I knew I was in for a basting of sorts.

I was not wrong. I suffered all the more because Ottaviano was there, and he was guaranteed to export this to Landuc, for it was hysterically funny and utterly charming. I particularly liked the end, at which—intentionally or not—the vanquished dragon's head and body exited left and the tail, which had been fidgeting on its own for a while, exited right, lashing splendidly.

Walter laughed himself sick through the whole farce. I resolved to get to him later and find out who'd really written it; it was far above the children who performed it. Shaoll was helpless, weeping with mirth, leaning on Walter, looking over at me and laughing harder from time to time. Ulrike smiled at some parts but seemed to miss many jokes entirely; she laughed more, blushing and glancing at me and giggling, after Ottaviano began whispering footnotes in her left ear. I laughed too—excruciatingly embarrassed at times, but I laughed.

After the play, the always-thoughtful Walter had arranged for a dinner to be laid for us in a small dining room upstairs in the house, and so Shaoll, Ulrike, Ottaviano, and I trailed after him to it. I would have liked to have left our cousin out, but Walter invited him and I couldn't contradict my brother in his own house.

"I thought you might like a few minutes of quiet," Walter said to Ulrike. "We've been handing you around like a new broadside. But it is only because we like you," he added with a grin.

"Thank you," she replied, and sank gratefully into the chair Ottaviano offered her. "It's all very . . . it's very nice . . . people are so friendly . . ."

"But it can be overwhelming," Walter concluded, patting her on the shoulder with one hand and pouring her a glassful of wine (Prissot Black Garnet) with the other. Good for warming winter-chilled bodies.

"I . . . thank you," she said, shyly, and sipped the wine.

Shaoll lifted a dishcover. "Venison!" she exclaimed, and looked inquiringly at Walter.

"From Belphoebe's bow," he said. "Her New Year's gift."

Prospero did not join us, so we dined without him. Ulrike, though unsure of herself, warmed to Walter, Shaoll, and Ottaviano and smiled more often during the meal. I thought she looked tired—her cheeks were flushed and she seemed mildly uncoordinated—or perhaps slightly drunk. Walter kept filling her glass with wine, though, and I wasn't about to embarrass her by asking if she wouldn't be better off with water.

"My," sighed Walter, over our second dessert, "what a pleasant interlude, but—"

Someone tapped at the door, then opened it. We all looked up and I rose to my feet, smiling, recognizing the man who leaned in.

"Voulouy!"

"Lord Gwydion." Lish Voulouy beamed and came in, followed a few steps behind by a pair of young women. We embraced and kissed one another, both speaking at once.

"I did not know you had come down—"

"I am representing the family—"

"—you should have told me, I would have been honored to host you—"

"—for the treaty meetings—"

"—not having seen you since I'm shamed to think when . . ."

"Why, but I couldn't guest at the Citadel, people might think we were getting preference."

"Of course not if it's business this time. Damn! When will you come down out of Haimance for pleasure?" I asked him, releasing him and looking into his good-natured, thin face. Voulouy is one of my favorite friends; he's of the Haimance Voulouy clan which had pioneered and flourished in vineyards and winemaking. He was quite right about not guesting at the Citadel, though the Voulouys are like family to us and everyone knows it.

"When will you come up?" He smiled. "It has been far too long, and the place is as hospitable as ever, but Haimance cannot come to you, Lord."

"I know. I know. I mean to come, every year, why, every season, and there's always a fresh broil here."

He shook his head mock-disapprovingly. "In Haimance we keep our broils low. But I did not come alone, either. . . . I think you may remember Tautau . . ."

"Tautau, sun and moon, yes . . ." I kissed the darker of the two women with him, and she kissed me back laughing at me.

"You might forget all Haimance, but I hope not me," Tautau said, and I laughed too. We were lovers for a few years before I had gone away to study at a University away in an Eddy-world in Pheyarcet; she had been living in the City then and had moved back to Haimance by the time I returned. There had been business and family affairs for her after that, and we had not pursued the intimacy.

"Here," said Tautau, "is a Voulouy you won't remember: Lishon, our youngest sister. This is her first trip to the City." Lishon was a typical-looking Haimance girl, lively, smiling, and playful. She and Ulrike regarded one another curiously.

"Welcome, Lishon," I said, "and this is *my* younger sister Ulrike," and there were more introductions and a few minutes of chatter until Walter proposed, "Shall we go and join the dancing?"

"Oh yes!" Shaoll said, beaming. "Ulrike, I shall teach you the steps, you will learn in a minute, they are not difficult, and you are light on your feet. You'll do well." She was a fine dancer herself, a perfect companion for a musician like Walter.

"I . . . I'll just watch, if that's all right," Ulrike said.

Ottaviano and I both glanced at her, surprised, and then at one another in a moment of mutually-recognized disbelief. Freia had loved to dance; it seemed Ulrike was not like her in many things.

"Indeed, it's not all right," Walter told her in a mock-stern tone.

"But, but . . ." She blushed. Tautau and Shaoll laughed.

"He's joking," Shaoll and Lishon assured Ulrike quickly, in unison.

"Walter is usually joking," Ottaviano said. "I'm feeling sedentary myself, m'lady cousin. If these gentlemen and ladies have an urge to trample the Old Year down with a dance, I will gladly keep you company the whiles . . ."

"Otto, I heard you promise Fedelm a dance," I said, "and I suspect she is waiting to claim it from you."

"I wasn't going to dance either," Lishon said, and Ulrike looked up. The girls looked at one another and Lishon went on, "Please, Tautau, can she—"

"We are going to sit in the gallery," Tautau said to me, smiling. "Lishon doesn't know many of the City dances and wanted to watch. She's a little shy."

I supposed she might be, but compared to Ulrike, she was positively gregarious.

"If you'd like to join us," Lish Voulouy said to my sister, "why, the more merrymakers the merrier the party."

I felt a twinge of guilty relief. I had several times seen a certain lady in the crowd, Evianne Perran, and she had several times seen me, and I wanted to see rather more of her than I could with an awkward younger sister on my arm. Tautau and Lish Voulouy were as reliable chaperons as I could ask for—not that girls in Argylle need chaperons, but clearly Ulrike wasn't ready to make her way in society.

Ulrike glanced at me and Walter.

"You don't need permission to sit out," I said as kindly as I could.

"If you're really not inclined to dance," Walter said, "of course you may sit it out. Some people can't dance after eating," he stood and stretched and smiled, "but you must excuse me. I'm not one of them. You must dance at the costume party tomorrow, though! No excuses," he tossed over his shoulder, and left.

Nervously, Ulrike asked, "Costume party?"

"It's great fun," I said. "It's held in the Vintners' Hall and all over the City. If you will excuse me also, sister, friends . . ." I added, smiling, "I have several engagements to discharge before I can sit overseeing the festivities in the dignified fashion becoming to my age and position—"

Lish made a choking rude noise, laughing. Otto snorted.

"—and Ottaviano here too has promises to keep; as a diplomat he must be conscious of his honor among us."

Thus I brought Ottaviano down to the dance with me and left Ulrike in the excellent company of our friends. However, I was delayed by one thing and another—parties and dances are rife with distraction—and so I did not collect Ulrike until the small hours of the morning. Indeed I did not think of her at all until it was time to find my cloak and leave, for hers lay under mine. I took both and went down, looking here and there in the rooms where people had settled in smaller intimate parties for conversation and music and stories, but she was in none of them. I continued down to the gallery where I had left her with the Voulouys.

She was sitting at a table by one of the latticework partitions, which make excellent screens for eavesdropping and whispered flirting. Neither she, Lishon, nor Ottaviano saw me coming toward them through the half-empty gallery; the girls were intent on him, giggling behind their fans and looking sidelong at one another. Lish and Tautau were nowhere to be seen, and I recalled suddenly that I had seen Lish dancing with Prezon Arvaud and Tautau with a fellow I didn't know. I had been so absorbed by other concerns, among them Evianne Perran, that they and Ulrike had not been associated in my mind. There was no reason for them to stay with her—I had not requested it openly. Still, I was irked, in the main at myself, and also at Ottaviano—the man was subtle, yet he had not taken the clear hint.

"Hullo," Lishon said pertly to me, with an uncommonly arch look which turned into a blush as I looked meaningly at the four empty wine bottles on the table with them. Black Garnet.

"Good evening. Ulrike, I have here something of which you shall have need anon," I said, displaying her cloak to her.

"Oh! It is late," she said, sounding confused, and stood, looking at Lishon and at Ottaviano who rose with her.

"Good-night, Otto," I said. "May the Old Year leave you softly." It was nearly gone; dawn was but a couple hours away.

"And may the New be generous to you," he said. "And to you, m'lady cousin. It has been very kind of you to tolerate me," he said, and bowed to her. "And you, Miss Voulouy."

"Lishon," Lishon said. "We do not Miss in Argylle."

"Indeed you do not." Ottaviano smiled.

I draped Ulrike's cloak around her; she had disentangled herself from the chairs without knocking one over or tripping. Lishon bade her an enthusiastic farewell until the morrow. With more polite words of parting, I guided my sister out of the gallery and out of Walter's house. Doubtless Ottaviano was guesting there.

Ulrike was unsteady on her feet from a combination of tiredness and wine, and I felt it prudent to put my arm around her to help her along over the icy patches of pavement lest she fall.

"I'm sorry," she said, holding my arm tightly, "I'm not . . . not used to . . . to . . ."

"Prissot Black Garnet is strong stuff," I agreed. "You should cut it with water, or just drink Tindler water . . ."

"What's . . . what's tinder water . . ." she said, trying to sound alert.

"Tindler is mineral water from Haimance. Mother liked it." Mother had known when to water her wine and when to stop altogether; most Argyllines do. Drunkenness is in poor taste.

"I'm sorry I'm so . . . wobbly."

I sighed. "It's all right, Ulrike." She would have to learn.

We navigated successfully over the Wye on the Iron Bridge and into the Citadel. Up the stairs, slowly, and then I put her in her rooms and turned to my own.

Along the hall, Prospero's door was open, his rooms lit. He stepped out as I fumbled with my keys.

"H'lo. G'night."

"Hullo, Gwydion."

"I'm not drunk," I said, dropping my keys. "Just tired." He nodded, skeptical. "Good."

I got the door open and he followed me in and closed it.

"What is Ottaviano doing here?"

"Partying," I replied wearily.

"I have eyes to see that. You spoke with him; wherefore hath he left Ollol? I knew nothing of't; was it done with your knowledge?"

I sat, yawning, and looked up at him. I shrugged. "Walter invited him. You know how he is. So he's here, partying. What's wrong with that?"

"The timing disturbs me," Prospero said.

"Timing?" I repeated. "New Year's?" I pulled off my shoes awkwardly.

"The day after Ulrike springs into our midst."

"Oh," I said, and tried to think about it. "He was here anyway. In Ollol."

"Your mother would not have suffered him within the City walls," Prospero reminded me. "He was poison in her sight. Nor am I overly fond of him myself."

"I don't trust him either. But he's just here for New Year's. For the parties. He's not coming near the Citadel or the Spring. He's over at Walter's. Walter will keep an eye on him. He knows. I can't worry about this now, Prospero; I'm too tired." I slumped back in the chair and yawned again. "Can it wait until morning?"

"As you wish," he said, frowning, and left.

⌒ 11 ⌒

IT WAS LATE MORNING WHEN I woke. I lay face-down among my pillows, thinking somewhat morose thoughts—Evianne had left by the time I'd gotten down to the dance. I supposed she had come with her brother and sister, who lived in Argylle City; Evianne lived on the coast south of Ollol, and we had been circling one another whenever possible with mutual consciousness of attraction since summer. Long, curly red hair; long, changeable blue eyes; long, graceful arms . . . It was aggravating that I hadn't been able to find her yesterday. I'd never had time to move the relationship from public to private places. I gave a few hard, uncharitable thoughts to Ulrike and then sighed and climbed out of my bed and started the bath filling.

After bathing, combing and brushing, and dressing, I hunted through my wardrobes and chests and found the black cloak, domino mask, and broad-brimmed hat I would wear that night. I used to be very fond of the fancy-dress parties of the second day of New Year's celebrations, the Day of Illusions, and then after Mother's death I had no heart for it, and now it was just too much trouble. So I had settled on this simple and concealingly anonymous garb.

I went down to the deserted kitchens and prepared breakfast for myself. Then I went for a long walk along the Wye, up toward Threshwood, to finish clearing the cobwebs from my brain. When I got back, I spent an hour or so in my office on the scant business that had come up during the past couple of days. In a fit of exceptional virtuousness, I even started flipping through the collection of papers I had had Anselm put together before New Year's, to begin writing the annual report which, following Mother's lead, I put together each year for my own reference. The Archive staff did another version for the Council and for public consumption which was a useful compendium of facts like wine production by region and house and variety, trade figures, harvest figures, and prices and so on; the reports Mother and now I assembled had less regular information in them, notes on trends to watch, editorial comments. Some years I found them a tedious duty and sometimes a snap.

I had not searched through the old ones and collated a report on the history of intrusions of unnatural beasts into Argylle. Even while I'd been recovering from Gemnamnon's battering, I'd had no time. I thought about that with a corner of my mind as I worked and decided to pass it off to the Archive staff when they had finished the annual report for the Council. It would be unfair to divert them from that now. Even though the visitations had stopped abruptly—as had the disturbances associated with Tython's infiltration of our Spring, following his removal—still it would be a useful thing to know, and there might even be a cycle in it or something of that sort. Most things had one somewhere.

As I noted down an outline of what I meant to write about Gemnamnon, there came a tap at my office door. I invoked the spell I had put on it to open it, and it swung quietly back to show a slightly wan Ulrike.

"Good morning," she said.

"Good afternoon," I replied, arching an eyebrow.

She blushed.

"How are you?" I asked, setting aside my pen.

"I, I'm fine, thank you . . ."

"If you are hungry," I said, "you can just go down to the kitchen and help yourself to whatever there is . . ."

Hesitantly, she nodded.

"Or," I sighed inwardly, "actually, I was beginning to feel a tad peckish myself . . . I'll go down with you."

Ulrike nodded again, relieved.

In the kitchen, I had a cheese-and-chutney sandwich and a glass of cider. Ulrike, with considerable effort, prepared scrambled eggs and bread-and-butter, warmed cold stewed fruit, and made a pot of tea. I watched her cooking with inward amusement. She was not very capable at it. However, Mother had always insisted that I be self-sufficient, and I did not intend to ease that standard for Ulrike, inept though she be. The girl ought to at least be able to cook a couple of eggs for herself.

She did manage to do that, and ate them while I had another sandwich and more cider. By the time we were done, the short winter afternoon was nearly gone; the light that came in through the high, narrow windows was blood-orange in color.

"We should be going along to the Vintners' Hall," I said.

"I, I don't have a costume," Ulrike said diffidently. "Perhaps I shouldn't . . ."

"Nonsense, Walter will have an extra for you," I urged her. "It is the Day of Illusions. Get your cloak and we'll go." I was beginning to lose patience with her hesitancy and lack of spirit.

I went up with her, donned a heavily gold-embroidered black velvet doublet, put on mask and cloak and hat, and went out. Ulrike had fetched her own cloak and was waiting in the hall; she jumped and gasped when I stepped out beside her, closing my door quietly behind me.

"What's wrong?"

"You . . . you startled me . . ."

I took her elbow and led her along, flashing a grin at myself in a mirror as we passed. "Indeed. You're in good company. Sometimes I startle myself," I told her.

Walter was still home. He said that he would fit Ulrike with a costume and take her over to the Guild; I was thereby freed to follow my fancy. My brother mentioned that Prospero had dropped by, earlier in the day, and that reminded me that I had intended to talk to him about Ottaviano that morning—it had fled my thoughts until now. Too late— Prospero was gone. Walter also said that Ottaviano was still about, dressed as the King in Green (a figure of ancient myth), but I didn't see him as I left the house in the rapidly-deepening winter darkness.

The streetlamps were lit. I paused a moment just outside the door and surveyed the street. People in coaches, carriages, and on foot, all guised as what they were not, what they thought they were, or what they would like to be . . . I turned left, following a whim, and wandered through the city, watching the revelers and joining the revelry from time to time. There were parties, dancing, open buffets at many of the merchants' and vintners' great houses; I slipped in and out, dancing awhile in one many-windowed crystal-hung ballroom with a tall, swaying lady dressed as a flame, all in rustling ribbons of silks colored in every shade from crimson to gold, and refused her whispered invitation to dance further, more privately, when the dance ended; I danced other dances, in other places, with other partners; I drank good wine and laughed and flirted and smiled and jested and wandered out into the streets again to see what more I could find to amuse me.

I passed the Vintners' Hall, but not yet, not yet; now I took the road to the Great Bridge and crossed it to the other side of the cold Wye, which reflected the colored-meteor fireworks shot over it from boats and moved slowly toward Ollol and the sea. There on the other bank was wilder, rougher partying; there were bonfires and mulled spiced wine and food and dancing and drinking and crowds of gaily-dressed celebrants. I drank when I was thirsty and danced when I met someone who attracted me and ate when I smelled something good; and I punched a half-drunken man who became too possessive of his dancing-partner, a dark sloe-eyed beauty dressed as a black cat who had rubbed up against me as we turned and turned again in the sensual, slow mahall dance, and I laughed at the cat and left there, desire quenched in the adrenaline of the fight. With a surreptitious word and a gesture I caused a great bonfire to burn blue and green and violet, agitating the crowd around it who speculated feverishly about what that could portend, and I met a bent old woman in red as I left that place, smiling to myself, who looked at me with seeing eyes and told me I had a gryphon behind me. I looked over my shoulder and saw nothing and laughed at her.

I recrossed the silent Wye, back to the City proper, where I danced again in houses and ballrooms, and I passed an hour in heated dalliance in someone's headily-perfumed darkened bedroom with a nameless, husky-voiced lady in a green-feathered mask and a wreath of red flowers who moved like a reed before the wind and who parted from me afterward with deep kisses and a whispered farewell. Then I drifted gradually toward the Vintners' Hall and made my way around the back, past numerous amorously-engaged couples in the garden that surrounded the Hall, and threaded my way into the ballroom through knots of conversation.

A pleasant afterglow of satiety lay on me. I took a glass from a servitor's tray and stood on the first balcony, looking up at the gaming and dining on the second and down at the dancing on the floor below. A slender lady in midnight-blue spangled with stars caught my attention, staring down at me from the upper balcony to my right; she wore a silver mask adorned with the crescent Moon, and I caught her eye for a second before she turned away.

I returned my gaze to the dancers below, who were winding about in three concentric circles, but as I dropped my eyes I saw another lady looking at me, across the floor from the other side of the first balcony. She wore feathers of bronze and red-gold and a golden-plumed bird-beaked half-mask, and I noted that she looked at me often, and I looked at her from time to time also as we both stood there watching the dance below. She smiled once, and so did I, and I began to feel a certain pleasant anticipation. Our eyes met repeatedly—oftener than chance would have it.

She glanced toward the exit after catching my gaze in hers yet again and smiled once more.

I smiled also and set my wineglass down. The crowd was thick. When I glanced over again, she was gone; but, feeling certain I'd read her aright, I made my way to the stairs and down.

I saw her passing through the outer doors just ahead of me. She glanced back as she descended the steps, smiled invitingly again, and turned right along the street. I caught up with her just between two streetlamps. She paused and turned and looked at me as I drew near.

Her costume was feathered. They were soft, downy feathers that stirred with each movement of her body, her breathing and pulse included, with longer, stiffer plumes adorning the mask and headdress. Her full lips were glossed with gold and her fair skin dusted with gold powder. Her graceful pale bare arms glistened golden within the long, slit-open feathered sleeves, and the lyre-shape of her body was not hidden by the rest of her garb, which was low-cut and close-fitting but gave nothing away. I could not guess what her hair color or eye color might be; she was a Gryphon tonight, brazen-plumed, touched with red and gold, Argylle's emblematic beast incarnate.

Neither of us spoke. She made no move toward me, either;

we regarded one another for just a few heartbeats, and she lifted her head slightly, showing a lovely throat, her lips slightly parting. Invitation and desire, conveyed in an instant. Her chest rose and fell a bit rapidly, and my own breathing began to speed up. I lowered my head in acquiescence and smiled slowly, keeping my eyes on hers.

She smiled also and turned and started away with a beckoning gesture. Intrigued, sparked with ardor and the promise of pleasure, I followed her.

We went along the street and through several small residential squares and alleys. Few others were out travelling by foot now, and they were all on the main roads; we saw no one else as we passed through Gouronnay Square and went down another alley. It was cold and still. At the corner of Gouronnay and the alley snow lay on top of a gryphon's-head wall fountain and in its basins below. The stars were clear above the housetops and streetlights.

My guide said nothing but went quickly, lightfoot dancing steps, without a sound. I hurried to keep pace with her; she glanced back from time to time and smiled at me, staying just out of reach, and I desired her all the more, tantalized by her smile, her graceful movements, and the sensuality conveyed thereby. I would have made love with her on a snowbank had she wished.

We emerged from a narrow side street into East River Lane, and she turned left and went rapidly along it toward the Boulevard that leads to the Citadel's Iron Bridge. I surmised that she was leading me to the Citadel, and shrugged inwardly—she must have recognized me. I did not care; I wanted her. She hastened to the corner and turned right, toward the Citadel, and I, smiling beneath my domino, liking the game and planning the ending in my mind, strode quickly to catch up to her and turned also.

The street was empty.

She was gone. I stopped, confounded, and stared up and down like a fool. Then I looked in the doorway of a shop on the corner, in the doorways of other shops up the street, and at the doors and windows of the townhouses. The golden Gryphon-lady was nowhere to be seen. I saw no lights, no movements. Not a sound broke the cold winter silence.

Was she standing somewhere out of sight, laughing up her sleeve at me, having beguiled me so? My disappointment was too crushing to allow for anger. I stepped back, out of the light's reach, and looked again for her, scanning the pavement. No sign . . .

A movement to the left caught my eye. Not wanting to be seen as I tried to collect my thoughts, I withdrew another step back into East River Lane. Two people on foot, coming toward me, toward the Citadel. I looked away, then looked again. They passed in and out of pools of illumination below the streetlamps. The one was costumed in green; the other, in dark colors and silver and a crescent Moon which flashed on her head.

I recalled, with a chill rush, that Ottaviano was dressed, according to Walter, as the King in Green. That must be Ulrike with him, masked as the Moon—yes. It was her I'd seen at the Vintners' Hall. Now she went toward the Citadel with him, arm in arm with Ottaviano whom our family does not trust and has held ever at arm's length. I frowned and waited until they were nearly abreast of me in the nearest streetlamp's light. Then I stepped out.

Ottaviano jumped half a foot, reaching for a sword or dagger that he wasn't wearing, and then uncertainly said, "Prospero . . . ?"

Ulrike, gasping with shock, exclaimed "Gwydion!" in the same moment. Behind the mask, her eyes were wide.

"Well-met indeed. I was just on my way home," I said, smiling and bowing slightly to her. "I trust you had a pleasant evening."

"I . . . Y-yes," she said, "thank you."

"It is most kind of you to accompany my sister thus far afoot, on a night when the hansoms are on holiday, but I shall spare you the rest of the journey," I said to Ottaviano.

Our eyes met, masks hiding our expressions. I moved forward and he turned to Ulrike.

"Good night, m'lady cousin, and thank you for your companionship this evening."

She took her left hand from his arm and, with half a movement, uncertainly offered him her right; he took it quickly and bowed over it, kissing it lightly I thought before releasing it.

Ulrike in a near-whisper said, "Good night, Otto."

I drew her hand through my arm and we went along the Boulevard and over the Iron Bridge. Regretfully I left my teasing Gryphon-lady to her own devices and took my foolish little sister home. Ulrike glanced back once to wave a small wave to Ottaviano, who stood beneath the light watching us go.

The third day of New Year's celebration and the first day of the year is more sober and less riotous than the last day of the Old Year and the Day of Illusions. It is the Day of Intentions, for giving practical gifts, whereas the two previous days are filled with playful presents and practical jokes. It is also a day for family gatherings. Our family assembles in the Citadel for a formal banquet with certain of our household's intimates and a few others, any guests who might be about, and the occasional (rare) diplomatic visitor. Thus, this year our table should include Ottaviano.

With the sight of Ottaviano with Ulrike fresh in my eyes, I wrote a note to myself to speak to Prospero first thing in the morning and left it in the washbasin before I slept. Thus the first thing I did after rising and dressing was to knock on his door. There was no answer, so I went down to breakfast wishing I'd remembered to talk to him the previous day and hoping he was home. The first day of the New Year is also sometimes occupied in figuring out how you got where you are and getting back to wherever you ought to be.

Ulrike was not there, but the breakfast room bore signs of having been visited already. When I was nearly through, the door opened and Prospero came in.

"Good morning. I'm sorry about yesterday, I forgot when I woke up—" I began.

He shrugged, poured himself coffee, and sat down with a glance at the door. "If it worries you not," he said, "then you're not worried."

"I am concerned. I find that we . . . are in a slightly awkward position. We cannot exclude Ottaviano today. It would be—"

"Smart," Prospero concluded, setting down his cup with a brittle clink. "You're too damned punctilious, Gwydion. What measures shall you take 'gainst his intrusion?"

"Put extra guards in the Core and at the Black Stair."

He snorted slightly and then shrugged again. "I'm a timorous old man," he said, with a tinge of emotion I could not identify.

He was neither, and we both knew it. "You think that's not enough."

"I have no opinion, nay, naught but dislike and distrust to guide me."

I wondered what Mother would have done. That was a conundrum: she was ever-generous, ever-courteous, and she couldn't stand Ottaviano. If Mother were here, the situation would not have arisen, because had Avril dared to send him to Argylle, either Walter wouldn't have invited Ottaviano to the City or Dewar would have bounced him as courteously as possible. In fact, Ottaviano probably wouldn't have tried to come if she were alive. He had always been very careful not to push things between himself and our family to the conflagration point, had always angled for a slightly better relationship.

Prospero broke my reverie, greeting Ulrike. I said Hullo and sank back into my thoughts. Prospero proposed a walk along the Wye to her, to which she agreed in her usual shy way, and they left after she breakfasted.

I decided I could not *not* have Ottaviano to the day's dinner. It would be extremely obvious and rude. No. However, I could and would put more guards on duty, and no matter what Prospero thought I couldn't do more and still be a good host. I rang and sent the servant who answered to tell Utrachet to meet me in my office in the next hour. Then I went there.

Utrachet nodded when I explained that I must regretfully call in some of the guards from their family festivities in order to tighten Core security. We worked out how many were needed and where to position them, and I sent him off to take care of it.

I did not tell him exactly why. While waiting, I'd framed it a number of times and the best I had come up with was that we had a guest of whose goodwill I was not entirely sure. Utrachet accepted this without questioning me—not that he ever did question me, but I felt my explanation was a bit sketchy. I supposed that the Seneschal knew us all well enough to know we didn't trust Ottaviano, but I also supposed that he understood that if I named no names, he shouldn't either.

That done, I fell again into working on my account of the dragon, carefully phrasing it. I did not put here the truth about Dewar. I knew that myself, and that was enough.

My report held my attention until the clock rang two. Then I stretched and put away my pen and inks and went into my rooms to dress more formally. Appearance counts more at these things than at the casual revels of the previous two days. Having passed final inspection at the looking glass, I went out, locking my door behind me. There seemed no one else around; I tapped on Ulrike's door, but she wasn't in or wasn't answering.

The high hall clock said quarter to three. The light from the windows was already dim. People would be gathering in the reception area in a few minutes; I was perfectly on time. I straightened my cuffs and lifted an eyebrow at my reflection in the face of the clock. I started down the Spiral, my soft shoes making a quick-paced padding echo like a heartbeat.

Voices rose up, a wash of conversations running around and around the walls, growing fainter as I descended. I looked over the banister to see who had arrived, and tripped on the stair, for in the moving light of the lamps my mother—

No. It was Ulrike, wearing one of Mother's gowns, one I ought not to have given her—one of her favorites, sea-green silk with a gauzy green overdress. She was emerging from the passageway which leads to the Great Hall where the Black Chair is.

The adrenaline left me weak and sick for an instant. I stepped away from the banister and stood, eyes closed, and for an instant only allowed the Spring which rushed upward and outward to subsume me. It was a comforting, upholding feeling, at once warm and cool, delicate and strong. I drew a shuddery breath and opened my eyes again, looked skyward at the windows around the top of the Core.

"Better?" someone asked solicitously.

I nodded and glanced over my shoulder. There was no one there.

Was I losing my mind? I shuddered and began hurrying around the Spiral again. If Ulrike had been designed, by some evil genius, to remind us of Freia, she was well-made, and if she was the natural product of a natural process, then she was a miracle, a very wonder: Freia come again. In justice I modified my thought: except when she opened her mouth to speak, she was the image of my mother, for the resemblance indeed was only superficial—but that superficial seeming was a powerful reminder of what we had lost forever.

It was almost worse this way, I mused. My feet had slowed to a deliberate pace as I thought. I did not look down again.

We would always be pained by the surface so reminiscent of Freia, because the interior, by comparison, was alien, blank, nothing. If only she had Mother's intelligence, her liveliness, her wisdom, or even the potential for them.

Another more worrying and immediate thought came to me: suppose Prospero's great fear were true, that she was an impostor, a clever faker come to trick us into giving her the Spring? She had been much in Ottaviano's company: Prospero surely feared that they were confederates, the woman enlisted by Ottaviano to engage our trust and open the way to the Spring for him when we had taken her there. More subtle than Dazhur, more dangerous, assailing our susceptibilities with weapons against which we would have no defense—if she were lying, what could we do? Execute her for misrepresentation? Exile? Exile might be most fitting, I thought. Death for a lie—that seemed harsh, yet the stakes of the lie were high and it might be wisest to make an example of her.

Or might the Spring take the matter unto itself, as the Stone of Morven in Phesaotois and the Well of Landuc in Pheyarcet have done on occasion, annihilating the unfit who presumed to partake of their potency?

I left the Spiral at a walkway that led to a corridor, taking a less direct way to the banqueting room where we would be dining so that I could think this through. What punishment would fit someone who wanted the Spring enough to lie for it, to impersonate the Lady of Argylle's own daughter?

And the answer came to me: the Spring itself.

My feet stopped and I stood very still, my heart hammering.

The Spring itself could kill her, yes, and it would—if she were cast to it as Freia had been. Unprotected, she would be destroyed, and by her death . . .

By her death Freia would live again.

Yes.

It was justice of the sort my mother had often handed

down from the Chair: give people just a little more than they meant to ask for. It was Argylle style; it was precedented. Mother herself would probably agree. If this Ulrike who wanted the Spring so much proved false, we could give it to her: give her to it, and redeem my mother.

Dinner proceeded smoothly, decorously; the Day of Intentions has everyone trying to strike optimistic notes to begin the coming year in a favorable key. The Voulouys joined us, and Lishon tried to flirt with me; I gravely told her in a private aside that I could not afford any appearance of favoring her family, given the sensitivity of the negotiations the Citadel and the Empire had in hand. She was sensible enough to take my meaning and behaved less kittenishly thereafter.

Ottaviano was a model of good deportment and made polite, neutral conversation with the people seated around him. I watched him and Ulrike, but he paid more notice to Lishon than to my sister, though Lishon's enthusiastic response to his attention might have been responsible for that.

Ulrike sat at my right hand. She knew little about wine— barely the basics—and, this being Argylle, wine was something on which everyone was ready to hold forth, so the talk in our vicinity went onto that track and stayed there, more or less, through the meal. I listened, not saying much, following three or four conversations and fragments at once: it is always good to know what other people think, although one needn't put much stock in it.

A curious exchange came between Ulrike and Lishon, who complimented my sister on her gown.

"It is very pretty," Ulrike said. "They gave it to me."

"Where did it come from?" Lishon asked her.

"I don't know."

"It was one of Mother's," I said.

"What!" Ulrike exclaimed, paling and looking down at the gown. "How?"

"Howso, how? It hung in her wardrobe," I said. "The

clothing shops are not open for business during the holiday, by and large."

"It looks nice though it's such an old dress," Lishon said.

Prospero glanced at her contemptuously—it was a tactless enough remark—and turned to Hicha beside him to ask about a book she had located for him.

"It is not so old as that," I shrugged, "and it suits . . . Why, Ulrike, what is it?"

"I, I didn't know," she said.

"Does it matter?" I asked her, puzzled. This was hardly elevated table-conversation, but her expression of mixed dismay and horror was hardly dinner fare either.

"I think it is not . . . to wear someone's clothes after they . . ." she said, unable to articulate her thoughts.

"I should think it would be rather uncomfortable to wear a dead person's clothes," Lishon said.

Tautau caught my eye and made an apologetic face. Lishon's manners would receive resounding and rapid correction when her sister had her alone later.

"Not if they fit," Ottaviano said, frowning at Lishon. "That sounds like a silly superstition to me."

"I didn't mean that," Lishon said, "it seems rather creepy, that's what it is. Isn't that it, Ulrike?"

"It is . . . odd," she said. "I did not know the dresses were Mother's." She looked at the gown again, clearly disliking it.

"Not like things from your sisters," Lishon continued, "that's different."

Shaoll saw the opening and mercifully redirected the conversation. "We'll take you out in the morning and go round the town shopping," she said. "One doesn't often have a chance to buy a whole new wardrobe! Even for someone else, especially for someone else, and on Walter's account too," said she, and glanced down the table at Walter mischievously.

"What?" Walter said, hearing his name.

"Shopping," said Shaoll. "It would be a fine New Year's gift to your sister to buy her a few frocks, wouldn't it?"

"A fine gift," Walter said. "I wonder if I have any money."

I laughed at his lugubrious expression; Walter usually doesn't have any money, officially; he gives it away and funds things and bails his friends out of debt, and it sinks away from him, water into sand. But everyone knows he's Walter, and so the unpaid bills come to his family at the Citadel—where, long ago when the pattern became clear to her, Mother arranged that there should ever be funds for Walter's use. Walter is not very clear on how it is that there is always, somehow, enough money, but somehow, there always is.

"Of course you do," Shaoll assured him.

Everyone laughed at that.

After dinner we retired to a music room for civilized entertainment. In the more casual setting I expected Ottaviano to once again approach Ulrike, but again Lishon Voulouy absorbed much of his attention. Perhaps he was self-conscious, since I had twice now interrupted them in colloquy.

I was still apprehending the consequences of Ulrike being, possibly, no true member of our family. It was hard to believe her naiveté could be shammed, but acting is a skill like others. Suspecting Ottaviano was natural; he had a name as a schemer. I heard him mention the Empire to someone and a fresh suspicion hit me—Ulrike could be an agent of Landuc, cunningly planted here by Avril. I pushed the problem away, as it threatened to preoccupy me: I couldn't worry about that and entertain my guests.

The evening passed quickly and very pleasantly with songs and instrumental pieces contributed by all (except Ulrike). Prospero once again turned the full force of his character on her and got her to behave more naturally, and perhaps his presence near her also kept Ottaviano at arm's length.

Ottaviano left with Walter, who would ride back to Ollol with him tonight. Nothing had happened. No one had so much as looked at the door to the Black Stair; though I'd watched Ottaviano and kept an ear cocked toward his conversation, nothing of sorcerous or political content had been mentioned. Ulrike, in Mother's green gown, bade me a polite good-night and went to her rooms.

⌒ *12* ⌒

THE DAYS THAT FOLLOWED NEW YEAR'S were true winter days, short and gray and wet. Prospero stayed in Ollol, inexorably mincing Ottaviano's hopes for a trading treaty that would put him high in the Emperor's favor, and Ulrike stayed in the City. Tautau and Lishon Voulouy and Shaoll earned my everlasting gratitude by commanding the vitally-important shopping for a wardrobe for Ulrike, whose taste was uninformed, though she favored flattering cloudy greys and blues of every shade. Her choice of colors made her look less like Mother, so that she did not continue to startle people when they glimpsed her unexpectedly.

She asked about Gaston, but never about the Spring. I suggested several times to her that she descend and drink, but she balked at the idea each time. Puzzled, I spoke of this to Prospero.

"She will not drink of the Spring," I said when we met over lunch at an inn between Ollol and Argylle.

He arched an eyebrow, sampling the wine in his glass. He swallowed, grimaced. "Will not?"

"Will not. I have offered more than once. She will not."

"Will not. 'Passing strange, that; if she'd see Gaston again, or Fenshuyan, needs must drink. You've told her so?"

"Oh, yes. Prospero, isn't it a point, so to speak, in her favor, that she did not leap at the first chance and do so? For surely a faker would."

He hmmmed in his throat and, thoughtfully, wiped out his empty wineglass and poured some of the white I had ordered for myself. "Much better. That's raw young red, best cellared another half-dozen years. Fool of a host knows not his business. —Ulrike. Yes. Perhaps so, Gwydion, perhaps so. What seems and what is do not always live in the same house. Could be she's all she says, your sister, his daughter, and all. She's not asked of Ottaviano?"

"Not a word. She goes about, just the way girls do, with other girls. Lishon Voulouy—"

Prospero snorted. "Cheeky chit."

"I must concur. But Ulrike's taken to her, and Tautau is perfectly pleased to look after them both and find them amusements. I cannot, I have forgotten what one does with seventeen-year-old girls."

"Swimming," Prospero suggested, and grinned like a devil so that I blushed. He laughed and poured me more wine. In my youth I had been in the habit of swimming after dark from the Citadel's Island to the Wyeside home of a certain young lady, and nobody who had heard the tale from my tutor had ever let me forget it.

"Shopping, more to her liking," I mumbled, and ate big pieces of fish, chewing hard.

Prospero's laughter ran down. "Ah well. So she's of the age where she flocks with the other geese: 'tis quite as likely that was her father's reason for shooing her here. Fine feathers and gabbling aren't his forte." He ate for a few minutes without talking. "You've heard naught of Gaston."

I shook my head, mouth full.

He made an impatient sound. "Bandersnatch," he said, or something like it. "Cannot have been mistaken, if he sent her here; I've thought over it, it's not to be done thus. But still we've no proof of her bona fides from him. What would you have done had she taken you at your word, inviting her to the Spring?" He glared at me.

"I'd have made some excuse, some delay." We had agreed, after all, that she should not drink until we had word of Gaston.

He shook his head, disapproving still. "Strange, strange that he sent her hither alone. Is he ashamed? Abashed? Wherefore?" he murmured, and took the last of the bread to his plate. "There's something here not fathomed yet," he decided, when the plate was immaculate and the bread eaten.

"The glaze," I suggested, pointing at the painted-on cherries and getting him back for the swimming joke.

"Hah. I'm not Dewar," said he, his mouth twisting and no amusement in his face. "Another dog out o' the kennel," he said, "howling at the moon."

"Surely he's all right," I said.

Prospero shot me a sharp look, quick and bleak.

"Probably he's just . . . busy. Lost count of the time."

"My son?" Prospero said derisively. True; Dewar was the master of clockwork and precision sorcery. He beckoned to the waiter, who came and cleared our table.

When the man had gone, I said, "Why would he send her here alone?"

"Ask him; I cannot guess. 'Tis unkind of him to do so. She's a comely child, just the thing he'd find a comfort. He'd rejoice to see Freia again in her . . . Indubitably not in Freia's gown, though," Prospero added, giving me another sharp look. "Do you put those away again."

"I did, sir."

"Good."

"It gave me a turn and a half too. I wasn't thinking. I'm sorry."

He nodded. We were brought dessert (a cake soaked with brandy and fruit) and the accompanying beverages, and we ate and drank without further talk.

After Prospero and I had said our farewells in the brassy late sunshine, I rode on Cosmo over the frozen road back home to the Citadel. The treaty would be ready in three days' time, and I would ride down to Ollol then and sign it with Ottaviano to witness. Then Ottaviano and Walter would return to Landuc and Avril would sign with Walter to witness, and so it would be concluded. Avril would not be pleased by the continued tight rein on commerce between us; Prospero had slackened nowhere.

The other matter in my mind as Cosmo's hooves thumped hollowly on the frozen mud was Ulrike, since we had just spoken of her at lunch. Though clad in different colors, different styles, different gowns, people still looked twice at her for her resemblance to our mother. As soon as she spoke the resemblance was gone, though, for the girl lacked Mother's judgement, her knowledge, her humor, her wit. She wanted constant guidance and cosseting. She was as unlike her mother as two people could be.

It was a great shame, I thought, that she was not like Mother. We could have used another sharp mind in the family; instead we had, it seemed—if she were ours and Prospero inclined to think she was—someone like Aunt Viola, who is not renowned for her intelligence. Viola has her own breezy charm, but Ulrike lacked even that.

Self-conscious and shy, she was nothing like Belphoebe or Marfisa, and I imagined they, when they met her in person, would find her amusing. Though averse to arms and graceful in form, she was not quick to learn dance steps and tended to be clumsy. I had seen her trip on her own gowns so often I'd feared she'd fall on the Spiral and had suggested kindly to her that she have them taken up a few fingers'-breadth. When I took her to the Spring, I thought, she would probably be so overcome or nervous that she would either faint or stumble and fall in.

Small loss, thought I, and then bit my lip. It would be murder, though someone would survive—Mother would, but Ulrike would not, her form animated by Freia's substance. It would be a public service of sorts, true, yet Gaston would hardly thank me for restoring his lady in such a way, even though he himself must be aware at how lustreless

Ulrike was. The comparison was inevitable, as was the conclusion.

I pushed the idea away. To execute a criminal impostor thus was one matter, but to assassinate a sister, even if she was an idiot, was another.

Thin golden sun came across the Spiral, nearly horizontal, as I descended one morning a few days after signing the treaty in Ollol. I had gone up to the top of the Citadel and watched the winter day begin, standing in the cold still air while darkness changed to light and seeing the stains of color creep onto the world—bloody crimsons and brazen oranges, presaging more snow. There had been nothing particular on my mind when I went up, though I find the heights a congenial thinking place; I had wanted to see the sunrise and the night's flight. When the sun was a hand's-breadth over the horizon, far away in the mild North, I went in and went down to find breakfast.

From overhead, a cold draft accompanied a black shadow which whistled in the air as it fell toward me where I stood on the stairs. I turned toward it and lifted my right arm, a gesture so practiced as to be ingrained. The bird, one of my black-and-gold-barred hawks, spread her wings and landed, staggering me.

It was one of the trio I had sent searching. Success, so soon? The cylinder on her leg had a blob of white wax over my black, which was broken. I stepped off the Spiral to a side corridor and into the first open room, which happened to be a formal reception room. The bird left my arm reluctantly and stood on the back of a chair. She did not appear to have had a hard journey. I murmured praises to her while I cracked open her capsule.

A tiny strip of white paper, torn from the bottom of my note, was enclosed. On it was written: *Yes, she is. W all affection, Gaston.* He had made his usual flourish in the signature, in miniature.

I sat down slowly, staring at it. Gaston's handwriting. The paper shone gold in the sun. I wished he'd Summoned me, or come here. Or written more. Yet, this was a great deal already: and Ulrike *was* indeed my sister. Had Gaston said otherwise, it would have been difficult to accept; all the evidence was for her. It was a great wonder, after so many years of death, that my mother should have a new daughter. Perhaps she would improve with time and effort.

My great pleasure and relief surprised me. I couldn't keep from smiling broadly, and I wanted to jump up and down and whoop. Instead I made myself sit very still, wiped the glee from my face, and then went down to eat when I was sure I was under control. First, though, I took the hawk out and hand-fed her at the mews, and I hummed to her as I did.

At the table, before Ulrike joined us, I remarked to Prospero that I had had confirmation of Ulrike's story.

"How?"

"A wee bird told me," I replied in a jesting tone.

He looked at me sidelong and lifted an eyebrow. "Ah-hah. 'Tis a relief anyway."

The snow outside my window was falling in thick, fluffy, clumped flakes. The fire leapt soundlessly behind the mica window in the stove door. Virgil, perched on the curtain-rod over the window, was looking down at the room below through wise half-closed eyes. Brahms, his dark head drawn down into his shoulders, golden eyes closed, slept on the bookshelves over the fireplace, a featureless feather lump. It was a quiet winter afternoon, perfectly suited for curling up and reading.

That was exactly what I was not doing.

"Will it hurt?" whispered Ulrike.

"Of course," I said.

"Oh."

"It hurts as much as cutting yourself usually does," I added, to explain myself.

"Oh," she said, and didn't say anything more, hugging herself.

On my worktable, fires burned with low, restrained roars in three pans arranged in a triangle. In a fourth pan in the center was a bar of gold. I took out my Master Key and set it ready on the bench beside a curved silver scalpel.

"Just do as I tell you when I tell you to do it, and don't do otherwise," I warned her, moistening my mouth with a sip of wine.

Ulrike, pale in a dark-blue dress, her left arm bare, long snug sleeve unbuttoned and rolled up above her elbow, nodded on the stool, wide-eyed.

"I may not actually speak," I said, "but you'll know."

I began the spell. After the standard cleansings and invocations, I tapped the serious power and shaped it to the form I wanted. Now the Master Key hung suspended in the form of the spell over the gold bar; the spell itself was visible to me as multicolored-gold basketwork around the Key and the bar and the fires, which were now hand-sized balls of flame like miniature suns. The sweat from my forehead stung my eyes—I'd forgotten to put on a headband—and I blinked and itched and struggled to keep my concentration on the forces I controlled. The fires were roaring. A distraction now would make my tower room, truncated, look like the business end of a reversed rocket.

I continued chanting and created the forms for the Keys I was making in the spell. The gold melted, glowing red-hot. I invoked Ulrike and described her to the spell, creating a space for her in the sorcery too, combining her with the Keys I would make and identifying her with them. Now . . .

I held out my left hand, reaching across the table above the red-hot metal, and commanded her to take it. A clammy, shaking hand was set in mine after almost too long; the force that abided in the spell surged and strained. I picked up the silver scalpel and nicked Ulrike's wrist. Her arm jerked in my grip; she might have squeaked or shrieked. I held her there, though, and her blood fell onto the molten gold and into the spell and when it was enough I released her, speaking words of acceptance and inclusion and completion.

The gold was white now, liquid and shining. I uttered the disposition of it and commanded it to go and at the same time, in the instant it went, I upended a silver ewer of water into the dish where the metal had been with more words.

The power, released suddenly, passed through me and off along the vent lines I'd established—a lifting, sexual rush that made me shiver and thrill. The three fires whoomfed and went out. Steam rose from the dish now filled with water.

I closed the spell, hands shaking in the gestures, and then took out my handkerchief and mopped the sweat off my face.

"That was not so fearsome, was it?" I said.

Ulrike made an odd, strained little sound. "But almost nothing . . . happened," she said. She was snow-white in spite of her comment. In fact she looked faint.

"There were things you could not see or feel happening," I said. "It was all on another . . . level. There are your Keys."

She nodded, but didn't look into the dish at which I gestured.

"They will be cool enough to handle in a moment," I assured her.

Ulrike nodded again, holding her wrist. "M-may I go get a bandage . . ."

"I've things here. Wait." I caught my breath, shrugged uncomfortably in my damp clothing. I keep medical supplies in my workroom, for my own use and for mending my birds when they need it from time to time.

When I'd bound up my sister's wrist, the Keys were cool enough to handle. I asked what she wanted to do with them.

"What do you mean? I'll give them to people, won't I?"

"Yes, but how? That's the question." I took one out and looked at it. It was a delicate, lacy thing, slender, the head shaped like a hornèd moon with a star between the points, closing it, and the wards like wavy rays. Rather nice. I had chosen the general shape, but the details came from Ulrike herself.

"Oh. I see." She frowned and rolled her sleeve down to button it. "I think," she said shyly, "for now, I . . . can I just give them to you and Grandfather and Walter? For now?"

"That's up to you. Here . . ." I counted out seven. "One for you, one for everyone else . . . an extra for yourself . . ." I hung one on my own ring of Keys and took out a leather bag to keep the rest in.

"Where do you put them . . ."

"In with the rest of the . . ." I was going to use Dewar's irreverent term, *family jewels,* and then supposed it would make her blush again, ". . . Keys, in storage. Come with me and I'll put together a set for you."

Ulrike said nothing while we went along to the strong-room. I nodded to the guard on duty there and opened the door. Lights leapt up in the wall sconces as we entered.

The extra Keys are kept in a cabinet in this repository for odd bits and pieces of stuff deemed, for sundry and sometimes whimsical reasons, too valuable to leave just lying around. The security of the place was debatable. Dewar had once laid complicated protective spells on it, but then Freia hadn't been able to get around them and had scolded him and made him lift them. She felt that the best warding was provided in part by obscurity, and anyway she trusted people, so she did no more than lock the strongroom with impressive chunks of metalware. That was early in Argylle's history, though, and I thought that perhaps I'd put down protective sorcery of my own. Now that I was supposed to use my judgement on things like that.

I unlocked the cabinet with a mundane sort of key (the lock and key did have a spell on them, such that they only worked for one who had drunk of the Spring, but that was hardly exhaustive security). The doors swung back. Inside, the cabinet was pigeonholed with little crystal-knobbed drawers. Each one held Keys for a member of the family, stored in an idiosyncratic order Freia had settled on. I opened them in order, took out a Key from each, and put them all side-by-side in a row on top of the chest; and, in that they represented us, they brought to mind a row of bodies, our family, laid out for identification.

My hand hovered in front of the last drawer, almost didn't open it, and then I did open it and took out one more. I put Ulrike's spare Keys in an empty drawer and locked up.

"Here," I said. "They're all quite easy to keep sorted out, you see . . ."

"I remember now. Father showed me his. This is his . . ."

At least he had shown her something. "That's Gaston's, yes. This is for the Citadel and this for the City. Here is Prospero's." An intricate, elegant knot shaped like a Key, or a Key shaped like a knot. "Alexander's. Marfisa's. Phoebe's. Walter's. Mine . . ." A featherish design at the top, clawlike wards at the bottom, and engraving along the barrel. "Uncle Dewar's, and Mother's."

"Mother's," she repeated.

I nodded, looking down at her face as she studied the Key. "Just so you have it."

Freia's Key is strangely similar to Dewar's in its labyrinthine wards, a negative image of her brother's, and the top is a cross-quartered circle, unadorned, smooth and rounded.

"I wish I had known my mother," Ulrike said, nearly inaudibly. "I dream of her sometimes. I think it is Mother."

"I wish you had too. She was the best the world could offer."

"She seems to have worked so hard, so constantly, here."

I nodded. "It was her life. Her public life."

"What was her private life? Utrachet said she had a garden, that it's still kept here . . ."

"Oh, my. Gardening, research in all kinds of fields, her family, music . . ."

"Research?" Ulrike looked up at me, puzzled.

"She surveyed out to the Border Range, back when the

world was new, surveys we still use to measure the Dominion. She did genetic and biological research, too; she loved plants and animals, she designed them and bred them or fashioned them from the Elements. It was she who brought vines to Argylle, when she first came to rule, and planted vineyards and began winemaking. She travelled . . . gods, she wandered farther afield than many of us, to Noroison, on every Road in Argylle and every little pocket-world between here and the Border . . . she loved music and dancing, she and Dewar danced beautifully together and sometimes, once in a while, they would sing, or she would sing with Prospero . . ." I looked at the Key. Smooth, seamless, whole. "She knew more about the way things fit together to make our world than I ever will, I think."

She studied Dewar's Key. "Nobody mentions Uncle Dewar here. Father wouldn't talk about him."

"He was my tutor," I said.

"Father did tell me that. Dewar is a sorcerer and he grew up in Phesaotois, and he taught you."

The things Gaston had told her sometimes told me more about Gaston than I'd ever known. "He's also Prospero's son. There's more of Landuc in him than Noroison, I think, and maybe more of Argylle than either. He's a gentle man and merciful, but dauntless; daring, but a careful, cautious planner. He has a great sense of humor," I had to add. My mouth twitched, suddenly remembering Dewar's silly pranks on anyone who happened to catch his attention and particularly on his sister. One year he had somehow—I still didn't know how—substituted live animals and plants for the cooked food under all the covered dishes at a dinner at Walter's house; the dining room had become a barnyard. Another year, during a particularly riotous party on the Day of Illusions, he had masked all the exterior doors and windows in Voulouy's house with illusions, so that those inside could not find their way out for hours, until the following dawn.

"Is he alive still?"

"I believe so."

"Father thought not."

I shook my head. "I would like to see him back here. Perhaps Fortuna will turn her Wheel about and bring him home. You would like him. He is a good man. Gaston was always distrustful of sorcery and sorcerers—same as Alexander, but more diplomatic—and I guess with good reason. . . . Dewar and Freia could put their heads together and come up with very dangerous . . . exploits."

Hesitantly, my sister asked, "Was Mother a sorceress?"

"Oh, not really. She called it hedge-witchery. She had a few tricks, but she wasn't interested in the Great Art. Dewar provided that if she needed it, as Prospero provided a certain diplomatic savoir faire and Gaston would provide a sword. Tools to her hand. She was good at hunches, though. Mother was always right." I smiled.

She sighed. "Someday maybe I'll understand."

I squeezed her shoulder quickly. "You're young. You'll get to know her with time." I wondered whether Mother knew Ulrike was here now, and what she thought of that.

Ulrike fingered her Keys. "Have you talked with Father?"

"He will come when he is ready. I shan't pester him." I crossed my fingers again as I spoke. Half-truths, half-lies . . . they grated on my sense of honor.

"He wouldn't talk much about Mother, either . . ." She sighed again.

"He loved her too well to talk about her, I think," I said gently. "Her death was a terrible shock to us. To you it is history. To me it was yesterday, and I still cannot imagine that she is not . . . travelling again somewhere on the Road." I looked away, at a tall, dusty clock which was apparently stored here because its works didn't. The benevolent, serene sun on its face was perpetually half-eclipsed by a smiling round pale moon. I wished it had stopped with both the sun and moon showing wholly, or just the sun, instead of with the moon attempting to supplant the unresisting sun.

"I'm sorry," Ulrike whispered.

"You must drink of the Spring, Ulrike," I said, closing the cabinet. "Now that you have Keys, it will be—"

"No!"

"No?" I looked down at her, nonplussed. "Ulrike, you will not be able to use these Keys here, nor to follow the Road or the Leys—"

"I . . . no, please. I . . . not yet," she said, chalky-pale again. "Not the Spring. Not . . . not yet."

Why such strong aversion? It was far easier than the Fire of Landuc, I had explained that to her once already. "Have it as you will, then," I said. "Or not."

⌒ 13 ⌒

MARFISA CAME TO ARGYLLE AGAIN, AT my asking, to meet Ulrike. I asked Alexander to come also, but he was busy in Montgard and could not. When I explained why I called him—that we had acquired a new sibling—he was irked.

"Naturally I would like to visit, to meet the girl," he said. "Damn. Marfisa—"

"She said she would be here in a few days," I said.

"I cannot easily leave now. You should have told me sooner." He drummed his fingers. "Well-a-day. It is discourtesy to Ulrike, too. Ulrike. What an odd name."

"I rather like it."

"It's a perfectly good name, just a bit odd."

"When do you think you will be able to attend here, Alex?"

He had not specified what business kept him, nor did I ask. With Alexander, it could be anything from war on three fronts at once to a lady about to succumb to his advances. He would weight them equally. Actually, he would place the lady above the war, because wars can be delegated.

Alexander paused, thinking. "In a month, possibly; realistically, two months."

"Mm," I said noncommittally. I recalled that Montgard's time spun slowly compared to Argylle's. "As you wish. I'll convey your respects and regrets."

"You've given her Keys, I assume."

"Yes. She just has the immediate family for now."

"Ask her to Summon me herself. She knows that much?"

"Yes. I will tell her. She has not yet drunk of the Spring, though. So it may be a while ere you hear from her." Repeatedly she had demurred, always leaving me feeling as though I was offering her poison instead of power. Most recently she had said something about not feeling herself ready yet. I could not force her, but it seemed silly to me.

My brother twisted his face in an irritated grimace. "Then give me her Key and I'll call her myself—why is it that things become complicated whenever you are part of them, Gwydion?"

"Indeed?" I said. I wasn't the one creating a difficulty here. I detached her Key from my set and held it up. "I'll send it by a carrier bird."

"I see it. Horns?" He frowned.

"A crescent moon."

"Excellent. I'll know it again. It is rude of me to delay introducing myself, but I have little liberty to rearrange the world here just now. Have you heard from Father?"

"Nothing new," I prevaricated. "He will be back when it suits him."

"I suppose. He is taking this too far. Perhaps I shall have a look around for him."

I didn't understand. "Too far?"

"Brooding over Freia's death. It is done. It is unnatural of him to deny it by avoiding us and Argylle and Landuc. He ought to be getting over it by now."

"Alexander, you're talking about *Mother*. Not some girl-friend who dumped him or whatever. Mother is different."

"There you go too," Alexander snapped. *"Was* different. *Is* dead. Sun and stars, Gwydion. Let it go. The Wheel has turned. You're old enough to know what death is about, aren't you?"

"I don't recall asking for a gratis consultation on my progress in grieving," I retorted. "Mind your own business."

We glared at one another, both offended.

"Just send me the Key, please, and I thank you for your news," growled Alexander finally, and I cut off the spell with a chopping gesture, flicking water at the flames.

For a minute or so afterward I stared into the firepan and made the fire burn in a nasty green, high, narrow column of flame, venting my anger on it. Easy for Alexander to sit in Montgard, Gaston's old city in the country of the same name, and sneer at those of us who tried to carry on here in Argylle. I snuffed the flame abruptly and rose and went off to the mews to get myself a carrier-bird to convey the Key to Alexander.

Ulrike's shyness and Marfisa's reserve meant that they were not exactly intimate, though Marfisa made clear efforts to make herself more accessible for Ulrike. They went riding when the weather permitted, but much of the time Marfisa lodged with fair, elevated Hicha, which was her custom and which brought Hicha's rare and lovely smile out. Marfisa's crippled leg still pained her, she admitted to me when I pressed her about the injury, and she dared not enter any combat with it so damaged, for she could not keep her seat. Two days after Marfisa came, Belphoebe arrived in the Citadel with a couple of small pots of some ointment she had concocted, which Marfisa was to use on the leg. One of Mother's recipes, she said, and Marfisa accepted gratefully.

Tellin accompanied Marfisa again, fetching and carrying for her and helping her mount and dismount when Marfisa would allow it. My sister's squire idolized Ulrike and spent her free time trying to befriend her, her light-green eyes wide with earnest goodwill and kindness, offering to practice fencing with Ulrike in the Landuc manner, which Tellin was just learning, or to shoot arrows at targets, or to go for a steeplechase ride.

None of these things suited Ulrike, and so instead Tellin chattered with her, telling her tall tales and trying to persuade her that coming with Marfisa and seeing the world would be capital fun. When the weather permitted the two went walking together, and I saw them sometimes, a funny pair, Tellin striding fast when she forgot herself and then trotting back to Ulrike, gesturing, picking up stones or snowballs and throwing them at birds, trees, or rocks, plainly talking nonstop about horses they passed, the snow, the Citadel, dogs, and everything under the sun.

I wished Ulrike were more like Tellin. There was a great deal to be said in favor of an optimistic outlook on life.

Belphoebe invited Ulrike to come into the wood with her, to see the place and hunt, and Ulrike nervously declined the invitation. One couldn't fault her for it; the wet of winter is hardly the time to see Threshwood at its best. Belphoebe, unoffended, returned alone to her trees and mountains.

My youngest sister seemed to prefer to spend time with Walter, but Walter is a busy man himself with his music and composing, and he wasn't available to shepherd Ulrike, though he did spend as much time as he could with her.

Marfisa had to return to Landuc after just a fortnight. Despite the ointment, which had already worked some improvement in her comfort and strength, the cold was painful to her, and it was summer in Landuc. So she left with apologies, promising to return when either she or the weather had mended. I wished she had stayed longer.

It was just a few days after that that Ulrike tapped on my door as I was finishing dressing. I had to sit in the Black Chair that day and so I was in a bit of a hurry.

"Best of the day to you," I said to her, swinging back the door.

"I hope I'm not interrupting—"

"No, as you see I'm up," I had a swallow of my lukewarm coffee, "and running . . ."

"I wanted to ask—"

"Fire away." I gulped the rest of the cup and poured another, warmer one.

"Alexander has invited me to visit him," she said. "Please, may I go?"

Startled, I hiccupped, or swallowed wrong, or something, and made a small explosive noise and then a large one. "I beg your pardon," I said. "To visit him? In Montgard?" I wished she had waited to tell me this; I had to think about the cases before the Chair.

"Yes . . ."

"You're quite free to go, of course," I said. "It's a lovely place." Even with Alexander there, I footnoted mentally. I supposed I should have foreseen something like this; Alexander wouldn't want me polluting her mind or some such drivel, and he wouldn't want to lose face by not seeming interested in the girl, and thus he would invite her to him since he could not come to Argylle. It was how he thought. I took a big bite out of an egg-glazed suncake pastry filled with soft sweet cheese. "When?"

"I thought," she said nervously, "I would very much like to see him, to see Montgard, Father told me about it a little bit . . . If . . . If . . ."

I set down cup and plate and looked at her. "You've not yet drunk of the Spring," I said. "That limits your travelling from Argylle. Is he coming after you? Opening a Way?"

"He says he cannot come, he is very involved in some difficult negotiations, but that if . . . if you or Grandf—or Prospero or . . ." she proposed tremulously.

"You want someone to take you there," I said, wiping my mouth and brushing crumbs from my sleeves.

Ulrike blushed. "It is rather an unreasonable thing to ask," she admitted meekly.

It certainly was. Prospero was in Haimance, warming his winter nights with the enviable company of one of the loveliest vintners, an affair which had been slow to catch but long- and hot-burning. Walter was in town, engrossed in rehearsals of a new choral piece and a visit from most of Shaoll's family, who had come to scrutinize him and now were trying to persuade him and Shaoll to move out of the city and come home to the family's silky-haired goats and market-garden. Belphoebe had left Threshwood to travel with Marfisa awhile. Belphoebe had been concerned over Marfisa's intention of going essentially alone—Tellin, though solicitous and mindful of her mistress's injury, was inexperienced. Offering to go with her sister and her esquire was Phoebe's way of making sure the two, both disinclined to acknowledge any weakness, got home in one piece. Her excuse to Marfisa had been a long-standing invitation from our Uncle Herne to hunt some particularly vicious beast with him.

That left me.

"He can open a Way for you whenever he pleases," I said. "But do let me know—"

"Oh, please, I . . . It is so far, I mean, I thought the journey was not so far—I'm sorry, it is a great deal of trouble," she said, utterly downcast.

I studied her, bemused. She had some unarticulated aversion to passing through a Way. Perhaps she was afraid of coming out in the wrong place—an understandable anxiety, given the trick Gaston had played upon her. To travel to Montgard by way of the Road, the long way around so to speak, did make a certain sense; Montgard was a good place for her to know how to get to. Moreover, perhaps the trip would spur her to drink of the Spring here so that she could travel freely in our domain as well as in Landuc's. Be that as it may, I was busy; I had to run the Dominion and indeed I had to do that directly.

"Let me think on it," I said. "I must go now. That is not a 'No,' merely an 'I have to think about it,' understand?" And I would think about it, but later, not now.

"Thank you," she nodded gratefully.

"You're welcome." Shooing her out ahead of me, I snapped my fingers and Virgil hopped down onto my shoulder. I locked the door and went off to settle the complaints of the citizenry in the Great Hall.

I kept my mind on my work and off Ulrike's request. The business of the Hall was concluded by midafternoon, the time being largely taken up with a complaint lodged by a group of citizens against the Council—they objected to the Council's plan to widen their street. It was a sticky sort of problem—the street would be more heavily travelled if widened, but on the other hand plenty of people were already using it as a shortcut between two squares instead of the commercial street a few blocks over. It was not a well-to-do neighborhood, which was probably why the case had come to me rather than being resolved in Council. Despite Mother's best efforts, the Council tends to be dominated by the wealthier Argyllines, largely because they have leisure for the endless arguments and more to gain from them. After listening to both sides, I sat back and thought for a few minutes.

"Your objection," I said finally to the neighborhood delegation, "is that the heavy usage changes the character of your neighborhood for the worse, and that encouraging this usage by widening the street will further change it."

"Yes, my Lord," said their spokesman.

"And you," I said to the Councillor who had come to explain that side, "desire that traffic shall flow smoothly in the city and that commerce not be hampered."

"The Council's position is that since the street is already heavily travelled, paving and widening it will not change the character of the neighborhood substantially," he said.

"My summary stands," I said drily. I was hampered by not being familiar with the neighborhood and street. Mother had been able to describe almost every street in the town. I did know some districts that well, but I'd never had time for an intensive study of the subject.

I poured myself wine and sipped it, thinking. The street was wide enough for a residential street. It was not wide enough to be a full-time thoroughfare. Shermyn Avenue was the commercial street not far away . . . Carefully I pictured the area to myself.

"The people who live on Numine Street," I asked the delegation, "what are their occupations?"

The delegation conferred in stagey whispers, puzzled.

"Largely," said the spokesman then, "we think most of us are mostly employed in the barge business, my Lord, in many capacities, and there are a lot who work in the Shermyn Avenue shops and a few clerks."

I added that to my picture of the area.

"Councillor Suibert," I said then, "I am always glad to know that the Council is concerned to keep Argylle prosperous and progressing. The campaign of street-widening and street-paving you have undertaken is an admirable thing and one I support fully. And your goal of moving traffic smoothly through the city, so that all may go easily about their business, is also one I support fully.

"The preservation of residential neighborhoods' character has also been something in which the Citadel has taken interest from time to time," I went on. "It troubles me to think that the shops of Shermyn Avenue may be losing custom as a result of people bypassing them and shortcutting through Numine Street, at the expense so to speak of Numine Street's peace and quiet, though Numine Street is a throughway like the others in its area. Therefore Numine Street shall become a double-dead street."

This was a peculiarly Argylline thing, a street that had a patch of park in the middle of its block so that the street led in from both sides and then ended at the park. It was commoner in older districts of the city.

"The Council will pave the street as planned, but not widen it, and the park shall be established under the auspices of the Parks and Gardens Office with the usual participation by the residents."

The residents appeared stunned. The Councillor looked resigned—historically, the Citadel usually squelched the Council when the interests of the lower classes were involved, so he'd probably expected to lose this one.

"But—" said one of the residents, sounding a little unhappy, and then shut up.

I smiled.

"I accept the decision without comment, my Lord," said Councillor Suibert, bowing.

"We yield our complaint, my Lord," said the spokesman for the group, bowing also.

They left the stairs, with much whispering among the citizens.

Utrachet stood. "Is there any who wishes to address the Black Chair for Justice?" he asked the Hall.

No one came forward.

"Justice is done," I said, relieved.

Mother had always liked giving people a bit more than they asked for. The residents of Numine Street probably had not intended to lose their throughway. They were now collectively responsible for the upkeep of the park in the middle, labor and expense, which would enhance the street and put a stop to the heavy traffic. The Council's idea of widening the street was a knee-jerk reaction, and so I wanted the Councillors to remember to examine the alternatives before flat-paving the whole town. I'd seen too many places like that in my travels along Landuc's Road.

Utrachet came up to me and we went back to the Citadel proper together while people cleared out of the Great Hall.

"I hesitate to mention this to you, my Lord, in your present mood," Utrachet began.

"My present mood is one of interest in what's for dinner," I said. "What is it?"

"The cellarer—"

"Oh, bloodrot," I muttered. We were running out of wine space under the Citadel; we had been for years. Mother had never been concerned about it. I knew Utrachet had spoken of it to her, and she had always said she had alternate arrangements ready against that time. But nobody knew what those were, and Mother had died before she had had to use them.

"The problem will be acute in three years, he tells me," Utrachet said. "If we are to expand, we must start soon."

"I'm not sure where we could expand to," I said. "The Catacombs? What if they . . . changed . . . you know they do at times . . . the Maze is quite unpredictable . . . what if we put wine down there and it vanished for a few years? Went past peak?"

Utrachet wasn't sure if I was joking or not. "There are some more stable sections," he said.

"There are. I dislike, also, the idea of the cellarer's staff tramping around down there. Frankly, the place is not for public consumption any more than my wine."

"The Spring. Yes. This is my objection also."

"We'll just have to drink more," I said.

Utrachet smiled. "Unfortunately I don't know that that will help. The problem is that the Haimance wines have done so well, but take so long to mature . . ."

"We went over this last year. I recall the details now." I thought about it. Damn. Gaston had always advocated expanding the cellars. Gaston knew wine so well it was joked that it ran in his veins, and he would have enjoyed designing and supervising the construction of additional Citadel storage space. I wasn't even sure if there were any quarter of the

Island left suited for such a project. "I must think about it. Remind me later."

"Yes, my Lord."

"Thank you, Utrachet." If I were lucky, he'd forget this until the cellarer mentioned it again.

Utrachet bowed slightly.

Anselm was lurking in my office with a stack of routine correspondence for me to sign; I read it all over, signed, and fled to my dinner. Nobody but me was there today. Feeling slightly rejected, I ate quickly and went back to my office to scribble a note to Hicha the Archivist asking for maps of every possible kind of the Citadel and Island and telling her why I wanted them, then sent Anselm off to look them up in the library here and in the Archives. Then I closed the door, retreated to my workroom, and sat in the window looking out.

The weather was cold and rainy.

Suddenly the idea of escorting Ulrike along the Road to Alexander's land did not seem so very unattractive. Montgard was in full bloom of summer now, horse races and picnics being the amusement of the day and masques and dances on the green the amusement of the night.

Uncharitable as it may sound, I also felt that Alexander should take a turn at hosting her. Prospero, Walter, Belphoebe, and I among us couldn't continually attend to her, and she was so shy and clingy that she'd rarely go out or make an acquaintance on her own. She was getting on my nerves. I liked her, she was a pleasant girl, but she wanted a lot of attention and I didn't have time or inclination to hold her hand and guide her through life a step at a time.

At least in deciding she wanted to visit Alexander she was showing some small degree of initiative. I did not know what he had said to her to persuade her to it, nor what Gaston had said about my oldest brother and Montgard—it must have been radiantly glowing. I could not help but remember that her attitude toward me was one of awed, even fearful, respect. However, Ulrike's fervent enthusiasm for travel was welcome, if unprecedented. I would never have expected her to choose an uncomfortable, long journey over simply waiting for Alexander to come here, but since she had done so, surely she should be encouraged and indulged.

Ideally, of course, her enthusiasm would extend to drinking of the Spring and going forth on her own. Her steadfast refusal was not only difficult to understand but difficult to accept. She was one of us, one of Argylle's family, and it was right that she join the accord, the union, of the Spring.

I set up a number of mental arguments to justify the trip while I stared out the window watching the rain fall on the snow.

When it seemed like a good idea, not a flight from tedium, I went to bed to sleep on it.

In the morning, it was sleeting.

"Oh, lovely," I muttered, looking at the ice outside, and shook my head.

Ulrike was writing a letter, reading another and replying to it, at the breakfast-table. She had become fast friends with Lishon Voulouy at New Year's, and they wrote back and forth every other day—or so it seemed. I couldn't imagine what they had to write so much about unless they were reporting on the business of everyone in town.

"Good morning, Gwydion," she said, looking up wide-eyed and covering her letters up with a start as I came in.

"Good morning, Ulrike." I poured myself coffee, propped my feet on one of the empty chairs, and began leafing through the newspaper. Ulrike had scavenged out the social and gossip pages. I snagged them back from her unapologetically and read the latest rumors and scandals and false allegations, then went on to the prosaic and dull news of ship arrivals and cargoes in Ollol, wine futures, and caravan reports. It tasted like cardboard in my mouth, the dry everydayness of it . . .

Irritated by the banality of the editorial comments, I folded the whole thing into a paper hat with a paper cockade and dropped it on my oblivious sister's head. Ulrike jumped.

"Gwydion!"

I laughed at her. "We leave tomorrow, or maybe the day after."

"What?"

"I'll take you to Montgard."

"You *will?*" she squeaked.

"I will."

"Oh, Gwydion!" Delighted, she jumped up, losing the paper hat, and ran around the table and gave me a hug around the neck and a kiss on the cheek.

"Hey!" I said, embarrassed by the unusual display. "Sit down, kid. Or better, make a list of things you need that you can fit in your saddlebags and go pack."

Ulrike released me. "I'm so glad! How can you leave?"

"Nothing important is happening," I said. Which was exactly true. It was all utterly ordinary.

I felt a little guilty about leaving town and sticking Walter with the job of substituting for me. I'd decided to work several tasks at once into the journey. Delivering Ulrike to Montgard meant that we had to cross the Border Ranges, so I would ride through the Border more slowly on my return and check the area out. Argylle had agents in several Eddies along the way, off the Road and near it, and I thought it might be good to shake them up a bit with a surprise visit. Mother had done that sort of thing, after all. Lastly, the origins of the monster plague were still unclear, although the best explanation still seemed to be that an Eddy had ruptured. Therefore I meant to do some sorcerous work and see if I could pinpoint any disruptions in the Spring's flow and then correlate the disruptions with beastly intrusions.

Thus I found ample justification for taking a trip out of

town. And I'd be gone no more than two months; finished or not, I felt I should return to Argylle after that.

Walter was entirely agreeable about taking over for that time. "You ought to visit Montgard for a while, Gwydion," he said when I talked to him about it later that day. "Enjoy yourself a bit."

"I might do that," I said in a probably-not tone of voice.

"I know you and Alex get along like paraffin and fire," he added with a little smile, "but in the event that he and Ulrike don't harmonize, you might bide there so you can bring her home."

"Perhaps. I hope this won't hamper your own work too much." Walter was fully as busy as I, with more interesting things. I felt guilty about pulling him away from them for a frivolous reason like this.

He laughed. "Let me worry about that, Gwydion. No, it will not. I can delegate some of the rehearsal time, and mainly what I'll be doing in the Citadel will be caretaking. The Council has been very meek since you shooed that dragon away. I doubt anything important will come up, just busy-work."

I hoped he wouldn't leave me a huge stack of unfinished business to attend to, and then I shrugged. That was the price of a holiday. And by the time I got back, the weather would be better and I'd have a fresh eye for things like the wine-cellar problem. Really, this was the best thing for me to do just now. Hadn't my tutor always counselled me that sometimes the only thing to do with a problem is to let be and review it later?

"Well enough, then," I said. "Don't drink me dry, and have fun, and all that."

"Always, Gwydion. When shall you leave?"

"I was thinking of leaving in two days. The full moon is then and there are lots of directions open."

Walter nodded. "Fine. I'll be ready."

"Come over tomorrow and we can go over current busi-

ness. There isn't much. Come in the afternoon and stay for
supper, if you can . . ."

"Sounds great. See you then."

In due course Walter came over. I briefed him on the
unfinished business I was leaving him and briefed him on the
stuff I didn't expect him to worry about so that he'd know
about it. Afterward we had a casual supper and sat around
drinking afterward telling each other embarrassing and
funny anecdotes about our friends and older relatives, and
finally we went off to bed after Walter gave me a lot of
messages for people he thought he knew in Montgard.

⌒ 14 ⌒

THE NEXT DAY WE LEFT AT midmorning. Shaoll and Walter ate
breakfast with us and bade us farewell at the Iron Bridge,
arm in arm, the picture of a happy couple. Looking at them,
I wished very much that I too had someone to wave good-bye
with like that. Anselm and Hicha the Archivist, with whom
I had done last-minute business at breakfast, waved from the
tall lily-and-rose decorated front doors of the Citadel, and
Ulrike waved back; I lifted my hand and then focused my
attention on the journey, closing my eyes and letting Cosmo
take us out at a slow walk.

Ulrike was sensibly dressed in breeches and a heavy cloak;
she had her hair up under a hat and looked like a boy at first
glance, which was smart of her if it was intentional. We
travelled light, carrying only a few spare clothes and some
food and water. I rode Cosmo and she had a sedate, good-
natured honey-colored palfrey named Daffodil. Virgil rode
my left shoulder contentedly, making brief forays away from
us from time to time to hunt for himself as we travelled on
the Road.

I had refreshed my memory of the route from an Ephemeris and a Map of Pheyarcet's Roads and Leys. Getting near Montgard was a straightforward (so to speak) enough journey; getting into it would be trickier. The place has few approaches. Gaston chose it for defensibility for reasons of his own and later he had found it a convenient and pleasant hideaway for rendezvousing with Freia, and later still a perfect secluded place to conceal their first-born children Alexander and Marfisa from the world. But he had long since stepped down from ruling as their Prince and handed it over to Alexander; Marfisa wasn't interested in it for herself and spent her time in other places, on her own affairs of which she said little. Alexander had dwelt there—when he wasn't in Landuc—ever since.

The route I intended to use from the Border to Montgard was not the most direct, but it had no seasonal or time-dependent Nexuses along it, and it passed through a couple of important Nodes. It was a relatively simple one with which Ulrike ought to be familiar. Our path to the Border from the Citadel I chose for its directness, on the principle that it is always good to know a fast way home to safety.

I began to feel the flow of the Spring which surrounded us. I sank into it, let it suffuse me and fit itself to me as I fit myself to it. The Spring was the center of everything, the center of my being, and from it radiated the Roads and the weaker Leys, the shifting pulses of a cycling tide. I turned Cosmo's head to the south, to ride along the Boulevard, and felt the constriction in the Road ahead at the South or Errethon Gate, felt the pulse of a Node not far outside the town and a relatively minor Nexus at a fountain as we passed it.

We rode through the town quickly to the Errethon Gate. As we passed through it I felt the disconcerting flicker that was the perimeter of the city pass by. Ulrike moved closer to me, riding beside me. I smiled at her.

"Feel that Node? That's the Crow's Tree," I told her, and then realized she couldn't feel it; she hadn't drunk of the Spring.

Ulrike shook her head.

"That one," I pointed at it, a solitary giant at a Y in the road ahead, which had been used as a gibbet from time to time and whose trunk was studded with nails, one for each hanged man or woman. It was laden with wet snow now, and snow whitened the usually black ground beneath its branches on which last year's leaves rattled like bones. The Y at which it stood had one arm that was paved and worn as this road that we were on now, and another arm that was little more than a track, the vaguest sunken outline of a way on the ground. "We'll bear right there," I added, and we did, and with that turn we left the Errethon Road of Argylle and moved onto the real Road, the Road that went by its own non-geometrical and mysterious ways to places that were not on this globe and places that were and to places that weren't really anyplace at all, the Road that rippled around us like the water of an insubstantial and powerful river, and that had its source, as all things in Argylle's domain did, in the Spring beneath the Citadel. We left no hoofprints in the snow beneath the oak.

Ulrike rode closer still to me. We passed phantom towns, unseen by our ghostly fellow-travellers; I felt the pulse and pound and pull of the Nodes and Nexuses and the leakage of the Leys we passed, and ignored them. This was the fastest and easiest way out of Argylle to the Border. There were a few knots (so to speak) in it, complicated Nexuses where we would have to say or do the right things or be there at the right time in order to go on, but by and large it was open Road. Pheyarcet's Roads are less straightforward than Argylle's, all in all; Panurgus built obstacles in certain places and modified the Road itself to improve Landuc's situation in the heart of Pheyarcet. Mother hadn't had the ability to do that, nor had Prospero evidently; at any rate Argylle's Dominion was much as it was in the beginning—which simplified travel considerably.

We rode at a good speed through wastelands and weird

landscapes and one place that terrified Ulrike so that she seized my hand as Daffodil shied with fear—a dark, humid, and warm spot of Nothingness where there was no sound nor direction nor sensation to be had, where there was nothing but the Road to carry us on.

I talked to Ulrike as we rode along, starting by asking if she had been in the Border Range between Landuc and Argylle before. She had not. So I told her something of that place.

"It is a strange environment," I said. "Things come and go there. There are fluxes that pass through, changing things. In the area called the Mountains of Madness . . . perhaps you had better just avoid it for now until you have a bit more experience."

"Are we going through there?"

"No. We're going to take the most direct route I could find across the Border. It will still take us a few days. We will pass the nights in the huts and waystations that are there. If we're lucky," I added hopefully, "there'll be a caravan going through." There would be stories and news and perhaps a trader or two I knew, fellowship in the dark starless nights.

"Father said there is a lot of trade up and down the Border, but he didn't know much of it . . . He said people from Landuc don't go there."

"They cannot pass the peaks on their side, that is true."

"Why is that?"

"That was one of the results of the Independence War," I said. "I can give you a book about it. It was one of the concessions Landuc made, that the Border is not under its influence. And it wasn't anyway—it is complicated."

Ulrike nodded. "Father said it was a dangerous place."

"Oh, not all that dangerous if you know where you're going. Which I do. And if you stick to the trail it's safe as houses."

"Is the trail charmed? Like the Road?"

"No, no, no. Of course not. There are no Roads in the

Border. Sorcery doesn't work there. Most sorcery," I corrected myself.

"Why not?" she asked.

"Because it's between. It's . . . it's neutral, you see," I said. "Picture . . . hm, picture two equal circles, interpenetrating. There's a vesica where they overlap. Rather than both of them dominating there, consider that the circles, one Argylle's Spring, one Landuc's Well, cancel each other out."

Ulrike digested this. "Can we use our Keys there?"

"Sometimes. It's unpredictable."

"That *is* dangerous, then," she decided.

I shrugged. "So is getting out of bed."

My sister blinked, taken off guard by this, and said nothing more.

We broke to rest the horses and have a snack in a dark, cool forest by a stream whose boulders were covered deeply with velvety blue moss. Virgil caught up with us (he'd been missing for an hour or so) and perched on Cosmo's saddle, preening meticulously. I took out the Map of Pheyarcet which I had brought with me and showed her our path from the Border to Montgard once we had crossed it.

"This is not so direct . . ." Ulrike said, tracing it with her finger. "Wouldn't this be better?"

"No. You see this Ley here which connects these two Nexuses? I don't know what kind of condition it's in. It is not in a much-travelled part of the world and it could be very difficult to follow. I am sticking to the Road on this trip, so that you will know a fast way into a safe place if you should need it."

"Oh . . ." Ulrike nodded with understanding.

"Yes. See, from this Nexus here, you could, if you wished, change course at the standing stone and head toward Landuc. If you wished. And here, at the well—see the mark?— here is an inn that is a popular place for people from Landuc to stay, a good place to run to if you're ever in trouble in that area. Look, you can take this Ley, or this leg of the Road, or this or this to get there . . ." and I showed her several spots of interest as we lunched.

She had never seen a Map of this kind before, though certainly Gaston had had at least one for each of the two realms, Argylle's and Landuc's, he moved in. I supposed he had been keeping Ulrike ignorant so that she would not make a beeline for Huhanwa when he had sent her forth from him. Heartless, some might say—but she did need to get out on her own. A cleverer person might recall details of the rides along Leys and the Road she said he had taken her on, might have noted the route they followed into Landuc, but Ulrike, a born follower, had not done those things, so Huhanwa's location was as great a mystery as ever. Perforce we must leave it thus. Gaston would come around in his own time, no matter what Alexander thought or said.

"And these are all the Roads, all the world there is," Ulrike said, sitting back on her heels.

"No, this is not all there is," I corrected her. "But this is all that we can use. The Road leads into places where we cannot survive without special protections, sorcerous or physical, against poison gases, extreme conditions of heat or cold, hostile places not for us. We think there is life there, but we are not inclined to investigate."

"If it is poisonous—"

"There are other kinds of life and living things than ours. We only see what is harmonious with us."

We mounted and rode on then, pushing on toward the Node where I meant to stop for a longer rest—a busy village with a few good inns, where two Leys crossed the Road. There we could sleep.

In due course and without incident of any kind we attained the village, chose an inn which featured a plump and cheery red pony on its sign, and took rooms there for the night. I sent Virgil off to keep watch from the roof.

The beer was very good and the food was fine country fare, substantial and filling. Since my sister had not drunk of

Argylle's Spring, the language was strange to her, and so Ulrike retired after we ate. I went for a stroll through the village and then listened, smoking a long clay pipe of the native tobacco, as the locals and other travellers traded stories and songs in the common room.

I slept well, a pleasant holiday-feeling stealing over me as I lay in my bed listening to the little night sounds without. Travelling is a seductive occupation. If I'd been alone, I'd have altered my journey somewhat, taken longer to get to Montgard than we would, but I supposed I could just drop Ulrike off there and then fare forth on my own business.

In the morning I purchased more food for us and we set out in a light rain, which was soon left behind. Our course moved back to the Road outside the village at an ancient cairn onto which we each tossed a rock before continuing on, attaining the Road thereby. I intended to push us now and make the Border our next stopover. Thus we rode harder, Virgil hanging onto the saddlebags behind me this time.

The Border is a stark and uninviting-looking place. The valley that runs between the two steep mountain ranges is not so unpleasant, but the mountains themselves are inhospitable and the trails are not for the faint-hearted. We entered the foothills as the light was fading from the sky and I hurried us along to a hut marked on my map, which we reached by lantern-light in the perfect blackness that is the Border night.

There was no one else there. It was the standard unattended wayfarer's hut for the mountains, built to provide refuge for any traveller who needed it, maintained by the donations of caravan merchants and traders' and craftsmen's guild associations. These huts are sprinkled about and are an essential part of the tracks that wind through the mountains; without them, few would travel those mountains because few would care to be out in the open at night.

Ulrike and I fed and watered the horses and left them in their side of the building (half for people, half for animals). There was peat, and it was chill in the stone hut, so I made a fire in the cylindrical stove. We ate cold meat and bread and rolled up in our cloaks on the uncushioned bunks without much talk. I tried to lighten Ulrike with suggestions of things she might do in Montgard, but she found the place oppressive and answered me distractedly, so I left it, played catch with Virgil for a few minutes to calm him down a bit (he dislikes the Border intensely), and then turned in.

The fire had gone out by morning. We yawned, had a bite and a drink and gave the horses the same, and started out again.

"We shall go over the pass, there," I pointed it out to my sister, "and be in the Valley at nightfall."

"It's so high!"

I nodded.

"The mountains of Huhanwa are not so high as this, and there are growing things there," she murmured, looking around at the arid rockscape.

"This is the way it is because the Spring's influence is almost nonexistent here," I said, and we followed a path marked with pillars of rough-dressed stone up the grey severe mountainside toward the deep-notched pass.

In the pass, we rested. We had taken longer than I'd expected to reach it, but we had plenty of time to get down to the Valley still. I took out a spyglass I had brought and surveyed the Valley.

"What do you see?" Ulrike asked me, shading her eyes and squinting in that direction also.

"A caravan I think across over there . . . yes. A goodly one, too. There is a waystation . . . it's hard to say how far off, distance doesn't mean much in here . . . anyway we shall stop there this night. I daresay they'll get there first if that's their destination. Going downhill here is as hard as going up and we must walk the horses." I closed the glass with a snap and put it back in its case.

"Beautiful, isn't it?" I added.

She looked around at the grey rock of the mountains, the

bleached-looking grass, the bone-white, directionless, bright sky, and said, "Um . . ."

"In its way."

"I guess so."

I laughed and got out a water-bottle for a drink. The wind hissed and whistled through the stones. Desolation of the purest, most sterile kind surrounded us, but the air was diamond-sharp and diamond-pure. I looked back, toward Argylle's Dominion, and ahead, into the Valley, and pulled my cloak around me to keep the cold, dry wind from my neck. Ulrike fidgeted with her saddlebags, had a drink also, and waited for me. Virgil had gone hunting for mice, though he knew as well as I there were none hereabouts.

I took a last look in the direction of Argylle and walked back toward her.

"We'd best—" I began, and Ulrike screamed and pointed, staring up and past me and starting away. Daffodil whinnied and reared and jumped away from her, pelting off down the mountainside, as I whirled to see something I did not want to see at all, now or ever.

Wings widespread, claws ready, Gemnamnon dropped into the pass.

⌒ 15 ⌒

DISBELIEF HELD ME PARALYZED FOR ONLY an instant. "Run!" I yelled to Ulrike. "Get out of here!" She was already running, though, and I ran too, out of the dragon's immediate reach. I stopped at the lip of the pass.

Ulrike didn't stop to ask questions; slipping and sliding, she raced down toward the Valley. I tried a lightning-bolt spell; it snapped weakly and did nothing. I tried a general-purpose explosive spell I had found handy in the past; it fizzled.

The dragon laughed but did not come closer than his landing-place.

"You are far from home, foolish sorcerer," he boomed, and casually fired a gout of flame at a rock, which exploded with the heat. I shielded my face with my cloak.

His eyes were healed. I drew my sword with a feeling of futility. I wore my gold-and-black mail over a light gambeson; I had no other body armor. Cosmo, bless his heart, hadn't run; he nudged me from behind. I jumped about a yard.

Gemnamnon laughed at me again. "Mount, mount, O Fool of Argylle," he encouraged me. "Perhaps I shall leave you here the nonce, for I know you cannot go far with your pathetic little sorceries, and come back for you when I have picked up that silly girl . . ." He laughed again, a deafening, numbing sound that filled the pass and bounced off the rocks, and he launched himself, laughing still, into the air. His wings stroked and made a great wind, and then he was airborne and swooping down toward the Valley.

Sick and giddy with fear for my sister, I ran to the edge of the Pass; I could not see Ulrike, but Gemnamnon was circling out and around . . .

"Ulrike! Your Keys! Try your Keys!" I screamed, panicking. "Ulrike! Use your Keys!" They might not work, but it was her only chance.

No answer, no sight of her. I shook. Below, Daffodil suddenly bolted into sight along a steep bit of the trail, and the dragon buzzed the horse and sent her, racing blindly in a panic, off the edge of the cliff. The animal's scream carried up to me.

Where was Ulrike?

"She's gone!" I cried to Gemnamnon, and I prayed it was true.

His laughter went on. He dropped to the mountainside again and began tearing at some rocks, tossing boulders as I might toss a football, and suddenly his mighty clawed foot paused in midair and then reached down more slowly and carefully.

I screamed "No!" as he picked Ulrike up. She was limp. Fainted, I hoped.

Gemnamnon laughed still as he went into the air again and flew up, up, around.

I could barely breathe. I wept with rage and frustration. There was nothing I could do to get her from him. My sorcery was no good, and my sword wasn't going to be much good either, and if Dewar were going to rescue us he would have done it already. I recognized that I was going to die, and a curiously calming clarity came with the thought; it would happen now, rather than later. I was glad that I had put things in a tidy state before leaving Argylle.

My horse nudged me again; I grabbed his bridle and said, "Get yourself out of here. You know the way home," and let go and slapped his rump. "Go!" I ordered him, and slapped him again. Cosmo took off without looking back, stones flying from beneath his hooves as he raced back through the pass toward Argylle. Relieved, probably. If he made it back to the Citadel, at least they would know there that something had happened to us.

The dragon finished his lazy victory rolls and plummeted into the pass again, making a neat three-point landing, still holding Ulrike carefully in one mighty set of claws. He hadn't crushed her. She wasn't moving, though.

Gemnamnon laughed at me still.

"You see, Fool of Argylle, how useless it is to oppose such as me. I am older than your Spring, and stronger than your sorcery, and I shall exist and persist long after you are dust and your realm has faded away into the Void. And that first shall be sooner, not later." He laughed again. He set Ulrike down before him and reared back, glaring down at me.

"Let her go," I said, shaking.

"You are a greater fool than you seemed," he sneered. "Let her go? As soon let you go."

"Release her! Or you shall have Gaston the Fireduke himself on your slot, lizard, and I think his reputation might have reached even your cotton-filled ears!"

"Gaston! The Duke is hardly a threat to make *me* shake," he laughed, and flamed and blew up another rock.

The noise of this apparently woke Ulrike. She jerked upright and then screamed and bolted, trying to get away. Gemnamnon plopped a clawed foot in front of her; she pulled up short and shrieked "Gwydion!"

"I . . . Let her *go!*" I screamed in impotent rage.

"For what?" he laughed. "For what, Fool of Argylle? For what?"

I had nothing to bargain with. Tears of impotent frustration stung my eyes.

"For your life," gravelled something as loudly as the dragon's laughter, off to my right.

My head moved so fast I nearly broke my neck. My breath went in and stopped halfway through my throat.

Gemnamnon's laugh rumbled to a halt.

Hunched, tense, and as big as Gemnamnon, golden and oozing power and confidence, wings half-spread, a Gryphon was perched on the top of the cliff that formed one side of the notched pass, and its eyes burned like two suns, and its beak and the claws on its massive feathered forelegs looked like bronze, glittering in the white light of the Border. The claws tightened slightly. Stone crumbled in them and rattled down, the only sound.

"These are *mine,*" rasped the Gryphon, and sat back on its haunches, which were covered in sulphur-colored downy feathers or fur. Its wings extended more fully, twitching, and its tail flicked from side to side.

The two beasts stared at one another, rigid and silent for a few dozen of my racing heartbeats.

I had seen gryphons before. This one was ten times the size of even the largest female. I forgot to breathe, looking at it.

Showing miraculous presence of mind, Ulrike suddenly

darted around the dragon's claws. He snatched at her, but she leapt aside, and he swatted at her again and again as she sprinted, faster than I'd seen even Belphoebe move, toward me and past me. I turned and followed her.

"Begone, children of Argylle!" cried the Gryphon. Gemnamnon answered with a thunderous noise that sent more rocks falling from precarious places. We heard the Gryphon scream and the dragon roar, and we did not linger to watch or place bets on the outcome.

Nearly flying ourselves, jumping from rock to rock and down the slope, we skidded and rolled and plunged while the howls and snarls of the monstrous fight filled our ears. We had gone about a quarter of a mile in maybe a quarter of a minute when I hurtled and stumbled and caught up to Ulrike as a rock moved under her foot and threw her aside. She steadied herself on my arm and started off again, dragging me.

"Keys," I gasped, my lungs aching, wanting to vomit from the fear, and pulled mine out. If they worked, we could get out of here, really out—

"The dragon!" she shrieked, distraught with fright, and I yanked her back and down and looked up just as a fountain of rocks and dirt blew up in the pass and the Gryphon and Gemnamnon took to the air both at once. Small stones, pebbles, and dust rained down on us. I shielded my head with my arm, crouching over her.

"We have a minute, and that's all we need," I said, keeping a death-tight grip on her arm lest she bolt and taking out my flint-and-steel. "Hold onto my arm!" I glanced up and saw that Gemnamnon had taken a long scoring down his side and that the Gryphon, though singed, appeared to be unharmed. Gemnamnon spotted us and started toward us, but the Gryphon intercepted him, raking a wing with its glittering foreclaws. Praying that we were in one of the Border's "hot spots" where lesser sorceries at least worked, I gibbered the spell to make contact with Alexander, whose Key was the one I'd grabbed first. For the fire I tore off my cloak and lit it, which caught and smoldered while I rattled off the Way-opening spell faster than I'd ever said anything. The time-consuming double spell was necessary to find Alexander and then to open a Way between us. I drew upon Ulrike's and my Keys and the spell was complete; the cloth burst into flames as sorcerous energy poured into the fire.

"Gwydion?" Alexander said, sounding startled, as the spell strengthened around us. He appeared, golden-tinted, in the flames. "Whatever are you—"

"Let us come to you!" I screamed, hearing the screams of the Gryphon doppling nearer, as Ulrike tried to bolt again and hauled me off balance. Bodies passed overhead, shadow-ing us; I didn't dare look up. A blast of heat; foul-smelling gas—the flames flattened down—

"Come then! Come!" our brother said, and he spoke the words easing the passage at his end, and I lifted and shoved the flailing Ulrike at him through the fire and followed her, falling into Alexander.

Water sloshed over me and steam hissed. I lost my footing and went down with a mighty splash, hearing Ulrike begin-ning to sob and howl with terror. A fountain had been Alex-ander's focus for the sending; we were in some garden. The fire, in the brief moment of connection, had made the steam. I thrashed to my feet, barking my knuckles.

Without saying anything, Alexander grabbed my arm and helped me out and half-dragged me over a white gravel path to a white bench supported by smirking white limestone putti. He had Ulrike encircled in his other arm, and she clung to him as a drowning man must hold onto a spar, making muffled, irrational noises in his shoulder. I was shaking now too, almost limp with fear and the delayed reaction. Alexan-der shoved me down onto the bench, staring at me and her alternately, and sat down with her and held her and shushed her, gripping my shoulder for a moment as I hauled myself back under control.

"What happened?" he asked after perhaps twenty minutes had passed and I had slumped back, eyes closed, still trembling.

"Dragon," I whispered.

Ulrike whimpered incoherently and Alexander patted her back and hushed her again.

"*The* dragon," he guessed.

"Gemnamnon."

"Where?"

"Border. Argylle side. In a pass."

He snorted softly and quieted Ulrike, who was starting to sob again.

"You're all right though," he said after a moment.

"Tell you . . . tell you . . . later . . ."

"You need a drink," Alexander said. "Can you walk?" He rose, picking Ulrike up. She put her arms around his neck and held on tightly, with her face still buried in his shoulder.

"Guess so." Still shaking, I got to my feet and followed him as he carried our sister through the garden, which was formally kept, across a wide lawn and through a conservatory and into a house I now recalled from other visits. The conservatory was new.

About four ounces of whisky later, Ulrike was calm enough to be put to bed. We did just that, pulling off her boots and outer clothing. Alexander assigned a maid to sit with her. I poured another stiff drink for myself, putting some water in this time.

"So what happened? You're not hurt, she's not hurt, you're both scared shitless," he observed, lifting his eyebrows.

"Alexander, I . . . ." I controlled my temper and my voice. "You'd have crapped yourself, buddy," I said after a moment. "The dragon dropped down on us like a hawk on a rabbit in a pass on the Argylle side of the Border Range. I

told Ulrike to run. She ran. My spells . . . I threw a couple
at him; they fizzled. You know it's hard to use sorcery there.
Gemnamnon laughed at me and went chasing after Ulrike
after a few taunts to me. He hauled apart the mountainside
to pull her out of a cave or cleft she'd run into below and
picked her up and flew around with her. I think she was
unconscious. I couldn't do a damn thing. Nothing. He
landed and boasted some more. I said that if he didn't let her
go Gaston would be hunting for him, and he sneered at that.
Ulrike came to and tried to run; he blocked her . . . it was like
a cat with a mouse, Alex . . . I couldn't do anything, nothing,
I had my sword and that's all and I couldn't—couldn't— I
screamed at him to let her go, and he asked, laughing, what
for—and this . . . a Gryphon answered him, for his life."

I stopped and had a gulp of whisky. "A Gryphon, Alex, as
big as the dragon, or bigger, and . . . and . . . nothing like the
Jagged Mountains' ones . . . bigger . . . brighter . . . It was
hanging onto the cliff side of the pass. It said that . . . we were
Argylle's . . . and told us to get out of there . . . we ran and
they . . . fought."

"Now *that* is something I would like to see," said Alexander.

I snorted a laugh, perhaps a bit high-pitched. "The hell
you would! I'll send you over and you can watch if you
please, and you can tell me about it from beyond the grave.
Gemnamnon was trying to buzz and torch us as we called
you. The Gryphon was interfering."

"Hm." Alexander frowned a little and slouched in his
chair. "Whence did the gryphon come? I have never heard of
them in the Border."

"It was no ordinary one. I know that much. It was—it was
like—" I shook my head. "Like looking into the sun," I
concluded.

My brother tipped his head back and considered me, and
I regarded him, and we didn't say anything while I finished
the whisky.

"I am glad you made it," he said finally.

"Me too. I shall have to go after that cursed creature now. We cannot have him in the Border."

"Where did you banish him to before?"

"Away, far away," I lied. "Not the Border. A wasteland."

Alexander's mouth twitched. "Evidently he found it not to his taste."

"Yes."

"Why did you not kill him?"

"What? Just now?" I stared at him.

"When you had him on Longview."

"I couldn't. I was barely able to do what I did." I wanted to steer the conversation in some other direction. That great ugly lie, as ugly as the dragon, made me just as uncomfortable. I was not a facile liar, lacking any practice, and the more I talked about that duel with Gemnamnon, the more I feared slipping up and being exposed by my lie. Although, if worse came to worst, it was no obvious harm to tell people the truth, still I had no way of knowing what Dewar was up to and I wanted to find that out for myself before trumpeting that I'd seen him. An archetypal sorcerer, with a sorcerer's ingrained secrecy, he wouldn't thank me for letting people know that he was using Ariel, or even that he was keeping himself well-informed on local affairs. "This is near Montgard, isn't it?" I asked.

"Yes, it is," he said.

"I thought I remembered the house. Isn't that a new conservatory? It looks handsomely done."

"Thank you. I had it built a couple years ago when I found I must spend more time here in the winters. It's very pleasant. Heated. Come, I'll show it to you," he said, rising, and I rose too.

"I think I'd like to put on dry clothes first, if I may," I said. I'd stripped off the wettest outer layer and my mail, but I was still clammy and warm.

"Of course. How unobservant of me. You frightened the

carp out of a year's growth, I'm sure," Alex remarked, and he led me to a guest room and got me dry clothing.

I changed and did a Lesser Summoning of Walter. Amazingly, I hadn't lost my bag of tricks.

"Hullo there," he said cheerily, reaching forward and lighting a couple more candles. The image in my mirror grew correspondingly in size and resolution. He was in one of the Citadel music rooms; I recognized the pianoforte at which he sat. "All's well, Gwydion."

"I'm afraid it may not be for long, Walt. We met Gemnamnon in the Border."

Walter stared at me, his bouncy good cheer becoming shocked concern. "The dragon?"

"The very same one," I said. "I shall be back soon. We are at Alex's house now."

"You're unhurt, though?"

"Yes. I'll tell you the full tale when I get there, but keep an eye to the skies and the outlying areas. Let Phoebe know we may have more trouble with the damned beast and ask her to hurry home with due caution when she can."

It was possible that the Gryphon had killed the dragon, but I wanted to take no chances. If he didn't turn up in Argylle, perhaps I ought to go looking for him.

Or I could just fall on my sword and deprive Gemnamnon of the pleasure of gutting me.

"Gwydion?"

"Thinking. Sorry. Um," I collected myself, "Ulrike will stay here; it's safer, I think, and on my way back I'll ask around and see if I can find anything more about him . . ."

Walter nodded. "Whatever you want, Gwydion. You're in command."

"Please tell Prospero about this also. He might want to think about getting his ass out of Haimance and down into Argylle City."

"He'll not like that." Walter grinned meaningfully.

I gestured impatiently. "Then she can visit, I don't give a

fig, but if I come home and find a burned-out city and Cita-del—"

"Surely we shall not come to that, Gwydion. If there is trouble or the rumor of it, I shall Summon you at once."

"Good. I had better go."

"All right. Safe journey, Gwydion."

"Good-bye, Walter. And thanks."

"It's no trouble." He shrugged, waving, good-natured again.

I snuffed the candle and sat down on the end of the bed.

I could not permit Gemnamnon to rampage around the Border or the Road. As Lord of Argylle, I was responsible not only for my immediate surroundings but for everything from the Spring to the Border. It was my job to form some plan to rid us of the dragon permanently and carry it out.

Where had that Gryphon come from? It was no ordinary one. The gryphons of the Jagged Mountains are scarce nowadays, and have been so since around the time of the Independence War; some plague crashed the population and it never recovered. They had long since retreated to the Western Wastes. I had seen two in my lifetime when travelling around out there with Belphoebe. Gryphons were not so big as that nor so powerful as that—the thing had been a veritable Node in and of itself, out of place in the Border, as out of place as Gemnamnon.

Maybe Prospero or Belphoebe would have some illumination to shed on that face of the encounter. I made a mental note to myself to ask them. The twins had never spent much time in Argylle and thus were not such good sources of lore and information, trivial and important, about the place.

Then I sighed. My holiday was shattered. I had been starting to really relish the idea of time off, time to myself, time to be Gwydion and not the Lord of Argylle, to be a nobody and just poke around on my own. If I lived through this, I swore I'd take a year off. If I lived.

16

ALEXANDER'S COUNTRY HOUSE WAS ONE OF those perfect places in which it is so comfortable to pass an hour, a day, or a year that the guest can hardly bear to leave. Particularly the guest who knows there is something large and dangerous waiting to pick a fight with him somewhere out in the wide world. I ought to have hit the Road again at once; instead, I delayed.

I spent most of the afternoon just walking around Alexander's garden; he left me alone and went and made himself agreeable to Ulrike, who had awakened and risen. When I strolled up to the house for the evening meal I found them laughing and talking together in a summerhouse with apéritifs and hors d'oeuvres. She showed remarkably few ill effects from her horrible introduction to the dragon, perhaps laughing a little brightly and talking a little too fast. Watching her as I approached, I was struck by the realization that we had gotten off lightly; at the very least, there could have been grave injuries. But there Ulrike was, almost as effervescent as Tellin, well and sound.

Alexander was charming her, I could see; she was happy to be charmed. He was petting and spoiling her, making plans to take her hither and yon and for parties and all that sort of thing, and he had shortened her name to Rikki, which was, I had to admit, rather cuter than the somewhat mournful Ulrike.

So I poured myself an apéritif, helped myself to little vegetables with dabs of this and that on them, and sat off to one side, listening to them with one ear and looking at the light and water playing together in a fountain not far off.

"Gwydion, be happy," Alexander said. "You are alive;

you are not presently filling a dragon's crop; moreover you have a most worthy opponent to challenge your swordplay and sorcery. Furthermore we are honored by the company of our delightful youngest sister."

Ulrike giggled. "Oh, Alex."

"Thus," Alexander went on, "Fortuna has given you everything a man of our blood could want. Stop moping, for heaven's sake. There is nothing you can do this minute, is there?"

I glared at him. "Alexander, I have to think of a way to either permanently discourage or destroy Gemnamnon. I prefer to do it sooner rather than later. I assume he is not sitting around composing quatrains on the elegance and surpassing excellence of some horse."

Alexander reddened. He had once done exactly that. He was drunk at the time, but Walter had heard about it and set the abominable poetry to music and sung it at a dinner party where Alexander was also a guest.

"Then get going on it," he said indifferently then. "Rid us of this scaly plague."

"You could offer assistance," I snapped.

"I am not the Lord of Argylle, and this is an Argylline difficulty," Alexander retorted. "I *would* suggest, *if* you were of a mind to listen, that you must either master him in his element or take him utterly out of it and vanquish him there. That is merely a philosophical chestnut, though, one which I am sure *you,* as notoriously clever as you are, have already applied to your possible solutions."

My reply to that was on my tongue when Ulrike interrupted me.

"Gwydion," she said, "Alexander was asking me just where Grandfa—where Prospero is visiting and I could not remember it; can you remind me of it please?"

"He is in Haimance," I said after a few seconds, "at Zhuéra Pellean's." I spoke through a tight jaw, though I saw perfectly well what she was trying to do. It was the right thing, to forestall a quarrel.

"That was it," she said. "Are the Voulouy family not related?"

"In some way or other," I said. "In Haimance, probably in several. It is a little turned in on itself, that district."

Alexander said something civil about the Pelleans, and the conversation went on in a more courteous and appropriate way.

"You've become quite domestic," I said to Alex the second day I was there. "The conservatory, the renovations . . . You are not thinking of marrying or anything like that, are you?" I said it lightly, banteringly, not offensively; it could be a touchy subject, but I was curious.

He laughed and then grinned. "Not in the slightest," he said, "never less than now, indeed. Why bother? I can get any benefit I would from having a wife from my staff or the local ladies, who count some uncommonly attractive creatures among their number. In fact, one of them is coming to lunch tomorrow with a couple of sisters and a cousin or two and some miscellaneous other friends and relations so that Rikki may begin making some acquaintances in the neighborhood."

"Which is the attractive one?" One of his mistresses, probably.

"You must judge for yourself. They are none of them bad-looking, I can tell you that. Any of them would be an ornament to the Palace in Landuc in any capacity."

"There's an idea," I said, "establish a harem . . ."

"As much work as having a wife," snorted Alexander, laughing. "And they'd ever be bickering and what-not too. Nay, the status quo contents me, and the status shall be quo for a long, long, *long* time to come."

"Good," I said. "Walter has been circling that weaver more and more closely."

"Walter has always been the domestic sort. Father and

Mother shouldn't have allowed him to run off and get married so young. It has skewed his thinking."

"He seems happy to me," I said.

"He's happy, but he's always looking for something he will never find," Alexander said. "Emily is gone. He shouldn't have married her. She was an ephemeron. He wanted, and he wants still, to find someone who will be there all his life, and it should be obvious that in our family this is the glaring exception, not the rule."

"Particularly considering the temperaments of our aunts and our lack of female cousins," I agreed, steering away from the subject of our parents with a gut instinct for avoidance. Talking with Alexander is like walking the wire for me.

"Speaking of female relations, Neyphile was setting little sticky lines for Uncle Fulgens lately," Alexander said.

I laughed at the idea.

"I know. The image that comes to my mind is of a Faphatan cat courting a bull. Fulgens found some urgent and engrossing business out of town and took to his heels."

"Wise of him."

"The woman is transparent. I wonder if she realizes that. Are you staying, then?"

I blinked at the change in topic. "No, I'll be off . . . perhaps tonight . . . have to check my Ephemeris. This isn't an easy spot to leave, and I want to ride along the Border on my way home and scout it out."

Alexander said only, "I believe the only way open to you is the dawn Gate outside Montgard."

When I consulted my Map and Ephemeris, I found he was right. I could shortcut down to the town on a Ley and go through a dawn Gate at a mound and a standing stone to get on the Road. At this season, this was the only opening within several days' travel, so I planned to do that. Alexander nodded when I told him this, gave me the name of a good inn in the town and a letter telling the Montgard town gatekeepers that I was to be permitted to come and go freely at any time, and showed me the Ley. Since, even with the Ley shortcut, it was a day's ride to the town, I was persuaded without difficulty to stay another night and leave in the morning. Regretfully I forwent the opportunity to see some of the prettiest girls in Montgard.

"Doesn't matter," Alexander shrugged, "the prettiest is already in the house. What a delightful doll she is, Gwydion."

"Isn't she," I agreed, shaking my head and smiling, "the quintessential sister, except our other sisters are nothing like her. She's so damn shy though."

"I can see that. That is why I thought I would introduce her to Lady Ammerle. She is a grandmotherly woman. I expect she will take Rikki right under her wing, and I'll have no further worries about introducing her anywhere."

"Try to get her to . . . you know . . . be a little more," I gestured, "or rather, a little less *mousy.*" My impulse to shake her at times nearly overmastered me. I wanted to shout, "Wake up! Look alive!" at her.

"Maybe she's just a mouse," Alexander said. "Some girls are."

"I cannot believe that Gaston would rear any species of mouse."

My brother shrugged again.

I left as planned in the morning on a fast, businesslike young blonde-maned mare of Alexander's who had plenty of Road trips to her credit. He asked that I return her as soon as I could, and I promised to do so. Her name was Hussy. Her saddlebags held a week's food and water, some extra clothing, and a letter Ulrike had written to her bosom friend in Haimance and which I had sworn to post when I got home. The letter probably recounted in hair-raising detail the trip hither. I was armed and armored as before, despite Alexander's suggestions that I get some heavier equipment.

"Alex, you've seen Gemnamnon. You saw what he did to

Marfisa. I know what he did to me. Armor is a formality against him. If I run into him alone without having some kind of plan or trap, I am simply going to die."

We stood in the grey-gravelled drive before Alexander's country house. I was taking my leave of them, and Alexander had brought up armor.

Ulrike looked frightened. "Gwydion, maybe you shouldn't go alone!"

"I must go alone. Alexander cannot leave just now and I can move faster alone anyway," I said, "and what I said about meeting the dragon alone probably also applies to meeting him with a friend or an army. There is nothing to be done. I am as well-prepared as I can be."

"He might not even meet the dragon," Alexander told Ulrike. "Don't worry about things you can't change, Rikki. This is Gwydion's choice. We all have the right to choose our risks and run them."

"Mother always used that as her last-ditch argument with Gaston," I remembered.

Alexander laughed. "It's a principle she didn't exactly invent, although she invoked it when it suited her. Safe journey, Gwydion."

"Safe journey," echoed Ulrike.

I mounted as they spoke. "Thank you. Au revoir," I said, and turned the mare's head as I nudged her sides with my heels. She trotted down the drive. Relief and dread jockeyed for position in my heart—relief at getting out of Alexander's house without our having one of our usual nasty arguments and at fobbing off responsibility for Ulrike for a little while, and dread at what I might encounter on the next Ley or Road segment I trod. I hoped Gemnamnon was not preying up and down the Border. He would be a nightmare of blood and terror to them.

The Ley track was a clear, easy-to-follow one; it led me straight down to the town and I left it when I recognized that I was about a mile from the town's gates. I rode in then like any other traveller and showed my pass-letter to the gate-keeper, who gave me directions to the inn Alexander recommended.

I half-feared it would be a fleabag brothel or some such prank of his, but it was a real inn: The Mermaid's Cups. The green-tressed Mermaid was combing her hair with a sultry pout on her lips and a mirror in her hand. The name was puzzling since Montgard is landlocked. I asked the host, as he showed me to a room, whence came the name, and he snickered and asked if I'd looked at both sides of the sign. I had not. Well, he said, that was where the name came from and it had been called that since the Old Lord's days and that was all he knew.

I went down and had a look at the sign and laughed out loud, for the reverse showed her with her hair up and dressed and her hands holding a seashell brassière which did not look adequate to cover her very generous breasts—one shell in each hand. Since the shells were of the pointed, spiralling sort and she held them at the narrow ends, they did look like wine-cups she was offering to the passerby.

"Very nice," I said to the landlord, and he chuckled and said there was a certain amiable lady who was said to be the spitting image of the Mermaid if I was interested, and I said thanks but no and had a beer and a meat pie and sat around listening to the local gossip, which was mostly uninteresting to me except when it touched on Alexander.

I spent a quiet night there, got up in time to make it out of town and onto the Road at the moment of access at the dawn Gate, and made good speed toward the Border. As I rode, I admitted to myself that I was afraid and braced myself for the things I might find there, and I tried to lay contingency plans for my escape or preservation if Gemnamnon should appear as he had before. There were not many courses open to me. Sorcery is unreliable in the Border. That closed most of the life-preserving avenues. And though

Hussy was fast, I didn't think she'd outrun Gemnamnon, even with an adrenaline boost.

Hussy made excellent time; she had amazing stamina and pounded along at a steady gallop. I praised her often and gave her rests to keep her sharp (and an apple at one stop) and wondered if Alexander could be induced to part with her or maybe one of her foals. Ulrike should have such a horse as this: already trained to Leys and the Road, fast, smart, and calm. It would be a fitting gift to give her come spring, when outings in Threshwood are as common as those on the Wye.

This turned my thoughts homeward. A half-panicked worrying over what might be happening there seized me with a series of horrible images. What if Gemnamnon had gone there? What if I returned to find him on my Citadel, over my brother Walter's body? What if he had laid waste the town or fired the forest? What could I do? How could I protect the whole City from such a monster?

There were guarding spells around the City already, of course, and there were simple wards on most farms and stronger ones on every village or town, but they wouldn't stop Gemnamnon. Could the warding spells be strengthened to a point where they *would* stop him? At least on the City proper? I would have to check. I suspected not, or not without substantially diverting the flow from the Spring to the rest of the world. What would such diversion of the sustaining power do to the Leys and the Road? Would they . . . fade? Or degrade? Or disappear altogether? Become intermittent, broken? There was no way to guess.

I gnawed at this problem for a long time while Hussy carried me along briskly. After fretting on the dilemma of whether to attack or to wait to be attacked again long enough for frustration to set in, I called a halt.

Hussy and I left the Ley and found ourselves a campsite in a desiccated country of yellow rocks turned incarnadine by the glowering sun. I picketed her. While she ate her oats and tried nibbling various of the local shrubs and grasses, I built a fire for myself and had dinner—a meat pie I'd brought from Montgard, a few tart early apples, a chunk of cheese. Then I drew a protective circle around us, horse and man, and cast three spells of warding for different kinds of threats into it.

That done, I wrapped myself in my cloak and lay beside my dying fire to watch the afternoon sky grow dark. It would be cold here tonight. I pillowed my head on a saddlebag and played the old first-star game. When I found it, a steady topaz spark near the zenith, I made a wish for peace and quiet and good health for everyone. That seemed like it might be general enough to do some good.

My sleep was light and uneasy. Indeed, I dreamt of lying awake. If you have never done that, be glad; it is as bad as dreaming of getting up again and again until you are ready to stay in bed when morning finally comes.

I dreamt that I lay by my little fire, which smoldered; I dreamt that I tossed and turned and I knew I did neither; I dreamt I fed the fire and tossed again . . .

I dreamt I was not alone.

Something colorless and shapeless moved outside the perimeter of my Circle. In my dream I sat up and watched it. It was interested in me; I felt that clearly. The interest was not that of the predator in the prey, of the hunter in its next meal, but an attentive curiosity.

"You are Gwydion of Argylle," it said.

I stiffened, surprised at being addressed. "Yes," I said.

"We are the Battlemaster. It is vital that we contact your father Gaston the Fireduke, but we cannot find him. We request assistance." The insubstantial thing paused near me in its walking around my circle. I regarded it, puzzled, and it seemed to gather power unto itself and became a more-perceptible blot in the darkness.

"The Battlemaster?" The name was foreign to me in sound and meaning. It didn't sound pleasant, however; it sounded like a name of someone who wished to pick a fight or finish one.

The thing said, "Ah. You may know us as Thiorn. Thiorn is one of our faces. Thiorn is a part of our identity. Battle-master was Freia's word for part of what we are, in your language."

Was this really Freia's friend, whom I knew of only by name, from some highly mechanized culture Freia had lived in long ago? My memory jigged. Thiorn. Freia had gone to visit Thiorn, before her death. They collaborated on genetic investigations and constructions, and Thiorn had commanded the armies of Argylle during the Independence War. "I can't help you. He's not talking to anyone," I answered, wondering what this had to do with Gaston.

Its, or their, voice was neutral, genderless, and soundless. I heard it in my head without the stirring of air to carry the sound to me. "He is not dead," they said.

I shrugged. "Alive a few months ago."

The Battlemaster continued to watch me. My circle had not reacted to their presence. "On what matter do you seek him? Is it one in which I may be of aid?" I asked.

"Possibly. Possibly. You are the nominal head of your family in his absence?"

"I suppose Prospero really is, but officially it's me."

Another silence. "The business touches Freia's death," the thought unspoken came.

Caution . . . I knew little about this asker . . . "I was there, yes."

"Good. She *is* dead?" they pressed.

"Twenty years and more." And still we miss her, I thought.

"Aha," or that sort of sentiment. "Describe the manner of her passing. Omit nothing."

"Beginning where?"

"Just the manner of her passing. We care not for your history."

I wondered how much the Battlemaster, or Thiorn, knew about us, and I gave a factual bare-bones answer. "She was thrown into the Spring of Argylle and it . . . destroyed her."

"The Spring destroyed her. You are not telling us something."

This was highly inconvenient. "I really cannot tell you more." I tried to suppress my thoughts.

"Do not trouble yourself," came the rejoinder. "We are just checking our facts, not probing."

"What's going on?"

"We really cannot tell you more."

Now I thought. Freia and Thiorn had been very close by all accounts. She had trusted her, or them it seemed. I just knew the name, not much more; Thiorn had been her general and ally in the Independence War, and the two of them had worked together on genetics; that certainly must mean Mother had been intimate with them.

They hadn't gone away; they were waiting, and I appreciated their courtesy in allowing me to think about how ready I was to trust them. "All right," I said. "The Spring absorbed her as it destroyed her. She is part of it now."

"It is an energy construct."

I had not thought of it thus before, but I supposed that was one way of seeing things. "That is essentially correct. Now what is afoot?"

A mental sigh—peculiar. "Someone has been rifling the Tamackay information banks."

"Information banks?"

"Storage of information about individuals who have had Tamackay therapy. Accelerated, controlled regeneration for the replacement or repair of damage to the physical body. Using means we associate with your kind, someone has extracted information about Freia. We were able to detect but not to prevent the violation." A pause. "You have conjectures. Please share them."

A meteoric flash of suspicion and intuition arced through

my mind. I had conjectures. I also had loyalties. "What would you do to this individual or individuals?"

"Discipline the criminal. Confiscate the information. It is confidential. It is not to be used without the owner's consent."

"We're talking about genetic information of some sort?" This was Freia's bailiwick; she had been fascinated by biology and her studies in genetics had been deep and ongoing.

"Correct. Genetic information describing Freia, such that it can be used to reconstruct her body. The mind, naturally, is another matter."

My suspicions became more solid, acquired a name and a sketchy outline—more substantial than my visitor. "Hell. Are you sure it's no one there?"

"We are certain," came the amused thought. "We would hardly expend the effort otherwise. This is costing us planets and suns."

"Why did you want Gaston?" I wondered.

"Under our law, her next of kin must decide the disposition of the information and must be informed of the violation."

It sounded legitimate. "Please promise me there will be no harm done to the culprit."

"You desire to shield this person? We begin to understand. We promise, with the proviso that if some . . . misapplication has occurred, we may take what measures we deem appropriate."

"Misapplication?"

"Genetic abuse."

I couldn't imagine what that would entail, but I thought I was probably against it. I said, "Very well. That is acceptable, and in that case I will help you."

"Agreed. Whom do you suspect?"

"Her brother, Dewar . . ." I hardly knew how to phrase it. "I think he is determined to free her from the Spring. It can be done by one of us killing himself or herself in Freia's place, providing a body for her. I'd guess he must be trying to work something out. Somehow. You did mention something about replacement of physical bodies . . ."

"Dewar." The mental tone was thoughtful.

"They were close. He went a little wild when she was killed."

Thinking, thinking—activity just a little too muted to come to me clearly. "We cannot maintain this contact much longer. Please come to Kavellron."

"I don't know where it is." Kavellron? A city? A country? A bar?

"You can find us." There came a feeling of snapping, as of an elastic overtaxed and returning to its own shape, and the Battlemaster was gone.

And I woke, a curious awakening, for on one level I felt my body sitting upright suddenly, staring around in the cold empty dark before my eyes had even opened properly, and on the other I sat as I had for the entirety of our conversation, looking at the place where the colorless, shapeless thing had been.

Hussy stood, staring at that spot, on the opposite side of the circle.

Was it a dream?

Just in case, knowing the fleeting nature of such, I opened my saddlebag, took out a little notebook and a pencil, and scribbled down the outline of the conversation. I tossed another piece of wood on the fire and observed that no wood was missing from my pile. The wood I put on hardly burned at all; it wouldn't catch. I tried another piece and that one flared up brightly, resin in the wood popping.

Kavellron.

That was what made this dream, or sending, a little, tiny bit convincing.

Kavellron was a name I had never heard before. Thiorn, or the Battlemaster, was. Thiorn's name appeared in chronicles of the Independence War, which were so obviously censored that there was no point asking Freia or Belphoebe what had been left out. I had asked Belphoebe exactly that once, and she said, "What is there is the record." The Battle-master was supposed to be the greatest military intelligence in existence.

And this also made my dream a little unconvincing too. I annotated the description of it: *Here I am, preoccupied with a serious Argylline problem, and my subconscious not only pops out a name associated with Argylle's great victory against a supposedly-invincible opponent (Landuc, then) but also suggests that my mother might be reincarnated. Wish fulfillment!*

"Take a rest, brain," I muttered, looking at my notes on the conversation. It was a rescue fantasy: that some miraculous ally would appear from nowhere and save me from the dragon.

Still. Kavellron. My mind usually did not invent nonsense words like that. And something about the context rang curiously true, although I had no evidence to support my guess that Dewar was slaving over a hot microscope (or whatever) somewhere, trying to build his sister a new body . . .

Ridiculous!

Yet . . . the Battlemaster . . . there was a real entity . . .

I reread my notes again, and the smallest uncertainty wove itself through my heartstrings.

Sendings can take many forms. I knew that the methods used in Argylle and Landuc and commonly in Noroison were not the only way of handling them. Perhaps this was a legitimate Sending of a nonconventional variety.

Perhaps pigs have six legs and wings too.

It's possible that somewhere they do, I countered my skeptical self.

I tapped the end of the pencil against my notebook and thought without structure, letting the whole business swirl around in my mind and settle into a decision. Then I put the notebook away, pulled my cloak around me, and snuggled back down onto the hard and cold ground to pursue the rest of my sleep.

⌐ 17 ⌐

IN THE MORNING I SADDLED HUSSY and got going fast, eating a couple of apples by way of breakfast. I returned to the Road and travelled slowly toward the Border, musing over my experience of the previous night. I had a strong urge to follow it up. This urge, I fully admitted to myself, was partly born of my desire to do anything but deal with the dragon Gemnamnon. The question was, how good an idea *was* it to pursue this now? What did Dewar intend? Was it so urgent that I ought to shirk the dragon problem?

That must be determined by what I found at the Border and in Argylle. My first responsibility was to my realm. Then I could engage myself with the problem of how to contact an entity about which I knew nothing in a place whose location was completely unknown to me. I did not even know on which side of the Border it lay.

So Alexander's excellent horse and I cantered on toward the Border. I put aside thoughts of Dewar and Mother and what-if, and I considered instead the lack of sorcery in the Border area. It is a dead zone, or nearly; the conditions that inhibit sorcery mean also that only the simplest technologies function. Mother had been an expert on it, because in her younger days she had spent much time there. She had even written up her notes in neat, usable form, a set of maps and guidebooks. Unfortunately, her lack of either interest or training in sorcery meant that she had not investigated that basic problem. Perhaps Dewar had, but he'd not mentioned it to me.

I had always accepted it as a limitation and never concerned myself with it; the Border was there to be crossed,
sometimes to be travelled for a few days with a caravan, once
in a great while to be visited for longer if one of the traders
invited one to stay. Now I saw it as a gaping lacuna in my
education. How was I to rule Argylle if I understood almost
nothing of the fundamental nature of an integral part of the
realm? For example, how could the Border exist at all if it
were not part of the Spring? How was it that an initiate of
Landuc's Well could not pass beyond the mountains on that
side? Where did the Border come from? What was there
before there was Argylle? Nothing?

Philosophical questions like this are another way of not
facing problems. I suppressed mine regretfully and forced
myself to think about Gemnamnon.

I had to either come up with something so powerful he
would respect it and leave us alone forever, or I had to
destroy him with something so powerful he couldn't beat it.
Figuring that out was the easy part. The difficult part was
producing the device. I fretted over the problem afresh until
I was once again running around it in decreasing circles, and
then I gave it up in frustration. I would consult Prospero and
Belphoebe when I got home. Perhaps they could help. Alexander, with a certain schadenfreude, had indicated he considered it my problem entirely, so I wouldn't bother asking him
this time. Let him look after Ulrike for the nonce.

Having succeeded in buying myself time, I stopped for
lunch at a dark stream ford and crossed it after making the
appropriate answer when challenged by the black-armored
knight who waited at the other side: one of the nastier Gates.
Then I continued on the Road to the Border.

It took another three days for me to reach the Border. I
performed a brief Lesser Summoning for Walter each night,
and each night he reported nothing new, no dragons, no
supernatural gryphons. Prospero had come to Argylle again,
he said.

I took precautions when I did this to ensure that detection of the spell at either side would be difficult, fearing that Gemnamnon might be monitoring me—I had no idea, after all, what his capabilities really were. Each evening I laid me down well-warded, and each night I slept undisturbed until morning, and each morning I saddled and mounted and rode away. The journey had lost all feeling of fun and holiday. It was part of my job now. There was no time for side-tripping, for exploration and impulse.

I stopped for the night at a hut which had been tenanted the previous night (judging from its condition) but which was mine alone now. A sound from the roof made me jump and flinch with a quick gripping of fear in my bowels, and then I cursed my nerves and laughed at myself.

It was Virgil, looking rather the worse for wear and very glad indeed to see me. I lifted him down from the eaves and petted him and carried him inside. I had assumed that, following the encounter with the dragon and the Gryphon, he would make his way home to Argylle and abide my coming there. But no, he had continued on the path I had chosen, toward Montgard, and then stopped here out of weakness because he had obviously had poor luck in the hunt. I scolded him and fed him and talked to him for a couple of hours, telling him what had befallen me since we had parted company, and he listened, as owls do, with his eyes mostly shut and his beak deep-sunk in his fluffy breast.

"So what do I do now?" I asked him. "How am I going to kill that monster? And this business with the Battlemaster and Dewar and Mother sounds like it might be urgent too. What do you think? I cannot do both at once."

Virgil pondered it awhile. I fed the fire profligately and warmed my feet.

Finally Virgil drew himself upright and shook out his feathers. He climbed up my arm to my shoulder and deftly pulled my Keys, which I carry when travelling on a chain around my neck, out of my shirt. Then he jumped down to my knee and selected one, offering it to me gravely.

"Mother?"

Virgil waited, staring at me orb-eyed.

I took the Key. "Mother is more important than the dragon?" My voice rose with incredulity.

He nodded twice, a very enthusiastic endorsement coming from him.

I shook my head. "That dragon is *killing* people, Virgil. I disagree with your priorities, and I think she would too."

Virgil turned his back and hunched his shoulders.

"Sorry," I said, "but I have a responsibility to the living as well as the dead, don't I?"

Nothing but a stiff little owl, ignoring me.

"Hmph," I said, annoyed, and pushed him off my knee; he flipped his wings and perched on the woodpile, and I shook out my cloak and wrapped it around my body and lay down.

No sorcerer can afford to quarrel long with his familiar. I had asked the opinion of mine and he had given it to me. I lay, eyes closed, weighing things again in my thoughts.

"Virgil," I said quietly after half an hour or so, "I don't like running away from things like this. It's not right. I owe a duty—"

He scared half the life out of me by jumping on my chest and grabbing for my Keys again.

"I get the message! Mother is important! Is she so much more important than everyone else?"

He chose two Keys and offered me them in his left claw— Mother's and my Master Key.

I looked at them a long time.

"She is *that* important," I said.

He nodded once, dropped the Keys, and returned to the woodpile.

Indeed! I lay back again myself and rolled onto my stomach. The heat of the fire felt good on my side.

Someone had stolen, the Battlemaster had said, genetic

information. Information that could be used to construct a body, they had said. I thought I knew who would do that and why: Dewar, trying to bring Freia back to life. But how could it be done? It seemed impossible to me, the most unnatural and awkward transition imaginable—from some kind of coded information to a person.

It made no sense. It would be better, I thought, to use an existing body. Like Ulrike's. I wondered, if Gaston *were* given the choice, what he would prefer: to have his wife again, or their immature and timorous daughter? He had been numb and distant after Mother's death, drawn into himself, cold ashes and charred old wood. What comfort could Ulrike be when he had lost the one he loved best?

Dewar, I thought, loved her as well. I had never realized how much until I had heard him speak to her image in the Spring just after her death, storming, his grief overflowing and drowning every other idea but that he wanted her back at any price. If it were possible to restore her to a body, he would do it for her—steal, lie, perhaps even murder.

However, in that he was little different from Gaston, who had more than once killed to protect Freia and, though theft and falsehood were foreign to his character, sorely missed her. Between them, they had all the determination and ruthlessness to accomplish anything, even reincarnation.

Had they, in fact, done so?

I turned and stared at the rough wooden ceiling.

Suppose, I thought, suppose Ulrike *was* a constructed body. Suppose Dewar had made her and Gaston reared her—not troubling much over her, for she was nothing but a vessel to be filled with better matter—and then sent her to Argylle, where his sorcerer partner would complete the work. It would explain her vacant personality, her vagueness, and Gaston's absence. Naturally, he would claim she was Freia's daughter in order to get her to the Spring. Perhaps Ulrike suspected something of this; that would explain her reluctance to approach it.

I wondered what was involved in the process of extricating Freia from the Spring. Was it as simple as her enthrallment? As simple as falling in? What would happen to Ulrike—would she become part of the Spring, then, in Mother's stead? It could not be so neat as that—or could it? No. I recalled that Freia had told Dewar that the one who followed her would be truly dead, not merely trapped. So since Ulrike was a blank construct, it wasn't murder: it was restoral.

If I had but known all this when first she entered the Citadel, I'd have taken her to the Spring at once and freed Freia. No one would have been the wiser, and Freia would be with us, and Gaston and my uncle would return, and all would be well, and I would have none of these problems that gnawed me now.

My sleep was uneasy. I woke again and again, thrashed around trying to get comfortable, and finally lay on my back miserably waiting for day. When light greyed the interior of the hut, I got up stiff and unrested and tottered off to saddle my horse. My stomach's knotted and sour state made me forgo breakfast.

At least I had something new to think about while I rode. On the one hand, Virgil was a creature of Argylle, and closer to the Spring in his way than I, more sensitive to and tolerant of its powers, and moreover I owed my uncle any help I could give him. On the other hand, I had a clear duty to Argylle's citizens not to fail them at this critical moment.

Yet. If I weren't going to listen to my familiar, why was I keeping him? I knew he was usually right. In all truth, I could not think of a time when I had solicited his view or used him to make a decision when he had been wrong.

Virgil himself sat behind me clutching the saddlebags, impassive, dreaming the half-dreams of an owl's half-sleep. I had soaked a lot of the dried meat from my food supplies and stuffed him with it last night and this morning. He didn't care for it, but it was better than starving.

I went slowly, looking in every direction at once, as I

288 ⟶ *Elizabeth Willey*

entered the Border Range. My preoccupation with Virgil's advice was given a frisson of urgency by my fear that the dragon might attack me at any moment. We were climbing toward a saddle, a long slanting gradual ascent, and I could see far along the sheer-seeming sides of the mountains. There was nothing untoward in sight. It was a normal trip thus far.

It continued normal while I seesawed back and forth about where my duty lay. When I found myself trying to frame explanations for Prospero and Walter for haring off down the Road looking for Kavellron and the Battlemaster, I realized that I was committing myself to that course little by little.

By then we were going down the other side, overlooking the serene Valley where a big caravan could be seen making its almost-imperceptible progress along the wide stone-paved road (a hair-fine line from here). There seemed to be a darkness in the Valley far, far away. Distance is difficult to judge there, so I couldn't be sure what it was or how far off it was. It was unusual: I was sure of that much.

I watched Hussy's footing, shifted my weight around to help her, and whistled under my breath. Her ears twitched back at me from time to time, letting me know she was paying attention. On the last long, shallow part of the track, Virgil rode on my shoulder, which meant he wasn't in a snit about my indecision. To amuse him and myself I sang a gory old ballad from Errethon. Hussy's ears swivelled around to listen too.

I sighed as we entered the grassland at the valley bottom. "All right, Virgil," I said, "I'm thinking about it still. If nothing happens with the dragon on our way home and nothing has happened there when we get there, then . . . I will try to find the Battlemaster."

Virgil made a *prrrrut* sound, pleased with himself. Hussy snorted. I nudged her and she blew out noisily and picked up her feet. We made it to the three barnlike structures that would be our resting place for the night long before dark.

After giving Hussy a thorough grooming and putting her in a stall away from the henza pens, which the caravan would fill when it arrived, I had a wash myself and went in and threw my saddlebags on a bunk. Virgil settled on the end of the bed for a nap. I looked up the caretakers, who were having fragrant hot tea in their quarters.

They were short, bipedal, and rust-furred, with long blackish claws and four agile digits on each hand. Their muzzles were nearly furless, studded with wiry black whiskers that curled tightly at the ends. Their clothing was of embroidered and studded leather. They knew me by reputation, though we hadn't met before.

"Dark Horse," said one, nodding to me. A cane rested beside him, carved and silver-inlaid blue wood. Names in the Border are of this sort, descriptive and sometimes derisive, often loaded with extra meaning.

"That's right," I said, bowing slightly. "I've a different horse today, though."

"Three Legs," the other introduced himself, rising stiffly and bowing also, "and this is Rough Going." Rough Going grunted and sipped the tea, not getting up. We spoke the Border creole.

Rough Going eyed me and nodded to a cushion. I nodded and sat down, accepting a hot metal cup of tea. It was good that I'd gotten here before the bustling caravan; it would give me time to get the news out of the caretakers without interruptions.

"Big caravan headed this way," I observed.

"Had a dry spell there," said Rough Going.

"Oh?"

They both looked at me.

I felt my cheeks color slightly. I thought of the peculiar darkness down the Valley from here. "Tell me about it," I suggested. "Trouble?"

The only humans who pass the Border are our family. It is well-known there that we come and go from places Beyond or Outside, as they call them, and we are regarded as not-entirely-natural and not-entirely-normal beings. The Border folk have an inkling that all the world is not as what they see, and some are curious about it sometimes, but they do not trouble themselves with it as a group.

"Strange things from Outside," said Rough Going, his eyes hard on me.

"A silver cloud, a golden cloud," said Three Legs. "A terrible storm of fire . . ."

I tasted the tea. It was flowery and slightly sweet.

"Fire and thunder near Five Ways." Rough Going nodded. "The fire burned four days' journey in each direction, near Five Ways. It is black now there."

I nodded slowly.

"Some say those were animals not clouds," Three Legs said, "but there are no animals as big as clouds."

"Unfortunately there are," I said.

"Hah," said Rough Going, with a satisfied grunt. "Clouds don't eat people."

"Fortunately they don't," I agreed.

Three Legs clicked his teeth three times, impatient or displeased at being proven wrong.

I hadn't thought about what to tell the Border inhabitants. I supposed the truth would do.

"There has been a large beast, a dragon, silver and purple and blue in color, hunting about," I said, "and making a nuisance of himself, killing many people Outside and now evidently here."

They looked at me, wrinkling their faces.

"Why here?" demanded Rough Going.

"I don't know," I said. "I encountered him myself," and I told them how Ulrike and I had been attacked in the pass, and how the Gryphon had fought Gemnamnon. Time is a slippery thing in the Border; I wanted to find out if Gemnamnon had been seen thereabouts since then, so I asked them how recently they had heard of the dragon.

"Last caravan to come through told of the fires," said Rough Going. "Then no traffic for days. You're the first traveller through since."

"Caravan coming in is coming from up the Valley," pointed out Three Legs.

"Dragon," Rough Going coughed the new word, "was down the Valley."

Maybe I'd better continue down the Valley with this caravan and see the damage. I might find Gemnamnon waiting. On the other hand, if the last travellers to come through had reported fires but no dragon, perhaps the Gryphon had routed him. Ulrike and I had seen no evidence of fires when we stood in the pass—most likely the fires were a by-product of that fight.

I sat with them awhile longer and finished the tea, then thanked them and went to my bunk. I suspected that Gemnamnon would have preyed more widely along the Valley floor if he were here. I told Virgil that we were going to be travelling along the Valley for a few days more at least. He fluffed and shot me an impatient glare.

"I'm not going back on my word," I said.

Virgil settled down again, mollified.

The henza caravan arrived. It was from far, far up the Valley and the merchants therein had heard only rumors, fairly factual ones without too much exaggeration. None had heard of any other dragon trouble in the Valley. Before going to sleep I talked to the leader, Polished Jade, about joining the group for a few days; he agreed genially and asked after Prospero, known here as Hard Fist.

"He's well," I said.

"Haven't seen him in a long time," he observed.

"Things have been busy."

Polished Jade twitched his left ear and nodded once. "See you in the morning, Dark Horse."

"Good night."

The sounds of singing and laughter in the other building

carried faintly to this one. I lay awake listening awhile, catching snatches of melody, and never noticed that I'd fallen asleep until I was awakened by the bustling of the merchants getting up and getting their gear together for the day's journey.

It took three days to reach the blackened area. To my eye, it appeared that Gemnamnon had started a grass fire which had run unchecked through the Valley until it reached a broad, Valley-wide swamp where water soaked the ground and the damp vegetation hadn't caught easily. We sat on one side of the swamp in the track and looked across its green lushness at a cinder-colored monochromatic desert.

"Won't cross it sitting on our henzas here," Polished Jade said at last, having taken in the sight and pondered it. "What do you think, Dark Horse? Is this safe?"

"I don't know if the dragon is ahead or not." I looked ahead, squinting, and shook my head. "I'm going to ride on ahead, Polished Jade."

"Alone?"

"Yes. Thanks for your company thus far."

"Let me send a couple of the—"

"No, they couldn't keep up with me." I smiled. "But thanks."

"Safe journey then," he said, an expression he'd picked up from Prospero.

I lifted a hand in farewell and nudged Hussy's sides. She, who had been bored silly by the stately pace of the henza caravan, took off like a shot, and I crouched low at her neck, enjoying the speed myself, grinning with the wind in my face. She raced across the swamp on the causeway and into the charred grassland. I pulled my cloak up over my nose and mouth to protect my face from the ashes and bits of cinder which a light wind kept suspended in the air.

A waystation became visible ahead of us after a long, flat-out run. I pulled gently on the reins, making Hussy slow down gradually, and we approached it at a trot. The caretakers came out, hearing us approach.

"There's a caravan behind me," I said. "Be here tonight."

"Good," said one.

"What happened here?"

"Fire. Burned the grass," said the other.

I nodded. "Anything odd since then?"

"No traffic from down the Valley."

Of course, that would be strange.

"I'm going on down then," I said.

They shrugged. "Whose caravan?" asked the first.

"Polished Jade."

"Hah," he said.

I got Hussy to gallop again without difficulty. Virgil was entirely put out by the rough ride and hunched himself down as close as possible to the saddlebags. We made it to the next waystation before the sky dimmed.

Disturbingly, this one was unattended. It was not unknown for the big stations to be without caretakers, but it was unusual. While light remained I looked around for signs of dragon-caused damage and found nothing conclusive. The stone buildings were all empty; I slept in the barn, up in the hayloft. Virgil flew up to a niche in the rock and stayed there, his head swivelling around hopefully. In the morning I set out down the Valley again and made the next station by midday.

This one was a ruin. There were two buildings here, one a barn, and outdoor holding pens for henza. The pens held charred henza bones. The dismantled and scattered condition of them suggested that the dragon had indeed dined here. I studied the skeletons carefully and concluded that the dragon had done so before the fire. The damage was consistent with that, with his jaws and claws crushing and ripping. Animals which are burned to death are not dispersed so, and there are no scavengers in the Valley to have done it.

I went into the barn, one corner of which had collapsed.

Virgil swooped ahead of me, silently reconnoitering. We found nothing alive there; I supposed that any henzas that had survived Gemnamnon's depredations had panicked and stampeded in the fire. There was a pile of luggage and goods, consistent with a small caravan of ten or twelve pack animals. That would mean three or four people with the caravan, probably. I left the building and looked at the long, low bunkhouse.

This was greatly damaged. It had been crushed or forcibly collapsed at one end and then partially excavated, stones lying far-scattered in disorder. Having seen the dragon go after Ulrike, I could easily believe he had done this.

My neck prickled. I looked up, back, around, from Range to Range. Silence and motionless stone.

I entered the upright part of the building cautiously, but I found no remains; there was only a pile of pack-bags by a set of bunks.

"I see no dragon here," I said to Virgil, who rode my shoulder now.

He closed his eyes.

"We'll go on to the next station," I decided.

We arrived there at nightfall. Two buildings, charred grass around them. I looked into the henza pens as I rode by and saw no signs of bone or carnage. A light glimmered by one of the buildings.

"Ho!" I called.

"Ho!" shouted back the light's bearer. "From up or down?" he asked.

"Up," I said. "I am glad to find someone here."

"Come in," he said, a stumpy, grey-muzzled old guy with pure white ears. "Put your animal in the barn."

"See you inside then."

There were eight people there. The dragon had not been seen since the fight with the Gryphon and the fire which had followed it. He had attacked a couple of caravans before that, in addition to the waystations I had found empty.

About twelve people were thought to have been killed altogether. This indicated to me that the dragon had not lurked here for long before Ulrike and I met him: had he been waiting for us?

They told me that the fire damage extended about two days' travel further ahead of me (one day for Hussy) and that the stations there had not been attacked.

Given this, I decided I could leave the Valley floor and get on with my trip back to Argylle.

Accordingly, the following day I left the lateral track that runs along the Valley like an artery and rode toward the Argylle side of the Border. Halfway up I paused for a look around. This was not the pass where Ulrike and I had been caught. I thought that one might be the next one down the Valley, judging from the positions of various of the peaks on the Landuc side.

At the top of the trail, another met it and there was a hut at the junction. The remaining good light was insufficient to get me out of the Border altogether, so I stopped.

Virgil was visibly impatient. I was feeling impatient myself now that I had the information I'd intended to get. The dragon Gemnamnon was not here now. He had not been here, apparently, since the Gryphon had fought him. I had found no close eyewitnesses to that fight, only the same nebulous account that Rough Going and Three Legs had given me.

The next day I left the Border Range behind me and found a Ley to follow toward a Nexus which put me on another Ley which led me to the Road. I sighed with relief as I rode onto that first Ley; the feeling of contact with the Spring was reassuring, and as soon as we were in a place with adequate fuel I stopped, built a fire, and opened a Way to the City: home.

I left Hussy at the stables with my heartfelt thanks, told the man who took her in to spoil her rotten, and went up to my quarters with Virgil, where I undressed and stretched out on the bed. Moments later I was asleep.

⌐ 18 ⌐

MY ROOMS WERE COLD. SOMETIME DURING the day I woke up enough to feel cold myself and pulled my cloak across the bed for extra warmth, too sleepy to get another blanket from the chest. When I awoke in truth, it was pitch-dark and chilly. I lay enjoying being in my own bed for a few minutes, and then I moved up from that primitive level of cognition to a higher one.

Virgil watched me expectantly from the foot of the bed. Time to make good on my promise.

Kavellron. How could I compose a spell of passage for a place I'd never been and about which I knew nothing? One couldn't leave the destination vague in these things; that was an error made just once, at the end of one's career.

I could ask Prospero and other family members about it, but as I looked that idea over it occurred to me that to do so would require some explanation.

I did not really want to sit down and tell Prospero that Dewar was working with Prospero's quondam familiar Ariel. I did not want to describe the scene between him and my mother's apparition or whatever she was in the Spring. It had a feeling of privateness to it, the whole affair. If Dewar had wanted his father Prospero to know, he would have told him. My sorcerer's professional courtesy demanded that I keep my mouth shut.

Professional courtesy was putting me on the spot, though. I knew the brief histories of the Independence War inside out, and I knew that Freia had allowed no hint as to the whereabouts of her allies to slip in. In case she needed them again, probably.

I got out of bed and took a bath, having a thorough scrub

and soak to get the accumulated travel grime off me. I tried not to think while I sloshed and lounged, but a thought did occur to me: Dewar, if he had been irritating these people, should perhaps be warned that they knew about his activities, whatever those were. He might have some advice on how I could handle them.

On climbing out of the bath, I attempted a Lesser Summoning for Dewar. Nothing, as ever. What had he and Ariel done to get themselves in so much trouble? The Battlemaster was not someone I would choose to annoy. They had beaten Landuc's best, and if they could somehow reach me to talk to me, without being initiated in the Well of Fire . . .

I tried a Lesser Summoning of Gaston. Next of kin, after all. Nothing.

I fingered my Keys. Might I try Ottaviano? No. I didn't think he knew more than I did about Dewar's whereabouts. Oriana? No, for the same reason. Prospero?

If I were to just level with Prospero, tell him everything, he might take it off my hands . . .

He might take deep offense, too, because I hadn't told him in the first place that his daughter persisted, standing on the threshold of life or death. He would certainly be furious that I hadn't told him about Dewar.

Belphoebe? She would listen and suggest I tell Prospero. So would Walter. Now that I thought about it, I didn't want to run into Prospero or Walter just now, and they were very likely both around. I had opened the bathroom window for a few minutes to air it out, and I had heard faint music from another room nearby when I'd done so. The prospect of the long and complicated circumlocutions that I'd have to conjure up was more exhausting to contemplate than the sorcery I planned.

I wished someone else in our small family had sorcerous talent like my own. I was isolated and without support. If only one of my siblings had taken up the Art as I had, I would have someone with whom to talk things over, to show me the flaws in my thinking as Dewar did when he was here: a trusted colleague, perhaps an apprentice of my own, at least someone who could be relied on not to judge me by lay standards.

But they hadn't, none of them. I grimaced in the Mirror and got up and dressed in clean clothes and different boots than the ones I'd been living in. As I dressed I ate the rest of the food from my saddlebags. Then I took a few implements from my workroom: my favorite wand, a triune balance, a little prism and a lens.

When working with the Spring directly, very little apparatus is used. For one thing, the level of power is such that it destroys most lesser tools—shatters Mirrors, breaks anything of glass or crystal, and heats and deforms metals. Water freezes and then sublimates; fire flares and burns intensely for a split second, leaving no ash behind. Wands such as the one I was using or other tools are made only to fine-tune, not to manipulate the power of the Spring in any substantial way; to place, so to speak, a thread spun by other means in position, not to spin the thread.

This doesn't matter, because when working with the Spring directly, if one knows what one is doing, one doesn't need props. If one does, one shouldn't be there. Theoretically the Spring will resist or even destroy the unfit itself. I have not seen this happen, but I have read descriptions of the deaths of several apprentices at the Stone of Blood on Morven in Noroison. Dewar made me read them before he would even consider initiating me there. I had never conceived of the Spring as having the same fatal potential until it had slain my mother.

Mother's death had seemed sudden, not instantaneous but very fast, and I had wondered, after writing my account of it in my journal, what it had been like for her. What had she felt in that terrible moment of falling, as Dewar had screamed and leapt forward, as I had howled and swung at Tython, as

Prospero had thrown the Black Sword? I'd never dare ask even if she were around to question.

There *was* music coming from Prospero's rooms; I heard it as I passed on tiptoe. Sounded like him and Walter both, singing and playing. Furtively, wanting to stop and go in and join them, feeling like a thief in my own house, I went down via a less-used stairway that lets one into the gardens. I didn't want to run into Utrachet or any others of the household, either. Let them all think I rested yet.

I left that stair before it ended, passing through a low, knobless door with only a keyhole in its fine-grained, finely-polished dark wood. My Master Key fit that hole perfectly and the door swung open at the touch of my hand. The Master Key is one of my uncle's little jokes. He was amused by the Landuc custom of Summoning-tokens being key-shaped and when he made Keys in Argylle he made a Key that was a key for opening certain locked things in the Citadel and around Argylle.

Closing that door behind me, I paused on the landing a moment to conjure an ignis fatuus. With that to show me the way, I continued along a narrow passageway that jogs this way and that around various rooms and segments of plumbing and chimneys and the like. It ends at another door as featureless as the first. I opened that one cautiously, looked left and right, and closed it behind me to go down an equally narrow, steep flight of stairs. Another door at the bottom leads to another passageway, a low one, and ends at a door made of a slab of stone. This one, which pivots on its central vertical axis, lets on a landing on the Black Stair. Down that and into the high-vaulted darkness below the world. I sought the Spring and found it.

It pulsed and danced in front of me, not dark and passive—active, excited, sparks and miniature comets coming and going in or above its black-opal non-surface. There was a soft, high-pitched sound as of a nearby but miniature waterfall.

I hadn't worked it directly since it had killed Freia. Of course I'd tapped it in my day-to-day sorceries, but I'd not used it for the higher levels of spells. I'd avoided them in fact.

I was sweating. Pure fear. I hadn't expected this. I set the lantern down with a bang by the bench. Three deep breaths—don't think about this, Gwydion, I told myself— and I called Virgil to assist me.

He swooped noiselessly down and perched on my left shoulder, his usual spot, and bit the top of my left ear gently with his hooked beak, a friendly gesture.

"Thanks," I said.

Another little bite and he straightened and adjusted his grip on my doublet's padded shoulder.

I took my wand from my sleeve and began.

The Spring felt as I remembered it; the Well and Stone were thin traces of their native might. I moved my wand and chanted loudly and softly and stood silent with concentration and passed power in and out of Virgil as I had ever done, and gradually a shining golden net formed over the Spring, around me where I now stood above it.

The construction was done. I was wrapped by and suspended within a spherical lacework of power, of different colors to the eye, different . . . tastes to the mind. A miniature Road-system, in short. The Spring made no special manifestations toward me; Freia, if she were there, was ignoring me.

Virgil was perched on the back of the Botanical Gardens bench, watching.

I caught my breath in that perfect, tense moment where all power hangs a moment at zenith, before speaking the final words that would make my spell seek Kavellron, then paused with the syllables unuttered on my tongue.

Here was one who really ought to know what Dewar had done. Next of kin, hell. Freia herself could decide what to do with him. Knit into the fabric of the Spring by the cords of the finding-spell I had made, I was now more intimately bonded to it than any other living thing in the universe which surged from here; the flow of the Spring through my spell and through me was exhilarating, invigorating, and sustaining. Hm. Maybe something could be done. Yes. If I could somehow get her to notice me, to talk to me as Dewar had done so long ago, if she were able, if she were there still as Freia and not some benignly indifferent preternatural force . . .

The tension of the energy in my incomplete spell swirled around and around me, pulling as an undertow, straining to return to its natural flow. It was as mighty as the ocean and as indifferent.

I exhaled and said, softly, "Mother, I need you."

No response. I could not hold the spell in suspense much longer; it would destroy me.

I closed my eyes and thought of her, breathed life into my fading memories. So much is lost in twenty years. I kept seeing the image from the photograph in my bedroom, Freia looking away from me, looking away . . .

I built her image before my mind's eye, yearning for her to look at me, to turn and speak: a Summoning from the heart without words.

The uncompleted spell snapped as a wire overdrawn. I felt it go; it tore at me to take me with it. Its energy whirled, sizzled, flew apart—and then the spell spun around me again, its force lessened and shape slightly altered; it now had an outlet, was a channel rather than a cul-de-sac.

"Gwydion," I heard, softly, a rustle, a whisper. The spell tightened around me, as if it would sheathe me in its cool, rippling satin, then relaxed.

My heart fluttered. My eyes opened. Startled, I looked around me. Nothing to see, no simulacrum or vision such as Dewar had gotten. "Mother?" I whispered.

"Yes."

"I need to tell you something and to ask you something." Talking to a disembodied voice that sounded in my ear was disturbing. I closed my eyes again, trembling violently. She was there, truly there, not dead but transformed. A chilly prickle went up and down my back. My shirt was clammy with anxious perspiration; it stuck to me beneath my doublet, making me feel colder.

"Ahhh," she sighed. I could almost feel breath against my cheek, and then I realized it was no breath, but a little pulse of the Spring. "What is it you need? Is not all well with you? Tell me."

"Dewar seems to have rebound Ariel." My voice shook, although I tried to keep it level and matter-of-fact. One doesn't talk to one's mother's ghost every day.

"That is true. Ariel serves him. Now ask . . ." The voice, though hers, was not wholly her voice; there was a richness in tone and timbre that no human voicebox could have produced: Freia's voice, enhanced and deepened.

I moistened my lips, eyes still closed; it was easier to concentrate on what she said thus, not on the wonder of her saying it. "I have been contacted by the Kavellray Battlemaster. Someone has stolen some kind of genetic information about you—"

"Oh, sun moon and stars," she whispered.

"—from them. They wanted to talk to Gaston, but they could not find him and settled on me as the kin they could reach. I thought you deserved to know too."

"When was this done?"

"I don't know about the theft. They, or Thiorn, contacted me a few days ago my time, when I was riding home from Montgard to Argylle, on the Landuc side of the Border, a Sending, very strangely done. They want me to come to them for further discussions."

"Thiorn. That is interesting. To find you must have cost them greatly; I did not think they could do such a thing. Yet it is no small matter to them, nor to me." She was silent. The Spring-currents in my spell moved over my skin rhythmically. "Thank you, Gwydion. Now, what is your question?"

I phrased my reply carefully. "Mother, I am fairly certain Dewar did it, with Ariel. It is easily within what I know of

Ariel's abilities. I do not want to lie to them, so I'll . . . I'll betray Dewar unless you wish otherwise. Do you?"

"I don't know. I truly do not know what he . . . He is rash. He is so . . ." The troubled words were delivered without the quaver of emotion I would have expected from a human throat, but she sighed again, a little gust of Spring-force. "I told him to do nothing. He will not listen. He hides from me in Pheyarcet or over the Limen in Phesaotois, and I cannot see what he does."

"Stubborn is the word."

"It does run in the family, doesn't it. He came here himself a little time past. That is how I know of Ariel. They were both here."

"When the dragon, Gemnamnon—"

"Yes."

"So has he been watching things here? Would you know?"

"He had Ariel watching you, yes. I said to him that that was uncouth, to forsake Argylle and still to spy so . . . poor Papa," she added aside, lower, perhaps not meant for my ear. "Ariel is here no more and Dewar has ceased that. He was worried about you, dear."

I had meant Gemnamnon, but this was equally interesting. "Kindly Uncle Dewar. I appreciate his concern. I was dead meat there, Mother."

"I was watching that fight too," she said apologetically. Her voice was acquiring more expression.

"Really? We ought to have sold tickets." For her sake now as well as my own, I was glad he'd saved me. Horrible, to watch your son and heir eaten slowly on your own mountain-top.

She actually laughed softly. "Now then. I must talk to Dewar and the Battlemaster and I would do it here, as the Border makes such a conference impossible there. You must tell the Battlemaster to incarnate and return with you. I shall try to reach Dewar."

Incarnate? "Can you do that?"

"If Ariel is within my demesnes, I can give him a message for Dewar. I know that Dewar is not here now, but I do not know where he is. I cannot pass the Border unless constrained to do so."

"What do you mean, constrained?"

"The Well and the Stone keep me from their demesnes; I cannot reconcile myself to them alone."

I nodded. "What if I commanded you to find Dewar after you opened the Way for me?"

"A moment; let me think on it. —How is Ulrike? She is not here."

"She is well. She is visiting Alexander in Montgard; he invited her to go there. You do not know?"

"I do not watch so closely as that." Pause. "Not usually. When people think about me very hard, it catches my attention."

I swallowed, squeezing my eyes tighter shut. Her voice made my heart ache in my chest. I wanted to open my eyes and see her there . . . "We think about you a lot," I whispered.

"Thank you. It keeps me together."

"As a personality?"

"Yes. —I find I must be actively constrained to pass my Border, Gwydion; you must guide me and protect me yourself. I do not think a spell alone would be adequate to the task; it requires a living being to control it. The forces keeping the universe in its present form are very strong."

Was that a joke? Hard to tell. "Pity. Very well, so must it be. I'll find the Battlemaster, get them to incarnate"—whatever that might mean—"and return with them. To the Spring?"

"Secretly. I would prefer that. I trust Thiorn, and none comes here, so it is safe. I have changed your spell a little, Gwydion, to make it easier for me . . . I can alter it further and send you to Kavellron, to a place I know they will receive you."

I was impressed, but this didn't seem to be the time to ask how she had learned to do that—although, being the Spring, I supposed she could do almost anything she wished. I said, "Yes. That is a good idea. While I am there, you do what you can to find Ariel. If you cannot, there are rather unpleasant but effective ways for me to haul Dewar in." I was sure he'd be furious, which was why it had always been out of the question before, but his sister outranked him, even dead. If she wanted his presence, he could not refuse it. Nor would he want to. He was not the Lady's Champion for no reason.

"A Great Summoning. Yes. Thank you, Gwydion."

I closed my eyes, synchronized myself with the spell's energy pulses, and spoke the words for Seeking, Opening, and Passage. Nothing more specific than the name, Kavellron, an omission that felt strange to me and that gave me a little twist of fear as I felt the spell act.

What if Freia made a mistake?

I brought my hands down in the gesture of termination and finished the spell. It flashed into action around me, and an electric-feeling charge ran over my skin. The air changed as I inhaled, in midbreath. I looked around. I stood alone in a grey, featureless room.

Almost at once, I hit my forehead with the heel of my hand. Damn it! I should have asked Freia about Gemnamnon! If she could watch me fighting him on Longview, if she knew that Dewar wasn't in Argylle's demesnes, she might know where the dragon was now or be able to find out. Distracted by Dewar's spying activities, I'd lost a chance at perfect information. Hell!

"Lord Gwydion. We were expecting you. Come in," sounded a voice, genderless, neutral. A grey doorway dissolved like mist on the Wye on a summer morning.

I went forward warily, looking around. Behind me, the grey room disappeared as the door reasserted itself. A few abstract-looking chairs and tables of a hard white metal-like substance were scattered around casually. The floor was tiled grey; there was bright, directionless light from the colorless walls. It reminded me of the Eddy where I had gone to study economics and accounting. I had not liked the place and I had not much liked economics and accounting either. Worst of all, their best wines had been only average compared to home.

I remained standing, looking for someone to talk to. "I have a message from Freia for the Battlemaster."

A person, a woman I realized after a few seconds, dark-skinned and dark-haired, appeared opposite me, standing, fading into sight as the door had. "That is us. From Freia?" she said—or seemed to say.

"Yes," I replied. "She's still a distinct personality and it's possible to talk to her under certain conditions." I examined the woman cautiously, trying not to be too obvious. She was not really there; she was an illusion of some kind.

The illusion frowned a little. Very naturalistic. "Indeed. Continue."

"She wants you to incarnate and accompany me to Argy-lle." Was this Thiorn, I wondered, this image?

The image twisted its mouth ruefully; its expressions mixed oddly with the toneless voice. "Inconvenient. However, since it is a theft investigation, we will comply. Obviously there is no other way we will get to the bottom of this. We cannot locate Dewar, and sending a simulacrum is too expensive— even if possible."

"I believe she knows what Dewar may be up to and is of two minds about it. I'll try to track him down, and you can discuss it, all three of you."

The Battlemaster snorted. "Freia always was keen for discussions. So be it. Can you give us any more information?"

"Only that Dewar has a very powerful Elemental ally he may have watching us right now."

The image shook its head. "We are sealed. Nothing in here that we don't know about."

"I got in."

"That place is unsealed. It is left open on purpose."

I frowned. "You seem to know a fair bit about us."

The image lifted its eyebrows. "We do. We were friends with your mother, remember?"

"Before my time, I think."

"No, she was here recently. Relatively speaking. Hm. What does she think of this business?"

"As I said, she seems to have a fair idea of what Dewar might be doing. I confess I don't."

"Hm. This is interesting, very interesting. Wait for us here. We'll be a while, incarnating."

The image faded away. A tray with some food and a pitcher of a bright-green beverage rose up on a table beside me, its top opening and receding like a telescope dome. "Make yourself comfortable," said the disembodied voice.

I took a chair, ate, drank.

I hoped that I had not signed Dewar's death warrant. I suspected Freia would stick up for him, no matter what he had done or tried to do.

For what seemed to be an hour or two, I dozed. When I woke, my chair had molded itself to a more comfortable reclining shape. I dozed again. Direct work on the Spring always makes me feel like a nap, no matter how well I prepare myself.

A light cough woke me. The dark-skinned, dark-haired woman stood before me again, dressed in a red tunic with a high collar and tight black leggings and boots. She looked powerful and strong, carrying herself with the air of confidence experience and fitness bring. Over her hair and in it lay a sort of net made of silvery chain with jewels sparkling in it here and there. I had the impression it was functional and not decorative. She was armed with peculiar-looking weapons at belt and thigh.

"I'm real, not a projection," she said. "Shall we go?"

"You're singular now?" I stood, stretched, rubbed my eyes and smoothed my hair.

"For convenience, yes. I'm Thiorn Tolgaren Lell-Garrhan, by the way. I was the most recent addition to the Battlemaster, so I'm the default incarnation. Lucky for your mother." She extended her hand and I took it. Warm, firm grip.

"How so?" I asked.

"I'm more flexible than a lot of these old warhorses. That's why they mixed me in, of course." She grinned. She had a wicked, wild, lively grin. I liked her better as an individual than as a plural entity's façade, and I wondered how much of the Battlemaster was in her still.

I shrugged, took out the tools of my profession, and opened the Way back to my rooms in the Citadel. It was quicker by far than a Road journey from here to there, though I was intensely curious as to where *here* was. Since Freia had conveyed me, I didn't know, and if I were to try to make my own way out, I'd have been able to backtrack. Thus the secrecy of the place remained inviolate because I was in a hurry.

Once through my Mirror of Ways, I led Thiorn to the Black Stair by the indirect covert route. It felt like midmorning; I smelled baking and saw sunlight streaming through a couple of high ventilation slits in one part of the hidden passage.

We went down into the Catacombs with a lantern. I had decided to be conservative about sorcery in front of Thiorn, as I always was in front of the uninitiated or strangers. I'd have avoided the Way, but since I had arrived by that method it couldn't be novel to them.

"I've never been down here," she remarked as we trotted down the Black Stair. "Never got around to it last time I visited."

"That was during the Independence War?"

"Yes. —Where's Gaston? I couldn't find him anywhere. I

didn't know him well, but I didn't think he'd be hard to find. Is he here?''

"No. We don't know where he is. He has avoided Argylle since Freia's death. We have not heard from him since a few years after it happened. He misses her.''

Thiorn nodded, looking vaguely preoccupied. "I'll have to look him up one of these days. Maybe I'll play a little hooky . . .''

"What do you mean?''

"Not go right back to Kavellron. It's good to do something new once in a while.''

I could not see her; she was behind me—but I could hear her grin.

She continued, "What's Dewar like, Gwydion? The Battlemaster doesn't have much feel for nutty people, and I personally don't know him well.''

"He's not nutty. He's . . . upset. Still. I think.''

"Upset?''

"I'd rather not talk about it. You can ask him yourself when you meet him.''

"Oh, I will.'' She chuckled. "I have a lot of things to ask him.''

⌐— 19 —⌐

I UNLOCKED THE DOOR AT THE bottom of the stairs and led Thiorn to the Spring. We had the place to ourselves. Virgil was gone. I stopped at the bench, bowed my head, and concentrated. Thiorn tipped her head on one side and closed her eyes.

The Spring splashed and sparked as it had on the day of Mother's death when Dewar had found her there. I threw my hand up before my face; Thiorn just squinted into the glare.

"Thiorn. You?'' Freia's voice suddenly echoed through the

dark, empty space around us. The Spring calmed, but seemed to quiver still.

"Me. Things have been quiet lately. They defrosted me and sent me off to do some detective work." Thiorn looked at the Spring, pacing around it slowly. "Interesting. How the hell did you do this?"

"It was an accident. I was thrown into it and it consumed me. Now I'm part of it forever."

"Forever. Eternity is a long time, Lady."

"The first twenty-three years haven't been so bad," she said more softly.

"You like it in there?" asked Thiorn, clearly thinking otherwise.

Silence. "It's not that unpleasant now that I'm used to it."

Thiorn snorted softly. "But there are things you might rather be doing."

Silence. "I have something important to do here."

In an almost accusing tone, Thiorn said, "You wouldn't have chosen this, though, I think, Freia."

"Probably not. But it appears to have been necessary."

Neither of them spoke for a few minutes. Thiorn continued to circle the Spring, eyeing it. I wondered how much she knew about it.

"Mother, did you find Dewar?" I asked.

A sigh. "I did encounter Ariel, but he fled across the Border before I could fasten on him and give him a message."

"I'll get him for us, then."

"A Great Summoning to Pheyarcet?"

"Yes."

"Please go a little ways away, then. It's very . . . uncomfortable for me to deal much with . . . Well things. Pheyarcet things. Even insulated by a spell."

"Of course." I picked up the lantern and walked away among the massive stone pillars, my light a homely inconsequential spark in the darkness. Were all the pillars hollow, or

only the one that held the Black Stair? Behind me I heard
Thiorn and Freia talking quietly. Old friends that they were,
they'd have a lot of catching up to do.

My footsteps bounced off the vaulting and echoed back to
me with metronomic regularity. When I couldn't hear the
voices any more, except as a faint echoey murmur, I stopped
and put the lantern down. Using my lantern for the flame, I
prepared the spell carefully. No weaknesses anywhere, and
all the power of the Spring to draw upon, so that he couldn't
fight back or block this. I chanted, spoke, named Dewar and
locked his Key into the structure of the spell.

The spell closed around me and the Key and began seeking
Dewar to complete itself. I sought with it, a racing, soaring
feeling of pure power rushing through my hands and head,
accompanied by the aching feeling of dissatisfaction from the
spell: it longed for Dewar, it existed for him and because of
him, and it had to find him, I had to find him . . .

My control of the spell began to feel tenuous. I was overex-
tended. Damn. I would have to stop and reconstruct. It was
too great a distance for a Great Summoning . . .

As I began to dissolve the Summoning then, I got a little
jolt through the Key. Immediately I returned to building the
spell up and as I surged into it, the lantern's flame flared. I
cried the final words, feeling opposition coming my way, as
with all the power of the Spring I Summoned Dewar to
appear before me. The aching dissatisfaction faded. The spell
was completed.

He struggled in the net of my sorcery.

The lantern flared again, cracking the glass, and with painful sympathetic fires running through me I had to withdraw.
I sent a probe toward Dewar. He sent a return shot so powerful it caused the lantern to explode—my head hurt now—and
left a burning puddle of oil on the floor. Another pulse, and
it flared waist-high before me. Pursuit! Good. I drew my net
back slowly, but Dewar began to squirm away. Reinforcing

the Summoning with a few quick words, I cast until I touched him again.

Anger! A smattering of fear. I had him, though, and now we wrestled. I was on my knees, gasping, hoping only that he recognized me and didn't get too rough. A Well-probe suddenly lashed back toward me, severing one of my lines of force, like losing an arm in a sword-fight because the spell and I were so closely intermingled.

I yelped with shock and pain, and my pain seemed to echo and another cry followed my own.

"Cut it out, Gwydion!" came to my ears.

"Speak to me right now or I'll come after you in person," I retorted.

A few hot, irritated bits of inexpressible emotion and hostile intent came, along with, "Since you ask so *nicely,* very well."

Snap! He pulled away and I released my net and waited, drenched with perspiration, shaking and panting with my back to the cold stone of the column. Something dripped on my hand. I touched my face and found a gash from the flying, shattering glass of the lantern.

A few seconds later there came the gentler feeling of a Lesser Summoning. The flames in the oil on the floor were fading, but they flared up and blossomed into a sheet to show me my uncle.

Dewar was wrapped in a too-small rose-colored satin robe, sitting on the side of a rumpled white circular bed hung with white, gauzy curtains. He was alone. The lighting was low and indirect. He too was dishevelled, panting, damp.

"You little asshole, you ruined my date," he said, glaring, and then grinned, shaking his head, tossing his hair out of his face. "Oh, well. Come easy, go easy."

"Sorry to spoil your fun," I said dryly. "Your sister wants a word with you Right Now."

"Oh," he said, and his eyes narrowed while his grin evaporated. Evidently this was not wholly unexpected. After a moment he sighed and stood. "I'll be right there," he said. "The Catacombs?"

"Nowhere else," I said. "The Spring. Five minutes."

He vanished. By the light of a wan ignis I walked slowly back to the Spring, which was agitated, darkness roiling in darkness. My footsteps were not so crisply regular this time.

"That hurt," Freia said tremulously.

Dewar's lashing at me and my spell had been transmitted to her, for she was the Spring. "I won," I said. "He shall join us."

Thiorn smiled, not very pleasantly. I sat down on the bench beside her and mopped my dewy brow and blotted the cut with my handkerchief in my shaking hand. Later I'd probably find the idea of interrupting smooth Uncle Dewar in a lover's boudoir far funnier than it was now. At the moment my head still hurt.

"Aha," Freia whispered suddenly.

Approaching footsteps sent Thiorn bounding to her feet. A fist-sized, faintly pulsating ignis accompanied Dewar. He had dressed hastily; as he walked toward us he was still stuffing his silky black-embroidered white shirttail in one-handed, the other hand holding a black shoulder-bag and a thin black staff I recognized as one of his favorite instruments. He moved with his characteristic fluid assurance.

Dewar stopped when he saw Thiorn. I felt a sudden flow of chill force on a very low level, unlike any sorcery I knew, from her toward him. It broke off when she nodded.

"He's the one," she said.

A cool draught moved around all of us, touching cheeks, ruffling sleeves, and faded away into the stillness of the Catacombs, but there was a curious stirring beside Dewar. Ariel.

I rose to make the introduction. Mother, good manners intact, preempted me.

"Dewar, you remember Thiorn Tolgaren Lell-Garrhan, the current incarnation of the Battlemaster of Kavellron," said Freia's voice behind us. I glanced back automatically, and jumped. She had manifested an image, an illusion of herself, just as on the day of her death or transfiguration. Red dress, dusty blue-green cloak, her hair in a loose knot.

My throat caught. I wanted to run to her and grab her out of the Spring where she stood on its nonexistent surface.

Dewar bowed, courtly and confident. "Unforgettable." He smiled.

"Thiorn, you'll recall Dewar, my brother."

Thiorn nodded, eyes half-closed, smiling a little. "Naturally." I hadn't known they'd met before.

Dewar joined us. Thiorn was as tall as he and looked him right in the eye. "I take it that's your . . . device," she said, glancing at Dewar's left side. His sleeve fluttered in a localized draft.

Dewar nodded. "Ariel, meet a tough lady."

"How do you do, madame," Ariel replied, a breathy whisper.

"You have stolen material from the Kavellray Tamackay library," Thiorn stated.

Dewar said nothing, but looked out at Freia.

"Dewar, *what* are you trying to do," she said, folding her arms.

"Get you out," he said.

"No," she said softly, pain in her voice and expression, shaking her head slowly.

"How?" asked Thiorn. "I ask as Freia's friend of long standing. Off the record."

He stroked his beard, studying Thiorn and deciding what to tell us. "Freia didn't ask for this," he said finally. "She's putting up with it because she feels she ought. That sleaze Panurgus—"

I couldn't help chuckling to hear our ancestor, the greatest of sovereigns, described so bluntly, and Freia smothered a giggle.

I said, "Panurgus? Is the dead king not really dead?" If so, his successor the Emperor Avril would be very unhappy to hear it. I set that aside for later consideration.

Dewar nodded without looking at me. "Right. He underwent a similar transformation, an apotheosis, voluntarily because he was dying anyway and his realm with him. Panurgus manipulated things here, I believe, so that a similar event would occur in Argylle."

"He denied this," Freia interjected hurriedly.

"When you asked, naturally; but I raised him and we discussed Josquin's visit and Dazhur," Dewar retorted. "Anyway, why he did it is something we could speculate on for hours, days. He claims that our Spring needs a guiding intelligence beyond what it has by its nature, to guard the interest of the realm."

"Interesting idea," Thiorn said.

Dewar lifted his eyebrows. "However, this seems a little unfair to me. Freia, a person known for her devotion to the Dominion and her dutiful attitude toward it, has been cozened, and I cannot countenance it. We got along without having a soul, so to speak, trapped in our Spring. Tython was an aberration, an exception to the rule."

"Tython?" Thiorn asked. "What's that?"

"Freia knows better than I," said Dewar, prompting her.

"Tython was here from the beginning," Freia said. "He was and was not of the Spring; Prospero rejected him on the night of his great sorcery of Making, and Tython endured and hid himself and nursed his grudge until Dazhur called into the world for an ally in her own hatred. For she was made on the Night of Making, but Prospero did not want her for a lover."

I was fascinated. I hadn't known some of this.

"The world's oldest motive," Thiorn observed.

"Nor did anyone else of our kin want to share the Spring with her," Freia continued, nodding, "so she sought ways to work ill, rather than be happy with the life she had been given. I always pitied her and paid her little attention, and I should have been more careful. She was not as weak as I thought. Phoebe recognized that Dazhur had touched some other power—she was not sure what it was—but now it seems that it was the Well of Fire, Panurgus, and that he tutored her. So Dewar says. Dazhur found the creature Tython whom Prospero had cast out of the Spring and shaped him crudely, and they learned to raise lesser and greater ills. Tython had a little power over the Spring because of his close association with it in the days before the Opening.

"I believe their ultimate plan was to reshape the world in such a way that the Spring would be sealed off into a pocket, which would starve off our Argylle and create, perhaps, something new elsewhere—under their command, the snake and the witch. They had made some progress with this when we interrupted them, and in the fight . . . In the fight Tython knocked me into the Spring."

"Which was what Panurgus wanted," Dewar said. "Dazhur was a deluded puppet."

"What's the point? What does it get you?" Thiorn asked.

"I watch," Freia said.

"Everything?"

"I guide. I consider. I will tell you things if you ask me."

Her brother nodded, folding his arms and regarding her. "A sibyl and a guardian. But not a very good one. Her spirit isn't in her work," Dewar went on. "I suspected as much when the dragon Gemnamnon was able to enter the very heart of Argylle and dwell on Mount Longview without Freia really noticing or doing anything, as she could and should have, to prevent it."

"I was preoccupied," she said defensively.

"Exactly. You've been fretting around trying to track down Gaston, causing all kinds of disturbances to boil up at the Border and into Pheyarcet and Phesaotois—unneighborly of you, stirring up their Eddies and jittering their Roads." He lifted an eyebrow at her. "Right? You've let quite a number of uglies slip past you, in fact. Careless of you. It took a dragon to catch your attention."

I opened my mouth and shut it. How could he know about that? He hadn't been here. Had *Dewar* been behind the plague of monsters visited on us? Had he *sent* Gemnamnon? All in an effort to get a rise out of his not-dead-but-transfigured sister? I began to give weight to Gaston's assessment of him: a little crazier than he seemed.

"Yes, but," Freia replied, still defensively, "I was worried about you too. We talked about this last year. I've been doing better since."

"You still don't like it, do you," he said gently.

No answer. Freia hugged herself, a misleadingly natural gesture, and almost hung her head.

"But," she began again, and stopped.

Thiorn's head was tipped again, her half-closed eyes on Dewar. "So what does this have to do with our little problem," she prompted him.

He flicked his left eyebrow up and down and returned his attention to her. "It is possible that she can be freed from the Spring. It is not as simple as her entrapment—there is a sorcerous procedure I've been working on which must accompany the, uh, sacrifice. But to get her soul out, there must be someplace to put her. Providing that is actually the easier of the two parts."

"A body," Thiorn said. "I see—"

"You idiot," Freia said. "You perfect *idiot!*" A fountain of hissing, tiny droplets burst up near us and fell back, each glowing a different red through a ruddy spectrum.

Dewar looked at her, eyebrows raised now. "It's possible!" he said, holding up a hand. "I've been working on it, and I've already succeeded—"

My breathing stuck. Ulrike. Was she Dewar's creature, then? Of course! That would explain her blankness; she wasn't meant to be real. He and Gaston, working together to create and nurture—

"Fool! What have you done?" Freia interrupted his words and my thoughts. The Spring boomed tidally from side to side. The oscillation made me queasy.

"What have I done? What do you mean?"

Freia seethed more restrainedly. "That information is obsolete! The Tamackay record!"

Thiorn looked surprised. "How so?"

"I spliced a series of mitochondrial genes into myself," she said.

"How?" Thiorn asked, still surprised.

"I didn't work with the Tamackay. You were busy relocating after the abdication and the facilities were disrupted and overburdened."

Thiorn said, "Oh! Was that why you visited?"

"Yes. I went on to another place with the right kind of knowledge."

Dewar opened his mouth and closed it. "Oh."

"Dear fool," she said, and the Spring calmed around her and left them staring, a bit helplessly, at one another.

Dewar was crestfallen. His lovely plan, spoilt . . .

"You *cannot* use those data," Freia said, shaking her head. "Remember I told you I was experimenting on myself, trying to . . . to make myself . . . stronger. I was aging . . . I succeeded. If you gave me a body based on the old sequences," she looked weary, "I'd have to go through it all again."

"Oh," he said, and sat down heavily on the Botanical Gardens bench, shoulders slumped.

"But Ulrike's already . . ." I said, and wasn't sure what I thought.

"What?" Dewar asked dully.

"Ulrike," I said. "Isn't she—"

"Ulrike?" my mother repeated, puzzled.

"Who?" Dewar asked, and he twisted to look at me. "Oh, your sister," he added indifferently. "What about her?"

We stared at one another. "I thought she was . . . Couldn't you just . . ." I said, nonplussed by his reaction.

"Gwydion!" Freia said, her voice echoing through all the darkness and going through my head like a cold wire.

Dewar said then, "Oh. Oh, hm." But his expression was not particularly disapproving. "Ulrike," he repeated. "You thought she was *my* work? A construct?"

"Um."

"I'm flattered," he decided, "and it's certainly an old practice to trade one life for another that way . . ." His voice trailed away. He swallowed.

"Don't. You. Dare," Freia rumbled from within the bubble of force. The Spring became a globular eruption of incandescent gold, concealing her; we all turned away, bright-edged shadows cutting the dark stone into silhouettes.

"No, no, naturally not," Dewar said hastily, turning back to her, shading his eyes and gesturing. "Please stop doing that; you're going to give us radiation poisoning." Despite the joke, he looked a bit pale and ill.

The Spring, with an air of insulted outrage, whumped as its unnatural illumination dimmed and calmed. It still shone, but less sunlike. Freia's image shimmered only faintly over it.

I looked away again, chagrined. Now that I looked at it here, in context, it did seem like madness to have entertained the idea that Ulrike was expendable for the sake of perpetuating Mother. I wished I had not said anything. It was a shameful thought to own.

"This puts a different, and rather tragicomic, face on things," Thiorn remarked, and sat down. My uncle snorted softly. "You are a well-meaning bunch of amateurs," she added, without condescension.

She produced a long, slender black pipe and filled it with a reddish powder from an ornate little black bottle, then lit it and smoked reflectively. Dewar ran his hands over his face and then rummaged a flat black case of cigarette-papers and a pouch of something green and dried out of his bag. He rolled a slender smoke. Thiorn offered him a light and he accepted.

"See, Freia, we need you," Dewar said after a few minutes, still a little weakly. "Such mischief children get into without supervision."

I turned and nearly hit him, stopping myself in time. Slowly I unclenched my fist. I was upset, shaking and angry; it was a child's rage, striking at someone else when my anger was at myself.

"It's all right," whispered something just at my ear, something Dewar and Thiorn plainly could not hear. "I understand," it added, Freia's voice very small.

I exhaled slowly. Across the Spring, Freia looked at me and smiled a little, sad smile that my uncle and our guest didn't see, as they were looking at one another. I smiled a little bit back, forgiven and ashamed. If Ulrike had not been so afraid of the Spring . . . It did not bear thinking of.

Again that long-familiar voice whispered at my ear. "Don't worry about it." A warm nothing touched my hand for a moment and vanished.

With a sigh, I leaned on the column behind the bench and took out my own pipe. The smoke rose up beyond the sphere of lantern-light into the vaulted dark.

Freia turned half-away, folding her arms again, looking down into the Spring to all appearances.

"So you can't get out without a host body to receive you," Thiorn said finally.

"Correct," Dewar replied for his sister. "According to Panurgus, someone can jump in the Spring with appropriate preliminaries and be immolated on her behalf, leaving her a body, and dying—really dying."

"There are surely better methods." Thiorn blew a smoke ring.

Dewar studied her, flicked an eyebrow, and said nothing.

"I myself am an example of a stored personality reincarnated," she pointed out. "Moreover, in my case I have to separate myself from a collective identity, a group mind if you will, to be reincarnated as me."

"Interesting," he said.

Another smoke ring. "Crude, crude, crude," she said finally. "There's a couple of ways I can see—"

"Wait a minute. What are you talking about?" Freia interrupted anxiously.

"This is an fascinating problem," Thiorn said. "Your brother picked the right time to rob us. I'm a sympathetic cop." She smiled crookedly.

Freia spread her hands and shook her head. "I have to stay here."

Thiorn leaned forward and jabbed the stem of her pipe at Freia's image. "No, you don't. For one thing, it was involuntary, and involuntary personality transfer is rape. For another, you're doing—according to Dewar who was telling the truth, or most of it—you're doing a crummy job. Better to leave it. For a third, you yourself would never support a society, a world structure, that relies on the misery and enslavement of one person to secure the happiness and safety of the rest." She leaned back. "This Panurgus character is your source of information?"

"Yes—"

"Don't trust him. He sounds like he has an interest in keeping you here. He also sounds like he doesn't understand the first thing about personality integrity and transfer procedures, never mind fundamental morality and human decency."

This sounded just like the beginning of one of Mother's classic anti-Landuc, anti-Noroison tirades. I hid my smile.

"Yow." Dewar smiled. "So you think we can do it."

"We? We who?" She looked him over. "I'm here to kill you, buster. Stealing personal genetic information is death. Clearly you should have talked to Freia about this first. Double rape is worse than single rape."

He drew back. Ariel hissed and a whirlwind sprang up,

stirring our hair and clothing. I felt a flow of power to them. An anxious expression came over Freia's face and she started to say something, lifting a hand.

"But, as I said," Thiorn went on, "I'm a sympathetic cop. There's ways around this. And I'm not going to do anything until we see what Freia wants to do. As the offended party, she has a say. If she were *really* dead it would be for me to decide on the spot."

"He meant well," Freia said softly. "And he got the wrong information anyway."

"So where is the correct information?" Dewar asked.

She crossed her arms again and looked down, shaking her head.

"Freia, this is an utterly unnatural state for you," Thiorn said, getting up and approaching the Spring. "I know you, and I can read you now, easily, and you're thinking about that very agreeable man you wed, Gaston, and your family, and a lot of things you miss, still, even though you think you shouldn't." She pointed her pipestem at Freia. "Dare to contradict me. I can think of a number of occasions when you've tried to place what you thought was duty before self-interest and been wrong."

"Freia is never wrong," Dewar grumbled, lighting another cigarette off his third.

"Sure she is. She's not contradicting me, is she?"

She wasn't. She had turned away.

"For example, wasn't I right about that time with Herron on Sthanis?" pursued Thiorn, grinning quickly.

Freia sighed. "You two," she said, her back still turned. "This isn't fair. I know what Gaston would say if he knew," she added in an undertone.

"He doesn't?" Thiorn asked, her voice rising. "Why not? Where is he?"

The Spring receded, light fading, and Freia was only dimly visible in the darkness over it. "I don't know," said she softly to the other side of the Catacombs. "Somewhere in Pheyar-cet."

"I can find him," Dewar said, smiling.

"Don't," Freia replied, shaking her head, her voice almost inaudible.

"Why not?" Dewar asked, in the gentle tone of someone reasoning with a small child.

She shook her head again. "He went away," she said, "I suppose he had a reason, and if he wanted to come back he would have done. He sent Ulrike alone . . . Find him for yourself if you wish, but not for me."

"He'd come right back if he knew. I could find him and tell him," Dewar suggested in the same tone.

"No. Too many people know already."

"Who knows?" Thiorn asked.

"Everyone who knows is right here, although Prospero may suspect something or know something he has not spoken of," I said.

They glanced back at me, Thiorn spinning quickly around.

"Gwydion, I'd forgotten you," Thiorn said. "You're quiet. What do you think? You're nominally in charge of this puddle of power."

"It worked perfectly without Mother. If she can be extricated without damaging it, I will render what assistance I may."

Thiorn turned back to Freia. "So Gaston doesn't know. *I* bet he'd say, get you out. There isn't a man alive who'd prefer his wife a martyred ghost given a choice of having her living and breathing beside him instead."

Dewar ducked his head, grinning quickly.

Freia turned back to us, shaking her head. "Papa wouldn't—"

"To hell with him!" her brother cut her off, jumping up, gesturing sharply. "Have you talked to him yourself? Let him know? Or has he tried to talk to you?"

"N-no," she admitted.

"It's not for him to approve or disapprove anything you do," Dewar said. "Leave him out of this; you know as well as I how he is, how he's always been. He'd say No, and I say you, your desires and your needs, should be considered first. Argylle was well enough with the Spring in its natural state! No harm can come of returning to that."

For a moment, they gazed at one another, and then Freia nodded. "You're right," she said. "I had liever not bring him into this."

Dewar nodded, and Thiorn came back to the bench. They sat down again. She said, "It is an interesting problem . . . As I understand it, if one of the initiated, who are all members of your immediate family, goes through certain preliminaries, he or she can draw on the power here and manipulate it."

"Yes," Dewar said.

"So, Freia, since you're part of it, what are you worth?" Thiorn went on. "What can you do?"

"I can do almost anything I want but leave Argylle's Dominion, the areas covered by the Road and Leys that have their source in Argylle's Spring, of my own accord. I cannot pass the Border, in short, without assistance from an initiate, who must arrange a . . . buffered reconciliation with the Well for me to do so, a balanced spell. It is easier for me to get to Phesaotois. Sometimes I can do that alone, but it is difficult."

"Suppose you put together a spell of Sending such that your personality, your identity, be transferred, sent, to an available host."

Silence. Freia considered. "I don't know. It's never been done. I can't see how it would be done."

"Sorcery is my bailiwick," Dewar reminded her. "I have been working on exactly this plan. I believe it can be done."

"We'll try that, then." Thiorn tapped her pipestem against her chin. "You'll have to point us toward your updated information. We can make you a new body and you can shift into it. Much better than relying on someone to sacrifice themselves for you, if less poetic."

Nobody looked at me, but I felt my cheeks grow warm I owed Ulrike an apology, unspoken but genuine.

"But Tython may take that opportunity to attempt to reenter Argylle," Freia protested.

"Tython is destroyed," Dewar said firmly. "When you fell in you annihilated him."

"C'mon, Freia. Give it a chance," Thiorn said. "Life is fun."

"I know it is." She looked down, around, up. "I see it all around me. If I had known you two were going to gang up on me, I would never have put you in the same room."

Dewar chuckled softly. Thiorn grinned.

Freia flicked out of view. Her voice went on. "In the city of Contrevis there is a spaceport. A man named Lars Holzen passes through there every fifty days. Mention my name to him and tell him I require the services of the Clinic. The keyword to identify yourself to him as truly a friend of mine is Renndamond. You will find everything you need among them; they too have perfected a version of the art of personality transfer. The place lies in an Eddy on Pheyarcet's Road."

Silence.

"So, Ariel," Dewar said, extinguishing his cigarette and pocketing the butts, "off you go."

I was envious. What might take me years to research, Dewar accomplished with an offhand command to his familiar Sylph.

"Gladly, Master. There's none can hide from my fingers." Ariel whooshed out. The stillness that followed was startling; I'd grown used to his constant stirring and draughting about.

"How long will he take to find it?" I asked.

"Don't know. It could be a while," Dewar admitted. "I think I'd better lie low still. This is not a project the general public needs to know about. Or anybody else, for that matter." He gave me a piercing, meaning look.

I understood perfectly: especially Prospero. "Definitely not." I stretched.

"We'll do the legwork," Thiorn said. "Dewar seems to have a vague idea of what is involved and you, Gwydion, can be our contact here."

"All right," I said. "You're going to build a body?"

"Yes. With the correct information, it'll be a snap." Thiorn smiled. "This Ariel, it can move through the worlds? See things, find things, tell you?"

"Correct," Dewar said. "When told what to look for."

"Too easy, almost. Hm. Freia had all these pieces. She could have put them together."

"Her sense of obligation doubtless impeded her," Dewar suggested. "Fortunately yours appears to be more malleable."

"Yes." She grinned at Dewar. "I'm hungry. Let's get a bite to eat and wait for this creature of yours to pop back up."

"I'd better go run the nation for a while," I said. "Apprise me of your progress, when you've made any."

Dewar grinned back at me. "Yes. Thanks, Gwydion."

"For what?"

"Ruining my date."

I laughed, took the lantern, and climbed back up to the Core.

⌐ 20 ⌐

"GWYDION!" PROSPERO CALLED TO ME FROM one of the catwalks above me.

"Hullo," I said, looking up.

He lifted his eyebrows with an *And?* expression.

After a moment's guilty anxiety, I recalled that I hadn't spoken to him or Walter since returning, and that they had no idea what I might have found out lately about Gemnamnon. And I kicked myself covertly. Distracted by the immediate, I'd forgotten, once again, to ask Freia if she knew any-

thing about him. Indeed, I could have asked Dewar for tips
on dealing with the damned beast, if I'd kept my wits about
me. I wasn't keeping my mind on my official job.

Prospero was coming down toward me, though, and
Dewar might not even be in the Catacombs any longer, and
I couldn't think of an excuse to run down there again after
obviously having just climbed up. In point of fact, I couldn't
think of much of an excuse for being down there anyway.

To buy time, I met him at the second floor, saying, "Let's
go somewhere less public."

"In all Argylle be few places more public," he replied,
looking up and down. He was in a good mood, it seemed.
"Come with me; I've undertaken to exercise droit du seigneur
'pon our pantry. Partake of the expedition and the spoils, if
you've stomach for it."

"Sounds like a fine plan to me." I suddenly realized that I
was famished. I couldn't remember when I'd last eaten. All
that sorcery takes it out of you, too.

So I followed Prospero down to the kitchen and we irritated the staff there considerably by getting underfoot while
they were trying to work. Bearing off a large, heavily-loaded
tray (I just kept adding things that looked good) and a bottle
of young wine, we made our retreat from there (pursued by
concerned cluckings from the principal chef Iviarre, who
thought I looked underfed and thus ought to take a custard-
tart too) to Prospero's study, which is a congenial place for
loafing.

He pulled back the curtains, looked out, and closed them
again. "Ugh. More snow. This winter shall we see more of't
than ever in my memory."

"Ugh." I opened the wine bottle.

"What were you about in the Catacombs?" he asked
abruptly, as he lit a three-globed oil lamp and brought it over
to the table where the tray waited.

My gaze by chance fell upon the corkscrew. I was inspired.
"Utrachet has been bothering me about the wine cellar prob-

lem," I lied glibly. "It occurred to me that if I could work out a way of protecting the area where the Spring is, I might be able to safely allow storage down there . . ."

Prospero grunted.

". . . I think it's innately too unstable though," I concluded, pouring. An uneasy feeling crept over me. My face felt warm. The false answer sat like lead on my tongue, tasted like lead too, and I reminded myself that I was obeying my mother's wishes. Though she had said, "Poor Papa," she and Dewar had concurred that all should be kept secret.

"Indeed; 'tis no more for public consumption than our wine. Next thing 'twould be some damn-fool tippling butler toppling in the blessed Spring." He clicked his tongue. "A touch too acid, this."

I checked the label, covering my guilty discomfort at his mention of the Spring. "Candobel," I said.

"Hm. How much have we?"

"Kind of a lot, I think. He had an unusually large production, didn't he?" I recalled figures, possibly inaccurate.

"Time's come, perhaps, for one of those endearing diplomatic gestures which do so much to foster goodwill 'twixt kings and kin." Prospero grinned sardonically.

I laughed, biting my lower lip. Argylle had, in the past, more or less dumped slightly inferior wines on our Landuc relatives, who rarely tasted Argylle's best. So far they hadn't caught on.

"We could certainly put something better in the space," I said.

"Were someone to consult the Ephemeris and see what anniversaries approach which would be fittingly commemorated with crisp autumn wine . . ." Prospero lifted an eyebrow, still smiling.

"I'll check, or have Anselm check. You're devious, Prospero." It wasn't really a cheat. Landuc would never know the difference, and the wine was still better than most of what they drank there.

I've outlived many fools," he said. "Hm. 'Tis better taken with food."

We pulled up a couple of leather-covered easy chairs and ate and drank without talking for a while. I consumed most of a smoked pheasant, a lot of other miscellaneous food, and a loaf of bread. Prospero watched me eat without comment after he finished his own more modest meal.

"Now, how fared you with Ulrike?" he asked, when I had slowed down and settled back with a glass of the wine.

"It was not pleasant."

"I'd imagine. Care to pass on the dragon's tale?"

"I'll gladly pass on the whole damned dragon, Prospero."

He looked at me, pained.

"Sorry. All right. I'm sure Walter tells it better than I do."

"Walter has fed me no more than the bare bones because," he said, "you gave scant meat, being tongue-tied and scatter-wit with fresh fright."

"I was not. Was I? I guess I might have been." I stared into the fire, remembered fear quickening my breathing. "We had climbed to a pass on the Argylle side of the Border . . ."

I did not gloss that we'd have been dead in our tracks but for the mysterious Gryphon which had championed us.

"You're certain it spoke?"

"Prospero, I would not invent something like that, not even to make a good story better."

"No," he said, "indeed, you would not. Hm. 'Tis a great curiosity."

"I don't think I've ever heard of a talking gryphon."

"Nor I. They screech, scream, squall, and squawk; betimes they hiss . . ." He shook his head.

"Maybe I hallucinated. I never asked Ulrike if she heard it too."

"It were a neat puzzle, if one did and t'other not, to say which heard phantom nothings. If phantom it was."

"I don't like dei ex machina," I said. "I want to know

where that Gryphon came from, where the dragon is now, where he's going to be."

"I agree with all my heart. Why then did you make such haste homeward?"

I blinked. "I thought he'd come here next."

Leaning back in his easy chair, Prospero regarded me, one eyebrow slightly arched. He stroked his neat spade beard with two fingers, waiting.

"I rode along the swath of destruction he left in the Valley," I said, "and they hadn't seen him since about then . . ."

Prospero lowered his head a millimeter, still gazing at me, still waiting.

"Should I have done more?" I asked, after a moment.

"You are the Lord of Argylle," he pointed out.

"My place is here when my realm is threatened."

"And when your realm is not threatened . . ." he said.

I felt a blush blossom slowly over my cheeks. I looked away from his unrelenting eyes. The fire popped in the stove.

"I suppose I could have . . . found out more . . ." I said after half an uncomfortable minute. "I . . ."

Ruthlessly, unforgivingly, I examined my own actions. I couldn't tell him about the Kavellron business, about Dewar and Freia, but all that was incidental—my course of action was set before any of that arose.

"I'm really afraid of that beast, Prospero," I said then. "He has it in for me. If that Gryphon didn't kill him, and I don't think it did, he's looking for me now."

Prospero shifted slightly, tipping his head back now. The lamplight touched the silver embroidery on his dark-blue doublet as he moved. He took a sip of wine and looked through his glass in the light.

"A man who'd conceal anything must first conceal nothing from himself," he said quietly after a moment. "I'd not grill you, Gwydion, nor scold you nor shame your fear—Gods, I fear him myself, to the soles of my feet, only a wittol would not. But you must not hide your fear and paint it over with good intentions to yourself. It cannot be reasoned away, only faced and outfaced. That's all."

My parents had told me similar things at various times. So had my tutor. I licked my lips and nodded, then had a swallow of wine.

"Yes," I said. "I'd forgotten that. Thanks."

He caught my eye and leaned forward suddenly, picking up the wine bottle and topping off our glasses with the last of it. "Just doing my job," he said with a slender smile.

"What job is that?"

"I know't when I see it," Prospero smiled more widely and we touched our glasses together and drank. His smile faded as he leaned back again. "This dragon has been most all my thought," he said slowly.

"Mine too. Tell me what you think."

Prospero snorted. "I think he'll be difficult to be rid of as Madanese pox."

I cleared my throat. "There are two methods: sorcery or weaponry of the conventional sort. The first has been more successful than the second. I don't know how much more sorcery I can pull out, though, Prospero. There isn't much that's more powerful than what I've thrown at him already."

He nodded.

"I'm not quite at my wit's end over it," I said. "There are hugely dangerous spells that would probably do him in. The difficulty is they'd probably have wide-ranging and completely unforeseeable side effects on the Dominion at large."

"I know the spells you speak of. I'd liever keep the world and kill the dragon, not banish both."

I nodded. "So that leaves conventional weaponry."

"So 'twould seem. Explosives . . ." he narrowed his eyes and looked at the glass-fronted stove where orange flames nodded.

"I don't know that much about them. Gaston would know

about bombs and the like. I haven't worked with them first-hand."

"Ah."

"Have you?"

"Yes."

"Then I delegate you to think about explosives that would give Gemnamnon the bellyache to end all bellyaching."

"Hah, I've already done't. Those incendiaries and disrupters I deem sufficient to split him crop-to-crupper would linger also, a vaporous miasma, and befoul the wider realm."

"Oh. Rather like sorcery."

"Mm-hm."

"There's always diplomacy," I said, slumping in my chair.

"Be of good cheer. I've expansive knowledge of explosives, and you've conned your sorcery well, but neither knows all his art."

"I'd not flatter myself so, certainly not."

"Nor I. 'Tis not unimaginable that the measure we need is known, and is but out of reach to us."

I understood. "I could dig around a bit . . ."

"You could, yes." He smiled. "Throw out a well-baited line and see what odd fish takes the hook."

"Dragons are more common in Phesaotois. Someone there might know something that wasn't in my books."

"Mm-hm."

I felt myself reddening again. I had hightailed it home because I was afraid of Gemnamnon. Now my error in doing so was staring me in the face, as was the inappropriateness of my bargain with Virgil. I should have done more legwork while I was away. I could have gone into Landuc itself, called on Oriana and buttered her up for information, could have ridden to Morven even . . .

"Gwydion," Prospero was saying.

"Huh?"

"You're granted a grace period. Use it wisely; its term is

unknown and its end is near-certain. Cast your will to the wind and follow it, or think swift and fast—but act."

I nodded. The clock chimed.

"Ah. I," he said, rising suddenly to his feet, "have an engagement at the theatre. If you'll excuse me . . ."

"Of course," said I, and stood too.

I envied Prospero. He went off to the theatre with Zhuéra Pellean, who was staying with a friend in the City, and I went off to my office to brood over my problems.

On the other hand, I mused, doodling gryphons, they were his problems too. Prospero had been careful not to give even the smallest bits of advice until this business had come up, though he'd not hesitated to point major things out to me when he thought I was missing them. He was letting me run the show, as he saw it, I supposed. But it was his Argylle, his home at risk here, and if I screwed this up the place he loved could be severely damaged.

If worse came to worst, he might boot me out of the Black Chair and take command until the crisis was past.

I didn't want it to come to that. If I were so incompetent as that, I'd deserve to be hanged. I didn't want this job, but, by the Spring, now that it was mine I had to do it.

Still, I envied him his theatre date and his lover and his nights of physical pleasure and relatively peaceful sleep. I had neglected my own connections in the past few months; I hadn't pursued Evianne hotly enough at New Year's; and lately word seemed to have gotten around that I wasn't available, because nobody had made me any offers lately.

I growled and wrecked the pen nib, splaying it out. I picked up another one.

Work hard, play hard, I thought. When I was through with this dragon, when his hide was being preserved and stuffed for my gloating pleasure, I would indulge every impulse I had.

I hoped I'd have a few good ones left by then.

Alexander had disparaged Walter's settled, snug pairing with Shaoll, but his own bed-hopping was the same thing, inverted and distributed. I wondered if Alex ever was too busy to hunt down a lover. If only I had someone around, I wouldn't be; it was the time-consuming business of getting started that I couldn't quite manage. It would be nice to have that refuge available. Someone who would work my body over and leave my brain refreshed, or even better someone like Shaoll who would deftly relieve me of a few of my duties into the bargain. And maybe a knack for sorcery . . . Wishful thinking.

How in the world had my mother, filling the Black Chair more competently than I was doing and with less help, ever found time for the even harder work of building and maintaining her rock-solid and marrow-deep love affair with Gaston? The job could not have changed much, but it took every minute of my waking time and many from my sleep. I supposed I could advertise that I was in the market for a full-time on-call lover. In Argylle that would be a joke, and it would lead to a lot more jokes, all at my expense. No thanks. All I had to do to get what I wanted was spend time looking for it. Almost nobody here, where procrastination and scenic detours and slow living were the rule, would believe that I didn't have time to visit Evianne Perran for a few months of courtship and play before consummating the affair. *Everybody* had time for sex. Even if they had no time to fill out their tax forms, they had time for sex. It was knit into the fabric of life as thoroughly as eating. Mother had shaped that into Argylle on purpose—and she had had Gaston.

I didn't even have time to think about sex. With another growl, I wrecked the new pen's nib too and then tossed it aside. My desk blotter was a mess of blots and splats. Anselm would replace it tomorrow morning. I went to my workroom and started pulling books off the shelves, and I sat down and stayed up until midnight and after, compiling a list of sorcer-

ers in Pheyarcct and Phesaotois who might know a way of
beating a dragon.

In the morning I took a sadistically cold shower-bath, because I had realized sometime as I slept that none of those
people would so much as give me the time of day without
gleefully charging me a heavy load of service or worse for it.
I couldn't just ask for help and get it, not unless the person
I asked owed me already. That was how the sorcery system
worked everywhere but with Dewar and me. I wasn't owed
any favors just now, either; our sorcerous colleagues tended
to avoid my tutor and me, not trusting us because he was
different and had made me that way.

I muttered obscenities, dried off and dressed, glared at
Prospero's door on my way to breakfast where I drank half
a pot of coffee all by myself. I learned from the kitchen lassie
who brought my food that Prospero hadn't come in last
night. Then I went up to my office and met with Anselm and
took care of a few things Walter hadn't wanted to proceed
with in my absence.

"There are four petitions to the Black Chair," Anselm
said.

By Hell's iron bells, as Prospero would say. "I just cannot
sit today, nor tomorrow in all likelihood," I said. "I must
study the dragon problem. Who knows I'm back, anyway?"

"The Citadel staff, of course—"

"I'm not back. As far as anybody's concerned I am not
here, I'm away, and I cannot be distracted. If any of the
petitions are urgent, ask Walter to take the Chair on my
behalf. He does it well enough." Prospero disliked taking the
Chair, and I did not want to stir him up by requesting he do
so when he was clearly preoccupied.

Anselm swallowed. "Very well, my Lord. Shall I so inform
him?"

"Yes."

"Is there . . . will you require me further today, my Lord?"

"I might. Why?"

"If I can be of assistance, I will gladly . . . do anything, my Lord," he said.

Anything? I wondered, and shook my head. "I just have to think. Run interference for me."

"Yes, sir." Anselm collected his papers blandly and left.

The unsigned note, written in tiny, anonymous printing, was crumpled. Virgil's claws had torn it, too. He had offered it to me apologetically; it had been attached to a powder-grey pigeon he had killed, hunting in the courtyard. The dove's blood-beaded corpse lay on my workbench.

> *Gwydion,*
> *What is needed is found*

I looked at it again and then dropped the shred of paper in the flame of a fat candle and watched it burn up.

"Thanks heaps," I said to it. "Summon me, can't you?"

It became black ashes suspended in clear melted wax in the ivory well where the flame was cradled.

I threw myself into my chair and drummed my fingers on the arm. Virgil picked up the dove and took it off to eat it in privacy, his duty done. I would have liked more information. Such as, where did he find it? And what were they going to do now? And why had he not Summoned me to tell me? Why the blackout on communications?

I considered another Great Summoning, but I didn't want to come across as a whingeing, incompetent kid who couldn't do anything on his own. Dewar wouldn't have left me holding anything I couldn't handle . . .

. . . well, but he might, I thought, sitting up. I wasn't his student any more. I was a colleague, a peer. My problems were mine and his were his. We happened to have a common area of concern just now in the problem of Freia's ambiguous state.

Nobody was going to hold my hand, I reminded myself. The Lord of Argylle had to come up with his own solutions. And an idea toward one of them came to me.

I bounced up and went into my workroom, opened the curtains, and started a Lesser Summoning at a Mirror of Vision. I used the second-best one in case it broke, which seemed possible considering the power I was playing with this time.

The flame rose up; the glass fogged; the Key was hot in my hands, almost unbearably hot. I concentrated and murmured the spell half-inaudibly.

It took a long time, until "Gwydion . . ." I heard softly. "Gwydion?"

"I have a question. You *did* say you'd answer questions."

"Answers of a sort, at least." Freia's voice became stronger. It seemed to come from behind me, not from the apparatus.

I did not turn around. "None of that riddle crap, if you please."

"Dear."

"I beg your pardon," I said, embarrassed by my testiness. I had no reason to be rude to my mother.

"You're upset about something . . ." she prompted me. "Ulrike?"

Why was she so worried about Ulrike? Ulrike was being fêted and entertained by Alexander. "This dragon, Gemnamnon. Is he in your Dominion now? Or the Border?"

She actually laughed, low and rich. "Oh, no. No, no, no. He won't be back here, I don't imagine. Don't worry about him."

"Really?" I said, not believing it. "How? Why?"

"I took care of him, dear. He has a lot of thinking to do. He'll not be in Argylle any time soon, if ever."

"You took care of him? May the Lord of Argylle ask what you did?"

"I sent him packing with a flea in his ear," she said, not

laughing now but audibly smiling. "He knows better than to return, the great bully."

"But what did you *do*, Mother?"

"Don't worry about it," she repeated, and her voice faded away from me rapidly with that phrase, so that the last word was more something I filled in than something I heard.

"Freia!"

The Mirror cracked as I yanked at the forces in the spell, and my sorcery came apart around me.

I made a loud, rude, exasperated noise, and then I laughed at myself. How typical of rulers and sorcerers both, to get an answer and demand more than the oracle was ready to give. I had an answer, which was more than I had had half an hour ago. I had a reassuring answer at that.

Quickly, while it was fresh in my mind, I transcribed the conversation in my notebook and then looked at it, considering the nuances. Mother, apparently, had expelled or pursued Gemnamnon from her Dominion, with a few tart words to speed him on his way.

"Don't worry about it." She'd said that twice. But what had she done?

Could I, should I just take this at face value and not worry about it? A dea ex machina solving my problem for me—

I caught my breath, eyes widening, catching my own glance in the cracked looking-glass and staring at myself in the act of revelation. Had I *seen* Mother getting rid of Gemnamnon? Had that been a manifestation of hers there in the pass? The gryphon is our realm's emblem, after all. A golden gryphon on blue is our flag. Why not conjure a gryphon to counter an enemy of Argylle? It made perfect, beautiful sense, and if I'd been doing something besides running in circles lately I might even have guessed it myself, knowing what I did. Could Mother, controlling all the power of the Spring as she did, project or invent or create a gryphon capable of damaging a dragon as I'd seen that one do? And the Gryphon had said "These are mine," and called us childrcn of Argyllc. Pcrhaps it had been meant more literally than I had interpreted it.

What else could she do? Or rather, what couldn't she do? Very few people would be dissatisfied by such power. Yet, as Thiorn had pointed out, there were many things a disembodied sibyl couldn't have: her lover, the taste of her apple-trees' fruit, and all the pleasures a body can feel.

"Wondrous convenient," I said to the broken Mirror, "but how do I explain this?"

I looked out the window. Water was dripping from the roof, a thin rivulet sparkling as it plunged past to splat in the courtyard below. The sound of thawing—early, but optimistic.

A slow smile curled over my lips. I went into the bedroom and picked up the picture beside my bed. "Thank you, Mother," I said softly.

No answer. I didn't expect one. She had told Dewar that she was paying more attention to what she was supposed to be doing. If keeping dragons at bay was part of that, it was entirely to my advantage that she do so.

Prospero had reminded me last night that I had a grace period. I still had it. I couldn't blurt out at once that the dragon was apparently scourged out of Argylle for the nonce; that would inevitably lead to explaining Freia's state. To keep trust with her and Dewar, I must think of an airtight explanation. I reckoned that I had until late spring, because Gemnamnon had been out of sight for months after the fight on Longview.

I could, in fact, take a holiday from the whole business, while pretending to do something about it. Did Prospero think I should leave town? Fine, I would. When I conveyed Ulrike to Montgard, I had originally planned to be away for a couple of months, and Walter had agreed to substitute for me then. Let us simply hold to the original agreement.

Lunch felt like a good idea. I left my rooms and went downstairs, meeting Anselm on the stairs. It occurred to me that I'd been rather curt with him this morning. Rude, even. I turned around and followed him to his office, which was unusually messy—unusual for it to be messy at all.

"Sir!" said Anselm, turning; he was arranging a slipping pile of rolled papers in tubes on a shelf.

"What is all this?" I asked, looking around.

"You had asked," he reminded me, "for maps and architectural plans—"

"Oh. This is all that?"

"Yes." He wiped a look of vindicated injury off his face and replaced it with ready-to-help-you.

I looked at the books, the scrolls, the blueprints, the model . . .

"Put it in the Cabinet Room," I said. "There's that big table there. Put it all there, sort it out a bit, and I'll go in and play with it. I had no idea there was this much."

"Neither did I. The Archivist did ask several times if you wanted everything. I thought it best to have everything."

"It usually is. Sometimes minor things show up in only one place."

"It was little trouble for her to find, because she had kept it together after the . . . after her late Ladyship had asked for it."

Oh, yes. Mother had done a similar roundup, trying to find maps of the Catacombs and the Maze. "So it's all indexed and so on. Hicha is indispensable. Get Villon to move it for you." I turned to go and remembered why I had come there. "Anselm," I said, turning back, "I was rather short-tempered this morning. Sorry. It wasn't you, it's the dragon."

Anselm shrugged slightly, smiled slightly, and picked up one of the books and looked at it. "No offense taken, Sir," he mumbled.

I started to go again.

"Uh, m'Lord," he began.

"Yes?"

"Nothing. Never mind . . ."

"Spit it out." I tried looking at him the way Prospero had looked at me yesterday. It worked.

"Uh. While you were away, I . . . The other day, I . . . it was very odd, Sir . . . Is it possible that there is a ghost in the Citadel?" he asked, his voice cracking.

"Why do you ask?" I inquired.

"Just a . . . a sort of a . . . a person who . . . who wasn't there when I looked twice . . ."

"If we have a ghost," I said after a moment, "I'm sure it's a friendly one."

"Sure, Sir?"

"Certain. Don't worry about it."

He nodded, relieved.

"Where?" I asked, turning around again.

"On the Citadel."

I nodded thoughtfully and left. I didn't ask what exactly he'd seen. I was certain I could have guessed.

The sun was still low, but bright as new silver. I took myself for a thinking walk that afternoon, up the muddy paths beside the watery-iced Wye to Threshwood, along a pleasant path there, and back. It was dark when I returned to the Citadel, lamps flaring up along the streets and ways of the City, barges passing the Wye with sidelights hung out. I felt wonderfully relieved. I could take the trip I had planned on when I'd ridden out with Ulrike, with the ultimate goal of locating Gemnamnon, and just knock around. Return Hussy to Alexander. Drop in on my cousin Josquin, perhaps. He's always glad to see you when you come for an hour or a year, and his country is nearly as agreeable as Argylle.

I talked to Prospero and Walter over dinner, indicated that I thought I should hit the Road and finish the investigations I'd started, and they nodded. Prospero looked approving and Walter cheerfully agreed to sit for me. My conscience twinged again about this fresh lie, but to tell them what was really going on was just impossible. There was no way to do so and preserve the confidences of Freia and Dewar, who did not want him informed as to what was afoot. If either had wanted him to know, she or he would have told him.

I took comfort in the knowledge that all would be told in time, when Freia was with us again, and that surely a blur of secrecy over such an undertaking would be forgiven.

Virgil gazed on me and closed his eyes, expressing no opinion when I told him we were travelling again.

The next morning I packed my bags, saddled Hussy and Cosmo both, and left. I tried not to look too cheerful as I did it.

"Be careful," Prospero said in the stable-yard, clasping my shoulders.

"I will."

" 'Tis no empty courtesy, Gwydion: I mean it."

"I do too."

His eyes searched mine and then he nodded. "I wish—"

"What would you wish if you could?" I asked him.

Prospero's hands tightened. "I wish that moonstruck son of mine would show himself here. 'Tis no slight on your ability—but we'd be stronger with than without him."

"I know. The more firepower we have the better. I'll keep an ear to the ground for him too."

His mouth thinned, grew taut. "O' course. I daresay you'll hear nary a footfall."

"Maybe I'll get lucky."

"You'll have need of more than Luck, Gwydion. Don't rely on Fortuna."

"Fickle bitch. Never. I'll be in touch."

He smiled, just a twitch of his lips, and let go of me. I hurried to mount and rode out without looking back, riding Cosmo this time, leading Hussy.

Guilt choked me, and a little voice railed at me: I ought to tell him, I ought to turn back and tell him right now. Everything. Mother couldn't mean to leave him hanging like this.

I closed my eyes, reminding myself that Prospero didn't

know Dewar was all right, his same self as he ever was, grinning and screwing around and cooking up sorcery that would astound the ages and baffle the adepts. And he didn't know Freia was practically looking over his shoulder. As far as Prospero knew, his daughter was dead and his son was as good as dead.

But I didn't turn back, and so I didn't tell him.

⌒— **21** —⌒

COSMO AND HUSSY LIKED ONE ANOTHER. I never got to the Border so fast before, for one thing; they raced all the way there. For another, she kept following him around, and he did the protective act when we stopped for the night.

"You're just like your great-to-the-twelfth-grandsire or whatever he was," I told Cosmo the next day.

He snorted.

"I mean it. They say half the horses in Argylle are descended from Hurricane. That doesn't happen by accident."

Cosmo whuffed. We were cantering across the Valley. He was letting Hussy set the pace.

I had a thought, a silly one, and started chuckling. Wouldn't it be a coup, a good joke on Alex, to return a Trojan horse—so to speak? I'd have rights on the foal, and thus Ulrike would get a horse of impeccable bloodline and, no doubt, superb performance as a gift from both of us brothers—a family present. Hm. I'd have to find out when Hussy would be in season and arrange to visit or to borrow her again or something. It was feasible. Unless Alexander was intending to breed her with one of his handsome bays, which was what I'd be planning if I owned her.

Good idea, I decided, but unworkable.

My first stop in Pheyarcet would be Montgard. There I'd leave Hussy and see how Ulrike was getting along. Then I would go as the wind blew me. I deliberately made no plan. It seemed pointless; something would come up, an omen, a sign that would push me on the right Road.

My inclination was to visit Josquin for ten days or so. I had been more disappointed than I had wanted to show that Ottaviano and not he had come to Argylle in the autumn; of the two, Josquin was far more to my liking, lighter of mood and a brighter companion, quick-witted, easygoing, and affectionate. We had always intended to take a holiday together—Josquin was a keen swimmer and diver and knew any number of good places for the sport—and I had ever been prevented by one circumstance or another from accepting his oft-repeated standing invitation to come visit.

I was curious about Gemnamnon's exact whereabouts, and if possible I wanted to locate him without sparking him. Although Freia had chased him off, I was sure he'd be back yet again. His pride would demand it, at the very least; I was sure he could not accept defeat. Finding the dragon would be my task after I'd visited Josquin. I had no itinerary other than that: two stops and a bit of work.

No sendings, summonings, or spooks imposed themselves on me. I arrived at Alexander's house, having followed the Ley up from Montgard town, late in the evening; my passletter had stood me in good stead there with the watch. Hussy recognized home and perked up; Cosmo had managed to wear her down over the past couple of days. I suspected my brother would be annoyed with me for returning a tired horse, but there was no help for it. I had kept them both tighter-reined on the Ley from town, but one could see that she'd been worn out thoroughly. No harm done. She'd taken no injury from it.

Alexander's servants were startled to see me again; however, they recognized Hussy and took the horses off to be cared for while a maid led me to a waiting room and another trotted off to bring Alexander from his dinner.

"Gwydion! You're the last person I expected to see."

"You did say you wanted your horse back."

"I did, but I thought it would be a few months rather than a handful of days."

"Then I'll take her and begone."

He laughed. "If you've not yet eaten . . ."

"No."

". . . and if you hurry upstairs to the room Clodia is turning out for you and have a quick scrub-up and change your clothes, you will be in time for the fourth course."

"How's the lady I left here in your care?"

"At dinner."

"I see. I'll be along then. Put the pretty girl to my right, please."

"I'm afraid she's taken," he grinned, and the maid rushed in with a curtsey—Clodia, obviously, and rather pretty herself—and brought me to my room.

I had a fast wash and changed my clothes, beating the fourth course by several minutes and thus having a taste of the third, tender little roasted birds baked in a tangy sauce. Alexander's guests were a few young men of the local nobility and their sisters or lady cousins, with a smattering of the more experienced of both sexes. Alexander did have the pretty lady for himself, too, a stately auburn-haired woman somewhat older than most of his other guests.

Ulrike smiled at me from the hostess's place at the end of the table. I would hardly have recognized her. She wore a modestly-cut but flattering gown of shimmery blue silk decorated with seed-pearls in a diamond pattern and had more pearls in her hair and at her throat. The gentlemen to either side of her were obviously dazzled. She said little during the meal, and that in her soft, diffident way, but they fell over one another to agree with and buttress her slightest opinion.

It was an excellent meal; I was glad I'd made it in on time for part of it.

"You did very well," Alexander said to her approvingly

later, when his guests had departed to disperse through the neighborhood.

"I hardly knew what to say," she said apologetically.

"You said it well nonetheless, Mouse," he assured her.

Ulrike looked at me. "Did you mail my letter?"

"Anselm did," I assured her.

"Thank you. Was there . . . was there any mail for me?"

"I'm afraid I didn't think to ask for it," I said. "I'm sorry."

"That's all right," she said, looking down and then up. "Have you come to take me home?" my sister asked.

"No, not at all. Perhaps on my way back. I have business here and there and if you need an escort I'll provide it. I can come by on my way to Argylle and collect you."

"Oh," she said. "But . . . but is it safe? To go?"

"Of course it's safe!" I said, exasperated.

"You have taken care of your dragon then?" Alexander asked.

"He will not be bothering Argylle for a while. I have yet to find and act on a permanent solution. That is somewhat of my business now."

"Ah."

Alexander obviously thought I was either dilly-dallying or running away from the fight. However, I'd seen what had happened to his and Marfisa's direct approach.

"Have you talked to Walter lately then?" I asked Ulrike, to leave the dragon.

"Yes," she said. "He said you came home and left again at once."

"Nothing unusual in that," I shrugged.

"When would you be honoring us with your company once more?" Alexander wondered.

"I can't give you a date. Anytime from a fortnight to a month or so from now."

He looked at Ulrike.

She said nothing.

"Rikki, would that be all right with you?" he prompted

her. "To leave whenever Gwydion can conduct you back to the City?"

"I . . . I don't . . . yes, that would be all right," she said. "Of course. I don't mean to be any bother. It's fine."

"You're no bother," Alexander said.

"Very well," I said. "I will try to give warning, but I can't guarantee it."

"Especially if you come tearing in with a dragon scorching your ass." Alexander half-grinned.

"I gave him your address and said you were eager to resume the acquaintance," I replied. "He said he had far more important people to eat."

"It's quite late," Ulrike said nervously. "If you'll excuse me, I think I'll say good-night."

"I'm tired myself," I said, standing and yawning. "Good night, brother, and sweet dreams, Rikki."

I stayed one day, giving Cosmo a rest, and then rode down the Ley into the town and out to the Road through the dawn gate there. The landlord at The Mermaid's Cups remembered me. I took the fastest route to Josquin's, but it still was a few days' travel.

The Heir of Landuc, son of the Emperor Avril and Empress Glencora, is also Prince of Madana, which means he is directly responsible for a huge chunk of land including a number of distinct former nations conquered or absorbed long ago, one of which is larger than Argylle proper and the rest of which add up to something about twice Argylle's size. However, Josquin has never been much for administration. He has lackeys who do the day-to-day work, the month-to-month work, and the year-to-year work, and Josquin himself ignores, by and large, what they do. When he does not, he is a ruler from his father's mold: impulsive, though less haughty, less capricious, of widely varying popularity but not so feared as Avril, perhaps because of his endearing and redeeming dislike of pomp and circumstance and ceremony.

He does not impose himself on his subjects; he allows them to impose themselves on him occasionally; he minds his business and trusts them to mind theirs, holding aloof save to dispense favors or mete out punishments in exceptional cases. I could not govern Argylle thus; though Argylle mostly governs itself, the Argyllines would not stand for such detachment, but Josquin does very well.

Leaving the Road and asking around once I had reached Madana, I heard that his whereabouts were presently unknown to the public. Not wanting to waste time roaming around tracking him down, I did a Lesser Summoning one evening in a small clearing where a stack of logs left by a lumbering team provided an arena for the antics of a family of the local black squirrels and a loud, territorial black-and-red bird which kept trying to drive them away. I built my fire on a bare-scraped patch of the moist ground; the smoke rose in a slow column in the gold evening light. The wood was damp, so it was hard to get a decent flame going at first, until the spell invigorated it. I altered the phrasing of the spell slightly to put the image in the smoke, since there was so much of it.

The smoke curled and glowed dimly. It knotted and roped and twisted; it took on color and firmer-appearing shape; it smoothed . . . it stopped, blocked by an impedance on Josquin's side. There was a receiving focus, but it was covered or blocked.

"Who Summons Josquin?" came the call.

"It is I, Gwydion."

"Gwydion! Wait just a minute . . ."

I waited a minute and a half. Then, smiling, his pale-blond hair cut short and looking damp, Josquin appeared, tugging on the collar of his loose, open-throated cobalt-blue shirt. He sported three gold rings in his left ear, one with a dewdrop-like cabochon diamond, which I saw as he ran his fingers through his hair.

"I need not interrupt you; I will Summon you again later," I said. "It is nowise urgent."

He shrugged. "I have learned to take sorcerers as they find me," he said. "Else they elude me later . . . I have heard that you are dead, maimed, injured slightly, wandering, and all things in between, Gwydion. I see you are none of them."

I laughed and spread my arms. "Alive and well. And wandering, in your neighborhood."

"Ah," he said, grinning quickly. "Are you really. Where?"

"I have no idea. Some forest off the Road in your end of the world, that's all. It occurred to me it had been a while since we had seen anything of each other, and I have time on my hands . . ."

"I have time on my hands too," he said, grinning again. "I'm in Massila. Do you know it?"

"I have seen it on maps. I have never been there."

"Oh, you must come join me then. If you are looking to spend time in frivolity and self-indulgence, Massila is a fine place for it. There is a Road that will bring you into the main town square, actually there are several Leys too but the one that comes from the North is the best to use if you can manage it. The eastern Ley is *rather* marshy and you should avoid it."

"Where shall I find you?"

"At the Red Flowers Tavern. It's near the New Docks on King Street. Big place. I'll bespeak a room for you."

"Thank you, Josquin. I take it this is not a Royal Progress."

He laughed. "You jest, Gwydion. I am incognito and losing money desperately at cards . . . Oh, I am going under the name of Jehan Demortre."

"We'll see if I can turn your luck, then," I said.

"It's a damned good thing I'm incognito doing it, too, or Father would pack me off to Argylle again." He twisted his mouth wryly. "And you not home this time either."

I laughed; in a series of card games which had become

famous all through Landuc, Josquin had lost a lot of money and some extremely valuable lands to his bastard half-brother Ottaviano. The Emperor Avril, incensed, had refused to allow the transfer and had punished them both: Josquin had been banished to Argylle for seven years (hardly a stiff sentence, as it turned out) while I was Gaston's esquire in Landuc, and Ottaviano had been sent on a long, perilous ocean voyage and tedious embassy.

Josquin laughed too. "Ah well. All's for the best, they say. Safe journey, Gwydion."

"Thank you," I said. "Au revoir."

I closed the spell and threw a handful of earth on the fire. It was late in the day. With my Map and Ephemeris I found Massila, then traced a route there. It was not far away; travelling all night to catch a moonset Gate and a dawn Gate, I could reach there by midday tomorrow. So Cosmo and I had a brief rest—a bite to eat and a nap—and as a gibbous golden moon began to light the clearing through the leaves of the trees to the east, I mounted and rode off toward the Road again.

Massila was a high-walled city which had overgrown its walls. Small sub-villages clustered around the gates, poorly-constructed and clearly meant to be sacrificed in the event of siege, fire, or pressing sanitary problems. I had passed through beautiful, fertile countryside on my way here, glimpsing stately villas and their prosperous dependent hamlets as well as herds of lazy white cattle and bands of sweating laborers in the fields: stereotypically Madanese.

I entered the city on the Ley and followed it to the town square Josquin had mentioned. Just now the square was the site of a noisy marketplace, though, so I left the Ley at an alley that took me to another street that led me to the square by way of a smaller one, which featured a fountain where a number of women young and old were doing laundry.

Once at the market, I rode slowly around the perimeter

and asked a fellow whose clothing and bearing marked him
as a sailor the way to the Red Flowers Tavern in King Street.
He gave me accurate directions and half an hour later I was
sitting down to breakfast with Josquin, known as Jehan
Demortre, having rousted him out of bed myself and evicted
a pouting, curly-brown-haired young guest.

We spent the rest of the day and half the night talking,
bringing our old intimacy up to date. He was eager to hear
about the dragon; I told him the official version of the tale,
leaving out Dewar and my intuition as to the Gryphon's
origins.

"Damn! You were lucky, then."

"I was lucky. I wish I had his head and hide stuffed and
mounted. He is a nuisance."

"My dear cousin, you are the only man alive who would
describe a dragon big enough to squash a building by sitting
on it as 'a nuisance.' Nay, I retract: Dewar would too. I am
surprised that Alexander has not taken up sword and shield
and ridden off to hack through his gullet."

"Alexander would be killed if he did," I said, "as Marfisa
nearly was. The beast is not to be beaten so easily as that.
He's no run-of-the-mill animal."

"I'll have to take your word for it. Gods! I'd like to get a
look at him. I cannot imagine one so big."

I recalled something Prospero had said. "Didn't you meet
a great dragon once yourself?"

"Oh, damn. Yes. I thought you'd be asking about that,"
he said, shaking his head. "That was an odd episode . . ."

"What happened?" I poured us both more wine.

"You're a thoughtful fellow," Josquin remarked, and
drank. "Ah. Or you know how to get a story out of a man.
Well, it was odd, very odd. I don't think he was less surprised
than I. I was on my way to Bripf'vorra, on the Road, and I'd
missed a Gate—slept too late that morning, but I'd a ringing
hangover anyway and I couldn't ride very fast. I got stranded

at dusk in a perfect little pit, one of those wattle-and-daub villages that's a step above the woods, but not a high one.

"I spent the night there and they told me all kinds of lies about themselves—you know how rustics are when they're trying to impress a traveller and keep from being robbed—and I pretended to swallow them all and treated my boorish hosts with great respect. They were all pretty ugly-looking and thoroughly unwashed, and there wasn't a one of them I'd have cared to plunder of anything. They had more fleas on their bodies than on their dogs.

"One of the tales they told me was that there was a mighty demon that lived in the hills west of the hovel. He'd not been there long, and they'd decided he was a judgement brought on them by immorality or some such folly, because he'd eaten a number of them and their neighbors with whom they'd been feuding ever since dirt was invented. Indeed I could see the beginnings of a religion building around the incident, whatever the truth of it was. I expressed sympathy, hoped he'd eat more of their neighbors than of them, and tried not to laugh when they described the demon's fatal farting and other bodily functions, which had impressed them more than his appetite.

"The next morning I left, heading west because that was where my Road lay. They were quite happy to see me go, probably figuring that if their demon got me they'd have a few days respite from him. There was a Node a few miles away in the hills and my Ephemeris told me there was a noon Gate there at a wind-eroded arch, no chance of missing it for I'd not slept late in the hovel; the dogs and children began howling at dawn. So off I rode.

"The first sign I found that hinted things might not be as well as I'd thought was a place where the vegetation was blackened and burned, but not scorched. Withered up. It reeked of sulphur and, though I rode past as fast as I could, I noticed that it was quite neatly defined and not the product of fire or some kind of volcanism—nothing I'd seen anyway.

I was about three miles from my Node and so I hurried, figuring I'd be better off out of here.

"My second warning smelled even worse. I hardly know how to describe it—it was everything foul and putrid, with an acid edge that made my eyes water. I smelled it before I saw it, a kind of flow of . . . well, as it turned out, of shit, a huge pile as big as a haystack. It crowned a low hill like a pervert's grave-monument. I couldn't believe my eyes, but my nose was convinced, and my horse was getting edgy. We put distance between us and the sewage fast.

"The Node was the highest hill in the area, but the Road ran through a canyon hard by it, cut out by a thread of a river way down below. I love things like that, so I rode along peering down when I could see through the bushes and catching glimpses of the diligent little stream of water patiently working away among the rocks. The Node was just ahead, but it wasn't noon, so I took my time to look at the water, and I was looking down for an instant when a dark shadow occluded the sun.

"My horse reared, nearly throwing me to the stream—nigh on a quarter-mile drop—and I, taken utterly off guard, fought with him and danced him around getting him under control again. Meanwhile a nasty-smelling draft was coming along the canyon toward me, from the Node, and when I finally got the spooked horse to behave himself I wrestled him to face west so we could complete our journey. He went forward reluctantly; I'd never used the spurs more than I did then to make him do it. We rounded a corner and the poor horse stopped cold, shivering with fear. I stopped spurring him because I suddenly didn't care to go forward either.

" 'We meet again,' said the dragon sitting in the road in front of me.

"I responded as many intelligent men would. I said, 'What?'

" 'We meet again,' the dragon said, trying for the same

effect and not getting it because I'd never seen the beast before and I'd have liever never seen him at all.

" 'I beg your pardon,' I finally managed to say, 'I don't believe we've been introduced.' Gwydion, stop laughing. I was scared pissless and I hardly knew what I was saying.

" 'Your memory is as short as your life,' the dragon remarked, and he breathed a bit of fire and incinerated a pitchy stunted tree, which popped and exploded.

"My horse backed up a few steps and I let him, and my mouth said, 'I do believe, Sir, that you are in error, for I assure you I have never seen you before.'

"The dragon advanced and then bounded upward so that he was sitting on an outcrop of rock over me, and my horse bolted—not far, because I reined him in. I'd realized—I was rational, you see, just sounded daft, really—that when the Gate opened at noon I could get on the Road and get away. It would just be for an instant, and I'd have to move fast, but it was my only chance. Noon was coming apace.

"The dragon addressed me again. He said, 'Indeed you are a fool,' and used his tail to clear away brush from the slope between us. 'Do you think,' he went on, 'to use the same trick twice? Do you take me for a fool? It is you who are the fool, Sir Otto.'

"Astonished, I sat there staring at him for an instant, and the thought that ran through my mind was that when I got my hands on Otto I was going to keelhaul him. All kinds of little ancillary thoughts about why he might have set the beast on me ran with that one, and meanwhile I was saying to the dragon, 'Sir, I assure you you are in error, for I have no quarrel with you, nor any desire for one, and if you are wise you shall bear yourself likewise. I am not this Sir Otto against whom you doubtless have just cause for complaint.'

"The dragon seemed nonplussed by my insistence that I was not Otto. He leaned forward, moving his head this way and that, and the tentacles on his head—did I mention them?—waved at me like anemone-fronds. 'It is a trick,' he said, and inched forward.

" 'I am Josquin of Madana, Sir,' I said, 'Prince Heir of Landuc, and all the world knows me and where I may be found, Sir, and I have never refused an honorable challenge, and if you will find some cause for quarrelling I shall gladly meet you, Sir, but I shall claim the right of the challenged to choose the ground and the weapon.' Noon was less than two minutes away. I wound the reins tighter around my hands and got ready to turn and bolt. I hoped the horse wouldn't go to pieces under me.

"The dragon was finding this more and more confusing. He said to himself, 'It's not quite right . . . Not quite the same . . .' and bent even closer to look at me. His huge head was just four paces away; his breath was suffocating.

"Somehow I'd gotten the upper hand; I only needed a minute more to keep it and my life. I said, 'Sir, if I may be of assistance to you in your challenge to this other gentleman for whom you have taken me, I shall. I must forewarn you, however, that any act of hostility against my person will bring reprisals from the highest authorities and considerable mockery upon yourself, if you will insist on confounding my identity with, evidently, that of my half-brother Baron Ottaviano of Ascolet.'

"The dragon reared back and roared. 'A very pretty speech,' he boomed, but he still looked perplexed. 'Your half-brother! A romancer's hackneyed fiction!'

"We are superficially only faintly similar,' I said, 'and essentially different.' I suppose dragons must see things very differently than we do; I'd never been taken for Otto, and I pray I never am again. 'You have made an honest error, Sir,' I said. 'Do not compound it.'

"I do not err!' he decided, and leapt forward.

"I'd been watching him, though, and I saw those huge muscles—you've seen one now yourself, you know how big they are—bunch up, getting ready for the spring. I whipped the horse's head around and, about five paces ahead of the dragon, my cloak smoldering and the horse flying in sheer panic, I raced away along the pathway. A natural irregular wind-eroded arch was the Gate. I lived eternity while the horse went over those fifty feet, stones flying under his hooves and the gas from the dragon sickening us both. He went under, and the dragon missed the moment, and I got away."

"Whew," I said, and I poured from the fresh bottle of wine. "What did you say to Otto?"

"I took him sailing and told him about it, and while he was laughing I put him overboard with the boom and the boat-hook," Josquin said, "midway between Point Perrot and Wicksnaw Neck. There's a buoy out there to mark the channel, and if he couldn't swim to the Neck or the Point he could hang onto it and howl for help from a passing fisherman. Dewar thought that was a perfectly splendid payback." He smiled, not entirely pleasantly.

"I don't think he'd have set the dragon on you deliberately," I said cautiously.

Josquin snorted. "No, he didn't. He explained later that it really had been the stupid dragon's fault, told me a long story—oh, he told you, did he? I didn't see any reason to apologize. If you're going to have any dealings with such a beast, they'd best end with its funeral. But it did put me off them. I'd been on a jag of hunting the lesser ones, and I gave it up after that. Didn't care to press my luck. I'd not care to go up against one alone. Indeed I'd not go with anyone but you or Dewar. I dare say he could take one on and live to tell about it."

"He never told me if he did," I said, which was literally if not morally true, and I hurried on. "Or Gaston . . ."

"Oh, well, he goes without saying, and usually does at that. —I'm going to ring for more food, you'll like the smoked fish paté. —Where is Dewar, anyway, Gwydion?

He's been out of sight for years. Did he go back to Phesaotois, heaven forbid?"

"I don't know," I said.

Josquin set down his glass and stared at me. "Really?" he
said, in a tone of disbelief.

"Well," I said, and looked down, away from his grey-blue
and unclouded gaze. I knew Josquin adored Dewar, his brilliant, dashing, exotic, and cavalier sorcerer cousin. There was
a natural affinity between them; when they were together,
one saw in the two duality and union at once, besides seeing
two of the most elegant men in the three worlds. "I know he
is alive. I know that. I do not know where he is. But he is
alive, and he is well. Don't tell anyone. He is keeping to
himself."

Josquin nodded. "He's in contact with you."

I shook my head. "Just once, recently. Same old Dewar, I
promise you."

"Well," Josquin said, and rolled his glass around moodily.
"Tell him I'd bloody well like to hear from him myself.
Damn it, I'd have looked after him after your poor mother
died, if I could have, but he'd gone off by the time I heard.
I know he's—he was fond of her. I've been terribly afraid
he'd . . . hurt himself." He twisted his mouth in a pained
grimace, a kind man rebuffed, and I thought his friendship
deserved better recognition than it had gotten. I put my
hands on his to stop him fidgeting with the glass. "I looked
for him," Jos said.

"He's a slippery fish, hard to hold," I said. "I would tell
you more if I knew it."

"But you don't know more."

I shook my head and, after a few heartbeats, changed the
subject. I had had a bellyful of Dewar, dragons, and worrying about Freia. This was my holiday. "Now tell me, what
has Massila to offer?"

Josquin tossed his head back, throwing off his mood or
covering it again. "Everything and anything you want. De-

cent wine, indecent women, every kind of man there is, and
fine weather; corrupt government and virtuous monks and
duels of honor . . ."

"I see," I smiled, leaning back in my chair. "And cards . . ."

"Hell, I shouldn't have said anything. I've just taken heavy
losses, but I'll win it back. I usually do. I can afford to take
the long view . . . Are you here for a while?"

"A few days," I said, "during which I mean to not think
about dragons."

The few days turned out to be twelve; I didn't really dare let
things go for much longer, and it is better to leave off before
one is surfeited on that type of holiday anyway. And I can do
quite a lot in twelve days, particularly with a companion like
Josquin, who had been in town a while and knew where to
find the best of everything. We renewed and re-cemented our
friendship, and, my inhibitions lightened by my share of four
bottles of wine we drank together one misty gold evening, I
insisted he come over to Argylle for a visit.

"Haven't been there since I don't know when," Josquin
said. "Since you were Gaston's squire. Sure. Sure. Didn't
think you liked visitors."

"Some visitors I like," I said. "The ones I don't like I don't
invite. It's my Dominion."

"That's how I feel about it, but it's harder for me to get rid
of the ones I don't want to have around," he said. "They visit
me anyway. Not you. You're *always* welcome."

"Thank you."

"Walter too. He came around a while ago. Nice to see him.
Happy days."

"Happy nights. He's home now. Sitting in for me. You'll
see him if you visit."

"Sure. Sure I'll visit you. Father'll like that. Dip . . .
Dimple . . . Dipple . . ."

"Diplomacy."

"That. Yeah. He likes that."

"I like that too."

"I feel pretty damn dip . . . dippelmatic. Is that bottle empty?"

"No. Here. Your health."

"Your happiness."

"Let's negotiate something."

"Sure. Practice. Like what?"

I thought about it. "Bet I can negotiate that earring off you," I suggested. It winked, twinkled, bobbed teasingly against Josquin's neck, just at the fringe of his fine fair hair. Josquin grinned. "It'll cost you," he said.

Late in the afternoon two days later Josquin and I said farewell to one another. We agreed that I would call him when I was back in Argylle and we'd work out the details then of getting him there.

"It will be springtime," I added thoughtfully.

"I love spring in Argylle! It's better than any other season, anywhere else. I'm looking forward to this, Gwydion. Safe journey."

"Thanks." We embraced and I mounted. Cosmo started off, eager to be going. I waved to Josquin, who waved back, and when I glanced over my shoulder at the corner I saw him still standing on the tavern's porch, gazing after me.

"That was fun," I told Cosmo when we were on the Road again.

He snorted.

"I know, I know. I'm trying to think of a way to get you a date with Hussy." And, perhaps because I hadn't been overtaxing my brain for a few days, the solution appeared fully-formed in my thoughts. "Of course! I have it!"

Cosmo's ears were expectant.

"I'll ask Alex to lend her to my sister to ride back to Argylle. Simple. Then I can just take a while to get her home again. How about that? A de facto abduction. He won't refuse her to Ulrike, I'm sure."

Cosmo whuffed, pleased.

"I take care of my friends," I said, patting his neck. "Wonder where Virgil's gotten to." I hadn't seen him since coming to Massila; before that, he had ridden quietly on the saddlebags or flown along ahead and behind me.

A couple of hours later Virgil rejoined us as we passed through a half-seen, vaguely-substanced city on the Road. He hooted softly from behind me and thumped down on the saddlebags. I said Hullo to him and went back to thinking about sorcery.

There had to be a way to locate Gemnamnon without him being aware of it. Conventional seeking spells would be too easily detected by the dragon. Simply riding around asking people was possible, but would take a long time. I didn't want to confront him now; I only wanted to know where he was. Freia's rapid disappearance had kept me from asking her, and possibly she could not have told me where the beast was anyway, if he were outside her Dominion.

The obvious solution was to go to Oriana, who had a vast collection of Mirrors of Vision and who was the acknowledged authority on spells of seeing and seeking. If anyone could help me, she could. However, Oriana's customary fee for her services—if she were in the mood to sell them—started at one year of service in her house and went upward from there. I did not like her enough to want to work for her for a year or more, though a dinner-party from time to time was tolerable. Perhaps I could invoke her vow to the Well, although I was the Lord of Argylle, and forestall her.

When I had come to this conclusion, I was riding toward a certain large Nexus through a dense and dark-shaded wood. The Road was made up of large slabs of stone here, mossed over from disuse. The place had a muffled, damp feeling. I reined in and pulled out my maps and looked for a route to Oriana's Castle of Glass.

Virgil woke up and hopped up to my shoulder, peering at the map with me.

"I'm going to ask Oriana to find Gemnamnon for me," I said.

Virgil clicked his beak.

"I can't stand her either. You have a better idea?"

My familiar spread his wings and settled again, turning his head to stare straight into my eyes.

"You'd go?"

A nod.

I thought about it. "I might find it inconvenient to be without you. And you might have trouble getting back to Argylle."

Virgil looked insulted. He half-opened his beak.

I chewed my lip. It would be good to avoid incurring the debt with Oriana if my diplomatic notion failed. I could under no circumstances bind myself in service. I cringed to imagine what she'd demand instead—I'd considered stopping somewhere and picking up jewelry and the like as a goodwill gesture—because she had demanded it once of Dewar and had made no secret of her interest in me. The idea didn't appeal to me. Beauteous as Oriana is, I prefer to keep myself out of such entanglements with my peers in sorcery.

"I'd head back to Argylle," I told him, "leaving you here on your own. You'd have to cross the Border."

He clicked his beak impatiently.

"If you really think you can do it, thereby sparing me a possibly very awkward situation with Oriana, then I'd prefer for you to do it," I decided. "However, if you have any doubts—"

Virgil screeched, an earsplitting derisive sound, and launched himself from my shoulder to swoop up to a branch overhanging the Road.

"Dandy," I said, rubbing my ear. "Fine. Do it and report back to me in Argylle when you're done. Find Gemnamnon without being found or noticed yourself."

He hooted, *uhuu, uhuu,* and flew off down the Road toward the Nexus, moving far faster than any mortal owl. I sat looking after him. He was certainly eager to go. I trusted his ability and discretion, and he was right—this was just the sort of dirty work a familiar was kept for.

Now I had nothing further to do with respect to the dragon, which felt strange. I checked everything over again as Cosmo cantered along the Road, trying to see what I had forgotten. I could find nothing. Prospero would certainly notice, whatever it might be. Was I running away again? It didn't look like it to me. I had delegated a piece of work to my familiar. That was all.

I wondered how Dewar was getting on. What would he be doing with Freia's information? With these Clinic people? How in the world did one construct a body, and how long did it take? Bodies are complicated things. One doesn't simply wire together spare parts. And how in the name of the Spring did one construct a *mindless* body?

The very thought brought up zombies, corpse-dissections at midnight crossroads, grave robbery, and a whole branch of magic that had always roiled my stomach somewhat. Respectable sorcerers might have a nodding acquaintance with the concepts, perhaps even with a practitioner, of necromancy, but few would care to engage in it and those who do, do not move in many magical social circles outside that of their necromantic colleagues. Alchemists are less ostracized and more highly regarded. Necromancers are the knackers of the magical world. I heartily hoped Dewar was not going in for such.

Cosmo and I passed the night in the barn of a dour farmer. He had me split wood and help him with a fence repair job in return. His wife was a bleached grey woman who packed me a generous bagful of food in the morning without saying a word to me. I wondered if they knew that the Road ran right past their house.

I often wonder this about people who live in close proximity to the Road or a Ley: how can they possibly be unaware of it? Yet it seems many, or most, are. I mentioned this to my mother once and she said it was just as well.

"Why?" I had asked, very surprised.

"Imagine the riffraff we'd have trafficking here and there. I am an elitist where sorcery is concerned. If they can't find it on their own, then they don't need to know about it and probably couldn't handle it properly if they did."

"I thought you were a democrat."

"Sometimes."

"Except where true power is concerned."

Freia had opened her mouth to reply, stopped herself, and then smiled. "You may be right. Sometimes. What do you think, Gwydion? Would you open the Road to all?"

I'd started to say Yes and then halted. "I don't know. I'd have to think about it."

"Think about it then. Tell me what you think sometime."

"I will."

That was many, many years ago, a golden summer afternoon boating home on the Wye from a picnic and botany day. I was still thinking about it.

Alexander was surprised to find me breakfasting in his house. I had ridden straight there, without stopping a night in the town of Montgard. His servants, accustomed now to me coming and going, had shown me to the table and served me without comment.

"What are you doing here so soon?"

"Eating." I had another bite of the excellent kedgeree.

He poured himself tea and looked at me with a certain irritation.

"I came to take the lady home with me as planned," I said.

"We weren't expecting you for days yet. Ulrike's not going to like leaving already."

"My business did not prove so demanding as I anticipated. It was a pleasant surprise to be wrong that way." And a pleasant business too, I thought. Just demanding enough. I grinned to myself.

"Hunh." Alexander served himself from the sideboard and sat down and ate also.

I reminded myself to get Hussy for Ulrike to ride. A good excuse would be that she was a stable, calm, fast, experienced horse, unlike the unfortunate Daffodil. When we got home—

A thought hit me between the eyes and made me sit up straight.

"Something wrong?" asked Alexander.

"I just thought of something . . ."

Maybe it wasn't a problem.

"Bully for you," he muttered, and put smoked salmon on his fork.

I bit back my retort. "Look, how has Ulrike been?" I asked softly.

He frowned. "Been? She's been fine."

Now I looked at him, irritated.

"You mean . . . socially?" Alexander asked.

"Kind of."

"Fine. Getting along. I think she was put off by arriving there at New Year's just in time for the carousing. Father seems to have been protective of her. Naturally—it's understandable." Alexander shrugged and drank tea.

"Do you think she could bear meeting another relative?"

"Depends. What, is Dewar coming back?" His expression became slightly pained and he began to shake his head. "He's a real—"

"Dewar's a good man. No, he's not back," I said, to prevent the argument, though I wondered why he would have jumped to that conclusion. "I had meant to bring Josquin to Argylle for a visit."

"Josquin." My brother set down his cup and looked at me.

How could he object to Jos? "I like him," I said, "and I think he'd find her amusing; she's like all those cousins of his in Madana. He knows how to make a good impression."

"Yes. Josquin. She said she met Ottaviano at New Year's." Slowly, his eyes narrowing, a calculating expression came over his face and he nodded.

I twisted my mouth ruefully. "I could have kicked Walt. Yes. I wish Avril had sent Josquin to negotiate, but he didn't." Otto, who was everything Josquin was not, was not exactly bad, but in comparison with his court-reared brother, he came off badly.

He tapped the edge of his plate with his fork in two-four time. "I think she'd find Josquin very agreeable. He's a gentleman, not overbearing, and he's been in Argylle before."

"He wouldn't mention her to anyone in Landuc, either, if I were to ask him not to. She should be able to choose when to go there herself. The rest of us did. Meeting Otto was an accident, and meeting Josquin will balance that out. He's a far pleasanter representative of that side of the family."

"Yes. Yes. Gwydion, you're smarter than you used to be. That's a good idea, inviting him over to visit. She can meet him there, in a safe place, supervised . . . a good idea." Alexander smiled. "I haven't seen Josquin in a while."

"Same old Josquin as he ever was, I gathered."

Alexander nodded again, still smiling, and returned to his breakfast. I returned to mine, a bit surprised by his enthusiastic reaction. I had expected him to say it was a bad idea, that she should meet people in her own time. Our rare accord pleased me. If we two who saw things so differently agreed, it was certainly the right thing to do.

Ulrike herself tripped in, squeaked with surprise, and gasped, "Gwydion!"

"Hullo," I greeted her. "Sleepyhead."

"I went for a walk," she said with an air of conscious moral superiority.

"Did you," Alexander said.

"Indeed I did. A lovely walk, because it's going to be hot today and I prefer to walk in the cool. Gwydion, I didn't think you . . . I mean—" She stopped and sat down.

"My business took less time than I thought it would, so I am ahead of schedule."

Plainly she was disappointed by having to leave.

"You need not leave if you prefer not to," I said. "Alexander can send you home through a Way whenever you wish."

She reacted as I expected her to, fearfully. "Oh—no, n-no, I . . . I guess . . . I guess I should go with you . . ."

I felt mean. It was cruel to tease her. She'd been badly frightened on the way to Montgard, and badly frightened going through a Way, and she had every excuse not to like either; moreover, I had toyed with the idea of killing her, and I wanted to make it up to her handsomely, if I could only think how.

I said, "Ulrike, it is up to you. It is safe to travel now; the dragon is not going to bother us. It will be a pleasant trip, not like the last one. But it is up to you."

"Mouse, it's spring in Argylle now," Alexander said. "The prettiest time. It's much nicer than winter."

"I haven't been gone that long," she said, her brows wrinkling together.

"Time flows faster there than here, because it is at the Spring, the quick center," I reminded her, pouring tea for us both.

"Thank you," she said softly, and sipped it.

"When were you planning on going?" asked Alexander.

"I rode all night to get here. Tomorrow morning, I suppose. The day after if you prefer."

He nodded. Ulrike looked at her tea-leaves. I had forgotten to strain the tea as I poured.

Alexander and Ulrike had been invited on an outing with friends; I declined to go and spent the day instead in my brother's cool dim library, browsing lethargically through collections of essays on miscellaneous topics bound in dark old leather. The printing press had not yet come to Montgard. These books were imported from somewhere else; they were printed on thick creamy linen paper, a pleasure to look at and touch.

We had a quiet dinner. I arranged for Ulrike to use Hussy; Alexander agreed and stipulated again that he wanted her back soon, and I said I would certainly return her at the earliest opportunity.

The following day, in good time and good order, Ulrike and I rode down to the town and took rooms at The Mermaid's Cups (Ulrike blushed) for the night. Our journey home through Pheyarcet and across the Border was so uneventful and peaceful as to be tedious. Still, that was good; Ulrike might have been permanently traumatized if we'd been set upon again. We took about ten days for the trip.

Spring was just putting soft touches of green to the trees and opening the first flowers on north-facing banks and in sunny gardens. I was glad to see it, glad that the winter and its dragon were gone for a season, glad that for the moment I had nothing to worry about but where I was going to put all my wine. With a feeling of noble resolve, I promised myself I would indeed take care of that this year. Ulrike set about reading and answering her hoard of plump letters from Haimance.

Virgil returned to me eighteen days after Ulrike and I arrived at the Citadel, just as the fruit trees began putting out tiny leaves. He indicated that Gemnamnon was in a distant part of Phesaotois, which was fine with me. I suspected he'd come from there in the first place. I hoped he stayed home from now on, and an anxious knot in my gut finally dissipated, leaving me wholly able to enjoy the weather.

A few days after that, upon receiving Prospero's hesitant approbation for the idea, I opened a Way for Josquin and brought him to Argylle.

Josquin was pleased to meet Ulrike; she was shy as ever but did manage to make small talk with him at dinner that night. Josquin understood the shyness at once and made careful and successful efforts to get past it. Soon Ulrike was as comfortable with him as with any of us. He settled into life in Argylle as if he had been born there.

In Argylle, the City of Gold, spring brings picnics and dances and outings and celebrations. It brings parties and boating on the Wye on warm days and everyone in town out driving or walking and chatting and smiling. Word had gotten around that the Lady's youngest daughter was home again, and this was of great interest to everyone. Whenever Ulrike went out for a walk along the Wye or through the town she was greeted warmly by complete strangers and welcomed, which she found disconcerting.

"They're so friendly," she said to me after we had weathered one such cheerful encounter.

"That's Argylle. Landuc's very different."

"Unfriendly?"

"Mmm, standoffish. Josquin's Madanese; he's not like most Landucians. I like it better here."

"And people are so . . ." she shook her head, ". . . ah, free with one another . . ." We were strolling along the riverbank, where rites of spring were in full swing in the parks, on the footpaths, and in the boats moored and floating. Ulrike blushed scarlet.

I grinned. "That's nice too, I think. A lot better than bottling it all up."

Spring also brings Walter's First of Spring party, which is more exclusive than but as famous as his New Year's revels. Ulrike did more than blush when she was propositioned there. Fortunately Walter was nearby and he caught my eye as he applied his diplomatic expertise to calming the dismay of all parties involved.

"Oh, dear," Hicha said to me. "I did tell Staron she should wait until she knows your sister better. But she's always been impatient."

I hurried over to help and, with a polite mumble, dragged Ulrike into a nearby sitting room and closed the door so she could recover her composure in privacy.

"I shouldn't have to put up with that!" she said. "No!"

"People are testing you, Rikki, finding your limits, seeing how you're different from the rest of us and Freia. That's all. Please don't make a scene. You've already made her feel very awkward." My sympathies were wholly with Staron, one of Hicha's partners, a complaisant and quick young woman.

"No! It's not right. No!" she cried.

"No, thank you," Walter corrected her, returning from his chat with the terribly embarrassed Staron. He closed the door quietly and knelt beside her chair, putting his hand on her shoulder. "That's all you need to say, dear Ulrike. No, thank you. Your mother," and he grinned, "had to say it quite a lot."

I chuckled. Ulrike didn't. "It's shocking! It's . . . it's . . . it's unnatural!" she wailed.

"Unnatural!" I repeated. "If sex isn't natural what is?"

My brother shot me a brief glare and shook his head. "It's life," Walter said to Ulrike, gently and definitely. "Just remember: No, thank you. And ninety-nine in a hundred will take that for an answer gracefully. The hundredth one gets turned to a cactus." He glanced at me and I nodded, resigned. "You probably won't have further . . . problems," he went on. "I'll spread the word if you like, make it clear that you are not interested."

"This is not a subject for, for gossip!" Ulrike burst into tears. "It's horrible! It's not!"

I was confused now. What was the problem? Walter hugged her and patted her back and soothed her. I looked at him, bewildered, over her shaking shoulders. *Later,* he mouthed.

"Gaston is strait-laced sometimes," he said when Ulrike had been persuaded to return to the party and had gone to wash her face first. "I suspect he, hm, did not mention a few things to her here and there, things that Mother would have told her. Such as the differences between Argylle and Landuc families. You know that Mother and Gaston were exceptional here, that Landuc's standard is not ours."

"Monogamous and male-female and that's all they'll admit to. I'm not sure what one *would* call standard in Argylle. People would laugh if one tried." Argyllines have families. Some people have big families. Some people have small families. Some are loose-knit associations like Hicha's, some tightly-organized to carry on a farm or business. Everybody has somebody; there are a few loners who don't travel with the herd, but they're a distinct type too, usually too busy with whatever they do to bother with building and maintaining family ties.

"That's the point. You grew up here. You have seen Landuc and places like it, though," Walter went on. "In such places sex is forbidden or regulated. I don't know this Fenshuyan from experience, but I'll warrant you it's run by the men, who own their women . . . She has to become accustomed to much."

"Do you think she's—" I started to say, amazed.

He cut me off. "It is none of our business to think, simply to make sure that the lady is not subjected to unwanted attentions. Mother had a perfect drop-dead glare she used on the ones who didn't take no for an answer, and then of course Dewar would turn around and smile at them rather nastily."

"Yes, I remember . . ." I grinned broadly, recalling a party one day on the river, a persistent suitor . . .

He began to chuckle and I joined in, remembering. "That ass got what he deserved. Never heard Gaston laugh so much in my whole life." Walter leaned on the doorjamb, laughing harder and harder. I wiped tears from my eyes. "The goat," he gasped. ". . . on the boat, oh, that was funny, oh . . . Can you do that?"

"I guess so. Yes, I can. Prefer not to."

We calmed down and massaged our aching sides. "Right," I said. "I shall do what I can, and you too."

"Yes. You know, it may be she'd be better off in Landuc..."

"She has not been keen on the idea of going there."

"No. But I believe she'll like it when she does." Walter snickered. "Or maybe I'll tell her the goat story."

⌒ *22* ⌒

DEWAR INVOKED ME WITH A LESSER Summoning a few days after the party. I was in my office; reluctant to take the risk of being overheard or interrupted, I hurried to my workroom, closed the door, and used a mirror to focus the spell.

It clouded and changed and cleared . . .

"Greetings," he said.

"Salutations. How are things?"

He smiled. "We found Lars Holzen, who introduced us to the people we needed to know at the Clinic, who have agreed to build a body for Freia, which they are doing."

"I thought this would be difficult, take a long time . . ." I said, taken aback.

My uncle shook his head. "Easy, easy, easy," Dewar crowed. "They keep tissue samples, not just sequence information. Frozen cell specimens."

"You can make a *person* from a few cells?" I asked, repelled.

"Yes, of course. What did you think I'd use, flowers? Snow? And they've done very interesting transfers: artificial people, originally with machine-based specially-designed task-focused identities, installed in custom bodies . . ." Dewar shook his head admiringly. "Fascinating!"

"People? This is done with people?"

He nodded. "Very much up Freia's alley. She's a wizard, in her own way."

"I'll say. —Mother did this kind of thing?"

"As she said, she augmented her own original genetic

package with genes, hm, borrowed from Prospero to improve her cellular metabolism. She didn't inherit a few important ones and the deficiency was beginning to have . . . serious effects."

"Borrowed genes?" Like borrowing a pen?

"Gaston got a little careless in one of their fencing sessions and scratched him," Dewar snickered, "and cleaned the blade onto a cloth she'd specially prepared. Then she analyzed the cells and extracted the bits she wanted. That picky work is even harder than working from scratch. Apparently here they suggested she simply build a new body and transfer into it, but she wasn't enthusiastic."

My skin crawled. I followed the gist, but the specifics were beyond me; perhaps I needed to study up on this, revolting though it sounded. "I'd imagine so."

Dewar guessed correctly at the source of my revulsion. "This isn't necromancy, Gwydion. Think of it as medicine on the grandest possible scale. It's healing. In fact it's not very different, if you think about it, from the, uh, usual way of making people. *You* started from only two cells, you know."

"Dewar, how can . . . how can there be . . . what about . . ." I couldn't even frame my questions properly, and so let pass unanswered his jab at my supposedly-deficient sex education.

"They retard the brain's cognitive development," he said briskly, as if he were explaining how cauliflower is blanched. "There isn't another person involved here. Don't worry about that."

"Still . . ."

"You're rather squeamish," Dewar observed. "Why?"

"It's . . . *unnatural.*"

"So is sorcery. So are many things you do, by somebody's standards somewhere."

I struggled to overcome my prejudice. Dewar shifted position, seeming to sit down.

"How . . . how are you going to . . . move her?" I asked finally.

"I'm still working on that."

"If I can do anything . . ."

Dewar nodded. "Of course I'd ask." He smiled. "Just keep doing what you're doing. You're doing it well."

I smiled wryly. "Any ideas as to where I can stash a lot of wine?"

"Stars, are we running out of room again? No. None. There's the Catacombs, but I'd prefer you not have a mason's crew running around down there just now."

Uh-hunh. I could see that becoming an exciting and controversial situation. "No, that's ruled out already. Prospero and I talked about it and nixed it."

"I honestly don't know," he said, shaking his head. "We have to drink more."

"If people spent more time at home, we would."

"True. You could reduce the Citadel's share, considering that Marfisa never collects hers, but that's a bad precedent. . . . I'm sure you'll find someplace. Not in my rooms though, please."

"How about under the bed?"

"Very well, a few cases of Corydol under the bed. Nice crusty dirty *old* ones." He grinned again, his eyes lighting for a moment.

I laughed. "Wrong. Thanks for calling, Dewar. Keep me informed."

"There's not much to inform about beyond this," he said, shrugging. "It's all routine from here on out."

Routine! I thought. Indeed.

Spring budded and bloomed around us, and my favorite days came, the warm days when the breeze off the Wye bathed the Citadel in the scent of blossoms from the Island's orchard. I opened windows and worked, dined, and just sat outside on the terraces and balconies, watching the birds.

Prospero went to Landuc to present the Emperor with an unexpected sweetener to the trading treaty he had closed with Ottaviano last winter: a large shipment of Candobel wine, for the Emperor to drink or sell as he saw fit. The gift had the pleasant side effect of liberating room in the Citadel's cellars for a luscious lot of Bevallin Coast Ember-wine, one of Mother's earliest and most successful varieties, which had the appealing quality (in our present pressed condition) of maturing in two years.

Josquin stayed on in Argylle, taking Ulrike around and amusing her and acting as a bodyguard to intercept the more-than-occasional offers for more-than-casual relations Ulrike still received. She did remember to say, "No, thank you," which I thought was progress. We all went around together often, Ulrike and Josquin and Walter and his usual collection of friends and I, picnicking, birding, riding, walking, boating. Josquin and I went night-swimming under full and crescent moons and raced our sculls through morning mists.

I was happy. I felt as if there had been some twisting worry in my life which had been solved away, and everything seemed to come easily to me.

We heard nothing from Gaston. Ulrike asked periodically about him, obviously wishing he would come home, and accepted our waiting policy unhappily.

I pointed out that if she drank of the Spring she could spend all her time trying to find him, either with Summonings or travelling on the Road, herself.

"No, thank you," she said, eyes widening, shaking her head quickly.

I stared at her and then laughed. It was probably the first real joke she had made, and I wasn't sure it was intentional, but it was funny. It wasn't intentional—she backed away from me.

"Gwydion!"

"Sorry, it just seemed funny for a moment. Then you'll have to wait with the rest of us."

Mother manifested herself in my rooms one rosy morning.

"Gwydion," I heard in the study.

At first I didn't recognize her voice and simply said, "Come in," stuffing the rest of my breakfast roll in my mouth. I thought it was someone with a message, maybe one of my sisters. I jumped and gasped when she mistily walked through the closed door. Then, coughing and choking, I had to wash down the roll very fast with a mouthful of coffee.

Mother fidgeted in and out of seeming solidity. "Gwydion, I am uneasy about this whole thing."

I swallowed again. "I can understand that, but I think you're in good hands."

"Panurgus says it will fail. He believes I shall extinguish myself."

"He wants you to back down."

She shimmered. "Perhaps he is right."

"Oh, Mother!"

"It has never been done before," she said.

"What would you have Dewar and Thiorn do? They are well along; he called me a month ago and told me so. It will not fail. He and Thiorn both have every reason to be careful, to succeed. You ought not to listen to Panurgus."

"That is just what Dewar said. I am committed to it, it seems; there is no other path for me   " She looked through me, then at me. "We must speak about—what comes afterward."

"Uh-hunh?" I had another sip of coffee to soothe my abused throat.

Afterward. I had thought about this myself. I had not wanted the Black Chair to be mine already. I had been ruling Argylle as a substitute while my mother was away down the Road, her proxy as Walter had recently been mine. I had not wanted it so soon, though it had been increasingly clear to me for years before that it was going to be mine someday. I had sat in it uncomfortably ever since.

My desire was that she would return, live here as before as the Lady of Argylle, and this could be just another weird, incomprehensible episode in our history, which already had a fair number, most of them associated with Freia.

Mother, however, had her own ideas. As ever.

"I shall not take Argylle again. You are doing well. I will substitute for you if you desire a sabbatical—as Prospero used to for me—but there are many things I still would like to do that I never did." She sounded defensive but quite definite.

I looked into my coffee cup. I chewed my lip. I stirred my coffee.

Nobody ever won this sort of argument with Freia. Prospero, Dewar, Gaston, even the Emperor Avril—they all backed down when she spoke in that firm tone. Despite the defensive note, I knew that if she said she would not do it, she was not going to do it.

And so I was stuck. I suppose I could have threatened to abdicate, but I suspect that neither she, Dewar, nor Prospero would have let me get away with it.

I moistened my lips and tried to sound hearty. "That's fine. I'm glad, in a way. I've gotten used to this."

Mother, with another of those disarmingly natural gestures, bent down in front of me and intercepted my gaze, which was trained on my boots at the end of the bed.

We regarded one another for a full minute, slightly-insubstantial mother and all-too-substantial son. Her eyes were strange, pure black iris and pupil, like the Spring itself.

I felt her looking right into me. I glanced away, unwilling to be studied too closely.

She straightened. "Good. I was not sure you were ready, but I see you are. The other matter is, that I would have you keep silent about this until it is done."

"As you wish."

"I do. Thiorn thinks Gaston should be told."

"What do you think, yourself?" It was gratifying to turn the tables and ask her one of her favorite questions.

Freia walked over to my dresser (making no reflection in the looking glass over it) and studied a vase of velvety-gold-and-cream mothflowers, her back to me. "Find him and tell him afterward, not before. Heaven only knows where he is or what he is doing. He may not care."

I was shocked. I didn't believe Gaston would go off and find someone else. "Mother! Of course he cares."

Her voice was very soft, and she shook her head. "He may have found someone else, dear. The Wheel does turn that way. It might be best for him so."

I shook my head. "No."

Still more softly, "You sound pretty sure."

I began again to say, *Of course,* and I stopped myself. Gaston was the core of her emotional universe. He knew that and provided solid, unquestioning support to her in those matters where her native stubbornness failed her. Gaston wasn't here, but somewhere in Pheyarcet, and of course she'd have no way of knowing what he thought or felt now. He had taken Ulrike away to hide her while she grew up, and that might portend all kinds of horrible things to Freia.

Had she opposed the idea of leaving the Spring because she thought Gaston didn't want her? Because she didn't think she mattered enough to him, to her father, to anyone? How could she doubt that we loved her?

I had to reassure her somehow. *Of course* wasn't enough.

"I think you're underestimating your importance to him. He was shattered, Mother. He still looks wretched when your name comes up, or anything about you."

"Have you spoken to him?" she demanded, turning around.

"No. Not since he was last here. He sent me a note when Ulrike came, via a bird I dispatched to find him. I think one reason he shooed her out of his life was that she looks a great deal like you and he misses you," I said.

Freia changed the subject. "I had a look at her. I think she resembles his mother."

I rummaged in my mental file of family faces. "Really?"

"Yes. There's a portrait of her in Landuc, in the Palace gallery, unless they moved it. Ulrike does have Prospero's coloring, but for the rest, she takes after her grandmother."

"Amorett? Maybe I'll have a look." I didn't think we had a portrait of Amorett here, which was an oversight. I thought I should get one. My mind skipped back to the beginning of the conversation. "Have you spoken with Dewar?"

She smiled a suppressed, amused smile. Her eyes danced. "A few days past. He appears to be enjoying himself greatly."

"They seemed to be going very quickly to me."

"It is a very swift Eddy. They are engaged in some stimulating theoretical debate, the two of them. Yes, it will be soon." Her smile faded, but did not disappear.

"I'd like to know."

"You will," she promised me, and then she became wholly serious again, drawing herself together, hugging her elbows and looking at me intently. "Finally, in my role as the family oracle."

I gestured expansively. "Prophesy away."

"Josquin has been about often, with Ulrike."

I blinked. "I had not thought of them as an item, but yes, I guess he has. He's visiting. I thought it would be good for her to meet him."

"She is young. She is still not used to society, to . . . to people. Keep an eye on it."

"Uh, all right." I wondered what I was supposed to do. *Keep an eye on it?*

She smiled and disappeared, a mist of colors evaporating. I had a spare hour and a half that afternoon between mediating a dispute among a group of western loggers and a road-planning meeting with a group of herders and farmers, so I used the time to make a Way to Landuc through my Mirror and asked for the portrait of Gaston's mother Amorett the Fair. It had been moved from its old spot in the family gallery—I suspected when the revelation of Gaston's marriage to Freia sent him out of favor with the Emperor for a while—and it took a few people scratching their heads to track it down on a back stair. I looked up at it.

Yes, the similarity was clear. Families are funny things. Amorett even had Ulrike's slightly hesitant expression and Gaston's faint smile, Ulrike's perfectly straight hair in Gaston's shade of brown, and Ulrike's physique: slender and graceful. But the resemblance could only be skin-deep; Amorett's demure mien had, I had heard, belied her capable and ruthless political abilities, and her penchant for scheming and plotting had kept her in royal favor and the royal bed long enough to produce two sons, Gaston and Herne, despite the insult this offered to Panurgus' Princess Consort Diote. Amorett only lost favor when she went a little too far, after Prospero was born to Diote, and attempted to murder the infant Prince who supplanted her own children. Ulrike, quailing and bashful, was nothing like her where it mattered—which was all to the good.

Prospero returned from Landuc on the First of Summer. I was on my way down the Spiral to a boating-party on the Wye and met him halfway, at a landing, as he climbed up.

"Welcome home," I said. "Auspicious timing! Care to join our party?"

He smiled. "Ah. I did but now meet Ulrike outside—"

"Yes, she loves the boats—"

"—with Josquin," he said, raising an eyebrow, "a pair of painted ducks in pretty plumage." The tame fat painted ducks which natter and bob around the Citadel's Iron Bridge are an indispensable part of Argylle's summers. I laughed at his analogy.

"She likes him," I said, "at least, she talks to him." What my mother had said about "keeping an eye on it" came back to me; I had not yet puzzled out what it meant. I was not about to chaperone them; I knew Josquin would be as good an escort for her as Walter or I, and she was learning to be more outgoing and less self-conscious from him. "I think he's a good influence," I added.

" 'Tis well he should be on someone," Prospero said dryly. "Nay, nay—I mean no insult, and indeed he's a better name here than in Landuc—"

"Prospero, really," I said, amused. "He's cultivated, good-mannered, well-spoken, and considerate. Do you think he'd lead her on some libertine's path of corruption? I suspect she's got enough sense to say No if he tried."

He chuckled. "It does seem that Gaston assured that an she know no word but one she know No; yet she knows to No her No sweetly, not contrarily. Has she drunk of the Spring?"

"She has not—"

All in an instant as I spoke, Prospero turned ash-pale and his knees buckled; his eyes closed as he fell forward.

With a horrified gasp of "Prospero!" I caught him and kept him from falling down. I lay him on his back on the landing, frightened, and began to seek his pulse. Why had he fainted—

Then I felt it too: a terrible surge of power flowing down into the Spring below us, sucking energy out of all of Argylle along the Road and the Leys, from Nodes and Nexuses, the great Source of All Being becoming instead a Vortex of All Being, drawing life back into itself—the tide ebbing and leaving death behind it. My head reeled. I grabbed the banister to keep from tumbling down the stairs.

The air changed without a wind to stir it, a movementless draft sinking past us. The temperature plummeted and the sunlight that lit the Core seemed to fade and lose its color and strength. Ringing shrilled in my ears. Something crashed to the ground somewhere below, and the sound was strangely muffled. My muscles weakened; I had difficulty holding myself upright on the railing and slowly knelt beside Prospero, who wasn't moving.

Dewar was trying something, damn him, and hadn't warned me!

"Prospero!" I shook him.

He was out cold, his pulse gone. No heartbeat. I drew upon the Spring, with a tremendous effort extracting a paltry amount of power from its reversed floodstream, and tried shocking his heart back in motion with small jolts of pure energy. I had read of this technique somewhere in a medical book of Mother's.

Once.

Twice.

Third time paid. His body jumped and his heart fluttered, then settled down.

I heard more distant sounds from below, unechoing and dulled. My vision tunnelled and the Citadel dimmed as the air continued growing colder. The banister on which I leaned was oddly unreal, like an object in a dream. Its shape seemed wrong. I tried to focus on Prospero's face and found that he seemed wrong too—perspective was misaligned; the stairs were strangely flat-seeming, their angles obliquing into nonexistence. Insubstantial—like Freia's image in my rooms as she disappeared . . .

I drew upon the Spring again, and was nearly sucked into it—or so it felt, like putting my hand from a boat into a powerful rushing current that sought to drag me off in its ropy sinews. There seemed to be a cascade of rainbow colors and shapes and shapelessness around me now—of disorganized sounds cacophonous and muted at once, every sound from the rustle of leaves to the splitting thunder of a storm, all equally weighted—emotions in a horrific confusion of terrors and loves and triumphs and rages and longings. The torrent hauled at me too, and I shoved it back from me and resisted, keeping my integrity against its tyrannical demand for me to yield. My eyes and head cleared.

Staggering, weakened, I lifted Prospero and carried him laboriously to a sitting room off the landing and put him on a sofa. Walking was lifting my feet and setting them down in an ocean of undertow and breakers pulling me in many different directions at once. Yet there was a feeling of slowing to the cataract—the rush was abating. The light returned and the temperature and moisture of the air increased as I went. There were weak cries and calls from the people of the Citadel, fearful queries.

Prospero groaned. His head moved to one side. I poured a glass of whisky and held it ready.

His hands moved hesitantly to his head, held it; his face, still white, contorted. "Aaaaah." After about a minute, he opened his eyes. "What devil's work this? Who hath dammed my world into such dead neap-tide? 'Tis unnatural, the Spring's denatured—what mishap's this?"

I feared I knew, but I was not sure. "I don't know. You had cardiac arrest. Drink."

Prospero nodded and knocked the whisky back in one gulp. "I must go to . . ." He seemed to run out of breath and took a couple deep slow breaths. "Some meddler's work. Dewar. I'll skin him alive and salt him." He tried to stand and sank back. "Aaagh. Can you feel't?"

"Yes. It was like a reverse power surge, but it has stopped. —Prospero, lie down! Please! You must rest!" I grabbed his shoulder and shoved him back, afraid he'd keel over again.

He subsided, swallowed, glared at me. "Perhaps . . . perhaps you've the right of it for the nonce. Have you your Keys to hand?"

"Ah, no, not with me . . ."

"Fetch them hither. Together we'll fathom the fouled Spring."

Damn. I couldn't refuse. "All right." I wished I'd had the foresight to make a Key for the Catacombs. I rushed to my workroom, grabbed my Keys, and did a hasty Lesser Summoning for Dewar. Nothing; a nebulous whiteness indicated he was using a broad array of screening and blocking spells to hide—still! However, the Spring flowed as ever when I tapped it. Everything looked as it ought. As if we'd dreamt and awakened . . . or perhaps we'd awakened, and dreamed again . . . I leaned on my worktable and rubbed my eyes. The tabletop was cold, hard, and undeniably real. I felt a chip on its edge I'd made once, dropping a heavy brass astrolabe. Real.

I could not delay longer; Prospero was waiting. I hurried back to him. "Got them. I tried Summoning Dewar; he's hidden, as usual."

He was massaging his temples, still reclining, eyes closed. "The bastard whelp was at the Spring itself; there we'll seek him now, and when I've laid him by the heels I shall break every meddling finger in both his monkey-hands."

This sounded unpleasantly like the sort of threat Prospero would follow through. However, I agreed with the sentiment. Dewar ought to have warned me, at least, even though he didn't want his father to know what he was about. I was in on this too.

Prospero was sitting up now. "Another glass. Of the same, and be quick."

I poured, though my medical judgement disagreed with his; he was my grandfather, after all. He swallowed it, hissed, and stood cautiously. "My head clanks and cracks like ill-forged metal. Ach. Come."

I walked in front of him in case he folded again. The Citadel was strangely empty; voices were buzzing down one of the side corridors, but Prospero shook his head when I looked that way. Best not to deal with anything but the immediate problem for the moment. We made slow progress down the stairs. I quietly opened the door at the bottom, though I doubted we'd find anyone. Prospero pushed past me and strode toward the Spring, seeming fully recovered.

He held his hand over it, and it leapt up, splashed insubstantial over and through his fingers, fell back, tinkling watery songs in the blackness. " 'Tis an alteration I cannot name, but clear and tangible to my hand," he said.

There was no one there. It lay as ever, dark, serene, alone. Alone.

Prospero scouted around the pillars, searching. I looked around near the Spring—for what, I don't know; Dewar was smart enough not to leave anything behind, certainly—and then I sat on the bench. I emptied my mind and reached for the Spring, looking for that feeling of friendly personality that had characterized Freia's tenancy.

Nobody home.

It had been nearly two hours since Prospero had collapsed. He came over and sat next to me.

" 'Tis altered. Someone has wrought some mutation in the very substance of it, and his change rings false to me," he said flatly. "Yet perhaps not so strange to thine ear as mine. Speak, Gwydion."

I felt my face redden and hoped the lantern-light didn't show it too much. "I agree, it feels different, and I agree, someone has done something, but I don't know what."

He sighed and looked me over. I met his gaze, not daring not to.

"Do not undertake to lie to me," he said coldly. "Thou hast nor countenance nor temper for deception, and secrets have been writ large on thy front this half-year and longer. I'll have the truth, the whole of it, and that instanter. Else shalt learn that I've not lost my claws."

The Spring enlivened suddenly; a crowned bluish splash erupted around the periphery, extending lines which knotted and intertwined of themselves over the darkness at the center. I felt the compulsion therein embodied press around me, close and claustrophobic. I also felt the pressure of a Lesser Summoning.

The timing could not have been better.

"Accept it," Prospero commanded me. The pressure from the Spring increased. My vision darkened at the edges, and the Spring drew my attention in.

"Gwydion?"

Dewar's voice, then Dewar's clean-shaven face, looking at me from the webwork in the Spring, which provided the ideal focus for his Summoning. Prospero's hand closed on my shoulder like a vise.

"Dewar," he said very quietly.

"Hello, Father," he said. "I think it worked." The power of the Spring was such that we could see where he was—a white-walled, white-cabineted room, incomprehensible apparatus on metal-topped benches before and behind him.

"Dost thou? What was't thou essayed—my death?" Prospero growled, rage hardening his voice.

"I wish you'd given advance notice," I said.

Prospero went on, "What design hast consummated? Speak now!"

Dewar looked at both of us and nodded. "What have you told him?" he asked me.

I was insulted by his lack of faith in my discretion. "Nothing." I bit the word off.

"Father, Freia was trapped in the Spring," he said. "We got her out. We think."

"Trapped? In the Spring?" Prospero looked at it, back at Dewar, and nodded slowly, his jaw tightening. He was still very, very angry. His hand felt as if it might break my collarbone if he got any angrier. "Aye. So. This answer serves for some few riddles."

"More than a few," Dewar agreed, impassive.

"Thou, thou knew'st of this from its inception." He looked at me, and I, unable to deny it, swallowed and could not lower my eyes. The Spring was climbing higher, higher, brilliant shafts of color shooting through the water as it twined and braided in a way I'd never seen before. "Why saidst thou naught to me?"

My voice shook, and I swallowed again before answering lamely. "It wouldn't have helped, would it?" I said. "Dewar only recently hit on a way of freeing her that looked as if it might work."

I found I could not tell him the true reason: that Freia and Dewar both had not wanted him to know. Not with Dewar overhearing, and probably never alone.

"Would not have helped! What remedy was there, and what matter whether there be remedy or none? I shall permit no bar 'twixt me and matters of my Spring," Prospero said. His hand tightened. I began ignoring the accompanying sensations. The tower of Spring-force fused into solidity as he continued, illuminating the whole of the Catacombs with white hard light as Prospero's voice rose steadily, "I care not a tinker's damn what thou mayst make o' the rest, but the Spring is *mine* and I am minded—"

"Father," Dewar said calmly, "we didn't think it would affect you. It didn't when she was transformed the first time. I am sorry."

" 'Twould not affect me! Why, am I sawdust and wood? Not affect me, and 'twas I opened the very Spring which sustains and bathes thee in its essence! What hast thou done, thou cold-blooded water-witted profligate thieving viper's son? What means this *we?* What scorpion-souled ingrate have I taken to my heart to poison me and all my works?" thundered Prospero, standing, releasing me, gesturing and making the Spring's visible force knit and knot itself higher, broader, more intricately—

Dewar caught his breath; I saw his throat work. He and Prospero stared at one another, and then Prospero gestured again and Dewar gasped, inhaled deeply once. "I'll come to you soon and tell you all the tale. Start to finish. Don't badger Gwydion; he knows only half the story."

"Within the hour present thy carcass at my rooms here," Prospero said curtly, gesturing.

"I don't—Yes, sir." Dewar vanished.

The structure in the Spring vanished too, falling like a silent, luminous waterspout and leaving nothing behind but an afterimage on my eyes. Prospero may have given up sorcery, but that must mean little when he had the Spring at his fingertips, responding to his wishes conscious and covert. I was shaking.

"Naturally," Prospero said in a conversational tone, turning to me, "I shall badger thee, O daughter's-son." He sat down again.

There was no refusing him. I omitted Dewar's more personal remarks to Freia as being immaterial and private, and everything about Ariel, but Prospero still frowned, though he grew calmer. At the end he said simply, "And it sat unshakable in your thought through all the years that nor Gaston nor I might be told? Wherefore this mistrust?"

"I didn't want to get his hopes up," I said. "Nor did Mother. She told me to tell no one anything till afterward, when we knew it had worked. I never thought of the connection between you and the Spring as being dangerous to you." It nearly had cost a life to redeem Freia's: her father's. "I am sorry, sir," I whispered.

He sighed, rubbing his forehead wearily. "What havoc's ever wrought with tenderest intention." And after a moment, "Poor Freia. What torment to her, what damnable impotence bestowed by greatest power. To see all and naught, blinded of the sight of two best-loved, ignorant whither Gaston and her suckling babe were fled. No deeper hell for a mother could be conceived by the best-schooled devil. Yet if Panurgus be indeed maintained in Landuc's Well, become Essence of Fire, he could have lightened her."

"I believe he would not. He opposed her release. He wanted her to reconcile herself to her position as . . . as an Essence, as you put it." If it were indeed a job that must be filled, someone with better aptitude must volunteer knowingly, I thought. Till then, it could stay empty.

"Mayhap there's some right of it on his side, but 'twas

ill-hap nonetheless." He stood and headed back to the door
and I followed him. He turned on me. "Do you think she'll
be won by this scheme of rescue?"

"I don't know enough to guess. But the feeling around the
Spring is different now."

"Aye. Vacant and purely vital; there's no heart beats there
now." He locked the door behind us and we went up. Prospero closeted himself in his apartment and I went to my
workroom and paced.

Three minutes before his hour was up, Dewar tapped at
my study door, opened it, and closed it behind him rapidly,
entering from my workroom where he had availed himself of
a Mirror.

"What did you tell him?" he asked me at once.

"What I know. Most of it."

He looked at me hard and nodded.

I was still furious with him myself and glared at him.
"Dewar, I had to restart his heart."

He paled. "I had no idea."

"Now you do. He's down the hall waiting for you. How is
she?"

"We'll not know for some time," he said, and left.

I hoped the discussion wouldn't become violent. Dewar
was an equable fellow, by and large, but Prospero had a hot
temper and ample provocation. There was nothing I could
do about it. I paced and fumed.

He had not kept me informed. He had not even told me at
the last minute, which would have helped. What had they
done? What effects would it have? This was going to be my
problem, dealing with the aftershocks of the disruption of the
Spring. It bothered me that he had left me holding the empty
bag—set me up, practically—and now it would be my job to
mend whatever he had broken.

It hadn't occurred to me that separating Freia from the
Spring that trapped her would have side effects. After all,
nothing of the sort had happened when she was consumed by

it. She was gone, and there was a pulse of energy, and that was all.

I was staring out the window, arms folded, when someone came in without knocking or calling. Turning, I saw that it was Prospero.

We regarded one another for a moment.

"Dewar will not know," he said after a moment, beginning to pace himself, "for several days what may be won by this gamble. In his frenzy he's overlooked that miscalculation o' the odds means that Freia's utterly lost beyond any redemption."

That hadn't occurred to me either. My breath caught.

"He seems fairly sure that the game is worth the candle," Prospero said.

"I think it is . . ."

"I deeply resent, and I suspect your father will be even greater pained, that Dewar, and you by your silence of consent, made this choice for all," Prospero said. "Did it not occur to you that you hazarded others' stakes in the play?"

I rubbed the toe of my shoe along the pattern at the edge of my rug. "Yes," I said. "In a way we all are interested parties, all of Freia's children and Gaston and you and Dewar, and in another way . . . it would have made it harder . . . harder for her to go through with it and harder for everyone if there had been even small hope . . ."

He stopped at the other window, beside me, and leaned on the sill staring out. "Dewar," he said, "hath told me the . . . consequence, the function, of her submersion in the Spring. And he admitted that to win her consent he had, in greater and lesser degrees, hoodwinked, bullied, and guided her as a will-o'-wisp might, banked on her trust and drained her will. If he has failed, if he has snuffed her out, I do not know what I shall do, but I know I shall be angry. And I shall bring him, and you, to reckon the debt."

I said nothing.

"Your father shall hear of this forthwith. It matters not a

clipped farthing if Freia survives or no; Gaston must know what befell her. Shall be for him to judge whether you should also tell your siblings and when."

"He does not need to know!" I said. "It will torment him if he realizes that he left her when he left Argylle and went wherever the hell he went with the baby, with Ulrike. He would never forgive himself."

"That is his burden, not yours. You shall find him and tell him." Prospero turned and fixed his commanding gaze on me.

I opened my mouth in startled protest. "What! How? He's been gone for years—"

"You are a sorcerer; you know as well as I how't may be compassed."

I objected, "Gaston may just kill me if I manage to pull him in before he discovers who Summons him."

"Fare the Road then and find him. I care not how you tell him, but he must know of this. It is just."

I stared back at him and then had to look down, losing the confrontation. "Yes, sir."

"Leave at once. I have told Dewar that he shall cease his shields and bars to Summonings. He asks that we Summon him only if need warrants; I have consented to that. Thus when you find Gaston, you shall tell him Dewar can be bespoke."

"That . . ."

"Yes."

"Gaston . . ." Gaston would reach down Dewar's throat and pull him inside-out if this failed, I thought. Freia was Dewar's sister, but she was Gaston's wife, and he had wagered everything on her himself before.

"Assuredly your father's of an age to face whatever may come," Prospero said angrily.

I just nodded, looking down still.

"And eke your uncle," he added.

There was no answer possible to this.

"If you had but thought a little more, Gwydion," he said softly, sounding very tired, "I would you had simply . . . thought a little more."

"I did think! I have thought about it until it has worn a rut in my head!" I cried.

"Then you were not thinking, you were ruminating!"

I flinched, bit back my answer.

Prospero looked at me as angrily as I looked at him and then, slowly, forced himself to relax. "Hie after Gaston," he said. "Safe journey. I'll take the Chair for you while you're absent."

He closed the door quietly behind him.

I threw things into a bag and changed my clothes, fuming still. Then I went to the mews and got two of my black-and-gold war-hawks. Virgil was waiting in a tree near the field where Cosmo was grazing with Hussy; I brought them both to me with a whistle.

"We're heading down the Road," I said, and let Cosmo out through the gate. Hussy trotted over to watch us go.

⌣— *23* —⌒

GASTON WAS PROBABLY STILL IN PHEYARCET, but to be sure I sent one of my best hawks to seek him through Argylle's Road and Leys. The other I took with me as I rode toward the Border.

I rode fast and hard and angry. I rode without paying much attention to my surroundings; I was wholly occupied with my inner monologue dealing with Prospero's dressing-down and Dewar's cavalier disregard and Gaston's possible reactions to the news that his wife was not dead but indeterminate. I resented being told off to break the news to him, for one thing. Dewar should do it. He knew what was going on, for heaven's sake; I had no idea what they'd done, how they'd done it, or what would come next. Prospero was being unfair to me. There was no way I'd be able to satisfy Gaston with the fragment of the truth I knew.

I muttered, "Gahrrr," as Cosmo jumped a hedge. Cosmo's ears flicked back, but he'd been with me long enough to distinguish a spontaneous remark from a command and changed neither gait nor direction. We were bucketing along an untidy, seldom-used Ley. Virgil was on the saddlebags—actually in one, having loosened the strap and climbed inside—wisely leaving me alone. The hawk flew overhead; I used her to survey the path before me.

I took just one rest stop on my way to the Border, drawing on the Spring to keep weariness at bay until I was bored with riding and wanted the halt as a change of pace. Cosmo, Spring-fed by nature, could gallop for a year at a time if I demanded it of him; he was pleased to stop too, though. I protected us with a Circle and slept badly within it, plagued by dreams of searching frantically for things in the Citadel, of trying to get to rooms that were not where they were supposed to be, and of being disoriented and lost in the City.

Ill-rested and ill-tempered, I resumed my journey and crossed into the Border, which I must take four days to pass. I thought up elaborate arguments with Prospero, Gaston, and my uncle as I rode; I defended my actions vigorously and justified them flawlessly; and I planned out a search path for my hawk to follow and another for Virgil and myself.

There were places where I was more and places where I was less likely to find Gaston. When I emerged into Pheyarcet I sent the hawk off on a route that covered part of them and followed the other route with Virgil, binding them both to seek Gaston until they found him. The hawk carried a note telling Gaston to Summon me at once. The owl, since I followed him, needed no note; I went with him because, since he was sensitive to my family, he might detect and locate Gaston more rapidly than the hawk.

I rode through wastelands and cities, devastations and

Edens, farmlands and ports. I followed the Road and Leys, crossed and recrossed Nexuses, and passed Nodes. I fumed to myself still. I did not Summon Dewar; he had my Key and he would let me know what was afoot if he had any residue of manners at all. I was curt with my horse and abrupt with my familiar.

On the ninth day Virgil swerved from the search path and took a Ley-track, a disused and difficult-to-perceive one which had nearly vanished from neglect. With the feeling of triumph that comes when the quarry is sighted, I turned Cosmo to follow him. We crunched through a second-growth woodland that must once have been farms, crisscrossed as it was by stone walls in meandering piles, passing a lone chimney standing in the ruined foundation of a long-gone house. The Ley became a faint cart-track, and the cart-track became a dirt road, and the dirt road became a hard-packed, graded road, smoothly contoured, at which the Ley petered out entirely.

I reined in and let Cosmo have a drink from a stony brook that chuckled along beside this gravelly, sandy artifact. Virgil waited in a white-trunked, yellow-leafed tree. We were in high, steep mountains.

"Is he hereabouts, then?"

A nod.

"Good work, Virgil."

A nod again.

"Modest you're not . . ."

Cosmo blew loudly into the water, lifted his head, and we scrambled up to the road and walked along it. Virgil hopped from tree to tree, leading at our pace, not his.

This road led us through more woodland where great trees lay cut and trimmed. Bright-painted machines for harvesting the trees stood idle; I paused for a look at them and went on. I had become familiar with such machines in an Eddy where I had worked for two years clearing forests; the ones I had known had been powered by temperamental steam engines, but these appeared to be internal-combustion. There was much solace to be had in such hard labor—perhaps Gaston was lumberjacking.

The sandy-gravelly road ended at one covered with hard, oily-smelling, slick black asphalt. The sun was behind me; the air was chill and dry. I rode Cosmo along slowly far over to one side, on the verge of the road where the sudden drop-offs permitted. Virgil led us up and up, climbing and winding along the mountainside. We passed other roads of various sorts leading away into the forest; we were passed several times by motor vehicles, large and small, and once by a helmeted man on a swift blue bicycle, who waved. I waved back, but he was already gone.

Virgil finally chose one of the tracks that led off to one side. This was barred with a gate obviously intended to exclude motorists; a foot-track led around to one side, and I led Cosmo around the barrier that way. There was a rutted and gullied, but passable, dirt road, and, figuring there were no motor vehicles around, I hurried along the middle. The sun was setting now. I would have preferred not to startle Gaston by coming on him in the dark, but it seemed I would have no choice.

It was dusk when Virgil suddenly swooped down to my right, off a cliff it seemed, and hooted twice. There was a faint tang of smoke in the air, which before had held only balsam and dry leaves. I slowed Cosmo and stopped, peering into the dimness; there were tall trees at the bottom of this steep bit, it seemed . . . Yes, the road curved down and around. I nudged my horse to a walk and went slowly down and among the trees. The sound of water and a glimmer of firelight were ahead. I conjured an ignis fatuus to light my way there.

Gaston had probably heard me approaching half a mile away. He was sitting on a rock by his campfire, waiting for his visitor to come closer. As I discerned his firelit form there, he saw me too, and he rose slowly to his feet, folding his arms, an amber statue in the moving light.

I drew in the reins when I was about twenty feet away.

"Gwydion," he said.

"Hullo, Gaston."

We regarded one another.

"Thy horse will find the grass upstream more than palatable, I suspect," he said after a moment.

I dismounted and led Cosmo off upstream; there was indeed a pleasant open grassy place where I left him after casting a Circle around him for the night. Virgil *uhuu*'d again somewhere in the darkness. The ignis led me back to Gaston, and then I banished it feeling that it was somehow inappropriate for the silence stirred by owls and insects and distant hunting calls of wolves and the darkness broken by Gaston's small fire.

He wore a high-necked knitted pullover of a dark crimson color, intricately stitched—the sort Mother used to make for all of us, knit in Council meetings. Probably it *was* one of hers. His boots were sturdy walking shoes and a pack leaned against a tree not far from the fire. We looked at one another again for a long moment.

"I cannot say," he said finally, smiling slowly, "that I am not happy to see thee," and he hugged me hard suddenly, as strong and solid and breath-taking as ever. I hugged him. We smiled at each other, and his eyes went over and over my face. "Sit down. Th'art tired. Let us sup first."

I sat, I blinked back a couple of sudden tears, I swallowed. Gaston took out food and a couple of cooking-pots, and I bestirred myself to open my saddlebags and wineskin and shared what I had also (including surpassingly excellent smoked sausages which we toasted on sticks and ate with bread soaking up their juices). Gaston made a pot of astringent herbal tea for us to drink with our meal. Whenever our eyes met we'd both smile uncontrollably, until finally he laughed and reached over and ruffled my hair up as if I were eight years old.

"Gaston," I said, ducking, embarrassed and pleased and wondering how to tell him what I must.

"Son."

That nearly did make me cry.

"Handsome earring," he commented.

"Got it in a place called Massila," I said, "when I visited Josquin there."

"I know Massila too well to ask what thou didst and how't liked thee," Gaston said, hiding his smile in his tea, but his eyes crinkled.

The full, horrible import of what I had to do struck me. Gaston had, clearly, been putting himself back together, stabilizing and coming to terms with the loss of his beloved Freia, and I was going to undo all that in ten words or fewer.

"Th'art come for a reason, I guess," he said then, reading my mind.

"It can wait until morning. It's not . . . it's not so urgent that it can't wait."

Gaston seemed about to contradict me, to order me to tell him what errand sent me to seek him out. He asked instead, "How didst thou find me?" curiously.

"Virgil."

"Ah."

"I don't think anyone else could have done it."

"Thy birds are apt for finding."

"Yes. I've never understood why no one else has birds."

"None hath thine affinity for them," he suggested, and poured more tea for me. "How goes it with Josquin, then?"

"Oh, well, very well . . ." and, reprieved, I launched into family gossip and anecdote. Gaston asked tidings of Ulrike next, and home, and I told him of my sister, of her visit to Alexander, about the dragon, about wine production and our storage problem. He shook his head over Gemnamnon's destruction in the Border and frowned to hear of Marfisa's maiming burns. And as for the wine . . .

"Cognac," he said.

"Cognac?" I repeated, an odd word.

" 'Twas long in my mind—indeed I spoke of it to thy mother, and she thought it full plausible—" a sadness flicked through his voice and he went on—"that Argylle might wisely wed the distiller's art to its vintners' natural genius. The soils along the coast, north of Ollol toward Bevallin, are well-suited to a vine called the Ugni Blanc. I had planted some at the Crespie estate, in a corner, to see how they fared—"

"The sour ones?" They produced a wine popularly described by the staff as pissing-poor. We no longer used the fruit for anything but compost.

He laughed. "Aye. Have they been pulled?"

"No. We thought a use might come for them and we never bothered. But the wine they yield, Gaston—" I shook my head.

"Take that thin stuff and when twice-distilled and aged in good wood you'll have something would make a Salamander spit, worth twenty times a bottle of middling wine," he said, in the tone of voice he used for describing a winning strategy on the battlefield.

My eyes opened wide as the idea made sense. "Whoof! I see. A kind of whisky. Firewater . . . Oh, no. Aged? No, that won't do—storage space is exactly the problem—"

"Eddies," he said.

"Eddies?" I repeated, lost.

"Find thou a quick, steadily-spinning Eddy-world, one where time's tread goes in, say, a fivefold increase over Argylle's. There are several I know of, where thy Spring purls and swirls swift."

I began to laugh, seeing all the plan: cook it down, age it, and sell it for twenty times the price of a similar volume of wine. And speedily done, thanks to the quick Eddy-aging. Fast money, and a product that couldn't fail.

"I see now," I said, "I see, and I thank you, Gaston. Why did you never start this?"

He shook his head, a little sadly. "No reason," he said, " 'twas an idea whose time I never found, one thy mother and I envisioned would divert us one day. But I gift thee freely with it now. And I look forward to thy success."

After that we sat watching the embers of the fire together for a long time until they were no more than a black-crusted glow. The long, drawn-out, mournful calls of wolves were thin lines of sound dividing the night into time. I jumped when Gaston put his hand on my arm, waking me.

"We'll talk more o' the morrow," he said softly.

I yawned. "Tomorrow. Yes."

The sun warmed me and woke me. I lay still, remembering where I was and with whom, and then took the punch of dread right in my gut. The worst was coming, and I could not postpone nor avoid it.

Gaston was sitting some distance away, reading in a small book, his back against a tree trunk. I stretched and rolled and got up, stretched again. A bath in the stream seemed like a very good idea. I went over to Gaston and told him I was going to take a swim.

He nodded. "There's a pleasant place up near where thou staked thy horse."

"Thanks."

" 'Tis right cold," he warned me, and he wasn't kidding.

My eyes closed and my breath caught when I put a foot in the water. It was barely liquid. There ought to have been ice at the banks. After a moment of steeling, in which I reminded myself that it would build my character and clean my body, I took the plunge, splashing in at this deeper spot at once, whooping after I came up for air, then panting frantically as my core temperature dropped.

Dressed, with my blood racing and my skin feeling three sizes smaller, I went back to Gaston. He had made a pot of strong black tea and rummaged out fruit and cheese and the rest of the bread I had with me. We breakfasted, watching birds flit around in the dark evergreens. The mountain rose beside and above us, higher still. It was a beautiful day, the sky a hard pure blue, the sun kind and ripe.

I waited until we had put things away.

"Um," I said, looking up at a great black-billed raven that watched us narrowly from the crown of a dead tree festooned with lichen.

"Yes," Gaston said.

I looked at him. I did not know where to begin.

"Tell me about it, then," he suggested, seeing my confusion, and took me over to his shaded spot, where we sat on tree roots. I picked up a stick and scratched in the rust-colored fallen needles.

"It's hard to explain," I said to the earth. "You'll find it . . . upsetting . . ."

"Hath aught befallen Ulrike?" he asked quickly.

"No. No, no, no. She's fine. It's about . . . Freia."

Gaston became quite still, waiting.

"I would never have . . . I didn't want to bring it up before, because I thought this was something that could only cause you pain," I said, "but Dewar . . . it was because of him that it's come up at all."

Gaston said nothing, and then, "Go on, Gwydion. I'm listening."

"Prospero said I must come and talk to you about it," I said. "I didn't really want to yet. This is all immaterial really. It's about Freia, Gaston. When . . . when Tython cast her into the Spring and the Spring . . . the Spring destroyed her, she wasn't . . . she wasn't really killed. It . . . captured part of her, the . . . the spirit, the mind, the soul, if you will, and she has been . . . inhabiting the Spring ever since."

Perfect stillness beside me. I dared not look at him.

"I knew about it because when Dewar disappeared later that day, after we came back up and told you, I was worried, he was so upset, so distraught, and then he was very quiet and I knew that he was going to do something. I followed him down to the Spring, and I saw that he'd built a great spell to send himself away. But he hadn't finished it yet. He told me to listen, to focus on the energies from the Spring. They were different. He called out for Freia then, and she . . . she appeared there.

"He talked to her and tried to touch her, but couldn't. She was a ghost. So to speak. An illusion. She said that she was part of the Spring now, transformed to . . . to some kind of Essential being, and that Panurgus . . . who is part of Landuc's Well in the same way . . . he said that there was no way to release her save for a living person to step into the Spring and replace her there, providing her with a . . . a . . . a body to inhabit. And he would not be saved as she was. I do not pretend to understand it all, Dewar seems to . . . For someone to die in order for her to live. She didn't want that. They argued, kind of, and he disappeared . . ."

"Ah." Gaston rubbed his chin.

"Yes . . . I just couldn't . . . tell anyone. It was pointless. What kind of person . . . Who in our family could we send to, to death, just to get Freia back? How could we trade life for death that way? I couldn't . . . I couldn't imagine anyone doing it. I knew I couldn't," I whispered. "I thought and thought about it. I tried to . . . get my courage up, a couple of times I went down and walked around and around the Spring . . . I just couldn't do it. I should have, and I couldn't."

I swallowed. "Then things just went along, and you went away and never returned either. I stayed in Argylle . . . recently though when I was coming home from Alexander's place, I had a . . . an odd dream . . ." and I told him about the Battlemaster and the theft of Freia's genetic codes and Dewar's guilt in that matter, leaving out Ariel—his familiar was only Dewar's concern. Gaston nodded slowly as I went on to tell of Thiorn's offer to help reconstruct a body and transfer Freia into it, of Freia's hesitant acquiescence, of her Sending to me and our conversation (not omitting what she had said about him), and of the day they had finally done this thing—or attempted it. "And that is where it hangs now, and Prospero insisted I must tell you at once. Dewar has not called me; you can call him—Prospero told him to permit Summonings henceforward. I do not know how . . . what happened. I fear it must have failed; it seems insane now . . ."

"If Thiorn be involved, it becomes both credible and . . . and possible," he said, in a measured, level voice.

"Are you angry?" I whispered, looking at him at last.

"I would have liked to have known, but I understand that thy motives were much as mine for keeping Ulrike out of sight. Not to burden, not to cumber, not to . . . impose." He smiled faintly. "Gwydion, let us not conceal such things from one another in the future. We are capable of bearing anxieties, sorrows, disappointments. All of us." He reached over and clasped my shoulder, looking into my eyes.

"I'm sorry. Yes." I sighed. "I'm afraid it didn't work, myself."

"I would have thee tell thy brothers and sisters."

I was not going to be very popular. "I would wait until we were sure. That was what Mother said too."

He looked at me. I looked down, feeling my neck grow warm.

"I'll tell them, since you request it," I said to the needles. "But if something . . . goes wrong, it will be very hard."

"Do not undervalue their courage, son. 'Tis difficult, but 'tis merited by their kinship and their trust."

"There's difficult and then there's . . ." I couldn't even think of a word for it—"cruelty, teasing, disappointment . . ."

"Nonetheless."

I nodded.

Gaston, his face impassive, stared off into the stainless sky. There was nothing more to say.

Gaston and I took affectionate leave of each other when I set out later in that day. I sent Virgil to seek and bring back to me my war-hawk, which still sought for Gaston, and rode slowly back to the Ley that had brought me here. Gaston did not say what he would do or what he had been doing; it looked to me as if he'd been hiking here, taking in the great natural beauty of the place. I hoped that, as he thought over what I had told him, he would not grow angry with me. He had sent me off with a gentle "Safe journey, Gwydion," and a firm, affectionate embrace.

My mission done, the Road held no attractions for me. I plotted out the fastest way back to Argylle. It had occurred to me that Dewar might bring Freia there if she were ill, and if she were all right she'd come there anyway, probably, to see Prospero, her children, Gaston—No.

Gaston. She would want to see him first. She knew the rest of us were well; we had all been where she could perceive us. Gaston she would want to see at once; Gaston was the trump card Thiorn and Dewar had played to win her out of the Spring again; Gaston was her great anchor to the corporeal.

I actually slowed Cosmo for a moment and almost turned him to go back and persuade Gaston to come home with me. If I put it so, he might agree . . . But he also might want to adjust alone, in privacy, to this strange idea of no longer being a widower. And also Freia's own fear jangled in the back of my mind: suppose he did have someone else, somewhere, now? He would have to settle that for himself. It would be better to leave him as I had, with what I knew, and trust him to do the right thing for himself and his lady.

So I continued on, not riding so hard as before but still making haste. Dewar had not Summoned me. I was irked about that. When I returned, I intended to Summon him and ask my questions about everything—and have answers.

There was no excuse for him to conceal anything now, except that it was a habit with him.

Virgil and my hawk joined me at a Nexus where I left the Ley and moved onto the Road instead. I passed one night on a beach, camped beside a tiny brook which ran through the dunes to a grey, slow-moving sea, another in a ruin of incalculable age half-buried and artistically overgrown, three nights in forests of differing types, and one in a blinding rainstorm crowded with Cosmo under a tilted slab of rock which formed an improvised cave.

I crossed the Border in four days, singing most of a long, complicated song cycle from Landuc to myself for amusement, and when we were in Argylle again Cosmo jogged along briskly, eager to get home, at a mile-eating pace.

In a desert all the colors of fire and stone, we stopped for water and a brief rest. There was a spring that was a Node here, giving water of exceptional purity and refreshment, and there was shade from a wind-carved arch which marked the spring's location. A few bushes fringed it with greenery.

I scooped water over my face, drank, and sat down on a rock. Virgil and the war-hawk waited on a pillar of stone. It occurred to me that I should get the other hawk back and send the lot of them home; they travelled faster than I and I had no need of their attendance. I called Virgil to me and told him to go find the other hawk and return to Argylle with her. When he was gone, I commanded this hawk to return to Argylle herself. She would arrive a day or so before I did. I threw her into the air, and she beat a moment and then, catching a thermal, ascended in a slow spiral and finally flew away, a straight line her path.

Watching her made me wish for wings myself. I had another drink and then mounted slowly and returned to the Road. Direct though it was, it was slower than flying.

We had not gone two miles and were still in an arid, stony landscape when Cosmo stopped cold and lifted his head, snuffing.

"What's up?" I whispered.

He moved his head from side to side and shivered.

I looked around, saw nothing; sniffed and smelled nothing; listened and heard nothing. Cosmo was shivering still, motionless, his head seeking. Something was bothering him, and that worried me. I focused on the Road's force and sank into it, feeling the flow and pulse of energy, feeling a hot spot not far ahead—Nexus or Node, perhaps?

As I recalled it, the map didn't show anything but that spring around here. I chewed my lip. This could be a side effect of that upset in the Spring.

The hot spot was there, a powerful and unfamiliar thing. It neither radiated nor absorbed. It was not a Node, not a Nexus—no, it was more alive than those, like an ignis—or a Salamander. I shuddered. A rogue Salamander, sucked into our world by the Spring's implosion, would be nearly as difficult to banish as the dragon. Yet it seemed quiet, for a Salamander. It couldn't be Gemnamnon; Virgil had seen him far, far away in Phesaotois, and I didn't think he could get from there to here so quickly.

"Let's have a look then," I said softly to Cosmo, and I reached over my shoulder and loosened my sword Talon in its scabbard. He lifted a hoof and put it down irresolutely. I nudged his sides. "Can't go forward without moving, old boy. C'mon. I'm here, you're here, and whatever it is isn't going anywhere."

Finally, after a fair amount of soft cajolery, he went stiffly onward. I was tense and cold now myself, and I rehearsed a few spells, quick ones, just in case.

We came over the lip of a small rise and descended into a high-walled valley. It seemed dim here; the dirt and stones were reddish, unpleasantly like dried blood, and the ground was lifeless and stony—a landscape consistent with a Salamander, which would devour everything down to bare rock. I saw not even a lichen. The sky overhead was brassy. There was no movement in the air, and the only sound was Cosmo's slow hooves. I breathed as quietly as possible, straining all my senses. The hot spot was just ahead, around the bend in this kinky valley.

The track the Road followed narrowed as it turned, becoming only a meter wide and barely discernible. I followed the pulse of the Road rather than the visible signs of a passage, looking around still—

The top of the ridge to my right moved.

Cosmo stopped again, tossing his head, and stared up at it, and I stared too as the ridge buckled up and acquired protuberances and moved sinuously and rumbled musically, a sound that grew in volume and bounced off the steep valley walls and buffeted me.

"Uh-oh," I said very softly to Cosmo.

ᴄ— 24 —ᴐ

A CLOUD OF RED DUST WENT up in the air as the ridge shook itself off and extended wings. I began murmuring the words of spells far more powerful than the ones I'd just prepared in my mind.

The problem was that the only ones short enough for me to be sure that I recalled them perfectly were insufficient to do any real harm to the dragon dropping down toward the valley bottom. There is a class of very simple and highly destructive spells—the kind that enable the user to level a mountain with a couple of words; but, as Dewar had said when he bailed me out the first time Gemnamnon and I met for a duel, they also have wide-ranging side effects on the surroundings—the Road, the Leys, the worlds. There is a place I have been with him that is just not there any longer because Dewar used a spell of that sort there. The Road leads up to it and stops, and one is left on the verge of a boiling chaos of disrupted being. It is necessary to use protective spells to get even that close.

Gemnamnon, leaving a cloudy trail of fine red dust, settled surprisingly softly in the canyon ahead of me. He looked at me from half-lidded eyes as he folded his wings.

Strangely, calm settled on me. My mind became clear enough for me to visualize certain pages in my grimoires and notebooks on which the spells I needed were written. The only thing lacking was time to prepare them.

Some part of my mind must have been out of control, though, because for an instant I wondered if Gemnamnon was going to rumble "Draw!" and lumber toward me in the fashion of fairy-tale gunslingers. There was no schoolmarm here, though, nor a saloon, which was too bad. I could have used a drink.

He regarded me coolly and waited. We both knew what this was about. I suspected I knew more about it than he did. Freia was no longer in the Spring, thus the Spring was no longer interested as it had been in my personal safety and health; Dewar was somewhere else: I would get no aid from unexpected quarters this time. Gemnamnon, I thought, studying his cool purples and silvers and blues, colors stained by the yellow light, must be aware that the Spring was changed recently. He must have tested the Border again and passed through it unopposed. Was he looking for me, I wondered, or on his way back to Argylle? I was not about to ask. What was I supposed to do now? Challenge? Retreat?

The nearest Ley was a few miles back, and the dragon blocked the Road. Forget flight. As for challenge, he was the invader in my territory. I had no quarrel with him as long as he stayed out of the Spring's Dominion—Argylle and the Border.

Still, the Spring was mine, not his. I was a son of Argylle, an initiate of the Spring whose force sustained the world around us here, and he could not touch that. I wasn't sure if a Spring outclassed the raw Elemental power Gemnamnon represented. Since Argylle's Gryphon had conquered the dragon in the Border, a neutral arena, perhaps the Spring had a slight advantage. And the thought of that Gryphon brought another thought on its wings: if Freia were still in the Spring, this could not happen. The meeting in the Border would have been the last.

What, if anything, had I learned in my previous encounters? Did he have weaknesses I could exploit, bad habits on which I could capitalize? I considered him dispassionately. He had a short temper. He liked playing with his prey. He tended to gloat. He did not necessarily pay attention to everything going on around him; Dewar and the Gryphon had both had no trouble surprising him. If I were to harm him badly enough he might retreat to fight again another day, as when I'd half-blinded him. *Might.* I suspected this was to the death, his or mine.

He had chosen this place to limit my actions, but he was limited too. It was narrow and high-sided; he'd have difficulty moving laterally up those slippery slopes of sand, even as I would. Could I use Cosmo to distract him? Perhaps.

The sun baked my shoulders. Talon was heavy. Usually I didn't notice the weight of my sword; it was just there, hanging off my back or my hip.

Considering him as a four-legged, winged animal with a long tail, I noted to myself that it took him time to turn around completely although his head could twist through more than 360° on that agile neck. I had no explosives handy to toss down his throat as Duke Nellor Trephayenne had done. Nor was he much for conversation, compared to Uvarkis' dragons or Ottaviano's. Either he didn't think we were worth talking to or he was a punk, an uncultured thug of a lout of a dragon. This was an interesting thought, and I toyed with it, waiting for him to do something besides watch me sidelong and preen. Perhaps Gemnamnon was a relatively young dragon looking for territory. That might account for his persistence. And his taking of things personally, his quickness to find offense, was something I have always thought of as a characteristic of the young and rare among the experienced.

Cosmo fidgeted and stamped. The dragon took this as a signal and lifted his head, set his haunches and opened his eyes more fully.

"This time we shall have done, petty sorcerer," he said, and a gout of green flame followed his words, long and focused, cutting the dry, hot air in an arc toward us.

Finally! I thought, and Cosmo must have felt much the same way. He stopped acting like a rabbit and got us out of the way of the flame while I repelled it with a reflective shield, bouncing it back toward the dragon. I couldn't hold the shield long, but I'd surprised him—perhaps he thought I'd be as toothless as in the Border. His left front foot took a bit of a scorch and he cut off the flame abruptly.

I drew Talon with a short, singing spell, the Golden Bees, and fired them off at him from the sword's point. Gemnamnon got most of them with a pouf that sent a diffuse cloud of acidic gas out his nostrils and shot a jet of the same foul stuff my way; it splashed short of the mark on the ground, and Cosmo retreated, backstepping quickly and awkwardly. I cast a raw bolt of power as he shot the jet of gas; it missed because of Cosmo's movement throwing my aim off.

This was feinting. We were neither of us giving our full effort to our strikes. I decided to throw out something more powerful, and shielded from a counterflame while performing a somewhat longer spell, a variant of Hubble's Bubble, which put a sphere of vacuum around Gemnamnon. It startled him; he had a sudden nosebleed and jumped away as air rushed into the vacuum with a loud concussive bang. The dragon snarled, shaking his head, and pounced (graceful despite his great size) down closer to me, firing a rapid series of small fireballs from his gullet, then tried to snort another gas but stopped.

I was busy shielding from the flames, but noticed the beginning of the gas-sneeze movement and noticed that he halted. Good! I snapped off three quick spells from Talon's point that punched at his head and then I wove a Fishnet, kicking Cosmo so that he carried me forward, in and out, a dancing quick feint, and dropped the Fishnet over his right front foot. It began to constrict, something it would do until it had formed into a ball again. Gemnamnon took a swing at me as I did this, though, and caught my left shoulder a glancing blow. I was knocked halfway over Cosmo's head, and Cosmo raced past the dragon, leapt his swishing tail three times, and turned to face him again as I regained my seat. My shoulder felt broken; it was numb and my arm unresponsively useless. I put my left hand behind my belt to hold it steady.

Gemnamnon laughed. I performed a complex, powerful spell of Dewar's called the Southern Rail which created a shrieking gale wind in a small area; it whammed into Gemnamnon as he blew more flame (still laughing) from his mouth and sent him tumbling head over tail.

"Hah!" I exclaimed, pleased with the unexpectedly good results—I'd expected that one just to pause him, not to actually move him.

He roared as he rolled to his feet, the spell howling away down the valley disharmoniously. I was getting the hang of this, though; the kinds of spells I thought of as fatal weren't always the same ones that actually bothered the dragon. I had an idea. As he leapt, wings partly opened, and fell on me, I made Cosmo run right past the flames which were terrifyingly hot despite my shielding, and threw a Stone spell up into his face, aiming for his manytoothed, tendril-adorned mouth.

Gemnamnon screamed and came after me, and a split second later I was unmounted, rolling, and Cosmo was galloping riderless back the way we'd come into this ambush. Life being what it is, I landed on my left shoulder, and I screamed as I rolled onto my knees. Tears of pain ran down my cheeks as I invoked a heavy-duty shielding spell because the dragon was taking another swing, the flat, open movement I'd use to squash a fly on a book. The force of the blow came through the spell to me; I gave way to it and let it knock me back, although that hurt like hell again, and used the movement to get to my feet, shielding again and calling up Block of Ice. His right foot was looking bad, scored by the Fishnet; I pointed Talon and Block of Ice at his left foot, which was swinging at me again.

It worked, again, and he snapped at me. My Stone spell had evidently paralyzed important bits of dragon oral apparatus, because if I were he and he were I, I'd have toasted me and eaten me by now, and he hadn't flamed lately. I ignored the pain in my shoulder and side and reinforced my shielding spell as I ran from him. He pursued clumsily on his damaged front feet. Gemnamnon's jaws closed on the air behind me with a low-frequency *thud* due to the shield.

I had to swerve up the slope to one side, slipping and fumbling in the sandy ground. I was looking desperately for cover; there was none to be seen. Cosmo was nowhere to be seen either. It was just as well. He could do nothing now, here.

Gemnamnon launched himself into the air and slammed down up the slope from me, setting off a small landslide. I lost my footing, struggling for balance. He roared triumphantly, pushing more dirt down with a sweep of his tail; I fell and rolled down the slope again, trying to protect my head with my right arm and failing. A rock bashed into my head, or maybe my head hit the rock, on the right side. My mouth tasted of blood. Managing to stop by braking with my feet, I spat and felt a tooth go. My right eye was hazed with red.

I swore and spat blood again. Talon was gone. Where had I dropped my sword? Didn't matter. Gemnamnon was lolloping down toward me, from side to side, and I threw up a shield, drew a bead on him with my bloody right forefinger, and mumbled the words to a spell I hadn't wanted to use, my mouth filling with blood again as I spoke.

Power rushed through me, a river of power from the Spring. I had trouble finishing what I was saying; my vision became hazy and I knew I would pass out, but I gasped painfully and finished the spell as the dragon reached me and swung his right foot to grab me. His foot and all the world around streaked out into distant places.

I was floating. That was the first thing I thought. It was not a pleasant floating. I vomited, which was not pleasant either. If you have never vomited in free-fall, I wholeheartedly recommend that you forgo the experience. I had done it before, so I knew how to avoid pushing my face in the mess I had created. It and I went off on different trajectories. It was a curious skill to have acquired while studying economics and accounting in that wretched sterile Eddy along the Road, but invaluable when needed—as now.

I hurt all over. It hurt to breathe, to move, and especially to puke. My face felt half gone. I seemed to be alive. I drew my legs up so that I was curled in a fetal ball as I floated, to present a smaller surface to whatever was here.

I could not distinguish shapes or colors where I was. It was unsolid, unformed, undefined—nothing stayed the same, if there was anything there at all, which there may not have been. It was easier not to look. I closed my eyes and groped for the feeling of the Spring, strained my senses to perceive a Road or Ley in my vicinity. I'd been right by the Road when I passed out. I could not find it.

What had happened? I supposed I had been too close to Gemnamnon when I blew him away. The spell I had riffed out of my mental deck of cards was the Disconnector. I had, in effect, dissolved Gemnamnon and a piece of the world around him—these things are hard to control. Fortunately it had stopped before I'd dissolved myself.

I whimpered. Home. I had to get out of here and home. I

was sick and I hurt a lot. What else was there about Disconnector? Would I hit the edge of the discombobulated area eventually, like washing up on a beach?

What was it Dewar had said that day we had looked at the place he'd destroyed with that spell . . . something about finitude, something about definition . . . Yes. It was possible to redefine the world inside the area one had, in essence, undefined, but it required such a drain from the Spring that he didn't think it was worth it. The Spring itself would slowly reconstruct the area over time.

I reached again for the Spring, but it wasn't available. I had cancelled its influence here, but if I was alive, there was Spring-force. Wasn't there?

It was hard to think. I struggled with my stomach, which wanted to empty itself again. I frowned and withdrew my thoughts into an unpained part of my mind. Dewar and I had stood on the edge. He threw a rock in. We watched it slow and drift and disappear into the souplike swirls. There had been a cliff at our feet. We had kicked a few rocks down; they bounced into the deconstruction also. One had bounced out, slowed, but come back and fallen against the cliff again, rolling down to a ledge. Dewar explained that the unbound matter slowly accreted to the still-solid. He pointed to a rock that had not been there on his last visit and before we left placed another ahead of it, at the very edge of the cliff, a marker.

So there must be an edge. I wondered how large an area I'd destroyed.

I stretched out my legs, and, eyes still closed, tried a sort of swimming. One-armed, it didn't work very well; I got no feeling of movement. I curled up again, pulling my scorched and torn cloak around me, and panted. Moving had made my body hurt more, much more than it had, and I tried to hold still. This I managed, not thinking about anything but my breaths, for a long time. I was unconscious or asleep for part of that time.

The jar that went through me woke me, or perhaps my own screaming did. I had fetched up against a wall of rock, and I grabbed and clutched at it frantically. It crumbled under my fingers; I scrabbled for a purchase and finally found it. It was sandy, gritty soil, like the soil in the place I'd destroyed. I lay my body against it and pulled myself together, then began crawling. I thought any direction would do.

I crawled for a while, stopped and rested, crawled again. I was stuck to the sandy wall now; as long as I kept myself close-pressed against it, I showed no inclination to drift away. I crawled intermittently for what seemed an hour.

Exhausted by this, I stopped for a long time and lay huddled. A thought crept out while I rested so and nuzzled my aching head. It whispered: *You fool, Gwydion. Try a Way now. This is concrete world here, so there must be a bit of the Spring to it.*

Fumbling and clumsy, I pulled my Keys from my tattered, blood-stained shirt. If I could open a Way to the Keystone in the Citadel, I'd be home free. Fire. The spell needed fire. I unclasped my cloak and pulled it into a pile—another good cloak gone. In agonizing slow motion I got my pouch of sorcerous tools from the left side of my belt and found the concentrated emergency flammables. I got a candle lit. I got the Key ready. I began whispering the spell, my diction furry and unclear, and mumbled it so badly that it didn't work. I tried again, the candle flame before my eyes where I sprawled on the red dirt.

This time I went slowly, concentrated, and enunciated everything no matter how it hurt my mouth. Blood moistened my tongue. The spell's construction sucked strength from me, but the flame burned brighter even as I again saw my vision darkening at the edges. The candle went up, wax and wick consumed by the Way's demand for fire, and the cloak ignited, and I looked through the flames into the Citadel, at the corridor where the Keystone is, or rather at the vine-carved stone baseboard. I lifted myself on my right arm and crawled forward.

I fell down, blacked out again.

The lute music was delightful: cool and precise plucking, a witty and graceful melody. I listened to it while I figured out how I was. The music stopped before I finished, and a door opened and closed. I heard movement, footsteps coming near.

"How is he?" A whisper.

"Still." Another.

Someone touched my wrist, which startled me so that I jumped and my eyes flew open. I shut them at once because it was so damn bright I was blinded.

"Draw those curtains!" Prospero ordered Walter, who rushed to do so. I had just glimpsed them at the edge of my dazzling vision of my bedroom ceiling. "Gwydion," he added, "forgive me for so rudely starting you from sleep. I knew not you lay near waking."

I tried to talk and found I couldn't. "Rnghf!"

"Your jaw's a mess. You look as though Fortuna herself rolled her Wheel over you," Walter said. "You'll not speak for a while, brother."

"Rrr," I managed, an impatient growl.

"Which shall be to us great hardship," Prospero said, "for ignorance as to what, in all the worlds beneath the winds, has passed with you leaves us groping and baffled . . ." I heard him pulling the bed hangings. "There, do you try your eyes again," he suggested.

I did. It was dimmer now, and my pupils happily adjusted without pain to show me Walter hovering behind Prospero, who was sitting in a chair beside the bed. Walter smiled at me, an enormous grin of relief. Reflexively I tried to smile back and stopped myself. It felt like a bad thing to do.

Prospero smiled also. "Now then. A guard found you by

the Keystone at dawn, a bloody dirty mess," he said. "Shall we play Twenty Questions?"

I tried moving my eyebrows, which didn't hurt too much but still pulled my skin. "Ungh."

"Yes is another grunt," Walter said, "and No is silence. Twenty Questions?"

"Ungh."

"Great." He smiled again.

"Did this happen in Pheyarcet?" Prospero asked.

I closed my eyes.

"No," murmured Walter.

"In the Border . . . ? In Argylle's Dominion . . . ?"

"Ungh." I looked at them again. Walter and Prospero glanced at one another.

"Did you have an accident, a fall or some such mishap?" Walter asked.

The last word in accidents, I wanted to say, but made no response. That wasn't what they meant.

"Were you attacked?" asked Prospero.

"Ungh."

"By a person . . . ? By an animal, or a pack of animals?"

"Ungh."

"Gemnamnon," whispered Walter.

"Ungh."

"Hellfire and hot coals!" exclaimed Prospero, and jumped up to pace.

"Was it near here?" Walter asked softly. "No? Far away?"

"Ungh."

"Very far away?"

I thought. Not very far, but not near . . .

"Somewhat far. Say, not at the Border but close."

"Ungh."

"Is he coming again to Argylle?"

I realized I did not know. I had no proof that I had destroyed him. He was, after all, an Elemental being. I might only have inconvenienced him.

"How could he know if the damned monster be coming or going?" snapped Prospero.

"True," Walter said. "Sorry. Ambiguous question."

I twitched my right hand. It was working, though clumsy. Slowly I moved it beneath the covers.

"You want to try writing?" asked my brother.

"Ungh."

"I'll fetch you things for writing, Gwydion. It would be faster, that's true."

"Ungh."

He went into my sitting room and I heard him go out. Prospero waited until the door closed and then came back to the bed.

"Found you Gaston?"

"Ungh."

"Good man." He gripped my right shoulder briefly. "Dewar reports," he went on in a quick undertone, "she seems to be there, in the body. They have sought for signs of her survival, but those are few yet; she lies shocked, stunned by the alteration. He's been told this is not unusual, nor cause for misgiving, for 'twill take time to unite incorporeal soul with earthly body. How long 't may be he knows not."

We regarded one another.

Walter came back in. He and Prospero propped me up and balanced a lap-desk under my right hand with paper and pencils ready. I wrote, *Walter, may I have wine please?*

"Son of Argylle!" he laughed, reading it. "Yes. I'll bring you wine, but watered."

Fair enough.

He went out again.

Miracle, I wrote quickly on another piece of paper and shoved it at Prospero.

He read it and nodded slowly. "I'll not believe till mine eyes, my hands, mine ear have all confirmed 'tis no dream but real," he said, "and I misdoubt still the wisdom oft. But 'tis wrought, for good or ill, and not to be undone."

Heard from G?

"No. Said he aught of coming here, of himself returning to the living world?"

I shook my head.

Prospero spread his hands. "I know not what's brewing with him. Dewar said he'd had no word—he seemed relieved by that silence, as well he might. Comes Walter."

Walter brought a pitcher of cool, light wine, a cup, and a straw. He held it while I sipped. There was an intravenous drip going into my left arm; it was glucosaline solution, Prospero said, and it would stay in until I could eat soup at least—a day or two or three.

Writing slowly, I told them what had happened with Gemnamnon.

"So no head, no hide, no dragon's-rump roasts, no trophies," Walter said mock-mournfully. "I don't know, Gwydion, perhaps we'll have to prosecute you under the Rare Species Protection Code. He was one of a kind, after all." He grinned.

So are you, I wrote. *You belch somewhat less toxic matter, and thus are more welcome in society.*

Walter laughed. "You're not in bad shape for all that," he said.

Ulrike came in the next afternoon with Josquin, shyly smiling at me.

"Hello," she said. "Your horse came back today. I thought you'd like to know that."

Thank you. That's good tidings. I thought he was gone for good.

"I found him," she said proudly. "He was in Threshwood, and I was riding Hussy there and we found him by a brook having a drink. He came home with us."

Josquin, sitting his chair wrong-way-round at the end of the bed, caught my eye and said, "Indeed, I've never seen a nag more grateful to see his stable. He positively fawned on the groom."

Good. Was he hurt?

Ulrike said, "No, not that I could see, he didn't limp, he was just dirty and his tack was a mess. The groom said he'd look after him."

I'm glad you found him. He might have decided to take a holiday.

Walter came and joined us with a guitar and strummed it softly; Ulrike patted my hand and didn't say anything more while Josquin gave me his daily dole of amusing gossip and observations on events in the City. Thereafter he visited me every morning for breakfast. Usually Ulrike and Walter dined with me, and Ulrike also came every evening in the last light of the long summer day and read to me for an hour in her soft, clear voice.

Prospero must not have told them about Mother yet, I guessed. Gaston had asked me to tell them, too, but I clutched a faint hope that Prospero had preempted me. Very likely he still intended to stick me with the job, as he'd had me go tell Gaston.

I was beginning to understand how Prospero thinks. That was indeed what he intended. He waited until I could eat to tell me.

"When your tongue's restored to its accustom'd nimbleness," he said, carefully undoing bandages, "you must exercise it in vigorous explanation."

I waited.

"Your siblings still must hear the tale of Freia's restoration," he went on.

I sighed.

"You shall tell them," he said, and his tone banned contradiction.

"Ungh."

"Good. This looks better, far better—albeit could hardly have been worse. You're drawing on the Spring."

"Ungh."

"Yes, it's coming nicely." His fingers were gentle and cool on my sensitive face. "Hm. Here was your jawbone broken; 'tis knitting as 't should. You're lacking a tooth in here; breaking, tore your gum, and I'd no choice but remove the rest, and stitch the gap and put a placeholder . . . Here you'll have a handsome scar a while. Was't a rock hit you?"

"Ungh."

"Thought so. Such local wounds seemed too particular for Gemnamnon's gross claws. Ribs and shoulder—they're cracked, whacked—and there's naught but suffering them to mend with time. No internal damage—you were lucky, damned lucky—nay, luck was naught of it. You were superb." He smiled at me suddenly. "Well done, Gwydion."

Finally I had done something right, I thought.

"Essay a word or two. Let not your jaw move overmuch."

"Aaah. Hm. Aches."

"Aye, so 'twill."

"I'm hungry," I said.

"Soup," Prospero replied sternly.

Dewar called a couple of days after my face-bandages came off. I'd postponed breaking the news to my sisters and brothers until I could speak clearly. I was in my workroom in my dressing-gown, writing up an account of my latest run-in with Gemnamnon in a notebook.

"Gwydion," he said from the Mirror as the spell completed.

"Hullo," I replied.

He blinked at me. "What hit you?"

"Dragon."

"I can tell it's a complicated story," he said after a moment, frowning slightly and then looking down. He bit his lip and went on, "I talked to Gaston just now. He said you'd hunted him out and told him . . ."

"Had to," I said. "Prospero insisted. And they both insist I tell the others."

He frowned in truth, his eyes hardening. "She didn't want that."

"So said I, but she's there and Prospero's here."

"I see your side of it, of course. Father can be a . . . oh, never mind."

I nodded. "How is she?"

"She's conscious, but not speaking or responding externally."

"So she knows you, but does not show it—"

"I have not seen her," he said.

"Then how—"

He went on, repressed emotion evident in the coldness of his voice, "They will not allow it. They have accepted Thiorn as a therapist of sorts. She is helping Freia accelerate the relearning. But I've not seen her yet myself. Gaston said he'd come, and I know they'll let him talk to her." He looked away.

Poor Dewar. Just as Freia had been barred from Gaston, so now Dewar was barred from her, forbidden to know firsthand how she fared or what she thought of him. I said, "I'd like to see her myself."

"I'll tell them that, but don't expect anything."

"What about doing a Lesser Summoning?"

Dewar tipped his head to one side and thought about it. "I don't know," he said finally. "I mean, I don't know whether she could handle it."

"Hm," I said. "Guess I won't try. And if anyone else does, I'll turn them to stone."

"It's probably best not to bother her."

When he had released me from the Summoning, I finished my writing and then took out my Keys. I had an unpleasant duty to perform. I'd procrastinated, excusing myself through bodily weakness, but I shouldn't postpone much longer. I supposed I could tell Walter and Ulrike together, since they were both here, but the others I'd have to Summon.

This I did. I reckoned that telling them one-on-one, rather than calling a family meeting, meant that they were less able to gang up on me and condemn me collectively, but it also meant repeating the tale until it sounded, to my ears, glib.

I began with the toughest: Alexander.

"You," he said, leaning forward and looking down at me through a fire. "Gwydion, by the Sun, I'm going to castrate that stud of yours—"

I couldn't help myself—though it hurt, though I knew it would only make him angrier, I began to laugh, the mood of the moment ruined by my brother's outrage. Cosmo had not been idle, it seemed. "Must have been the wind," I said, and forced my laughter to stop. "That's not what I must tell you—"

"That mare is worth—"

"Oh, Alex. The foal will be a fine animal. Let us train it and give it to Ulrike. She has none of her own yet, and it will please her. Or do you find some fault in Cosmo's bloodline?"

"Your Cosmo's bloodline and your own—" he began, and to his credit he stopped himself, because I was ready to interrupt him with harder words. "What do you want to tell me that one of your louse-ridden birds cannot bring?"

When I finished he shook his head and broke the spell without saying anything. He was shocked, and I suspected when his shock receded he'd be more furious than ever before. Phoebe just nodded slowly. "It explains much," she murmured. Marfisa reacted much as Alexander, with but a hint of visible anger. I had no stomach for a quarrel; I had decided to let them abuse me and excoriate me if they would, but no one did, which was disconcerting.

I sent Anselm to get Walter and Ulrike and spoke to them in my rooms before dinner. Walter was shocked and then delighted. Ulrike was flabbergasted and at once asked when she would see Freia.

"Not for a while," I said, and I repeated my policy statement on Summonings.

"Good idea," Walter said, "she'd get no rest with everyone pestering her all the time. Gwydion . . ." and he shook his head slowly, rather as Alexander had.

"What?" I asked, irritably.

"The things you do . . ." was all he said, and he left, still shaking his head.

"I do what I have to do," I muttered at the door.

"Gwydion, may I tell Josquin?" asked Ulrike softly.

"No. Let us wait and be sure. I know nothing of this; it is all Dewar's doing. Anything could go wrong. Tell no one, discuss it with no one."

She nodded obediently and sat staring at her hands. "The Spring . . ." she said as if a thought had vocalized itself without her noticing.

"Hm?" But it brought something to mind, something I felt I should be more forceful about. "Rikki, you should drink of the Spring. You should have done so long since." Our family was so small, so fragile in comparison to Argylle's extended clans, and it was hard to believe we had gained instead of losing. The gain should be confirmed.

Ulrike's fingers twisted together. "I'm afraid to," she whispered.

"What do you fear?" I sat down beside her on the divan.

She continued knotting and unknotting her fingers, but I knew her well enough now to see that she would speak when she had her nerve up. I waited.

"When . . . Father took me to Landuc," she said, almost inaudibly, "I . . . he led me there . . . and I approached the Well as he commanded, and afterward . . . when I was in its fire . . ." She stopped.

"Many people have visions," I said, hoping to help.

"Father told me that, and explained that I should not be

afraid but . . . but . . . it was not like a vision . . ." Ulrike moistened her lips and went on, "it was a voice, a voice that said, 'Beware lest the sorcerers and the Spring of Argylle use thee as thy mother.' I saw darkness and grew dizzy and I thought I was falling . . ."—she was shaking now—"and then it . . . it stopped and I was back, with Father beside me, and I could not tell him what I had heard, I was reeling so. And he sent me away to Argylle then . . ."

"Oh, my," I said, understanding. "As you thought, to your death. Ulrike, you should have said something. Right away. What a— What did you hear again?"

" 'Beware lest the sorcerers and the Spring of Argylle use thee as thy mother,' " she repeated, gulping. "Gwydion, I do not want to fall in as she did!"

"No, no, no," I said, and patted her shoulder. "You won't. I swear it. In fact I . . ." I stopped, the phrase turning in my mind, and my stomach lurched. My hands began to shake. "That bastard," I said softly. "Panurgus." How had he known?

"The dead king?"

"It was a man's voice you heard?"

"Just a voice."

I said, more to myself than to her, "He thought Dewar would try to use you to bring Mother out again."

She went white. I should not have spoken.

"Ulrike, he would not! Ever! Nothing of the kind! That says more about Panurgus than Uncle Dewar, believe me— Dewar's a good man, a kind man, and he would never harm you. Nor would he push you in the Spring, nor would anyone else. Believe me. Do you believe me?" She had to believe me . . .

Ulrike, after a moment, nodded hesitantly.

I swallowed and squeezed her hands in mine with gratitude. "Thank you. We are not murderers and necromancers, Rikki. Dewar may be eccentric, but he wanted Freia to be herself, not a bizarre amalgam of herself and someone else.

He is above the kind of . . . perversion that Panurgus suggested. —You do see how that can be read two ways?"

"Yes . . ."

"He meant it thus, certainly," I said. "Remind me not to subscribe to Landuc's oracles."

⎯ *25* ⌐

ULRIKE DRANK OF THE SPRING THE morning after our talk. I filled the cup for her myself, a special, simple golden chalice kept in the room where the Keys and the frozen clock rested. We did this without audience, the two of us, because she wished it so.

"Wouldn't you like to have the others there?" I asked her, puzzled, when she said that.

"No," she said, "n-no, I— Just you."

"Why not?" I asked. My parents, Walter, Phoebe, and Dewar had been there to embrace and kiss me when I had drunk; Walter had had all his siblings and Freia and Gaston. To do it solitarily seemed furtive, stealthy. I felt that Prospero ought at the very least to be there also. "Why not Prospero, even," I suggested, "or Walter?"

"He's . . . Grandfather has been so angry . . ." she said, "so cross lately, I . . . I . . ."

Prospero had been curt and closed with everyone. "He can be that way," I said. "As you wish, then, Rikki. But if you want someone else, anyone would be honored. I am honored that you ask me." I was honored and relieved. The sick idea that I had weighed her murder to give her mother a new life gnawed my conscience. As for Prospero, his distemper was its own reward; he could not complain of the slight when he had been snapping and snarling at the household and family since the day Freia had been freed from the Spring. "What about Alex?" I suggested. She liked him more than I, and it was her day.

"He—I don't think so," she said, "he was cross about me keeping his horse . . ."

"Hussy? That's not your fault." Damn Alex's temper.

"He came to get her while you were ill," Ulrike said, turning an exceptional shade of crimson, "and when we went to the paddock, she, I mean your horse, they—He was very angry."

"Oh," I said, and snickered. "That's life. She's a good horse and so is Cosmo. Why don't you tell Alexander you want the foal? He'll give it to you if you ask."

Her eyes widened, and she looked interested. "I will then. He said all kinds of . . . bad things about it. He won't want it, poor thing. But I don't think he'd like to come to Argylle again, Gwydion; he said he wouldn't, and I . . . I ought to drink soon, oughtn't I."

"When?" I asked her.

"Does it take very long?"

"Minutes."

Ulrike seemed surprised. "It took a long time at the Well."

"Our Spring is a less controlled thing," I said. "There's nothing to do but drink. Why don't we go down right now?"

Her eyes widened and then she swallowed, straightened a little, and squared her slender shoulders. "Yes," she said. "Right now."

She already knew what Prospero had reminded me of recently: you must not hide your fear and paint it over with good intentions to yourself. It cannot be reasoned away, only faced and outfaced.

So I fetched the chalice and Ulrike a cloak against the chill underground, and we walked down the Spiral and the Black Stair, around and around cased in night-dark stone. At the bottom, I led her slowly to the Spring, letting her feel the space and the solitude. I could feel more than that, the out-flow of the Spring itself, but to her this was only empty.

"It's so big . . ." she whispered, and her whisper ran up to the vaulted roof and trembled.

"Vast," I said softly, "and unmeasured."

"How can it all be hollow under the Citadel . . ."

"I do not know. I have wondered that also. It is part of the way the world is. If I ever find out, I'll tell you," I added, and pressed her hand on my arm against my side.

The park bench, incongruous and mundane, elicited no comment from her. I brought her to the edge of the Spring, which was, as ever, calmly and steadily pouring unseen substance into the world. I wondered whether, had Freia still been within it when Ulrike approached, it would have become excited. Probably not. Mother has better sense than that.

"Just stand here," I said, and reached over the Spring with the chalice. I closed my eyes and Summoned the Spring, and suddenly my arm and the chalice were drenched in the geyser of water—real, wet, visible water—which the Spring's force became.

"Oh!"

We were showered by droplets, bathed in light.

"Drink and know the world," I offered, and she steeled herself, her narrow jaw clenching for an instant, and took the chalice and sipped. I kept my hand on the cup lest she drop it, but she did not; she sipped, swallowed—it just tastes like very fresh sweet fine water—and then drank all. The geyser still shot up, pattered down on us, misted our hair and dewed our lashes. Ulrike lowered the chalice and looked up at me, and she smiled, her eyes shining.

On the tenth day after Ulrike drank, I was rudely awakened by someone knocking over a stool in my workroom and cursing fluently. I sat bolt upright, staring, as Dewar came in.

"Don't leave furniture in front of a Mirror of Ways," he snapped at me, rubbing his shin, limping slightly.

"On the contrary," I said, "it proves an effective alert of

unauthorized usage. What's wrong with your own Mirrors?"

"They're in another room," he retorted, "and if I come here to talk to you privately, do I want twelve servants and my father to bump into me?"

"Small chance of that at the break of dawn."

He looked out the window, twitching the draperies aside. Sun streamed in. I rubbed my eyes. Farewell to those last tag ends of dreams . . .

"Pretty day, too," Dewar said wistfully, and then grinned, turning from the window. "Did they come here?"

"Who?"

He began laughing wildly. He flopped into a chair and got himself under control. "I'm sorry. It's too funny. I'll have to go back and pick up Thiorn. I had to tell you. They didn't come here, of course."

"Who?" I demanded, tossing a pillow at him. "Talk!"

"Gaston," he said, wiping tears from his eyes. "Gaston came to me via a Way; we arranged it so. He looked rigid, absolutely stone-faced, as he does when he's very angry. You know. And I thought he was angry at me but no, he was calm, just wanted to see Freia at once. And these therapists— picture Gaston, armed as he customarily is, mail and a helmet, Chanteuse du Mort sheathed and longer than one of the nurses is tall, looking at these soft people in white and telling them he would see Freia now, thank you. *Now.* What matter that she is asleep, he has seen her sleep before. And so on. Oh, you should have seen it. Gratifying, really."

"I take it they were the ones keeping you out too."

"Yes. I was intimidated . . . I confess I was not entirely sure what would happen afterward, and they knew what they were about . . . and Thiorn seemed to be backing them up, so I accepted the ban—not to jar anyone's elbow, as it were. Not Gaston. Thiorn came in when it looked ready to get unpleasant—I was arguing for him, contending he had more right than anyone to see her, to talk to her, and Thiorn walked in and smoothed everyone's tempers. They're very impressed by her. Hell, I'm very impressed by her. Gaston went off with Thiorn.

"Perhaps an hour and a quarter later there's a tremendous hue and cry, a clanging damned klaxon and people running around madly. I immediately thought he must have killed someone. They're physically nonviolent, but good at mind-games, and he has no patience with that. Thiorn came in holding her sides and laughing. 'He's wonderful, wonderful, I love that man so,' she kept saying. It turns out that Gaston said he would like to be alone with Freia. The nurses wanted him to disarm. He picked one nurse up in each hand, put them out, and closed the door, blocking it somehow. Thiorn shrugged and sat outside to wait; the nurses scurried off in a tizzy. Some doctor came by after a while to ask Thiorn what was up. Thiorn said, 'Conjugal visit.' The doctor didn't un-derstand and opened the door with a special key before Thiorn could stop her. There was nobody there but the em-bers of a fire in the corner by the window, and the fools threw water on that and set off their own smoke-detection system—that was the alarm, a fire-warning thing."

I started laughing too.

"They've told me Freia is conscious and can speak now," he said. "I'd guess she told Gaston to get her out. He burned a table, opened a Way, and picked her up and left. What I like about him is that he knows what he wants, and he goes and gets it. No politics. No maneuvering."

"It will be a while before we hear from them," I said.

"Yes. Pity. I would've liked to talk to her for a minute myself." He found a cigarette-case in his pocket, lit one, and chuckled softly. "Life is back to normal, I think."

"Something like it, anyway."

Dewar came to breakfast with me. Prospero and Ulrike were stunned to find him there, comfortable as if he had never been anywhere else, sitting at table greedily eating apricot pastries and drinking cup after cup of dangerously dark tea. He told his tale with a wicked gleam in his eye. Prospero smiled. Ulrike appeared to have mixed feelings.

"Why didn't they come here?" she asked. "I would like to see Mother. And Father."

"Ulrike," I said, "it is a hard truth we have all had to learn, every one of us, starting with Alexander and Marfisa. We come second. For either of them, the other comes first."

"True," Dewar murmured, "quite true." Prospero nodded.

Ulrike looked at Dewar. I wondered what Gaston had told her about him. "But I have never met her. And it is more than half a year since I saw Father."

Prospero lifted an eyebrow and leaned back, saying nothing.

Dewar stared at her, shocked. "Ulrike, my niece," he said, with not inconsiderable condescension, "Twenty-three years is a long time too, isn't it?"

She frowned a little. "But . . ."

Dewar shook his head slowly. "Gwydion was right. And so it should be. Ties of blood are strong, and important too, but the ties you choose are even stronger." He looked at her through narrowed eyes, assaying her. "How old are you?"

"I guess—I guess I must be eighteen or twenty. Time felt different—swifter—here, when I came."

"They spent ten times that falling in love," he said in a tight voice. "They spent fifteen times that concealing their relationship and their children from all Landuc and Argylle, and not one of us suspected a thing. Including me, and I'm popularly supposed to know everything about my sister. A year is *nothing*. Twenty is something. Especially when you're unhappy. I bet we won't see them for five years, minimum, Argylle time, and we won't hear much from them either." Dewar shrugged. "So what? They have their lives and we have ours."

"I have a right to know my mother!" she cried.

He leaned forward, holding her eyes, shaking his head

again. "You have *years* to know your mother. It's not that she doesn't love you, kid. She spent all twenty-three years beating at the Border between Pheyarcet and the Dominion, trying to find you and Gaston. She's found him. She knows you're safe, happy even. She'll get hold of you when she's ready. He comes first."

Ulrike looked ready to burst into tears.

"Talk to Phoebe about it," Dewar said, slumping back. "She might be able to explain it more clearly."

I thought he'd made things very clear; Belphoebe would only say the same thing in slightly different words.

After breakfast, I tagged after my uncle as he went to examine his workroom. Ulrike had obediently ridden off to find Belphoebe in Threshwood.

Dewar still seemed slightly amazed at Ulrike's naiveté. "What does she think they're going to be doing," he asked me rhetorically, "playing cribbage?"

He puffed a cloud of dust off a row of glass jars. I coughed and opened a window.

"I think she had a very sheltered childhood. —Dewar, you need to clean up in here . . ."

"*Sheltered* is one thing. *Oblivious* is another. Sea and stars. I bet she found social customs here a bit shocking. —Yes, I guess I do."

"She did. She has made an effort to get used to them. —If you didn't leave it locked up so, the staff would do it."

"Hmph. I've got to go bail Thiorn out from the righteous wrath of the regenerative profession. I'll be in touch. I'd like a holiday. —I don't like people mucking around in here when I'm away. I ought to look up housekeeping magic. Freia has some sort of charms around her rooms that keep things from getting this . . . funky. Pheugh. You still mixed up with those twins?" He grinned knowingly.

I cleared my throat of dust and sat on a three-legged stool by his black-marble-topped workbench. "How did you know

about . . . Never mind. —No, the staff cleans Freia's rooms.
—I want to ask you a question you won't like."

Dewar studied me for a moment and nodded. "Go
ahead."

"Did Prospero really free Ariel?"

He studied me another moment. "He told him to go where
he list and do what he would, that he would make no further
calls upon him. Verbatim. I had pleaded with Father not to
fully release him; I thought he might come in handy someday. As he has. Let's keep that very, very quiet, all right? If
Prospero knew . . ." His voice trailed away. He looked down
at the workbench and drew a swirl in the dust, eyed it criti-
cally, shook his head.

"Of course. I just wondered." I pushed a dusty pencil
aside. It left a clean spot beneath it. "Come back sometime
. . . sometime soon. Josquin's sailing bug has bitten me too.
We could go around the Isles. Catch up a bit."

Dewar set down a round, polished chunk of crystal in
which something blue and distorted floated, a slow, brilliant
smile coming over his face. He nodded. "That would be very
nice. Yes. I'll call you and we can arrange something like
that. It's been a long time, Gwydion." We gazed at each
other until I smiled too. "It's good to see you," he said very
softly, and then he looked away.

With his sleeve, he wiped dust from a silver-framed Mirror
of Ways and began setting up the apparatus to perform the
spell. "By the way," he added, after he kindled the fire with
a word and lifted his hands to gesture, "if it's not too much
trouble, would you be so kind as to have this place cleaned?"
And he lifted an eyebrow as he grinned again.

Dewar and I didn't sail around the Isles; we didn't have time.
Instead, when he returned to Argylle a week later, we went
on a coasting trip down to Errethon and spent days exploring
the fjords and fishing and swimming, the sort of voyage we
had often made when I was his student. We returned just

ahead of the first of the autumn storms, slipping into Ollol's snug harbor as the waves got bigger and bigger and the wind more and more powerful.

In pouring rain, we made our boat fast to the dock and decided a pub crawl was the only way to celebrate. Hours later we were skidding along the water-slick pier back to the boat to recover, lit by a blue-green ignis fatuus that was having trouble tracking us. Dewar laughed like a maniac as he slipped on the dock planks and fell into the pool of water in the boat's cockpit. I did slightly better and was actually standing and trying to open the cabin door when he sat bolt upright and yelled, "Hello, beautiful!"

I looked around. Nobody there.

"Oh, just fine!" he said. He lost control of the ignis fatuus and it winked out, doubtless relieved to be shut of us. I ineptly conjured a new one, which was dimmer and smaller, reflecting my own dimmed mental state.

"Who is it?" I asked.

He grabbed my ankle. I lost my balance and toppled, clutching the boom to let myself down on one of the benches. A moment later a Lesser Summoning fastened on the ignis I'd just conjured up, and it glowed softly and expanded to a round haze, feeding on the energy of the Summoning.

"Dewar," my mother was saying, her expression pained, "You are *drunk.*" She paused a moment and added, smiling now, "But you always were a cute drunk."

Dewar chuckled. "And you're a fun one. How the hell are you. You look *gorgeous,* gorgeous."

"Mother!" I said, and pushed my hair out of my eyes.

"Gwydion! I should have guessed either you or Otto would be handy." Freia was shaking her head ruefully, laughing. Her hair was short and curled around her face and neck softly. She was wearing loose indigo robes, lined with white and bordered with silver, and she seemed to bend toward us, toward the flame she used for her Summoning.

I caught my breath. I had forgotten how beautiful Freia

was, or perhaps I had never really noticed, seeing her constantly.

"I presume things are calm in the Citadel, since you two are three sheets to the wind at the docks," she went on in a teasing tone.

"Oh, they're fine," Dewar said. "Everything's fine. Fine. You're fine too."

"I shall call again when you're capable of a straight conversation."

Dewar grinned. "Come find out how straight a conversation I'm capable of."

Freia laughed again, shaking her head, and vanished with a gesture.

"Awww, *shit,*" he moaned. "She's mad at me now."

"Let's get inside, Dewar." I knew that if I stayed sitting down much longer, I'd be in the bilge beside my colleague.

He swayed to his feet and leaned, actually half-draped his body, on the boom. "I didn't mean to be *rude.*"

I splashed over to the cabin door, broke the latch to open it, and dragged Dewar in.

"I'm *always* saying the wrong thing," he mourned. "Stuffing my big feet in my fat mouth. Ought to cut my tongue out."

"She thinks you're cute. She's not mad at you."

"I think she's cute too. I'll be damned if I don't. Actually I'll be damned if I do, right? No, that's not it. Already damned. Shit!" He sat on his bunk with his head in his hands.

I tried to dry myself off and realized that I was still clothed. I undressed and threw my soaked clothing out onto the deck with a vague idea that it would dry faster outside.

"Gwydion," said Dewar, suddenly getting an idea, "I'm sleeping up forward tonight."

"Fine," I said. "Don't fall off."

"I mean in the bow berth."

This could be used as extra sleeping quarters if necessary, being fitted with cushions. "I don't care where you sleep."

"You're a *gentleman,*" he told me. "A real gentleman. You make me proud. Where's my stuff got to?"

"Breadbox," I reminded him, falling onto my own bunk and fighting with the blanket.

He rattled around in the tin breadbox, spilling everything, and then retreated unsteadily to the sail-locker by way of the head. I dismissed the ignis fatuus, which had followed me in. Dewar thumped into something and swore blue in three languages and then called for Ariel.

I fell asleep rapidly. Hours later, I woke. My head was beginning to throb. The rain had stopped; the storm, typically, had swept past. I decided I needed more rest and turned over to get it. I thought I heard laughter, but it might have been water against the hull, and I dropped off to sleep again.

Coffee smell. It woke me. I sniffed at it, enjoying it, and then noticed I felt very bad. Dewar was cussing quietly.

"Damn it, no. Red and white stripes. Try again, Ariel."

I moved my head carefully. He was sitting on the bunk and had a collection of corked brown glass pill bottles in front of him.

A sharp, headache-jarring pop followed, and another bottle fell into Dewar's lap.

Dewar inspected it briefly. "Come now. This is *not* it. I cannot read the label."

"You've given me scant guide," complained Ariel.

Someone chuckled softly.

"Wha'?" I said thickly.

"It's a lousy morning," Dewar said. "I'm Summoning her. I'm sorry, but this is an emergency."

"Send Ariel," the person who chuckled suggested.

He frowned. "All right. Ariel?"

"Yes, Master." Ariel sounded put upon.

"Go find Freia. Tell her I want those great red and white capsules she had. She'll know the ones. Make sure she's alone before you talk to her."

"Yes, Master." He popped out with a gusty martyred sigh.

"Whozzat," I said.

"Hi, Gwydion. Coffee?" Thiorn bent to look in my face.

"Yeah."

"No," said Dewar. "Coffee is out. No."

"What?" she said. "But you wanted it."

"Not until I get those pills."

"What are these pills?" she asked.

"They're *great.*"

Dewar was clearly still feeling the effects of last night.

"You do not need to pollute yourself any further. You're barely managing what you have." Thiorn was half-laughing.

Dewar growled something I didn't catch. I put my face back into the pillow and noticed that the rocking of the boat was nauseating. I tried to forget I had noticed that.

Ariel reappeared. "Her Ladyship told me exactly where to seek: in the Citadel pharmacy." A concussive bang, and a bottle plopped on the bunk. "Here. Anything else?" he added sulkily.

"No. Thanks, Ariel."

"She said one per twenty kilos of body mass. She was laughing." Ariel whisked out, hissing through the door.

"Arrrgh. I'll never hear the end of this one. Heigh-ho. Down they go." Dewar swallowed his and handed me five. "Eat your vitamins, dear boy."

I leaned on my elbow and looked at them. "What is it."

"Hangover cure. Freia invented it, I think. Used it to finance her research down the Road early on. Long story."

"Water," I said. Thiorn handed me a cup. I took the pills, drank, and lay down again, closing my eyes.

"Good idea," my uncle said, and from the sound of it retreated again to the sail loft.

Thiorn followed him.

Oh, I thought, and went back to sleep.

* * *

When we had recovered—about an hour and a half later—
Dewar helped me clean up the cabin and deck and told me
he wanted to take the boat out again with Thiorn. "We'd like
to try a fairly long trip."

"Have fun," I said, nodding.

"I was think—" He stopped and held up his hand, then
moved away, pulled a candle stub out, and lit it. He opened
one of the brass running lights quickly and lit that from the
candle, sitting down before it. "Good morning," he said, and
made a dismissing gesture behind his back at me.

I went below. "Where's Dewar?" Thiorn asked, looking
up from the green-covered bunk. She was examining the
contents of Ariel's collection of remedies and specifics.

"Someone has Summoned him."

"Ah. I think these won't kill you. Any of them."

"I'll pass, I think," I said.

She shrugged. "What's life if you don't experiment once in
a while, I say. It's not an inconvenience if we steal your
boat?"

"I'll not be using it." I shrugged and kept the regret from
my voice.

She smiled. "I'm playing hooky, as I threatened," she said.
"Let them stew. I checked back in, said I had resolved the
theft satisfactorily, and disappeared with Dewar before they
could pin me down." She laughed quietly.

"They? Who are they?"

"The others. The Battlemaster. Now I'm out of it, myself
again, and I'm finding it as good as it ever was. I owe Dewar
much for giving me the chance to escape."

"Will they not pursue you? You can simply . . . leave?" I
said doubtfully.

"Let us say, they cannot pursue me. I was the one who was
able to reach and find you, because I knew things the others
did not—things I had learned about you, about the way the
Road and the Well and the Spring work, from your mother.

I had kept it from them and took all of it with me, you see."
She grinned, feral and intense.

I thought about this for a moment, frowning. "Like the
volumes in a library . . ." I said after a moment, half-aloud.

Thiorn nodded once. "Not a bad analogy. They know they
knew, but they no longer know. Live volumes. They cross-
check, cross-reference to one another, and pulling one out
doesn't cripple the rest—but it removes what was in that
volume."

"But you've done this before, haven't you? During the
Independence War," I said.

"Well, not exactly. I hadn't been fully . . . incorporated
into the Battlemaster then; I dominated it. The process of
assimilation takes a very long time. During the War I could
use the Battlemaster's knowledge, but it did not have mine.
Indeed it never does. Full subsumption is suicide—there have
been a few of those, but I'm not going to be one. Splitting
and running like this is, ah, unprecedented. Of course they're
furious, but I was bored, bored, bored." She snorted with
disgust.

"You'll never be bored with Dewar around," I said. "He
seems to attract things."

Her wicked smile came back, and she glanced at the var-
nished, closed hatch. "Yes. I knew another guy like that. He
was a good friend of Freia's. Always something happening,
often not of his doing, but sometimes he'd stir it up just for
fun." She opened a capsule and sniffed, then tasted the contents. "Salicylic acid and B-complex. Whoa. And caffeine,
among other things."

Overhead, Dewar laughed.

We looked up. "It's Freia," Thiorn said. "By the way, is
she going to abdicate or what?"

"You mean from Argylle . . . As far as she's concerned, she
says, she's done. If I want to take a holiday and roam, she'll
substitute for me, but I'm the Lord of Argylle."

"Big responsibility."

I shrugged. "Not really. It runs itself, mostly, now. I expect that she'll stay away for a good while, so that it is very clear that she is not ruling. People will have trouble getting used to the idea."

"You don't, though."

"No. I've been brought up for this, I think." I found cheese and bread in the breadbox and made a sandwich. "Although Dewar brought me up as much as my parents," I added, chewing.

"He mentioned that you were his student."

"Years and years. That was fun. But it always was clear that my place was in Argylle."

"Nice to know where you fit in," she said.

Dewar thumped on the cabin, a vigorous tattoo. "Your mother says hello," he said, sticking his head in, "and since nothing is happening she won't be around for a while. A long while. A very long while. She still seems . . . dazed."

"Not surprising," Thiorn said. "It'll take her months yet. Big transition."

I finished my sandwich, getting to my feet. "I'll be going now," I said to Dewar. "This was a good trip."

"It was. Let's do it again. I know great places to sail. I think you've never been to the Cape of Storms, up north."

"No, I haven't." I dusted the crumbs off my hands and climbed up the ladder. "So long," I said to Thiorn, "and thank you."

She nodded.

Dewar and I stood on the dock a moment, regarding one another.

"Freia said to tell you she'll talk to you soon," he said after a moment.

"Thanks."

We looked at each other.

"Safe journey, Dewar," I said finally, and he clasped my shoulders a moment, and then we embraced.

"Don't work too hard, Gwydion. It's supposed to be fun, isn't it?"

"I don't think I work too hard. I don't play hard enough, that's all."

His laugh ruffled my hair. "Yeah. Right. This has been good, to play with you again. I missed you." He hugged me harder, forced himself to relax a little, and kissed me on both cheeks.

"I missed you too. Not just because I didn't know what I was doing, but because I missed you."

There were tears brightening his eyes, I saw them when I turned my head. I hate saying good-bye. Part of me wanted to beg him not to go. I squelched it.

"Disappearing is an occupational hazard with sorcerers," Dewar said, as if reading my mind. "We all do it, all the time. You'll find out."

"Is that the last thing you have to tell me?" I said, an old joke.

Dewar's smile faded and he looked serious, then shook his head. "No. No. I can't imagine what that will be, Gwydion." He hugged me again, smiled into my face and shook his head again, then turned me around deftly and gave me a shove. "Away with thee, sister's-son, and my blessing with thee."

I shouldered my bag, walked up the dock, and looked back once when I was going down the pier, but Dewar was nowhere to be seen.

⌐— 26 —⌐

ANONYMOUS, LOOKING LIKE ANY SAILOR HOME with his bag on his back, I found a coach at an inn and rode home to the City. I walked to the Citadel from the Wyebridge Inn where it left me. It had been good, sailing and talking with my tutor-uncle-friend. I put my bag down on my bed and unpacked it slowly myself rather than having Villon do it. Melancholy over the end of this golden summer vacation, already wishing Dewar were still around to talk to as he always had been when I was his student, I went into my workroom, went out again, picked things up and put them down in my sitting room, and then went back to the bedroom and opened the windows to look into the garden.

I left the bedroom and went down the narrow tower stair that serves the family quarters of the Citadel only. It lets us in and out of the gardens and courtyard. From there I drifted along the paths until I ended up at a green-painted gate in a hedge, which I opened and went through. Mother's garden.

It was perfectly tended, as always, but by the staff nowadays, not by Freia. I hoped she would be back again to enjoy it. I found a bed of late-blooming lilies and picked some, heavy-headed golden flowers on stiff stalks, and then I returned to my apartment and put them in a vase with water on the nightstand beside the picture of my mother and her brother. They looked well there, and their scent filled the room. I sat down on the bed, gazing at them and not thinking anything particular, just soaking in my mood.

So absorbed was I in myself that I did not really hear the click of my workroom door for several seconds. Then I started and glanced up, lifting my eyebrows, and then stopped.

Freia smiled, a small, slightly shy smile—rather like Ulrike's. She leaned against the tall dark door, which she'd closed. Her dress was long, a sort of robe over a loose chemise, in the poppy-orange and golds of the lilies. Short-haired, head tilted, her brows raised a little . . .

"I hope I'm not intruding," she said softly, as if she had never been gone.

I shook my head. "Come in—I mean . . ."

She was real, really there, not an image, an illusion, a hallucination. It wasn't possible. It was. She was there.

I uncrossed my legs and stood and went to her, and Freia

smiled up at me, looking me up and down and into my face.

"I was just . . ." I started, and couldn't finish. Instead I put my arms around her, because she was hugging me tightly.

"Dear me, have you grown?" she joked, and we laughed.

I blurted, "You look about seventeen. Maybe you need to grow yourself." She was solid, warm, breathing—real.

"That's about right," she said, smiling.

She did. The fine lines around her eyes were gone; the touch of grey that had been in her hair, just a few silver strands at her temples, was gone; the lines that years of care had worn into her forehead were gone; the physical marks of her long, not-always-easy life were erased, cancelled; and she seemed no older than Ulrike. But for the expression that had already settled around her eyes and mouth, one would have thought her so young, too. No seventeen-year-old girl had ever been so wise.

I trembled once, intensely, and she squeezed me again.

"Gwydion, my love," she said, and wiped tears quickly from her eyes with one hand, keeping the other on my arm. "I'm happy to see you, Gwydion."

"Come sit down," I said, and we sat on the window seat and looked at one another.

"You look wonderfully well. Much better," my mother said, putting her hand on my bearded cheek. "That holiday did you a world of good, I can see."

"It did. I have just been regretting that it was over." I took her hand and held it in both of mine—I had forgotten how much smaller than I my mother is, how her head barely comes up to my chin and how her hands are but two-thirds as big as mine. Her hands were warm. She was real.

"All holidays end," Freia reminded me.

I nodded. "Are you on holiday now?"

"Yes. A long one. I think it will be a few years, Gwydion, but I wanted to see you—really see you—and know that all is well with you . . . You know, with a beard now that you're older you look so like Papa it's scary." She was still looking at me closely, inventorying me.

"He says he keeps thinking he's walking into a looking glass."

She reached up, stroking and smoothing my slightly-shaggy hair into place. "Where did you come by this diamond earring? It makes you a bit rakish . . ."

"Oh, Mother . . ." I chuckled.

". . . but it suits you. I guess I don't want to know"—she smiled—"and it's none of my business—"

I shrugged. "Prospero says that children never stop being their parents' business."

"That's rich coming from him." Freia sniffed. "I'll have to remember that. Hmph. Anyway."

The change in her tone of voice meant, *down to business.*

"Dewar said you had had trouble with Gemnamnon again. He would tell me no more than just that. What has happened?"

"Oh." I nodded, looked away, looked back. "Cup of wine?" I'd need something to moisten my mouth for this long yarn.

"Why, yes, thank you."

I got one for each of us. "As good as it ever was, or better," I said, handing Freia hers.

"I should hope so."

I sat down again and gave her the dragon tale, beginning to end, with everything in its proper place.

"He should not have come back," Freia said, frowning, when I had wound down.

"But you weren't keeping him off, once you had left the Spring."

"Just that once—"

"Aha, so that *was* you."

"Shhh." Freia smiled mischievously and tipped her head back. "Don't give it away."

"I thought it must have been you. You were magnificent."

"I was furious. I still am. If he is still around, you let me know. We shall think of a way to quash him for good. I can't imagine he'd have survived your Disconnector spell. Think, dear: an Elemental is still made of something—he's just not mixed in nature."

"Dewar said so too. I wasn't sure whether that made a difference, that he was Elemental—"

"It does not," she said firmly.

"Needless to say, I shall agree with you both until we are all proven wrong." I smiled, thinking how utterly typical this conversation was, how normal.

"Wise of you."

I thought of another question, one I'd meant to ask somebody for a while. "Mother, in the past I have been told that the Spring will kill anyone not a member of our immediate family who drinks of it. Is that true?"

"Y-yes," she said slowly.

"Then how did Gaston survive?"

"Why are you wondering this?" She scrutinized me.

"When Ulrike first came here, we couldn't figure out if she was really your child or not—"

"Oh, I see. Ah . . . I suppose I can tell you this, but, Gwydion, you must not . . . We must not become like Pheyarcet, or worse, like Phesaotois. I implore you to keep it hushed and never to use it."

I began to promise I would not, and instead said, "I know that protecting the Spring must be my first care. I would not taint it or Argylle by sharing it carelessly."

She was satisfied. "Let that always be in your heart, in your thought, Gwydion, and all else becomes easy." Freia took a swallow of wine, tasted it well before she went on. "The truth of it is that any initiate can attune another, just as at the Well or Stone. All the Elements are equal: equal in strength, in dominion, in importance; none may take precedence over the others—this is not conventional sorcerous wisdom, but I know it is so. The Spring will kill the newcomer if the burden of the power be too great or if the candidate be inharmonious; I have been told the Others will also. Yet there's a way around that too."

I waited for her to finish.

"I worked it out myself," she said after a moment, organizing her thoughts, looking down at her hands. "Dewar told me later I was taking a terrible risk, but he also thought it made perfect sense. When Gaston and I wed, you see, we used a very old ceremony in Montgard."

"You've lost me, Mother."

"It involved, among other things, a drop of blood in a cup of wine—"

"Ha! Now I follow. You became affined, so to speak, to Gaston, and he to you."

"Yes. So Dewar said, and so we saw it then. Dewar wasn't here when we did it, of course, it was right after . . . Avril's falling-out with Gaston.—I'm not a *complete* idiot about sorcery, you know, and neither is Gaston." She looked at me sharply.

I diplomatically said, "No, but that is quite a connection to make—"

"It was apparent to me anyway. And to Gaston when I put it to him. So, since I was attuned to Argylle's Spring when we wed, he was already . . . not attuned himself, but . . . I cannot think of a handsome technical word for it."

"Harmonized, perhaps."

"Yes. Thus drinking of the Spring, for him, was as passing Landuc's Fire is for children of Well-initiated parents; they are unscathed, unlike those with no previous trace of the Well. A latent ability is awakened."

"That must be quite a wedding ceremony," I teased her, to lighten things up.

She laughed, blushing. "Brief but binding. Well-suited to the principals, a poor show for the guests."

I laughed with her, and the strangeness of it caught me again. "I can't believe I'm sitting here talking to you."

"You are. When I go you'll have two wine-cups to prove it." Freia clicked her cup on mine; we saluted one another silently and drank, and she was serious again. "How is Ulrike?"

"She is well. She has drunk of the Spring."

". . . yes . . ."

"She is very eager to see you."

Freia smiled. "I know. Gaston and I have decided she shall come to me, to us, and soon; it will be a few months, perhaps half a year, by your clock. I missed her so . . ." Her smile softened and became sad. "All grown now—it isn't fair. You, Dewar, Papa—you haven't changed, Gaston hasn't changed, but I have changed and she has." She shook her head, fingering her cup's engraving. "There is so much to say, and so little time to say it before she takes wing on her own."

"She speaks of you often." To leave an infant, small and helpless, and return to a young woman—yes, I thought, that would be hard.

Mother caught her lower lip between her teeth and looked down at her hands. She patted mine absently. "As for Ulrike," she said, "Ottaviano was here around New Year's . . ."

"Oh. Hell. Yes, Walter invited him. Avril had sent him to renegotiate the Empire–Dominion Compact."

"I just wondered what was going on. I misliked the way he pounced on her," she added, lifting her chin.

And something in the gesture, the topic, and the set of her mouth clicked.

"Gryphon," I said, involuntarily.

"I beg your pardon?"

"That was you too!"

Freia looked away, and her throat and neck became red.

I opened my mouth and closed it. "That night," I said finally, "that was one big letdown, let me tell you, lady." I began laughing and blushing too. "What a perfect patsy I was . . ."

Freia didn't say anything, but still blushed.

"I'm sorry," I said, "I'm laughing at me, not at you—again, you were magnificent. I fear you know me too well."

"Anyway," she said, "he's not to be trusted. She is too young to know."

She was discomfited. I squeezed her shoulder and leaned forward to look around at her. "Freia," I said, "thank you for caring about us and keeping an eye on us."

"Little good I did you, nor may I do more now." She still didn't look at me.

"You were good enough for me, but to have you out is better. You did the right thing, Freia. Never doubt it. Please do not doubt that. Dewar was right. We need you alive and breathing more than we need you . . . otherwise."

She turned her head back, very serious, still flushed. "I hope so."

"I am more certain of that than I am of anything else in the world."

"You're kind. So all's well . . ."

"Don't worry about anything. Go back to Gaston and relax and do what you will and never worry about us."

"I think I can do all of that but that last."

"Then the Lord of Argylle will command it of you."

Freia smiled at me and reached up and kissed me on my bearded cheek. "Good," she said. "So be it then."

I blushed, embarrassed by my flippancy. "I didn't mean—"

"I hope to heaven you did, dear." Mother set her cup down and stood. "I must go, Gwydion. If something comes up, send a bird to me."

"I won't," I promised, standing also, and shook my head, looking down at her.

After a wide-eyed moment, she nodded. "You're right."

I smiled and bent down and kissed her on both cheeks, Argylle's way, and she kissed me back and told me to take care of myself.

"Always," I said. "Give my love to Gaston. I liked seeing him."

Freia nodded. "Good-bye for now," she said, and opened my workroom door. I thought she must be going to see Prospero, or perhaps Ulrike, and I followed her just in time to see her vanish into a Mirror of Ways without any preliminaries.

Hm. She must have learned a few shortcuts in the Spring.

I closed the door again and went back and picked up the wine-cups and looked at them. No, she'd really been here—I could still feel her kiss on my cheek, hear her voice in my ear.

I set the cups down, had a whiff from the lilies, and went to my office. On my desk was a note from Utrachet citing figures from the new wine-share agreement which Prospero had negotiated and asking, very frankly, where in Hell my Lordship intended to store the stuff, for there assuredly would be no room in Argylle. Grinning, I reached for my Map.

Acknowledgments

The author gratefully acknowledges the contributions of

- Greer Ilene Gilman and Delia Sherman for taking something which was good and showing her the flaws which kept it from being—well, as good as possible under the circumstances;

- Valerie Smith for confident guidance which steered the author from the pyrite path of folly and spared her the tarry slough of despond which lies at its end;

- Michael Swanwick and Marianne Porter for sounds, soundings, and sound advice;

- Laura Anne Gilman, who got more and less than she bargained for—*Excelsior,* Laura Anne, and sincere thanks; and

- Liz Lavalley and Gail Roberts, who are friends in need, indeed, and who may read again at last what they read first.